The Last Saturday in July

Sharon Black

POOLBEG

This book is a work of fiction. References to real people, events, establishments, organisations, or locales are intended only to provide a sense of authenticity, and are used fictitiously. All other characters, and all incidents and dialogue, are drawn from the author's imagination and are not to be construed as real.

Published 2023 by Poolbeg Press Ltd.
123 Grange Hill, Baldoyle,
Dublin 13, Ireland
Email: poolbeg@poolbeg.com

© Sharon Black 2023

© Poolbeg Press Ltd. 2023, copyright for editing, typesetting, layout, design, ebook and cover image.

The moral right of the author has been asserted.
A catalogue record for this book is available from the British Library.

ISBN 978-1-78199 510-5

All rights reserved. No part of this publication may be reproduced or transmitted in any form or by any means, electronic or mechanical, including photography, recording, or any information storage or retrieval system, without permission in writing from the publisher. The book is sold subject to the condition that it shall not, by way of trade or otherwise, be lent, resold or otherwise circulated without the publisher's prior consent in any form of binding or cover other than that in which it is published and without a similar condition, including this condition, being imposed on the subsequent purchaser.

www.poolbeg.com

About the Author

A recovered journalist, Sharon Black is a member of Writing.ie, and both a Writers Ink and Curtis Brown Creative alumna.

When she's not writing, she reads, walks, sees friends and drinks a lot of Italian coffee. She is an active member of a long-running book club where books and wine are consumed in roughly equal amounts. She loves old Hollywood films, every romantic comedy ever made and edgy stand-up.

In recent years, she has become close friends with Google Maps, thanks to her appalling sense of direction. She is highly allergic to shopping. Except for bag-shopping. She can be found on Facebook and Instagram as SharonBlackWriter, and on Twitter as SBlackwriter.

Sharon lives in a Dublin coastal village, with her husband and family.

Acknowledgements

My thanks to Paula Campbell and all the publishing team at Poolbeg Press, especially my amazing editor Gaye Shortland, who understood exactly what was needed to make this so much better. Thanks also to Paula Campbell and David Prendergast for my wonderful cover – I love it!

A special thank-you to the Writers Ink group, in particular Vanessa Fox O'Loughlin and Maria McHale who run it. Vanessa has continued to encourage me and her advice for writers is always generous and readily given.

Many thanks too, to the Curtis Brown Creative team, including Abbie Greaves and Abby Parsons who, through one of their online courses, offered constructive feedback and support in the late editing stages.

The writing community is a very warm and welcoming one, but I particularly want to give a shout-out to Carmel Harrington who has been so kind down the years.

While I'm at it, I'd like to thank my writing 'sisters' Lucy O'Callaghan and Ruth O'Leary. And a shout-out to my reading sisters at the book club!

There were a number of people who read earlier versions of this book – I promise you this is a much better version – so thanks to

Anna Farrell, Stephanie Culliton and Analiese Culliton for their valuable feedback.

To my wonderful friend, Margaret Downes. I love that you insisted on driving me to that writers' retreat all those years ago and stayed to participate with me.

Almost there. Much love to my husband Gary, my two daughters and my son. And to my wider family: my parents, my brothers, nieces, nephews and in-laws, and especially my aunts and uncles who kept me well stocked in books as I was growing up.

Finally, to you, the reader for choosing this book. I am deeply grateful.

Dedication

For my lovely mum and dad, Colette and Paul Black

Chapter 1

'FOR the last time, Kate, I was totally cool about being put on that ferry to the Isle of Man. Like, would it even be a hen party without a practical joke?' Jess Bradley tipped back her head in the loos of the Charleston Hotel Group offices and squeezed a couple of eye-drops into her right eye.

Kate flicked her a look in the mirrored wall as she slicked on some lipstick. 'Jess, I've known you since we were twelve, and your eye always does that twitching thing when you're lying.'

'It's Monday. They're twitching because I'm tired. Hence the drops.' Jess took a deep breath and held it while she aimed the tiny bottle towards her left eye.

'Really?' Kate looked doubtful.

'Of course.' Jess swiped the corners of her eyes and straightened up to flash her best friend a bright smile.

Kate sighed. 'Fine, but I still feel bad. It was my job to arrange everything, and that was not on the itinerary.'

'I love that you're a control freak.' Jess scrutinised her slightly frizzy, mouse-coloured hair and decided to tie it back. It made her feel more professional – sometimes it was the little things. 'Why do you think I asked you to be my bridesmaid? Anyway, it wasn't like I was in any danger. Zoe was with me.'

Kate looked slightly mollified, and Jess's insides squeezed with guilt.

'No offence to your sister, Jess, but that doesn't make me feel much better. I didn't even know she'd planned it until the last minute.' Kate tucked her dark bob behind her ears. 'Seriously, I tried to tell her it was a stupid idea, but she said it'd be a total laugh.'

Jess vaguely remembered Zoe giggling and telling the others that they'd be fine, only for her to pass out drunk on the bed as soon as she and Jess had checked into that hotel on the Isle of Man. She'd be strongly tempted to kill her sister, if Zoe wasn't a photographer who'd agreed to do her wedding pictures free of charge.

'Yeah, well, you know Zoe once she gets an idea.' Jess shuddered. 'To be honest, I'm still not over that TikTok video.'

As sole bridesmaid, Kate had organised Jess's hen party. On Saturday night they'd all gone to a Chinese restaurant in the city centre before hitting a club. Zoe had pushed Jess into the middle of the floor, where Jess had gone full-on Taylor Swift. And then there'd been more drinking. After that, Jess had been a lot less Taylor Swift and a lot more Cardi B. According to Zoe, she already had fifty thousand views.

Jess felt a fresh wave of nausea. She reminded herself that on the surface things could be worse. Her fiancé Simon, bless him, wasn't on social media, and even if he accidentally stumbled on the video, he probably wouldn't recognise her. After she'd lost her L-plates and cute veil, Zoe had made her wear a red wig, which had made her look like Pretty Woman's less attractive cousin. Kate wouldn't say a word, obviously. She was a total sweetheart. 'Have fun,' Kate had said. 'Go wild!' Well, she'd ticked that box. Now all Jess wanted was to forget it had ever happened.

'Trust me, it was the best weekend ever.' Jess spoke more firmly this time.

Kate pursed her lips. 'If you say so. What about Simon? Did he miss you?'

Unwilling to meet Kate's eyes, Jess rooted through her bag as they walked back through the lobby of the modern office building by the Grand Canal, its cream walls and pale wooden floors warmed by the early-morning sun slanting in through the huge glass doors.

'*Uh*, I think he was too busy working to even notice.' Jess found a Twix and offered some to Kate.

Kate scrunched up her nose. 'No, thanks, I've just had breakfast.' She hit the call button for the lift. 'Don't be so hard on Simon. I think it's great he's so dedicated.'

'*Hmm*.' Jess was munching through her Twix. She'd always found it attractive that Simon was a successful solicitor, but the man specialised in company law. The way Kate went on, it sounded like he did pro-bono work for refugees.

'Jess?' Emily, the new receptionist, waved frantically.

Jess gave a little wave in return. 'I'd better go see what's wrong.'

Kate looked over at Emily and rolled her eyes. 'She's probably broken a fake nail – the girl's a total drama queen.'

Jess said nothing. Sometimes Kate could be a teensy bit judgey. 'I'll go tackle my spreadsheets. See you at lunch.'

Kate's eyes widened. 'Can you believe your wedding is so close?'

'*Ha ha*, don't remind me.' Jess caught Kate's puzzled expression and forced a quick smile. 'I mean, it's so exciting.'

The lift arrived and Kate stepped inside, still frowning.

Jess waited until the doors closed and the lift was whisking Kate up to Accounts, before she sagged against the wall.

That had been the worst weekend of her life. After she'd thrown up the contents of her stomach over the side of the ferry and they'd reached dry land, she'd had to mind Zoe, who'd pulled a Sleeping Beauty at the first chance she'd got. Which was exactly what Jess should have done.

Instead, she'd gone to the hotel bar where she'd had a few more drinks and a personality transplant, before hooking up with that guy, Declan. Jess fanned her face rapidly with her hand. They really needed to turn up the air conditioning in here. Nobody knew. Not Zoe, who assumed Jess had spent the night asleep beside her. Not Kate. Certainly not Simon. Mind-blowing sex aside, it was the worst thing she'd ever done, and she clearly needed to have her head examined.

At thirty, she was the youngest marketing manager Charleston Group Hotels had ever had. She also had a wonderful, thoughtful and clever fiancé who was all set to marry her at the end of the month. And she'd almost destroyed everything with a stupid one-night stand.

It was way too late for regrets. All she could do now was to spend the rest of her life making it up to Simon. He just wouldn't know it. Because she'd already decided that her hen weekend was a secret she would take to her grave.

Chapter 2

EMILY was close to tears when Jess got to the reception desk, and Jess just hoped that whatever had happened could be sorted before Frank Charleston found out. The previous week, he'd asked Emily to order a cheeseboard for an afternoon meeting, but Emily had misheard, and had instead delivered Chinese food to a boardroom of bewildered executives.

Jess dropped her voice. 'Emily? What's wrong?'

The younger woman glanced around. 'I've completely screwed up,' she whispered frantically. 'And it's way worse than the food thingy. This is really serious. I could lose my job!'

Jess couldn't risk another headache. She'd already maxed out on painkillers after The Worst Hangover in History. 'Emily, whatever it is, we'll fix it.'

'Some guy called Ian Finnegan rang for you.'

'Right, he's the new events manager at Linford Castle. Did he leave a message?'

Emily rubbed her eyes, smudging dark eyeliner. 'Isn't that the five-star hotel in Mayo the group bought, that's like hundreds of years old? Do you think it's haunted?'

If there'd been as much as a whiff of a haunting, Jess would know about it. And the Linford Curse didn't count. 'Definitely not. What happened with Ian Finnegan?'

Emily sniffled. 'You're going to kill me.'

'I won't, just tell me what you did.'

'Right. So, I told him you weren't in yet, but he asked if he could leave a voicemail. And I thought I'd put him through to your office, but I accidentally put him on hold.'

'Not too dreadful.'

'My ex-boyfriend was on hold on the other line.'

'Crap.'

'I know.' Emily's bottom lip quivered. 'I ended up telling Ian Finnegan that he was a total prick, and that I'd faked all my orgasms and if he ever called me again, I'd –'

'*Stop!*' Jess massaged her temples. 'That *is* a bit of a problem.'

'I'm so sorry, Jess.' Emily's voice broke. 'You've been so lovely to me since I started, but I'm terrified that if Mr Charleston finds out …'

'Nobody's going to find out. Let me think.' Jess tried to focus. 'What did Ian Finnegan say, by the way?'

'Nothing. He just listened to my rant and then he hung up. That's when I discovered my stupid ex was still on the other line. Do you think he'll complain to Mr Charleston?'

'I'm not sure, I've only spoken with him a couple of times on the phone. I've never met him. Hang on, I have an idea.'

Jess scrolled through her contacts and rang Ian's mobile from the phone on Emily's desk.

As soon as he answered, she adopted a broad Australian accent. 'Hello, Mr Finnegan? I'm phoning you from the Charleston Group. We've had some problems with crossed lines on our phones this morning, so we're contacting everyone who … You did? I'm so sorry – we've reported it, and we hope to have it sorted as quickly as possible. Yes, of course, I can put you through now. Thank you for your patience.' She nodded to Emily, who transferred the call to Jess's voicemail.

'I definitely transferred him that time.' Emily beamed. 'You were brilliant, thank you.'

Jess was pretty sure Hungover Jess was far from brilliant. 'It's just hard to think when you're upset, but maybe don't make personal calls at work, if it's easier?'

'Maybe.' Emily seemed to consider this, then flapped her hands in front of Jess's face. 'I nearly forgot; I heard something exciting about Linford Castle. Although ...' she bit her lip, 'I wonder should I say anything?'

Jess stifled a sigh. 'I think it's okay to tell me.'

'Cool beans.' Emily leaned a bit closer. 'So, I heard a rumour this morning that some Hollywood celebrities have booked Linford for a massive wedding at the end of this month.'

Jess shook her head. 'I'd have heard.' Her mobile rang and she checked the caller ID before swiping. 'Jess Bradley.' She listened for a moment. 'I'll be there, thanks.' She hung up. 'That was Frank Charleston's secretary. There's a meeting in ten minutes. Listen, if anyone's looking for me ...' She hesitated.

Emily nodded furiously. 'I'll be able to transfer them, I promise.'

Jess smiled. 'Great. Thanks, Emily. Catch you later.'

Jess slipped into her office and pulled the blind. Since the weekend, everything seemed to be moving far too fast. Her own wedding, which had seemed ages away, was now in less than a month. She wished ... no, what else was there to wish for? She and Simon had been together for three years. And he'd been there for her and her family, right through her dad's two-and-a-half-year battle with cancer. After her dad had got the all-clear six months ago, Simon had proposed. For Jess's family, it had been a double celebration. Almost everyone agreed that she and Simon were a perfect match.

But now this. She'd never cheated on Simon before, and she still had no idea why it had happened now. She'd drunk too much, and that guy Declan had been … oh God, she had to stop thinking about him. The fact was, she wasn't a teenager anymore. She was a grown woman.

She dialled her voicemail and listened to the brief message Ian had left. *Jess, Ian Finnegan here, glad I got through. Chat when I see you later.* She checked her diary: there was nothing about Ian coming to Dublin. She'd phone him back after the meeting. Right now, her chest felt so tight.

Five minutes of yoga should sort her. She stepped out of her heels onto the thinly carpeted floor and tried to concentrate on breathing. *In – two, three – belly out. Out – two, three – belly in.* She placed a hand on her tummy.

Her knee-skimming skirt was cutting into her after the stress of the last few months had sent her sugar-cravings soaring. Which was bad enough, given her mother's dire warnings about diabetes, but she'd be in real trouble if she couldn't fit into her wedding dress. Why had she let her mother persuade her to buy something that resembled an eighteenth-century instrument of torture? She didn't care who the designer was – she'd never worn a corset in her life. Now she had to spend the last Saturday in July looking like a time-travelling virgin sacrifice.

Stop it, Jess. Don't think. Just breathe.

There was a sharp knock on the door and their head of finance stuck his head in. 'Meeting's about to start, Jess.'

'I'll be there in a minute.' Jess slid her feet back into her shoes and grabbed her phone and notebook, before heading to the boardroom one floor below. She could hear chatter and laughter as she approached the open door, and stopped for a moment to check her appearance, wondering briefly when she'd start to feel like she belonged at these meetings.

Adopting a confident smile, she slipped inside, her senses assailed by the competing smells of furniture polish and fresh coffee. She quickly scanned the room. Frank Charleston, chief executive of the Group, filled a large chair at one end of a long, gleaming table, while several department heads poured hot drinks and helped themselves to pastries. The only person she couldn't place was the well-groomed, grey-haired man sitting two seats up from Frank. She greeted a few people and slipped into an empty chair, just as Frank got to his feet.

An expectant hush fell.

'Thank you, everyone, for gathering so quickly this morning. I'm delighted to announce that we have some very exciting news about our latest hotel. One that will put Linford Castle on the world map.' He cleared his throat. 'As you're all aware, this group took a huge risk when we bought Linford Castle. At the time, it was barely holding on to three stars, and badly in need of structural repairs. After restoring it to resemble a grand Victorian house, we reopened it six months ago as a five-star hotel. Today, I can announce that our gamble has paid off.' He turned to the grey-haired man Jess had spotted when she came in. 'I'd like to introduce you all to Ian Finnegan, Linford's recently appointed events manager.'

Jess squirmed as Ian got to his feet, buttoning his jacket over a bright-pink shirt and dark-pink tie before looking around.

'Good morning, everyone.' His strong Kerry accent raised a few smiles. 'A couple of months ago, I got a call from an American celebrity couple, to see if Linford would be available at the end of this month. Obviously, it was very short notice, but nothing we couldn't manage. The couple want to hire the hotel for a week, starting with a three-day wedding for two hundred guests, and they've negotiated a very generous deal.'

'How generous?' someone said.

There were a few chuckles.

Two hundred people? That meant every guest cottage on the estate would be used to accommodate them.

Jess raised her hand. 'Ian, who are the couple?'

He turned to her. 'Chelsea Deneuve, the American reality TV star, and her fiancé Leo Dinardia, who owns a string of casinos in Vegas.'

Ian gave a genial smile, as everyone around the table began to speak over each other.

'*Wow!*'

'Christ, they're only engaged about a minute!'

'They're getting married in Linford?'

'We couldn't pay for this kind of publicity!'

Jess knew that management at Linford wouldn't have had many bookings to rearrange, to accommodate the wedding. The west of Ireland hotel was pitched at the very top end of the market, and business had been slow.

Frank looked to her. 'This will be the wedding of the year, Jess. I want you to personally take charge of things from our end, manage the marketing and publicity and liaise with Ian. It's the opportunity we've been waiting for.'

'Of course, Frank.' Jess wondered if he knew the hotel had been nicknamed Frank's Folly. Or if he cared that most people thought buying a rundown, four-hundred-year-old castle in Mayo and giving it a full Victorian makeover had been an ego project, one unlikely to turn a profit for a long time. Not to mention the Linford Curse, thanks to its record number of wedding disasters. But if this celebrity wedding was a success, none of that would matter: the slate would be wiped clean.

Jess raised her hand again. 'Ian, what day is the wedding?'

'Saturday, July 28th.' Ian helped himself to some more tea.

That was the day she was getting married.

Chapter 3

'I REFUSE to feel guilty anymore.' Kate ordered a flat white and a latte at Butlers Café later that morning. 'It's your own fault.'

Jess pulled herself back to the moment. 'What is?'

'The hen weekend.'

'What?' Had Kate somehow found out? She seemed very calm.

'You said you wanted one last wild weekend.' Kate put their coffees on a tray. 'Anyway, you didn't actually get yourself into any trouble.'

'Right.' Jess wished she would just stop talking about it. 'I'll have a blueberry muffin too. Let me get this.'

Jess paid and they sat down.

'Thanks.' Kate tucked some hair behind her ears, frowning as Jess rubbed at her eyes. 'Don't do that, you'll get stretchy skin, and don't tell me it's your hay fever.'

Sometimes Jess forgot how bossy Kate was. Although she knew she meant well. She tried blinking hard instead.

'So, have you forgiven Zoe yet?'

Jess grimaced. 'Mam rang me a while ago. Apparently, Zoe told her that we all went out for a nice meal, had a couple of glasses of wine and decided to call it a night. So naturally Mam assumes we all got completely wasted and slept with every man within a ten-mile radius.' She winced as the words left her mouth, but Kate didn't seem to notice.

'So, are the rumours about Linford true?'

Jess bit into her muffin and wiped away some crumbs. 'Yup! Frank called a meeting earlier. *California Girlfriends* star, Chelsea Deneuve, is marrying,' Jess did air-quotes with her fingers, '"Vegas King" Leo Dinardia.'

She thought briefly back over the past hour. After the meeting, Frank had introduced her to Ian Finnegan.

To her mortification, Ian's eyes had lit up.

'A pleasure to finally meet you in person, Jess.'

He'd given her a tiny wink, which she didn't know how to interpret. She had stuttered something vaguely intelligible in reply, hoping he didn't get a chance to talk to Emily.

Luckily, Emily seemed to have forgotten about the phone call.

'*Omigod!* I can't believe Chelsea Deneuve is getting married here in Ireland. You have to get selfies, Jess. Seriously, *California Girlfriends* is the best reality TV, and Chelsea totally deserved her win as Most Popular Girlfriend last year. Although I'm betting on Brandi this year.'

Jess had decided to humour her. 'Brandi?'

'Chelsea's younger half-sister – same mam. They're, like, super-competitive.'

The reception phone had rung, saving Jess from having to hear any more about Chelsea and her sister.

Kate looked thoughtful. 'You won't have to meet them, will you?'

Jess scrunched up her nose. 'I'm not sure, Frank wants me to liaise with Ian Finnegan. Although I'm sure the couple will have their own publicity people.' She shrugged. 'He probably thinks I'll market Linford better if I can get a handle on this. I know the wedding will be huge but Linford is really special, you know? Is it mad that I want it to be more than just a wedding venue? I mean, I know I've got the history and the whole Victorian thing too, but ..." Jess trailed off. It was the first time she had admitted she was struggling with the new marketing campaign.

Kate just laughed. 'How hard can it be? It's a posh castle and you're flogging it to the one per cent. And if it's just going to be used for celebrity weddings, so what?' Before Jess could object, she added, 'How did they manage to keep it a secret?'

'Ian Finnegan and Frank were sworn to secrecy, apparently.' Jess grinned at Kate's expression. 'They're flying in two hundred guests for a three-day wedding.'

'Jesus, the press will have a field day!'

'I know, it'll be amazing. They'll need loads of security, though, especially as Bobbie Grayson has bought exclusive media rights to the whole affair.' Tiny alarm bells had started to ring inside Jess's head, over the two-weddings-on-the-one-day scenario. And it didn't help that in all likelihood she was probably still slightly in shock after the weekend. She wrapped her hands around her cup. 'How's Luke?'

Kate visibly brightened. 'Spoiled rotten by Dad. They spent Saturday at the beach and spent Sunday watching football and getting takeaway. Luke said he beat Dad in four out of five chess games. Did you know Dad pays Luke a fiver for every match he wins? The boy's only nine, for Heaven's sake!'

Jess laughed, relaxing slightly.

After Kate had become pregnant in college, her parents had built her a tiny one-bed in their end-of-terrace garden. When Kate's mother died, her dad had moved Kate and Luke into the family home, while he settled next door. Jess knew that he'd do anything for them.

Kate checked the time. 'Come on, we should get back.'

They walked back to the office, a light breeze coming across the Grand Canal.

'Look, aren't they gorgeous?' Jess pointed to a couple of swans on the near bank.

'*Hmm*, they're always there.' Kate tugged her blazer around her slim frame. 'I just realised – that wedding is probably around the same time as yours.'

'*Um*, yeah, same day.'

'*What?*' Kate sounded shocked. 'Did you say anything?'

Jess avoided her eyes. 'Of course not. It's not like I'll be needed at the celebrity wedding – my focus is Linford itself. And, anyway, I'm not sure anyone knows I'm actually getting married.'

Kate gave her a look. 'Remind me why you haven't told people, Jess? It's weird.'

Jess felt herself tense. 'It's not weird. Simon wants a winter honeymoon, so there's no need to say anything for now. Plus, I've only been marketing manager for nine months. I don't want Frank thinking I'm distracted.'

'Let's hope you're not distracted on the day. What if something goes wrong and Frank depends on you to fix the problem?' Kate's eyes narrowed. 'Plus, your wedding is only about twenty miles from Linford – word of it might get round, as news does in country places.' When Jess didn't answer, Kate asked, 'Are you okay?'

God, she was so far from okay. She wished she could confide in Kate. But it was bad enough that she'd cheated on Simon – there was no way she could ask Kate to keep such a huge secret.

'Just a bit wrecked.' Jess managed a smile. 'Catch you later.'

Jess closed her office door and sat down to view the Linford Castle website. It included a drawing of the original sixteenth-century castle, photos charting its recent upgrade, and a short video of the hotel's highlights since its reopening. While Linford was beautiful, it was, as Kate pointed out, a destination hotel for the rich and, even with deals, they'd struggled to fill the twenty castle bedrooms. During the winter months, they'd managed to cost-rent some of their cottages to writers and artists, but Jess knew the group was desperate to start making real money from the place.

The previous owners had faced structural problems, not to mention the endless upkeep of an old castle. Then there was the Linford Curse, which, if legend were to be believed, had started in 1937 with a young runaway bride, Lady Helen Linford. When the castle reopened as a hotel fifty years later, those brave enough to marry in Linford's tiny chapel or in the castle itself had experienced everything from unexpected appearances by ex-spouses and jilted fiancées, to full-scale reception brawls.

The final straw had been when a groom went into anaphylactic shock and died during the wedding dinner. After a massive lawsuit, Linford's finances had never recovered, and the Charleston group had snapped it up at a bargain price. Since they'd reopened, there hadn't been a single wedding booking.

There was a knock on the door and Frank Charleston stuck his head in. 'Do you have a minute?'

'Sure.' Jess started to stand but Frank waved her back down and arranged himself carefully in the other chair.

'I'm flying out to our head offices in Switzerland tomorrow, and I wanted to ask a small favour.'

'Go ahead.'

'My nephew, Adam Rourke, is coming to work with us for a while. Would you believe he's never been to our Dublin office?'

Jess resisted an urge to groan. She knew exactly what was coming.

'So, he'll be here tomorrow, and I've asked him to work with you.'

Jess nodded politely. 'Is he on work experience?'

Frank hooted with laughter. 'Ah no, he's a bit older than that. He's even out of college.' He winked, and Jess made sure to keep smiling. 'He'll be helping you with this celebrity wedding.'

'Ah, brilliant.' Clearly, Frank had lost his mind. She had enough to do without babysitting the chief executive's entitled nephew.

Frank opened his hands in an expansive gesture. 'You've probably guessed why I've asked you to be hands-on with this, Jess. We threw a ton of money at Linford, and we've been operating at a loss since day one. Like it or not, this celebrity gig will help inform our image. To begin with, anyway. Long-term, we can't be relying on celebrities. Classy clients, Jess, that's what we need. People who appreciate its history and beauty, as well as its luxury.' He tapped the side of his nose. 'I'll leave you to dream up the magic.'

Frank stood and Jess scrambled to her feet.

'I'm excited to get stuck in,' she said.

'Excellent.' He cleared his throat. 'By the way, before the meeting, Ian Finnegan mentioned something about a problem with our phones. I asked our new receptionist, but the poor girl seems to be a bit dumbstruck around me.'

Jess wiped her hands on her skirt as she pretended to think.

'Yeah, there might have been, but they seem fine now.'

'*Hmm*, good stuff.' Frank shook her hand. 'Always lovely to see you, Jess. And don't worry about Adam, he'll be invaluable.'

Jess gave a bright smile. 'I look forward to meeting him.'

Chapter 4

SIMON came into the bathroom that evening and wrapped his arms around Jess from behind. He smiled and rested his narrow chin on top of her head, his silky, fair hair flopping across his forehead.

Jess tied a double knot in her bathrobe and tried not to look guilty. Simon had been asleep by the time she'd got back the previous night and, as usual, he'd been gone by the time she woke this morning. Now she met his pale-blue eyes in the mirror above the sink. She was a terrible person, who didn't deserve this thoughtful, caring, wonderful –

'You smell amazing.' He buried his nose in her hair.

'Thanks.' Jess swallowed hard. 'Actually, I was just about to take a quick shower.'

'Will I join you?'

Shower sex? In the three years they'd been together, that had never happened. Maybe he was trying to save water again. Like that time shortly after she'd moved in when there'd been a national water shortage and he'd insisted they shower together every day. Which had definitely been fun, especially as it had nothing to do with saving water. But the only time they'd attempted actual sex in the shower, Simon had slipped and sprained his wrist.

Now, his hand landed on her hip, and started to trail up to her breast.

His timing was atrocious. It was way too soon after … she squeezed her eyes shut, trying to shove the memory of her one-night stand firmly from her mind. Even to think about Declan was dangerous.

She turned around, hardly daring to meet Simon's eyes. 'Maybe we shouldn't? If we're going to your parents for dinner. They're kind of sticklers for timekeeping.' She offered an apologetic smile.

Simon leaned in to kiss her lightly. 'That's extremely thoughtful of you. *Um*, have you thought any more about us starting a family?'

He looked so hopeful that Jess tried not to visibly tense, as a familiar feeling of panic slithered through her.

'It's such an important decision, Simon, and we shouldn't rush it. Especially as I've just been promoted at work.'

Simon adjusted his round, wire-rimmed glasses on his nose. 'That was nine months ago. I'd say you've more than proved yourself.' He sighed. 'Promise me you'll keep thinking about it? I want us both to be on board for this. You're already thirty, and studies show the older a woman gets –'

'*Simon!*'

He blinked.

'Sorry, I didn't mean to shout.' Jess pushed her hands into the pockets of her robe. 'It's just, well, we've been through all this before and, you know, thirty isn't old. We've still loads of time.'

'Well, yes, but it probably won't happen the minute we start trying.' His voice faltered. 'And it's not like we haven't lived together.' He blinked again, his fair eyebrows disappearing under his fringe.

Oh God, she dreaded that look. As an only child, Simon was

obsessed with having a family. Especially as his own parents had married late and had, by all accounts, been lucky to have him. But she couldn't take any more guilt.

'I promise I'll think about it.' She managed another smile.

Simon pulled her to him and kissed her again, this time for a bit longer. Jess closed her eyes and remembered how much she loved him.

He released her. 'You take your shower and I'll go find a nice bottle of wine for Pops.' He squinted past her. 'Is that a bowl of sweets on the shelf?'

'*Er*, no.' Jess glanced around. 'Miniature soaps, all different scents.' She beamed. 'What do you think? I thought they were a bit more homely.'

Simon laughed. 'Than the liquid soap in the dispenser?' He gave her one last quick kiss. 'They're fine.'

After he left, Jess got undressed and stepped under the hot water. She reached for the shower gel, wondering how many showers it would take to feel clean again. She wasn't sure which was worse: that she'd had a one-night stand, or that every moment since she'd been lying to the man she was about to marry.

Simon was the best thing that had ever happened to her, and he deserved her honesty as well as her love. But, for both their sakes, she had to forget about her hen weekend, and focus on making things right with him.

But she couldn't do it at the expense of her career. She'd worked long and hard to get this job, and she couldn't mess it up by starting a family right now. Maybe things would be different in a year or two. She and Simon were so right for each other – this was just one obstacle they needed to overcome.

* * *

One of these days, Jess thought, she would walk through the door of Simon's gracious family home in Killiney and feel completely at home. It would probably happen after they were married. Obviously not immediately after – that seemed a bit soon. But it would definitely start to get easier. She'd be family then, and Professor Úna McCardle-Donohue and her husband, retired Judge Edward Donohue, would be her parents-in-law.

She suppressed a tiny sigh as she sipped her white wine and looked around the drawing room, with its papered walls and beautifully framed landscape paintings. She clearly remembered the first time Simon had brought her to meet them.

His mother, in a taupe cashmere jumper and perfectly pressed beige trousers, had ushered her towards a rather uncomfortable antique sofa.

There Jess had perched, drinking rapidly cooling tea from a china cup, while Úna had effortlessly steered the conversation. Simon's mother could probably give classes in small talk. Which was not something she'd always been able to boast. According to Simon, she'd been a reserved woman, happy only to discuss her academic interests. Her charity work had completely changed her.

Jess was surprised that Úna had retired so young from lecturing and thrown herself into what Úna termed 'worthy causes'. In an effort to find some common ground, she'd mentioned that her own mother did voluntary work. To her credit, Úna hadn't batted an eyelid when Jess explained that Carmel served tea in the parish hall after 10 o'clock Mass on a Sunday. Unless she'd been working the night shift at St Vincent's hospital, where she was a staff nurse, in which case she'd be in bed.

After that first visit, she'd asked Simon if his parents had a TV. He'd seemed a bit surprised at the question, but told her that they had an old, rather small television in the winter study. Jess imagined that most people with drawing rooms and winter studies lived on large estates and rode to hounds, or whatever the modern equivalent was, but she'd said nothing. Still, Úna and Edward were thoughtful and polite and, although Úna tended to be bossy, she'd always been kind.

She wasn't exactly sure how her own parents felt about them. Her dad was a hardworking, practical man, who treated everyone exactly the same way. On his first visit to their Killiney home, he'd spotted the greenhouses at the rear of the two-acre garden and asked the judge to give him a tour. The two men had spent a pleasant half hour discussing seedlings and organic slug deterrents.

Her mother had fared less well. Apparently, things had started promisingly when Úna complimented Carmel by declaring that nurses were the backbone of the Irish health system but had quickly deteriorated when she added that nursing was a vocation. Carmel hated people who subscribed to that theory, because she claimed it was always used as an excuse for poor pay and even poorer working conditions.

Jess also knew her mother resented it when Úna talked endlessly about her latest charity event. Nor could Carmel understand how Úna could listen to Mozart for hours on end 'because The Judge likes it', but claimed not to know who Daniel O'Donnell was.

As far as Waterford-born Carmel Bradley was concerned, Daniel O'Donnell was a national treasure, and she didn't have time for anyone who pretended not to have heard of him. Carmel had had a bit of a rant after that first meeting. 'Who calls their husband "The Judge"?'

'Well, he was actually a judge, Mam,' Jess had said.

Her mother had rolled her eyes. 'Total affectation. Can you imagine me referring to your dad as "The Electrician"? People would think I'd gone soft in the head.'

Now Jess sipped her drink and listened to Úna's latest charitable exploits. In a moment, her future mother-in-law would be urging her to come to a fundraising lunch or buy tickets for a charity ball. After she and Simon got engaged, Úna had suggested she might like to join one or two of her charities. But while Jess was happy to buy raffle tickets and sit through the odd charity lunch, she drew the line at being on committees with her future mother-in-law.

At the other end of the double reception room, Simon finally made his move on the antique chess board. He and Edward always had a chess game on the go, and each of them made a single move when Simon visited.

As the two men argued good-naturedly about the weekend's rugby, Jess glanced over and caught Simon's eye. He sent her a tiny wink, and she reminded herself again how lucky she was, and how utterly stupid she'd been.

He came back to where Jess and his mother were sitting, and Jess used the brief break in Úna's monologue to change the conversation. 'How was your day, Simon?'

'Good.' He handed his mother another gin and tonic. 'I'm in the Central District Court with a new case and it's quite interesting.'

Jess waited for Simon to expand, before she remembered he couldn't talk about any of his cases. He stood now, tall and straight like Edward, a glass of wine in one hand, the other behind his back.

She'd always thought he looked a little bit like a young, slightly skinnier Hugh Grant, with his angular features and floppy hair. If Hugh Grant wore Harry Potter-style glasses and was a smart, successful solicitor.

He smiled at her. 'What about yours, Jess?'

She sat up a bit straighter. 'Really exciting, actually. There's going to be a huge celebrity wedding in Linford Castle at the end of the month and –'

'That place has the best golf course in Ireland.' Simon pushed his glasses up his nose. 'Could you swing us a weekend deal there, darling?'

She hated golf! Still, they hadn't taken a break away in ages. And since they were putting off their honeymoon until winter, a weekend at Linford would be fun. Plus, the castle had its own stables, so she could probably ride every day.

'I can try. The hotel has amazing facilities. Seriously, the spa is to die for, and they put in a pool in this huge Victorian-style dome. Anyway, this celebrity wedding is –'

She was cut off as Simon's phone rang.

'Sorry, excuse me.' He gave her shoulder a squeeze and left the room.

Jess took another tiny sip of wine. Maybe she should shut up about the celebrity wedding. He wouldn't have a clue who the celebrities were, and even less interest.

She knew it wasn't Simon's fault. Compared to her own family, Simon's was very highbrow.

'Jess, dear, I just wondered what way you'll be wearing your hair for the wedding?' Úna said.

Jess pulled her left hand through her thick frizz, wishing she'd been born with hair like Zoe or Kate, whose own manes seemed to be forever silky, shiny and frizz-free. 'I haven't actually decided yet.' She hoped Úna would just drop the subject. But judging by Úna's expression, she was only getting started.

Now she dropped her voice conspiratorially. 'Well, what sort of veil do you have? Don't worry, I won't mention a word to Simon.'

'*Um*, I'm not wearing a veil.'

For a moment, Úna seemed to be stunned into silence. 'Maybe you just haven't seen the right veil yet, Jess,' she said finally. 'And it doesn't have to be a long one, remember. Some of the short veils are lovely. But you will need something, especially as you're not having flowers.'

Before Jess had a chance to answer, Simon returned. 'That was about a potential client. He'll be in Dublin next week. Jess and I are having him over for dinner with my boss.'

Úna swivelled to look at Jess and she nodded vigorously.

Oh god, that was next week, thought Jess. How had she forgotten? Apparently the client didn't particularly like going to restaurants when he travelled, so Simon had persuaded his boss that he and Jess would be delighted to have them at their place. Which – to be fair – he'd run by her in advance. Only at the time she'd agreed to it, she hadn't quite realised that it was happening the same month as their wedding!

He sat down. 'It'll be worth millions to the firm if I can get him. I'd say it would secure my partnership.'

Úna reached over and squeezed his hand. 'I have no doubt, darling. How are those dance lessons going, by the way? Have you two perfected your waltz?'

Jess waited for Simon to reply. When Úna had told them she

had a special early wedding gift for them, the last thing Jess had expected was ten ballroom-dancing lessons.

Simon pushed his glasses up his nose. 'Extremely well, what do you think, Jess?'

Jess managed a positive-sounding murmur. Simon, as far as she knew, never lied to his mother, so he obviously believed that only stepping on her toes half a dozen times during the class was huge progress. Although it probably was. After their first couple of classes, the bruises on her feet had been so bad that Simon had bought her a very generous voucher for their local beauty salon by way of apology.

Úna looked pleased. 'Jess, did you see my suggestions for music for the wedding? I know you two have the church organised, but I've given you some lovely ideas for the champagne reception, as well as beautiful waltz music.' She patted her fine hair, cut into a feathered style around her face. 'All very tasteful, I promise.'

Jess kept a smile pasted to her face. Since their engagement, Úna had taken to sending frequent emails with suggestions about everything from the length of the speeches (longer than three minutes was vulgar) to a selection of suitable wedding singers (separate ones for the church and the hotel) and string quartets.

Jess didn't mind that Úna had insisted on having so much say, especially as Simon was an only child. But having to make sure that everything was in good taste, or rather, Úna's taste, was a bit exhausting.

Simon pushed his fringe out of the way. 'I forgot to ask – how did Luke get on over the weekend with his granddad?'

'Kate said her dad spoilt him.' Jess latched on to the change of subject. In the past three years, Simon had become like a brother to Kate, while Luke regarded him as a favourite uncle. 'He can hardly wait to be a groomsman.'

'Kate's a terrific mother.' Simon's tone was warm. 'Luke's a credit to her.'

In the adjacent room, Edward carefully slid a vinyl record from its cover and placed it on an old turntable. Moments later, the opening bars of some vaguely familiar classical music filled the house.

'Is that "Air on the G string"?' It was the only Bach piece Jess knew.

Simon listened for a moment. 'No, it's his Fugue in G Minor. But you were in the right key-park.' He chuckled at his little joke.

'Everyone all right for drinkies?' Edward called.

Úna waggled her glass in his direction. 'All fine, dear.' She turned to Jess. 'What about you, Jess?'

Jess smiled and nodded. It had taken months of biting the inside of her cheek hard not to laugh when Edward spoke, given that he always sounded like a character from a PG Wodehouse novel.

Úna patted Jess's arm. 'Simon was telling me that you girls had a lovely weekend. It sounded very enjoyable.' She turned to Simon. 'Speaking of the wedding, the Judge and I bumped into the Feely-Martins at a charity golf lunch. You remember them, don't you, darling? You were in school with Jolyean.'

Jolyean Feely-Martin, Jess thought. Why did parents do that to their kids?

'Yes – we played Ultimate Frisbee together in school. And we were on a couple of chess tournaments together, although he was a lot better than me. The last I heard he'd been offered a lecturer's post in Cambridge. How is he?'

Úna's hand fluttered to her ever-present string of pearls. 'Apparently he's going through a horrible divorce, but that's neither here nor there. Mavis has accepted an invitation to be chairperson of the Irish Society of 20th Century War Memorabilia, and as you know I'm very involved, so I think it would be good to invite her and Archie to the wedding.'

Crap, she couldn't be serious. Jess waited for Simon to say something, but he just nodded vaguely. She spoke up herself, trying to sound reasonable. 'Would it not be rude to ask them at this stage, Úna?'

'Oh gosh, no. The Feely-Martins never stand on ceremony. Completely down-to-earth people like us.'

Jess took a mouthful of wine and coughed as it went down the wrong way.

'Are you all right, Jess?' Simon's eyebrows disappeared under his fringe.

'Yes, fine thanks.'

She couldn't really say no. Once Úna had recovered from the shock of what she considered a rather sudden engagement, she and Edward had insisted on helping out financially. 'I know it's traditional for the Father of the Bride to foot the bill, so I trust we're not offending you,' Edward had said to Tom, peering over the top of his glasses. 'Úna and I are delighted that Jess will be our daughter-in-law, and it would be an honour to help out.' And that was that.

'But, you see, there's a problem, Úna,' said Jess. 'We already have a hundred people. The hotel can't fit anymore.'

Úna waved her hand airily. 'Well, they'll just have to squash them in, or else we leave two other people out.'

Jess gaped at her. 'But everyone's already been invited.'

'Anything is possible, Jess, and these people are very important.' She patted Jess's knee. 'Now, I do believe the casserole is ready. Don't worry, if the hotel is dreadfully strict about numbers, you can always tell a couple of your friends to pop along a bit later instead.' She stood and smoothed down her long, pleated skirt. 'These things can always be sorted.'

Maybe the hotel could squeeze in another couple of people. Although when they'd chosen Burlington House, she remembered the events manager emphasising their boutique experience. Which, Jess knew, was hotel-speak for small numbers.

She'd wanted to marry in Dublin where their family and friends were, and where she could have got a staff discount in one of the Charleston Group hotels. But Úna, for all her Dublin affectations, was from Mayo, and she and Edward had married in Ballygobbin.

It was Úna who'd suggested they take a look at Ballygobbin's quaint village church and the nearby four-star Burlington House, which, in fairness to her, was far better value than a boutique hotel in Dublin.

Simon pulled Jess aside before they joined his parents in the dining room and pressed his mouth close to her ear. 'Let's not stay too late.'

She turned and met his eyes, trying not to panic. An early night was Simon's shorthand for sex. Not that long ago, she could hardly wait to get the man out of his Calvin Klein boxer briefs. Right now, all she wanted was to put her feet up with a glass of wine and a giant bar of Cadburys, and watch *Celebrity Come Dancing*. Guilt was a total mood killer.

'Jess?' Simon gave a tiny wink.

Jess managed a wobbly smile. 'Sounds good.'

Maybe if she just kept reminding herself how incredibly lucky she was, she'd eventually forget about the hen weekend.

It would be like it had never happened. In fact, she remembered that Declan had mentioned something about going back to Switzerland, so there was no chance she'd ever run into him again.

Úna caught her eye. 'Jess, do you feel well? You're quite flushed.'

'*Um*, it's just the wine. Excuse me.'

Jess slipped out of the room, relieved to escape for a few minutes. In Úna and Edward's pristine black-and-white tiled guest bathroom, she ran the cold water over her wrists, closed her eyes, and tried a few deep breaths. God, yoga was completely useless in these situations.

She opened her eyes and stared at herself in the bevelled mirror above the basin.

Chill out, Jess. It was probably completely normal to freak out after what she'd done. In fact, if she wasn't freaking out, she'd be some sort of sociopath. But she had to stop doubting her relationship with Simon: they loved each other. Ever since they'd met at her cousin's wedding, Simon had been a steady, dependable part of her life.

Which, after a number of shitty relationships, had been sexy and reassuring.

And although she'd hesitated for a moment when he'd proposed, she'd quickly reminded herself that marrying Simon was a smart, grown-up choice. Kate was right: she was lucky. Her life was almost perfect. And it would be utterly perfect when she married him at the end of the month. She'd be a fool to let anything interfere with that.

Chapter 5

LOOKING after a celebrity wedding would be exciting, Jess decided the following day. Everyone loved a wedding, and a celebrity one would help her kick-start a successful, long-term marketing plan for the hotel. It was quite simple: if Chelsea and Leo were happy to overlook Linford's unfortunate wedding history, everyone else would follow.

She'd start with a professional wedding photo-shoot at the castle. It was the ultimate romantic combination, and they could use photos and video footage on their website and across their social-media platforms. She rang Ian's direct line.

'Jess!' Ian's voice boomed down the phone. 'How can I help?'

She filled him in. 'What's your quietest time between now and the celebrity wedding?'

'Let's see.' Ian hummed to himself as he tapped away at a keyboard. 'How about the second last week of the month? That would suit ourselves.'

Jess thought for a moment. Ideally, she'd prefer to get it done sooner but, after the embarrassing phone incident, she was keen to stay on the right side of Ian Finnegan.

'That'll give me plenty of time,' she said.

'Grand, you let me know if there's anything I can do.'

After Jess hung up, she messaged Zoe. **You free the week after next for a day's work?**

Details? Zoe messaged back.

A wedding shoot at Linford Castle for the marketing campaign. But you'll need some help, it's a big job.

Send me the spec. Finn just called in. Talk soon.

Jess was glad she hadn't rung her. She might have been tempted to say something bitchy about Zoe's boyfriend. He'd probably dropped by to borrow money. At twenty-eight, Finn Murphy was a struggling dancer and performance artist, and was permanently broke.

Her mobile rang, and Jess cheered up as she saw Moira Bradley's name flash up on the screen.

'Nana, how are things?'

'Fine, dear. I'm about to head out to my sculpture class so I won't delay. I rang to say I was talking to your mother, and I heard you've too many people coming to your wedding – so, if you need to, you can leave me out.'

Jess tried to think. She'd only been talking to Úna last night. Had Úna rung her mother since then? 'Nana, you must be confused, of course you're coming.'

'I may be eighty-two, dear, but I have all my marbles and I'm never confused.'

Jess grinned. Her dad's mother was her last remaining grandparent. She lived on her own on the outskirts of Wicklow town and had always been strong-willed. The last thing Jess needed was her to dig her heels in over the wedding.

'Nana, you're at the top table, remember? I won't get married without you there.'

Moira chuckled. 'I was hoping you'd say that. Now, when are you coming to see me? I have a new bust.'

'What?'

'A sculpture, Jess, of our art teacher. My best so far. Mind you, he's very easy to look at and he's recently divorced. Mid-fifties, so probably a bit young for me, but I can look all I like.'

She giggled and Jess giggled too. She and Zoe were Moira's only grandchildren, and they'd always been close.

'I'll come out after work some evening next week.' There was almost no point trying to arrange to call at the weekend. Moira had a social life that rivalled her own.

'Good. I'll send you a text and let you know what evenings suit. Love you.'

Moira hung up, and Jess spotted a WhatsApp from Simon. **David arriving this week. Told him we'd meet him for a quiet drink.** Jess smiled and sent a couple of drinks emojis. David was Simon's oldest friend and best man for the wedding. Having lived in London for the past four years, he was moving home. Most importantly, he was single and, as far as Jess was concerned, his first job was to meet the bridesmaid.

Jess started to slump around 4 o'clock. She clicked out of the proposal she was writing, to check her emails. There was one from Kate, reminding her about Luke's tenth birthday party at the weekend. She'd promised to help out at a kids' adventure centre. There was also one from Úna, with the subject line **Veil suggestions and drinks after dinner.** With a small sigh, she opened it.

Jess, there's a lovely wedding shop in Dalkey village which stocks a very select line of veils. The owner Cora and I play bridge

together, so if you'd prefer I didn't accompany you, do mention me.

Oh God, maybe it would just be easier to wear a veil, and to ask Úna to help her choose one. Except at this rate she wouldn't get to make a single decision by herself about her wedding day. And she didn't want to wear a stupid veil. Jess read the next bit.

On a separate note, I wonder should we ask the hotel to offer brandy and port at the tables after the meal? Do let me know ASAP. Úna

Jess frowned. Did people still drink brandy and port after dinner? It seemed weirdly formal and old-fashioned, but she didn't want to offend Úna, and it was probably better to give in on something. **The drinks suggestions sound great. Will you let the banqueting manager know, or will I? Jess.** After a moment, she decided to add an *x* after her name. Úna never included kisses in texts or emails, but Jess figured she should make an effort now she was joining the family. She hit send, then slid open the top drawer of her desk and took out a Mars bar. Time for a coffee.

Jess was nearly out the door when the office line rang.

She wavered, then snatched it up.

'Hi, Jess, Emily here.'

'Hi, Emily.' Jess waited. She'd learned it wasn't a good idea to rush Emily.

Emily lowered her voice dramatically. 'There's the cutest guy down here to see you.'

Emily thought every man under forty was cute. Had Simon finished early and decided to drop by? Simon was cute: in a sort of overgrown, floppy, schoolboy kind of way. It was also highly unlikely he'd dropped by out of the blue.

'Did you get a name?'

'Adam Rourke. *Omigod*, Jess, he's so fit!'

Adam Rourke ... Adam Rourke ... *shit!* She'd completely forgotten about Frank's nephew. Jess smothered a sigh. 'I'll be down in a couple of minutes.'

Emily seemed engrossed in her phone when Jess arrived at Reception. Jess glanced quickly around the foyer and spotted a tall, dark-haired man, sitting with his back to the reception desk.

'Emily,' Jess whispered, leaning over the desk.

Emily jumped guiltily and pulled out some air pods.

'Sorry, just looking at Chelsea's latest TikTok. Have you seen it?'

Jess shook her head. 'I'm not on TikTok.'

Emily looked a bit confused. 'You should really follow Chelsea and Brandi. They're, like, so inspirational.'

'*Um*, yeah, I'll have a look. Hang on, who's Brandi?'

'Brandi Oliver? I told you – she's Chelsea's younger half-sister? Like, they're basically the only reason why everyone's watching *California Girlfriends* at the moment, because they had this, like, massive fight about two months ago, and now they're both trying to get each other kicked off the show.' Before Jess could say anything, Emily went on, 'So, Chelsea's made a TikTok about her wedding and the Linford Curse. Did you know that Helen Linford ran away with her maid on the morning of her wedding? Mad, right?'

'Did she actually use the words "*Linford Curse*"?' Jess kept her voice low. 'Never mind. Listen, tell Adam Rourke I'm in a meeting and I'll see him in a few minutes. I need a coffee before I deal with him.'

Emily's eyes drifted past Jess and colour rushed to her face. '*Er, incoming!*' she muttered.

'If you don't mind, I'll join you for that coffee and we can have a chat.'

Jess spun around to see the man in question behind her. He was clean-shaven, and immaculately dressed in a dark-grey suit and crisp, white shirt.

She felt faint.

That face, and every other part of him, were etched in her memory. It was the guy she'd slept with on the Isle of Man.

Chapter 6

ADAM Rourke's dark-blue eyes met hers. Jess watched his expression change rapidly from confusion and disbelief to amusement. At least one of them thought it was funny.

He extended his hand. 'Lovely to meet you, Jess.'

Jess wiped her sweaty hand quickly on her skirt and reluctantly placed it in his. '*You're Adam Rourke?*' The words came out as a squeak. Why was he staring at her like that? Shit, now she was having a problem breathing. She pulled back from his grasp and did a deep into-the-tummy yoga breath, before realising it made her skirt tighter. This was a bad dream.

And why had he lied about his name? *Say something, Jess.* 'Your uncle said you'd be coming to work with us, but I thought you were just out of college.' Oh great, if that was the best she had, she might as well chuck it all in now.

He smirked. 'When did you think that?'

Ha-bloody-ha.

Emily was staring at them.

Any moment now, Jess's face would burst into flames. Forcing herself to stay calm, she turned and crossed the foyer.

But Adam reached the door a fraction of a second before her and opened it before stepping aside. 'After you.'

Jess folded her arms tightly across her chest, every nerve in her body tingling as she stepped past him.

Wordlessly, they crossed the road to Butlers, as Jess struggled to think. If she'd learned nothing else from yoga, it was that brain fog was the first symptom of panic.

At the counter, Adam turned to her. 'What would you like?'

Right now, she'd love an entire bottle of gin. 'A latte, please.'

'One latte, one black coffee.'

They stood in silence as the coffees were made, then Adam gestured to a table nearby. 'Let's sit down.'

Jess's legs were like jelly as she slid onto a chair, surreptitiously glancing at her left hand. She'd worn her engagement ring for two days after Simon had given it to her, before almost leaving it behind in the loos, when she'd taken it off to wash her hands. After that, she'd told Simon she didn't want to risk losing it and had tucked it away in its box.

Adam met her eyes across the table. 'It's good to meet you … again.'

If there was any justice at all, Jess thought, the ground would open obligingly for her. Or better still, for him. Why couldn't she even get a one-night stand right? She wondered how much he remembered, or how much he'd guessed. Maybe he assumed that she regularly went clubbing in a white tutu and neon-pink T-shirt, with **RIDE-IN-TRAINING** in big iron-on letters across her chest. After the **B** had fallen off, her T-shirt had made no sense. Although no doubt Declan-slash-Adam figured it made perfect sense.

Jess stared at her coffee and realised she'd gone right off it. She folded her arms more tightly around her. 'Why did you tell me your name was Declan?'

'*Ah*. It's actually my first name, so it's on my passport. I'm sorry,

I didn't mean to lie, it just seemed easier to use it when we were on the ferry together and then, well, at the hotel.' He looked a bit sheepish. 'Adam is my middle name, but it's the one I use.'

Just not for a drunken one-night stand. Jess focused on the small table between them. 'I had no idea who you were.'

'Me neither. Look, it was just one of those things. We were attracted to each other, and we had sex.' He shrugged.

Jess blinked hard and concentrated on keeping her voice steady. 'Don't mention it, I'd forgotten about it.'

'Really?'

She looked up. Clearly, she wasn't fooling him for a moment. Hardly able to meet his eye, she did her best to sound dismissive. 'As you said, it was sex, nothing more. And nothing special.'

His eyes narrowed, but he finished his coffee before he spoke again.

'Glad I made an impression. I guess we'll write it off to experience.'

Briefly, Jess wondered how it was possible to feel this hot and sweaty without exercise. Taking a deep breath, she adopted her most dignified tone.

'Don't let me keep you, I want to finish my coffee.'

'I'll need somewhere to work,' he said briskly, 'What's your office like?'

She'd rather quit than work at close quarters with him. 'Tiny. I'm sure you'll find somewhere, though.'

'Fine. As soon as you can, let's talk about this wedding. It's the reason I'm here.'

The reminder pulled Jess straight back to reality. The chemistry might have sizzled between them that one night, but in the cold light of day Declan Adam Rourke was all business. Which would make working with him easier.

She spoke coolly. 'I have to go down to Linford on Friday afternoon to meet the couple and their wedding planner. They're flying in to see the hotel. I'll know more after that.'

'Perfect, we can go together, I'll drive.'

'There's no need for both of us to go.' She tried not to sound panicky.

Adam gave her a long look. 'Jess, I'm sure you grasp the enormity of this for the group. We've poured millions into Linford and all eyes will be on this wedding. If the high rollers like what they see, they'll come. But we need to make it pay. Fast.'

'I completely understand.' What kind of moron did he think she was? And why was he being so obnoxious? There was absolutely no way she was going to let anything slip about her own wedding now. 'It's my job to market the Irish hotels.'

He lifted an eyebrow. 'We need something special for Linford.'

Crap, she'd been right, Frank wasn't sure she could pull this off by herself. It was a depressing thought.

'Fine, we'll go together.'

Adam smiled, and her tummy did a treacherous flip.

He stood up. 'Catch you later.'

Jess slumped in the chair after he left. One night! What were the chances? And now he was here to spy. At least she hadn't told Frank she was getting married, especially with both weddings on the same day. She hoped Kate didn't let anything slip. She had a sudden, horrible thought: what if Adam had a girlfriend too? He could be just as attached as she was.

God, what was she thinking? Why would it matter? They'd both had too much to drink and made a stupid mistake. Luckily, he seemed willing to forget about it. She just had to pretend it never happened.

Chapter 7

JESS put the phone down and stretched, trying to ease the tension out of her neck and shoulders the following morning. She'd organised everything for the upcoming photo shoot at Linford Castle and put one of their regular photo-stylists in touch with Zoe. Her office phone rang, and she braced herself for problems with the arrangements. But it was her mother.

'Hi, Mam! Why didn't you ring my mobile?'

Carmel tutted. 'I'm having to phone from the landline because my mobile's out of battery and we've got this new bundle package, and your dad nearly hit the roof when he saw the first bill. Do you know how much it costs to phone a mobile from a landline? Let me see, I have the bill here.'

Jess could hear her mother rummaging about and muttering to herself. 'Mam, it's fine, just tell me why you rang.'

'It's Úna.' Carmel sounded a bit huffy. 'She's pushing me to tell her about the final numbers from our side because, according to herself, there's more people she needs to invite. Now, I know she and Edward have been very fair about splitting the cost, not that we needed it, but I won't be pushed around. We agreed to split the guest list exactly in half. She's breaking her side of the agreement.'

Her mother made it sound like peacekeeping attempts in the

Middle East. Jess wondered if Úna was talking about the Feely-Martins or if she'd suddenly discovered more people she wanted to invite.

'I'll mention it to Simon, Mam.'

'Oh Jess, what's poor Simon going to do? I love the boy but, honestly, he's devoted to his mother. I'd do it myself but Úna never answers her mobile, so I have to phone the landline and half the time I get stuck talking to Edward. God bless him, I'm sure he's a good man, but he's hopeless on the phone, and he never passes on messages.'

Jess could see this going from bad to worse. 'Leave it with me, I'll see what I can do.'

'Good girl.' Carmel sounded relieved. 'And will you ever have a quiet word with Zoe? I don't know what's got into her, but I can't look at her these days only she's snapping the head off me. It's worse than having a teenager around the house again.'

'That's the problem, Mam. She's been living at home too long.' Jess flicked open a fresh page in the notebook on her desk and started to doodle a little figure lying on a couch.

'Oh, will you stop, Jess. You know what your Auntie Anne says about twenty-five being the new eighteen. And she should know, being a teacher.'

Jess had no idea how her Auntie Anne would know this. She was a secondary school teacher, and she and Uncle Paddy had never had children. Despite this, her mother always asked her for advice.

'I'll talk to her on Saturday, Mam. We're coming for dinner, remember?'

'I know. Just don't mention anything about Úna in front of poor Simon. I don't want to upset him.'

Jess suppressed a sigh. 'I won't. I have to go. Love you.' She hung up and exhaled slowly, wondering why her mother always referred to him as 'poor Simon'.

Immediately, her phone rang again immediately, and she snatched it up without checking the caller ID. 'Mam, I really have to work now.'

'Hello, Jess? It's Ian Finnegan.'

Jess winced. 'Sorry, Ian, how can I help?'

'Bit of a change of plan, Jess. Our celebrity couple are flying in now on Saturday morning, so they'll be with us around midday. Does that suit?'

'No problem, I'll be down before they arrive.'

When Jess hung up she sent Adam an email to let him know. With any luck, Saturday wouldn't suit him, and she'd be spared his company. Then she messaged Kate. She hadn't talked to her since Adam's arrival. Now she had to make sure that Kate didn't say the wrong thing, without letting her know why.

It was getting complicated.

A while later, they slipped into the last seats at the bar in Pizza Pizazz.

'I thought we were having sushi,' said Kate.

'Would you prefer sushi?'

'Pizza's fine for me.' Kate was cheerful. 'Although maybe we should both steer clear of the deluxe special with extra cheese, at least until after the wedding.'

'I won't have the extra cheese.' Jess shifted uncomfortably, hating any reminder of the weight battle she'd fought right through her teenage years. 'So,' she adopted a deliberately casual tone, 'have you met Frank Charleston's nephew?'

Kate opened her breadsticks. 'Not yet why?'

To hell with casual. Jess leaned across the table and lowered her voice. 'The guy has been sent to spy. Frank is freaking out about the marketing of Linford, and suddenly doesn't trust me to do my job. He's a total pain.'

Kate frowned. 'Frank?'

'No, his nephew, Adam Rourke.'

'So, you had a formal meeting?'

'We had a coffee at Butlers.'

'No wonder you're suspicious.'

'Kate, take me seriously. I really don't want to work with this guy.'

Kate crunched down on a breadstick. 'You're not making any sense.'

This was the perfect moment to confess her Isle of Man one-night stand. But the more she thought about it, the worse it seemed.

Kate peered at her. 'Are you okay, Jess? You've gone a bit pale.'

'I'm fine.' Jess took a breath. 'Sorry. Look, it's just this guy was working at the company's head office in Switzerland, and he was meant to be coming over later this year. But Frank asked him to step in now because of the Linford wedding. Don't you think that's a bit off?'

'Not really. What I don't understand is why you're getting involved in that wedding.' Kate tucked her hair behind her ears. 'Don't they have a full-time events manager?'

'Ian Finnegan, yeah. But this is our first big event.' Jess sat up a bit straighter and undid the button on her skirt. That felt a bit better: maybe she wouldn't eat the whole pizza. 'Anyway, Frank wants me involved, remember?'

Kate shrugged. 'So now you've got help.'

'I still wish I wasn't working with him.'

Kate folded the empty breadstick packet into a small, neat square before tucking it under the salt. 'You've only met him – how can you not trust him?'

'It's just a feeling.' Jess chose her words carefully. 'I think it's safer to keep everything completely professional between us, so I'm not even going to mention that I'm engaged. I don't want him knowing anything personal about me.'

Kate shot her a quizzical look. '*What* is going on?'

'Nothing, look, please don't mention me at all.' Jess thought quickly. 'He's Frank's nephew and I don't want him reporting back, so don't tell him anything about my private life, promise?'

'Fine, you lunatic.' Kate shook her head. 'Now, can we change the subject?'

'Absolutely.' Jess beamed. 'Did I tell you that Simon's best man is coming back to Dublin for good this week? And he's single!'

'That's nice.' Kate studied the menu.

'Kate?'

She looked up. 'What?'

'Wouldn't you like to meet someone?'

Kate raised one dark eyebrow. 'So now you're trying to set me up with someone I've never met. Because as two sad single people we must be perfect for each other.'

'Kate!' Jess gave a burst of surprised laughter.

'Sorry.' Kate twirled her mother's ring around her finger. 'I picked up a dress, by the way.'

Jess beamed. 'For the wedding? What's it like?' Letting Kate choose her own dress for the wedding had been one of her better decisions, because as far as Jess could see most bridesmaid's dresses were awful.

'I have a picture.' Kate took out her phone and shuffled through a dozen pictures of Luke playing football, before finding a photo of herself wearing a full-length, silver-grey silk dress, with spaghetti straps and a side slit just past the knee.

'Oh, it's stunning!' Jess felt a pang of envy.

Kate smiled a bit shyly. 'You don't mind that I didn't ask you to come shopping with me?'

Jess shook her head. 'Don't be silly, I know it was something your sisters-in-law wanted to do for you.'

Kate put away her phone. 'So, what are you going to eat? You could have one of the no-cheese pizzas.'

'I'd forgotten they were a thing.' Jess pulled a face.

Kate glanced over the menu again. 'Actually, they mustn't do them here. Pity.'

'Tragic.' Jess cheered up, putting away the menu. 'It doesn't matter, honestly, I've already accepted that wearing that dress and eating will be mutually exclusive.'

She and Kate exchanged a grin and Kate called the waitress over.

Jess wished she didn't have to involve Kate in her lie. But asking her not to share anything personal with Adam was still better than coming clean with her.

From now on, there'd be no more lies. She'd be a good friend, a loving fiancée and an ideal daughter-in-law-to-be. And on the last Saturday of the month, she and Simon would have the perfect wedding.

Chapter 8

'GINA, you know they're keeping their theme a secret, but I can guarantee there won't be any circus animals. Just llamas. And white horses, and white doves and puppies.' Jess listened to the English reporter for a moment. 'I don't know the colour of the puppies, they're on loan for the day. No, as far as we know, none of the British royals are on the guest list.'

Jess propped the phone between her ear and shoulder and tried to open the sash window in her office. It wouldn't budge. But she was pretty sure she'd managed to strain her wrist. There was a knock on the door. 'Is that it for now, Gina? She took a breath. 'I'm sure Leo and Chelsea's own publicity people will be able to … right, thanks.'

She hung up and called, '*Come in!*'

Adam walked in. 'Morning. *Wow*, it's roasting in here! Mind if I open the window?'

'Be my guest.' Jess sat down, acutely aware of Adam's proximity as he gave the bottom of the window a sharp tap, before pushing it open.

'Tell me if you're in a draught.' He leaned against the window frame and slipped his hands into his pockets. 'How's it going?'

'Great.'

Jess wished Adam would sit down. It was difficult to concentrate with him standing there, taking up so much space in her office. He was too tall, or something. Although he was probably only a couple of inches taller than Simon. Too broad, then. God, she couldn't go there. *Focus, Jess.*

'There's a good buzz about Linford.'

Adam walked back around the desk and sat down. 'I wanted to talk about our image.'

'Right, well, I have some ideas.' Jess sat up straighter, and tried her best not to stare as Adam shrugged out of his jacket and loosened his tie.

'Sorry, go ahead.' He rolled up his shirtsleeves, revealing surprisingly tanned, muscled arms.

She hadn't really noticed that when they ...

He lifted an eyebrow, and she felt her face warm.

'Now?' she asked.

Adam folded his arms. 'Now would be good.'

'*Um*, well, I have it on file.' Jess fumbled at her keyboard, wondering why her brain had suddenly stopped communicating with her fingers. 'Just give me a minute.'

'Why don't you give me the elevator pitch?'

Jess grabbed a pencil and started to doodle a miniature castle in her notebook. 'Right, so, obviously, I thought I'd play on its history, and the fact that it's a luxury destination hotel on the Wild Atlantic Way.'

She looked up at him when he didn't respond.

'I think your elevator pitch might need some work,' he said then.

She tried not to glare at him. 'The key is its history, and its immersive Victorian experience.'

Adam waved his hand dismissively. 'Forget the history – it's enough to confine that to our website. The only bit anyone is interested in is Helen Linford running off with her maid. Which brings us right back to the Linford Curse. That's why this wedding is so important. Celebrities. Bobbie Grayson's behind-the-scenes documentary movie. And no chance of anything going wrong. This is the real money.'

'Maybe.' Jess drew a flag in one of her castle turrets. 'But that won't solidify our image. Long-term, Frank agrees that we want guests who know the difference between a watch tower and a water tank.'

Adam shrugged. 'So?'

She wouldn't give him the satisfaction of getting annoyed. Instead, she smiled sweetly. 'Maybe you haven't had a chance to look at the marketing I've done for Linford since we reopened? The media coverage, the new website, our strong social-media presence. I haven't been sitting around hoping for a celebrity wedding. Yes, this will raise our profile quickly, but we can't just depend on celebrities.'

'No, but we need to ensure a steady stream of income.' Adam spoke patiently. 'So, you need an angle.'

'Right, and a five-star hotel that looks like a fairy-tale castle is a good place to start.' Jess started to draw a tiny horse, but her pencil-tip snapped on the page. 'I won't have any problems selling that.'

Adam sat forward. 'You know, I hate to burst your bubble, Jess, but people can stay in five-star hotels anywhere in the world. They don't have to come to the rain-soaked shores of the west of Ireland. And most people don't actually care that much about history, either.' He glanced down at her drawing. 'You draw pretty well.'

Before Jess could respond, Adam took out his phone.

'Have you seen what's trending on Twitter? The celebrity wedding and the Linford curse. Do you know that twenty years ago Linford's owners allowed a wedding between two big crime families to go ahead? They weren't even halfway through the reception before a huge fight broke out: twelve ambulances called, and thirty-five arrests made. There were no weddings for three years after that, because nobody wanted to go near the bloody place.'

Jess managed not to roll her eyes.

Adam sighed. 'The last wedding we had at Linford, the groom died from –'

'Anaphylactic shock, I know.' Jess looked grim. 'And the wedding before that was annulled, because the bride kissed the best man on the altar straight after the ceremony. What's your point, Adam?'

He put away his phone. 'My point is that people think the castle is jinxed. We've been open six months and advertising wedding deals even before we opened. This is our first booking, and Linford should be packing them in. The great hall and the orangery are at opposite ends of the castle, so we could even have two weddings at a time.'

'Well, Frank seems to think that Chelsea and Leo's wedding will be the magic wand that'll wave away the curse,' Jess said.

Adam nodded. 'I think he's right, and it'd be a relief. But it may not be enough. So, we need to work on that high-concept idea.' He stretched and pushed both hands back through his hair. 'You've a great view from this office.'

Jess latched on gratefully to the change of subject. 'Where are you working?'

'I found a small office beside the boardroom. No view, though.'

She felt a stab of guilt. 'Still, better you have your own space –

we'd have been on top of each other here.' Heat flashed to her cheeks as soon as the words were out. What was wrong with her?

Adam smirked, but mercifully he got up to leave.

'By the way, let's keep the press pack very simple. We want to generate speculation. Not to mention that we have to keep their theme a secret.'

And there he was, back to his condescending self. If there was anything worse than Simon implying that her job was just something to do until they had children, it was Adam telling her how to do it.

She gave a tight smile. 'Don't worry about a thing.'

'I won't. Catch you later.'

He left and Jess muttered a couple of swear words. She couldn't afford to look insecure in front of Adam. Frank prided himself on a small, strong team of people at the top.

No matter why Adam was here, she couldn't afford to hang around waiting for his approval. She answered directly to Frank and there was nothing to prevent her putting together a proposal for him.

Chapter 9

'JESS, are you ready?' Kate knocked once and stuck her head around the door of Jess's office that lunchtime.

Jess looked up.

'We're going out? Brilliant, hang on.'

Hastily, she shoved the chicken sandwich with low-fat mayonnaise on wholemeal bread into her desk drawer. She'd made it that morning in an effort to eat healthier lunches and lose a few pounds before the wedding. Healthy eating could wait – right now she'd kill for a panini.

They took the stairs and emerged into the foyer.

'So, where are we going for lunch?' Jess placed a hand over her rumbling tummy.

'The Modern across town. We're meeting Úna and your mam, remember?' Kate's phone buzzed and she replied quickly to a text.

How had she nearly forgotten about that? 'Of course I remember.' She ignored Kate's sceptical look. 'What? How could I forget a lunch?'

'There you are, love.' Carmel waved almost maniacally at Jess, from a table in the middle of the room, as she and Kate arrived. The restaurant was early 1930s Art Deco style, and the two mothers were sitting at a linen-covered table with a Tiffany lamp centrepiece.

Jess noticed her mother's relief as they reached them.

'Úna and I have been having a lovely catch-up, haven't we, Úna?' Which was code for 'Where the hell have you been, I've been stuck trying to make small talk'.

Jess and Úna air-kissed before she turned and hugged her mother tightly, feeling her relax as she embraced her.

Úna turned to Kate and took both her hands in hers. 'Lovely to see you again, Kate. How's your little boy?'

Kate's face lit up. 'Great form, thanks, Úna. Beating his granddad at chess.'

'Isn't that wonderful? Does he ever play with Simon? I have an idea – why don't you bring him over sometime to play against Edward? I'll have lemonade and cake.'

Kate's face turned pink. 'Honestly? I think he'd love that.'

'That's settled, so. Edward and I will really look forward to that.'

Behind Úna, Carmel raised her eyebrows at Jess. She knew exactly what her mother was thinking. No sooner would she and Simon say, 'I do', but Úna would be dropping hints about them starting a family. It also struck her that it was probably the first time she'd heard Úna refer to her husband as Edward.

'Well, isn't this nice?' Carmel beamed as Jess and Kate sat down. 'Just the four of us. Now, let's catch that young fellah's eye, and get some drinks. Should we order a bottle of white?'

'Oh, I never drink in the middle of the day.' Úna clasped her hands together on the table. 'I'll have sparkling water.'

'I don't make a habit of it either, but it's a special lunch and I made sure to leave the car at home,' Carmel said.

'I'd better not drink when I'm going back to work.' Kate shrugged apologetically.

Carmel's smile faded as she turned to Jess.

God, she couldn't let her mother drink by herself – she'd look like an alcoholic.

'Let's order a glass each, Mam.' Jess beckoned the waiter over.

Once they'd given their drinks order, Jess cleared her throat, grateful to have something concrete to focus on.

'So, I thought this would be a good time to chat about a few details of the wedding day.'

'Speaking of which, Jess, did you get my email earlier?' Úna said.

'*Um*, yes, the one about the after-dinner drinks?' Jess made an effort to sound enthusiastic. 'I replied to say that's fine. Do you want me to –'

'No, you let me handle that.' Úna waved her hand airily. 'You've enough to think about.'

'What's that about after-dinner drinks?' Carmel looked at Jess. 'Sure, won't people just go to the bar and get what they want after dinner?'

Úna touched the string of pearls at her neck. 'Jess and I just thought it would be a lovely gesture to offer brandy and port at the tables afterwards, didn't we, Jess?'

No, we bloody didn't. 'Absolutely.' Jess avoided her mother's eye. 'So, Úna, you know that Mam, Zoe, Kate and I will all be getting our hair and make-up done at the hotel? I was hoping you could join us.'

Úna raised a hand almost unconsciously to her fair hair. 'Oh, I usually just wash and dry it myself – it's an easy style to keep. But Jess, dear, have you given any more thought to having a veil?'

'I don't think Jess is having a veil,' Carmel replied crisply. 'You decided against one, didn't you, love?'

Jess suppressed a sigh. 'I'll have something in my hair on the day.'

'What something? Are you wearing it loose?' Úna's eyes narrowed, and Jess guessed she was having visions of a bohemian-style bride. Which couldn't be further from the truth.

'I've been helping Jess with ideas for her hair,' Kate said, and Jess shot her a grateful look.

It was a total lie, but Úna looked relieved as she patted Kate's hand.

The waiter returned with their drinks and the women took a moment to give their food orders. When he left again, Carmel turned to Úna. 'You have to think of yourself too, Úna. Simon will only be getting married once, so you might as well go all out.'

Carmel delivered this in the sort of cheerful, no-nonsense tone Jess always imagined she used on her most stubborn patients.

Kate pulled out her phone and tapped on a file marked **Wedding**. 'We're booked in for hair and make-up in the hotel's beauty salon at 12.30. It's no problem to add one more person.'

Úna looked like she was about to object but instead she thanked Kate graciously, and added, 'How are we for numbers? Has everyone RSVP'd?'

Carmel cleared her throat. 'We're just waiting for three or four people from Tom's side of the family. I don't want to be hassling them. I'm sure they'll be in touch soon.'

Úna gave a small gasp. 'At this stage? Have they no idea how much planning goes into a wedding?'

'I'm quite sure they do, Úna – they're just fairly laid back, that's all.'

Carmel's unspoken inference hung in the air, and Jess wondered what had possessed Kate to organise a lunch with both mothers, then felt immediately guilty. Kate was a brilliant friend and, as far as Jess could tell, she was doing everything a bridesmaid was supposed to do.

She searched around for a safe topic. 'I got an email to say the cake is ready and will be sent down to Burlington House the day before the wedding.'

'I just hope they're very careful with it,' Úna said pointedly.

Jess knew she'd been a bit put out when Jess and Simon had opted for a profiterole mountain, rather than the traditional fruit cake Úna had suggested.

The food arrived and Úna took gentle control of the conversation, making sure everyone was included. It was a people-management strategy Jess had often seen her use, and she was happy to let her take charge, especially as she watched Kate blossom under Úna's genuine interest in Luke. She knew Kate missed her own mother badly, and the two women had always got on well.

As they left the restaurant, Úna took an envelope out of her bag and handed it to Carmel. 'Before I forget, perhaps you'd give this to Zoe? It's a list of people and groups we'd like to have included in photos at the wedding.'

'I'll make sure she gets it.' Carmel put the envelope into her own bag.

'Tell me,' Úna said, 'are she and her boyfriend still an item?'

Jess guessed that Úna was asking in case someone could be dropped from the bride's side of the guest list.

'Finn?' Carmel pursed her lips. 'Still very much together.'

'Simon tells me he's some sort of artist.'

'A performance artist.'

'Oh.' Úna frowned.

Carmel pulled the belt around her summer jacket. 'Actually, he and his troupe are giving a performance in town on Friday night.'

'Well, that's encouraging. I hope it goes well.'

'You'd be more than welcome to come along,' Carmel said.

'Isn't Finn's stuff very experimental?' Kate said quickly.

Jess tried to catch Kate's eye. What was she doing?

'I'm sure Úna can make up her own mind.' Carmel smoothed down her jacket.

'Well, obviously The Judge and I like to support the arts whenever we can.'

Carmel rummaged in her handbag and found a small flyer.

'Here's the details, Theatre Underground on the quays.'

Úna's hand fluttered to her throat. 'Is it easy to get parking? We might have to take a taxi.'

'You and Edward don't live too far from us.' Carmel seemed pleased to have the upper hand. 'Why don't I collect you both at seven?'

Kate was quiet as they walked back to the office, and Jess wondered if she'd been a bit hurt by the way Carmel had responded to her comment about Finn. After Kate's mother died, Carmel had treated her like another daughter but, the fact was, Kate wasn't her daughter. Jess sighed. She mustn't overthink it. Kate was a weird mix of inner strength and incredible neediness, and sometimes it could be a bit exhausting.

By the time she closed her office door behind her, she felt ridiculously tense.

Locking the door, she slipped off her shoes, lay down on her back and popped open the top button of her skirt. Wriggling close to the skirting so that her bottom just touched it, she stretched her legs up against the wall. She closed her eyes and tried to focus on her breathing. A few minutes later, she opened her eyes and stared up at the ceiling.

It was no good, she couldn't relax. There was a constant niggle of worry about the celebrity wedding. Which made no sense, since the Linford staff would have everything in hand, and Chelsea was bound to have an entourage. Nothing could go wrong.

Meanwhile, thanks to Kate and Zoe and the two mothers, her own wedding was falling perfectly into place. Really, all she had to do was turn up and marry Simon. But for some reason, she couldn't shake the feeling that her job and her personal life were on a collision course for the last Saturday of the month.

Chapter 10

JESS finished a video call the following morning with Ian, Zoe and Gemma, the stylist they'd engaged for the upcoming photo and video shoot at the hotel. She'd been a bit disappointed when Ian had advised her to avoid the swans on Linford's river for the shoot, because one of the sous chefs had had to get a tetanus shot after the female swan bit him on the arse. Apparently, she'd only been defending her cygnets. Still, getting selfies with wildlife seemed fraught with danger.

Frank, meanwhile, still hadn't replied to her email outlining her marketing proposal for Linford. Her campaign for TV and social media was a good jumping-off point but she couldn't do anything without his approval.

In an effort to include Kate in the excitement of a new campaign, Jess had filled her in, but she got the distinct impression that she wasn't interested. In fact, ever since her engagement to Simon, Kate had been blinkered to everything except making sure her two best friends had the perfect wedding. Jess knew she should be grateful: Kate was an amazing bridesmaid. But recently Jess had realised just how close Kate was to Simon, which meant there was no way she could tell Kate what she'd done.

The truth was that Kate's whole world revolved around Luke and her dad, Jess and Simon. The last time she'd even dated was when one of the other accountants had set her up with her cousin. Afterwards, Kate had bluntly told her colleague she didn't care how many eligible cousins she had, she wasn't going on any more awful blind dates. Kate deserved some male attention from somebody other than her dad, her son and her best friend's fiancé.

Jess messaged David. **Organising drinks so you can meet a few people. Would next Monday or Tuesday evening suit? Jess. X**

'Jess?'

She looked up to find Adam leaning against the doorjamb, his hands in his trouser pockets.

'What's up?'

He lifted an eyebrow. 'Maybe I should ask you the same thing.'

'What do you mean?'

He didn't respond.

Jess wished he'd just come in and sit down – he was way too distracting posing by the door.

'Come in, why don't you?' she said sharply.

He came and stood in front of her desk, hands still in his pockets.

He seemed to be gathering his thoughts.

'How do you view our relationship?' he said then.

'Sorry?'

'Our working relationship.'

'I haven't given it much thought.' It was a bit worrying how good she'd recently become at lying.

'You went over my head with your marketing ideas for Linford.'

Jess folded her arms. 'I work directly for Frank, not you.'

Adam's tone was patient. 'We're working as a team, Jess. I want us to be on the same page about Linford. Your idea was fine, but —'

Jess cut across him. 'My idea was a TV and social media ad campaign using actors in Victorian costume pretending to be guests at Linford Castle. We'd have a montage showing all the amazing facilities at the hotel, and the voiceover would say something about the experience being so authentic that guests feel like they've stepped back in time. The way I saw it was that we'd show people in their ordinary clothes walk up to the door and as soon as they step inside, their clothes, their hair, even their mannerisms all magically change.' She hated herself for sounding defensive. 'I'm simply doing my job. And I know it's a good idea.' She stopped, feeling a bit sick. 'How did you know? Did Frank say something to you?'

'No, I broke into your computer and went through your emails.' Adam rolled his eyes. 'Frank mentioned it in passing, he wanted my opinion on it.'

'He should have told me that you were my new line manager.' Shit, now she just sounded stupid.

Adam pinched the bridge of his nose. 'I'm not, Jess — stop being so defensive. If anything, I'm the one who should feel annoyed here. Frank assumed I knew about this. You didn't bother to tell me.'

And now he was gaslighting her.

'You were completely opposed to my ideas when I mentioned them,' she said.

'You didn't mention any ideas. Well, you did, but let's face it, they were a bit waffly.'

Jess took a breath. 'I told you I had a plan, and you started going on about how we should treat a four-hundred-year-old, beautifully restored castle as a theme park for tasteless celebrities.'

Adam raised an eyebrow. 'When exactly did I say that?'

'When you started going on about Bobbie Grayson and her making a movie of the celebrity wedding. As if we've been waiting this whole time for a bunch of celebrities to descend on us and give us buckets of money.'

Adam burst out laughing.

Jess swallowed hard. 'What's so funny?'

'You are. I didn't realise you were such a snob.'

'I'm not, I'm just stating the obvious. If I was a snob,' Jess warmed to the theme, 'I wouldn't have suggested we try to make Linford Castle more accessible.'

Adam shook his head. 'Linford is the ultimate playground, that's what we're selling.'

She knew he was deliberately misunderstanding her. 'You make it sound like Vegas.'

'What's wrong with Vegas?'

And now he was winding her up. 'It's fake. And gaudy.' She threw up her hands. 'And, I don't know, too easy to get married by mistake.'

His eyes glinted. 'And wake up the following morning with a ten-dollar ring on your finger, and a stranger beside you in the bed?'

Jess reddened, and Adam had the grace to look sorry.

'All I'm saying is Vegas is fun, Jess.' His tone softened. 'People know what they're getting.'

'People will know what they're getting with Linford. And it's authentic.'

'Like the Linford Curse? Come on, Jess, we're selling escapism.'

Jess took a deep breath, and reminded herself that managing people was part of her job. 'I think we both actually want the same thing.'

Adam studied her a moment. 'What I want is to market the place to a wealthy global audience. What you want is to give a history lesson. It's a five-star hotel, not a visitor centre.'

He had to be the most annoying person she'd ever worked with.

'Just think about it,' Adam continued. 'If we're to turn a profit, Linford will always be about the big events and the international market: Europe, America, Asia.'

Which was why her proposed ad campaign was perfect! Except that he was completely ignoring what made Linford Castle special.

'Look, I've quite a lot to do this morning,' Adam said. 'Do you want to talk about it over lunch? We can work here, I'll bring food.'

It sounded more appealing than Jess wanted to admit, but she remembered just in time that she had to meet Simon at Occasions on D'Olier Street, so they could choose their wedding favours. Finally, they were about to do the most fun planning since their cake-tasting. And this time, it would just be the two of them. Operation Be a Better Fiancée: *tick!*

'Sorry, I have other plans.' She tried not to look smug.

'Pity.' He turned to leave. 'Do you think Emily likes pizza? I'm having some delivered.'

God, she'd kill for a pizza. She adopted her most disinterested expression – he was clearly looking for a reaction. Simon would never behave so childishly. Although Simon didn't like pizza. Still, that wasn't the point.

Adam winked. 'I'd better go down and see if it's here. Catch you later. Enjoy your lunch.'

As discreetly as possible, she pushed her folded arms into her stomach, hoping Adam couldn't hear it rumble. 'I will.'

Adam left, and Jess checked the time. Ten past one! Shit, she was late, and it was all Adam's fault. She wouldn't even have time to eat now. She'd slung her bag across her body before she remembered the chicken sandwich from the previous day. Opening her desk drawer, she eyed the chocolate before grabbing the sandwich bag and unzipping it, sniffing cautiously. It'd be fine.

Outside, the lift was opening, and she waited for it to empty, before jumping in. She took a large bite of the sandwich.

Better to eat it as quickly as possible – she'd have to try to get a taxi now.

'Hi, I was starting to worry.' Simon pulled her in for a quick kiss, as she arrived at Occasions.

'I know, yeah, I'm sorry.'

Jess took a deep breath, determined to forget about work for a while. The next three-quarters of an hour was about making memories, choosing small, thoughtful gifts that their guests would treasure forever. At least, that's what it read on the shop's website.

'You must be Jess and Simon.' A dapper, middle-aged man in a three-piece suit, complete with buttonhole, approached, smiling widely. 'I'm Ken and I'll be assisting you today. Lovely to meet you both. Now, you've booked an hour, so let's get started.'

Simon pushed his glasses up his nose. 'Actually, I have to be back at the office by ten past two.'

'But I've been on the website and I've narrowed down our choices,' Jess said hurriedly.

Ken frowned. 'That's a bit tight, but we'll do our very best.' He tapped on the iPad he was carrying. 'Let me open our order form and we'll make a start.'

Jess pointed out the items she had selected and discussed each with Simon who seemed hesitant about them. Ken made suggestions and displayed other possibilities.

'Maybe everyone would just like to take home a slice of cake,' Simon said eventually. He turned to Jess as Ken clicked onto a page showing a selection of decorative sweet boxes. 'I don't think I've ever eaten the cake at a wedding.'

'We have profiteroles, remember?' Jess said. 'They'll be demolished.' She slipped her hand into Simon's. 'I just think we should be picking things that say "Jess and Simon", you know?'

Simon looked confused. 'Things with our names on them?'

Ken made a delicate sound in his throat. 'I think what your fiancée means is that she'd like your wedding souvenirs to be special to you both, to reflect your personalities, your relationship and your unique day.'

Jess was starting to like Ken more and more. 'I love those vintage-y-looking cups with the candles in them. And those tiny heart-shaped soaps and the little packets of tea that can be monogrammed with our initials.' Maybe they could give everyone a goody bag? They could have five things in each bag. No, seven. And the items didn't all have to be from here. They could throw in a giant bar of chocolate and a little packet of mints. People would love it.

'I think we'll choose one small token for each place setting,' Simon said. 'Perhaps one of those little bundles of sugared almonds. They're simple and tasteful. And people don't want …' he seemed to be searching for a suitable word, 'odd bits they might feel obliged to keep afterwards.' He turned to Jess. 'What do you think?'

Jess stared at him. *Bundles of sugared almonds?* Úna would approve, of course.

Simon got to his feet. 'I'm afraid I have to go, Jess. Can you look after it from here?'

'Absolutely.' Jess gave a bright smile. 'No problem.'

'Thanks, darling.' He bent down and pecked her cheek. 'See you this evening.' He straightened and stuck his hand out to Ken. 'Thank you so much for your help.'

Jess tried not to feel too disappointed as she watched Simon leave. She turned back to Ken, who gave a diplomatic smile.

'Shall we look at those sugared almonds?' he said.

Jess sighed. Feck it, it was her wedding too. 'And those miniature bottles of mead too, please.'

Chapter 11

WHAT had possessed her to eat a chicken sandwich that she'd kept in a drawer overnight? Jess could almost hear her mother warning her about the hazards of food safety and salmonella poisoning. She'd clearly lost her mind. And judging by the sinister gurgling noises, she was about to lose the contents of her stomach. She sat as still as she could on the sofa, as Simon walked from one room to another, putting things away and talking about something she wasn't following.

The man really was obsessed with tidying. Which was great, she reminded herself, given how bad she was at it. As he came back into the living room to examine his tie in the mirror above the fireplace, Jess tried to remember where he was going. Maybe he'd arranged to meet David for a drink. Although wearing a tie to the pub was a bit formal, even for Simon.

Pain and nausea were coming in waves now, and she hoped desperately that the throwing-up part wouldn't start until after Simon left. He'd never been good around her when she was sick.

'Aren't you getting ready?' Simon turned away from the mirror to look at her.

She looked at him blankly.

'The opera?' he said.

Shit, the opera! She'd promised to go. Offered, in fact: Operation Be a Better Fiancée.

'I was thinking, if we get to the theatre early, we could have a glass of wine first.' He gave her an expectant look.

'Oh, great.' She waited until Simon disappeared back to the bedroom. Okay, she'd be fine, she'd just take it slowly. She made an effort to stand, but another wave of nausea surged through her, and she crumpled back onto the sofa, before sliding further onto the polished oak floor. That felt better, it was cooler down here. She'd just crawl instead.

'Jess? What are you doing?'

She looked up.

Simon looked startled as he peered down at her from the doorway.

'I'm going to be sick.'

'*What? Hang on!*'

Before she could do anything, he pulled her to her feet and practically dragged her to the bathroom. She fell to her knees and heard the door click behind him as he left, She hung over the toilet bowl and vomited. After a few minutes, she pulled herself up, gasping, and leaned back against the tiled walls, pressing her hand experimentally against her tummy.

Simon knocked on the door, then nudged it open and looked around. 'How are you feeling?'

'A bit better now that I've thrown up.'

'I'm just thinking, is there any chance …?'

'That I'll pass it on to you?'

'No.' Simon hesitated. 'I just wondered if you might be pregnant.'

Jess groaned. 'No, it's the dodgy chicken sandwich I had at lunch.'

'Oh.' Simon's face fell. 'You poor thing. Can I get you anything?'

She put her head in her hands. 'I'm not sure if I'm up to tonight. Sorry. I'm a terrible girlfriend.'

'Don't be silly, you can't help being sick.' He gave a tentative smile. 'I'll see if they can sell the tickets as returns.'

He was the loveliest person on the planet. She felt a rush of gratitude along with a warm feeling in her tummy, that she recognised just in time.

As she hung over the toilet bowl again, she heard Simon leave. He came back a few moments later with a glass of fizzy water and handed it to her.

'Thanks.' Jess took the glass with shaky hands and sipped cautiously. 'Why don't you ask your dad to go? I'll be fine here, honestly.'

Simon pushed his glasses up his nose. 'I can't leave you on your own when you're sick.'

'Yes, you can, really, I'd prefer it.'

'Are you sure?'

'Positive.' Jess managed a reassuring smile.

Was that a flash of relief on Simon's face? She didn't move as he walked back into the living room to call his dad, only to return moments later.

'The folks have a previous engagement.'

Jess peered up at him. 'Is there anyone else you could ask?'

She was about to suggest David, when Simon said, 'Actually, Kate mentioned that she likes the opera.'

'She does?' Jess couldn't remember Kate ever liking opera, but she'd probably been humouring him. And it would solve the immediate problem. 'You should ask her.'

Simon scrolled through his phone. 'Kate? Hi, it's me.'

He walked out of the room again, looking happier when he reappeared.

'She said she'd meet me there.'

'Brilliant.' Jess's stomach swirled and she tried to take small breaths. 'Go, or you'll be late.'

'Do you want me to help you to bed first?'

'I'd better stay here for a while.'

'I'll leave my phone on silent. Message me and I'll come straight home. Promise me?'

'I promise.' She managed another smile.

Simon seemed satisfied. 'Love you.'

'Love you too.'

Jess heard the front door close just before she threw up again.

Sipping as much fizzy water as she dared, she found her phone and headed to the bedroom. She should probably sleep but she felt a lot better than she had ten minutes ago. She propped herself up against the pillows and checked her emails. There was one new one from Ian, confirming that all the hot-air-balloon operators had been vetted. *Wow*, the man worked late!

Jess opened Google Maps, popped Linford Castle in the search bar and zoomed in. They planned to set up the balloons in the far east field, where the river was. She made some quick calculations: it was about a mile from the hotel, too long for most guests to walk. Linford had about half a dozen Victorian-style coaches, but they could definitely do with more. She opened her emails and hit compose.

Hi Ian,

With the hot-air-ballooning happening a mile from the hotel, would it be possible to hire more horses and buggies? In general,

it might be an idea to have more for the wedding. What do you think?

Jess

As an afterthought, she looped Adam in and sent it off.

To her surprise, Adam replied almost immediately. **That sounds great, if you think it's possible, Ian?**

Maybe he felt bad about earlier, she thought, as another wave of nausea sent her running back to the loo. Sitting against the white-tiled wall, she hugged her knees to her chest and rested her head on top of her knees. Adam was clearly keen to work as a team. And she had to admit that it was strangely comforting to work with him, even if he was her one-night stand.

She sat for a while until the nausea subsided, before cleaning her teeth.

Back in the bedroom, she peeled off her clothes, pulled on an old T-shirt and climbed back into bed, grateful for the blackout curtains at the window. She had to remember to thank Kate for tonight. But as she drifted into sleep, her last thoughts were of Adam.

Chapter 12

'YOU'RE sure you should be at work?' Kate frowned at Jess over her coffee the following morning.

Butlers was buzzing, and they were perched on stools at one end of the high counters that ran along the windows.

Jess slouched as she sipped her second cup of black tea. 'Yeah, it was just a dodgy chicken sandwich I had for lunch yesterday.'

Kate looked appalled. 'Where did you buy it? Because you need to tell them they're poisoning their customers.'

'Yeah, no, definitely.'

'So, do you think you're up to Finn's performance tonight?'

'Yeah, I should be fine. You'll be there, right?'

'I'm not sure.'

'Why? What's up?'

'Nothing.' Kate tucked her hair behind her ear. 'Maybe it'd be better for you and Simon to just go together, without me tagging along.'

Jess stared at her. 'It's not a date night, Kate: it's Finn's gig. There'll be loads of people there – of course you should come.' She drank some more tea. 'Thanks for coming to the rescue last night, by the way. I'd say three hours of German opera was grim.'

'Actually, it was lovely.' Kate shrugged.

'If you say so.'

'Were you talking to Simon this morning?'

'Nope, he's always up and gone before me. Why?'

Kate gave her a strange look. 'I think you should try to like opera, that's all. I mean, Simon loves it.'

An unexpected wave of nausea curled through Jess's stomach. She'd never eat chicken again: maybe she'd become vegetarian.

'We've separate interests, Kate. I don't expect Simon to go out riding with me.'

Kate started to tidy up the counter. 'Not all of us got riding lessons when we were kids, Jess. You wouldn't catch me dead on a horse.'

'Maybe you could be Simon's opera buddy.' Jess tried to make it sound like a joke. 'Ignore me, sorry, I barely slept.'

'God, you poor thing.' Kate gave a small shake of her head. 'Look, tell me to mind my own business, but all I'm saying is that it's important for couples to have shared interests. And, you know, be careful not to take Simon for granted.'

'I don't.' Jess belched loudly. 'God, sorry, that was awful. Still, I feel a bit better after it.'

Kate grinned. 'We'd better get back. By the way, I've offered to do the accounts for one of Úna's charities.'

'Are you getting paid?'

'No, it's voluntary.'

'That was generous of you.' Jess stretched carefully, hoping Kate hadn't felt pressured.

'Simon mentioned it, and I thought it'd be good to get involved in something outside work.'

Kate's phone rang and she checked the caller ID.

'It's Carl, he probably wants to talk to me about those figures I sent him yesterday. I'm going to run, see you guys tonight.'

Back at the office, Jess mulled over what Kate had said. Obviously, Kate was wrong, because she didn't take Simon for granted. Except for that one night. Which didn't count, because she knew it had been a mistake, and she'd regretted it ever since. But she also had to stop thinking about it and put it behind her.

Turning to a new page of an A4 notepad, she doodled a quick sketch of a castle, with a driveway, a river and trees. She'd loved art at school, and even though she'd decided against art college, doodling usually helped her to brainstorm.

The problem was this time it wasn't working. Marketing Linford Castle should be child's play. Even Kate thought so. Especially now it was to host a celebrity wedding. But even that didn't distinguish Linford from other beautiful old castles, now high-grade hotels, that offered lavish, fairy-tale weddings.

She wondered if they'd ever be able to use its history to their advantage. To date, no matter how cleverly she'd tried to present it, the general public tended to zero in on Lady Helen Linford's non-wedding in July 1937.

Jess added a little figure in a wedding dress and veil, running out of the castle. Helen Linford's disappearance was still a mystery. On the morning of her wedding, her maid went to help the twenty-one-year-old get ready. When her mother went to look for her a while later, the wedding dress was still on the bed, and both Helen and her maid were gone. Neither was ever found. Despite the family's attempts to pretend that Helen had been taken ill and sent to a sanatorium, rumours quickly spread that she and her maid had fled the country.

Most people nowadays speculated that the two young women had fallen in love and had lived abroad as 'companions' for the rest of their lives. Either way, Lady Helen Linford was the castle's infamous runaway bride, and the Linford family never had another wedding at the castle.

Jess's phone rang and she clicked out of the file, swiping to answer Simon's call. 'Hi.'

'How are you feeling, darling?'

She smiled. Simon rarely rang during work, so he'd obviously been worried about her. 'Much better, thank you.'

'Are you sure? Because if you're still feeling a bit sick, we can always skip tonight. I'm sure Finn will understand.'

Jess swivelled her chair around to look out the window. There was no sign of the swans on the canal. 'I'd feel bad, Simon. I think they need as much support as possible.'

'Oh, okay.' Simon sounded resigned. 'The thing is, I was talking with Kate last night and she agrees that Mum and Pops will probably hate it. So, it's better they give it a miss.'

How had Kate managed to get herself in the middle of this? Although, knowing Kate, she'd have simply been honest with Simon if he'd asked.

Jess's stomach rumbled loudly, and she pressed cautiously on it, as she attempted to sound reasonable. 'Your parents are grown-ups, Simon, you should let them decide. I have to go. I'll see you this evening.'

Jess hung up before Simon could say anything else and put her phone in her desk drawer. The only upside of a dodgy stomach was that she couldn't face chocolate. Her tummy gave another rumble, and she pushed away from her desk. She'd buy some plain crackers, make herself some tea and grab a quiet ten minutes.

* * *

'Jess, are you sure this is the right place?' Simon stumbled on the winding stairs that led to Theatre Underground on the Quays that Friday evening. '*Ouch, Christ!*'

Jess, who was walking in front of him, turned and peered back around the curve of the steps. 'You all right?'

Simon rubbed his forehead. 'I think I can feel a lump coming up.'

'Oh.' Jess squinted. 'You poor thing – we should get something on that.'

They emerged into a dimly lit, cavernous room, already half-full with a mostly young crowd who were chatting and drinking. A bar ran along the back wall and tables and chairs, many of them half hidden behind huge stone pillars, were arranged to face the small open area they'd just walked through.

'Is there another room?' Simon looked around.

'I think this is it.' Jess gestured towards the modestly sized performance space.

Simon's eyebrows shot up under his fringe, and Jess guessed what he was thinking. If it were full tonight, Edward could feel claustrophobic. Maybe she should have let Simon discourage them.

'I'll get some ice, hang on.' Jess hurried over to the bar and came back a few moments later with a glass of ice and some paper napkins. She wrapped an ice cube and handed it to Simon, who pressed it against the lump.

'Thanks. Oh, there's Kate.' He waved her over with his free hand. Kate looked very un-Kate-like as she approached them, smoothing down an eye-catching dress with a bright butterfly design.

'You look amazing.' Jess wondered if she should have made more of an effort.

'Thanks.' Kate turned to Simon. 'What happened?'

'Nothing, I'm fine, just bumped my head. Look …' He lowered the ice cube.

'Luke did that last week on the football pitch.' Kate shot him a look of sympathy. 'You really need to keep that ice on the bump.'

Simon handed the wrapped ice cube to her. 'Would you?'

Kate wrapped another napkin around it and placed it carefully on Simon's forehead. 'I'm going to apply a bit of pressure.'

Jess wondered if she should get a drink and let Kate fuss for another while. Sometimes she felt like an outsider around them.

After what seemed like ages, Simon drew back. 'Thanks, that feels better.' He touched his forehead gingerly. 'You look lovely, by the way.'

Was Kate blushing, Jess wondered. It was hard to tell under all the make-up. Kate rarely wore much make-up, apart from lipstick and a tiny bit of blusher. And she so rarely bought herself new clothes, she was obviously delighted someone had noticed.

Kate clasped her hands behind her back. 'You'll be pleased to know that I've been trying to persuade Jess to give opera a chance.'

'Kate!' Jess felt a flicker of irritation.

Kate shot her a bemused look. 'What?'

Simon chuckled. 'I usually bribe her with a glass of wine beforehand.'

Kate laughed and Jess forced herself not to react. It never bothered her that Simon and Kate were close, but sometimes she felt like a kid around the grown-ups when they ganged up on her.

'Well, we're in the right place, anyway.'

Jess turned, brightening up as she saw her dad helping Moira carefully through the dimly lit room. Always delighted to make an entrance, her nana's round, five-foot figure was draped in a loose, red, stripy shirt over pink palazzo trousers.

'Dad, Nana.' Jess gave them each a hug, relieved at the distraction. She drew back, wondering what was different about Moira. 'Nana, you've dyed your hair pink!'

Moira beamed. 'The hairdresser did. I told him I didn't want an old lady blue-rinse! Now, let me look at all you lovely young people. Simon, you're even more handsome than the last time I clapped eyes on you. Isn't he, Kate?'

The bright spots of colour on the tips of Simon's ears spread to an all-over flush.

Tom looked around. 'It'll be a bit of a tight squeeze for Finn and his troupe, won't it?'

'Will they all be in leotards and tights like last time?' Moira winked at Jess, who tried to keep a straight face.

'I'm not sure, Nana.'

'There's always hope. Maybe we should get a table right near the front, Tom.'

Tom shook his head. 'Mum, behave yourself.'

Jess grinned and caught Simon's eye, as he pushed his glasses firmly onto his nose.

'Shall I get some drinks?'

'I'll give you a hand, Simon.' Tom turned to Moira. 'Mum, will you be all right? Why don't you sit down?'

Moira waved him away. 'I'll be fine. Pink gin and lemonade for me, please. All the trimmings.'

Simon looked relieved as he and Tom went to the bar.

Moira put her hand on Kate's arm. 'How is Luke?' Without waiting for her to answer, she added, 'And what about this best man of Simon's? Jess was telling me he's single and he's returning to Dublin. Have you met him yet? Is he handsome?'

'Kate hasn't met him yet, but I can tell you he's lovely,' Jess said.

Kate turned all her attention on Moira, ignoring the question about David but chatting warmly to her about Luke for the next few minutes.

Zoe joined them, her blonde hair in a messy topknot, cameras slung around her neck.

'Thanks for coming, girls. Hi, Nana.' She kissed her on the cheek, taking care the cameras didn't bump her.

Simon and Tom came back with drinks.

'Hello, love, you're looking very professional.' Tom grinned at Zoe and handed Moira her gin.

Zoe only then seemed to notice Kate properly. 'Hey, look at you, I nearly fancy you myself. Maybe don't stand so close to poor Simon, he's already sweating.'

Jess didn't think it was possible for Simon to go any redder, but the man could blush for Ireland. She glared at Zoe, who completely ignored her.

'Where are Mam and Dad?' Zoe said.

'Your mam went to collect Simon's parents.' Moira gave a little sigh. 'Would you like something to drink, dear? We can get you one of these.' She held up her gin.

'No, I'm cool, Nana. I need a clear head when I'm working. This'll be one for their portfolio.'

'Are they in costume?' Moira peered around.

'They're changing in the loos behind the bar.' Zoe turned to Jess. 'I'm stunned that Simon's parents are coming. Still, bums on seats. Oh, while I think of it,' she pulled Jess slightly to one side, 'I dropped in earlier, when they were all rehearsing.'

Jess lowered her voice. 'Shit, were they all right?'

Zoe huffed out a breath. 'Of course they were, they were brilliant.'

'Right, sorry.'

'Anyway, Finn introduced me to this couple who dance in the troupe. They live in Limerick, and they're selling this old cottage that one of them inherited.'

Something caught Jess's eye and she nudged Zoe just as Finn appeared from the back of the room and strode over.

'Say nothing for now,' Zoe hissed.

Jess flicked her a confused look. 'About what?'

Zoe didn't get a chance to answer because a moment later Finn towered over them.

At 6-foot-three, Finn had the lean, wiry body of a dancer. He wore his long, thick hair loose and, with his heavy stage make-up, including horizontal stripes across his nose and cheeks, he looked like he was about to take part in Mardi Gras. Jess was grateful he was wearing a dressing gown over his leotard. She wasn't sure if Moira was up to so much excitement, this close up.

'Hey, girls!' He gave Jess and Kate a small wave. 'Hi, Moira, thanks so much for coming.'

Finn grinned broadly and Moira flushed.

'Wouldn't miss it for the world, dear. You look wonderful.'

Finn wiped his hands on his dressing gown. 'Any media here yet?'

Jess was careful not to react. Unless Finn had persuaded the local free sheet to send one of its trainees, there was absolutely no chance anyone from the press would show.

'*Er*, not yet.' Zoe looked around, as if she expected a camera crew from RTÉ to arrive at any moment. 'But don't worry, I'll send photos to all the press desks.'

Finn gave a heavy sigh and scratched his crotch. To be fair to him, Jess thought, it was very warm in the room, and the striped nylon tights sticking out underneath the knee-length robe looked quite itchy. Simon, who was standing close to him, started to edge carefully away.

'Simon, why don't you sit down here with Tom and me?' Moira said, patting the seat beside her.

'*Smile, everyone!*' Zoe pointed the camera in their direction and Jess, Kate and Finn huddled into a group beside Moira, Simon and Tom. She snapped a few photos and looked towards the door. 'I hope Mam gets here in time with your parents, Simon.'

Simon put down the drinks on one of the tables and pushed his glasses up nervously. 'I'm really not sure Mum and Pops are going to enjoy this.'

Jess was starting to feel they'd hate every minute. But it was too late now. She gave her brightest smile. 'They'll love it.'

To her relief, Carmel arrived with Simon's parents a few minutes later.

Simon stood quickly to help them to the table beside them.

'Thank you, Simon.' Úna peered closer at his forehead. 'Good grief, what have you done to your head? You've got a big lump on it.' She turned to Jess. 'What has he done to his head, Jess?'

'Well, once Jess didn't do it, that's the main thing.' Moira raised her fishbowl glass of gin. 'Úna, you should get a couple of these into you.'

Jess suppressed a giggle at Úna's expression. Simon's parents had only met her nana twice before, and she was the only person Jess knew who could put Úna on the back foot.

Jess leaned towards them. 'Thanks for coming, I know Finn will appreciate it.'

Úna sat down next to Simon, her hand fluttering to her neck. 'Such an unusual venue.' She turned to Edward. 'We've never been here, have we, Judge?'

Edward made some small clearing noises in his throat, as he peered over his wire-rimmed glasses. 'Well, no, it's not normally the sort of place . . .' He trailed off and squinted harder. 'Where exactly is the stage?'

As Jess started to point out the performance space they'd just walked through, the lights went out and the audience chatter dropped to excited whispers. A noise behind them made them turn, and Jess could just make out the shapes of the performers as they moved along by the wall to the top of the room. The first strains of some discordant classical music filled the air and, as a spotlight lit the stage, Jess heard a distinct gasp from Úna.

The twenty performers, men and women, wore sheer body stockings, over which were artfully placed feathers, tails, claws and wings, while elaborate bird and animal masks completed the effect. They began to dance, twisting and writhing, stretching and arcing around the small stage, as they stroked each other's heads, arms and torsos.

To Jess's left, Simon shifted in his chair. She didn't dare look across, in case she caught Úna or Edward's eye.

At the table behind her, a couple of people snorted with laugher. Jess glanced over at Zoe, who grinned and gave her the thumbs-up. Thank God, it was meant to be funny.

She met Moira's eye, who raised her glass in a salute, before downing the rest of her drink and settling back in her chair.

Jess turned her attention back to the stage.

She'd been unsure what to expect but, while their performance was eccentric, it was also brilliant.

As the music reached a crescendo, Edward suddenly scraped back his chair and got to his feet. Úna tried to pull him back down again.

'I have to leave.' His voice carried above the surrounding tables and a number of people turned to look.

'Oh dear, sorry.' Úna sounded flustered.

Simon leaned close to Jess's ear. 'I'll have to take my parents home. Will you ask one of the others to drop you back, please?'

'*You're leaving now?*' Jess hissed.

'Yes, I must.'

'Go out the back, Simon, otherwise you'll have to cross the stage.'

But Úna and Edward were already halfway out of the room, excusing themselves in loud whispers at practically every table.

As Simon stumbled after them, Kate leaned towards Jess. 'It's fine, everyone will understand.' She gave her arm a reassuring squeeze.

Jess wasn't so sure about Zoe and Finn. Helplessly, she watched Simon steer his parents towards the back of the room, and out through the emergency exit. Mortified, she snuck a look at her parents. As she met her dad's eyes, he gave a little wink. She could only imagine what he was thinking.

Simon had been right about his parents. She wished she'd listened to him. Now, she'd ruined his night too. Unless he'd been secretly grateful for an excuse to leave. The thought annoyed her. Even worse was knowing that Kate's instincts about tonight had been better than hers.

Jess sighed. She'd apologise to Simon later. For now, she'd just try to enjoy the rest of the evening.

Chapter 13

JESS felt a bit subdued as she drove to Linford with Adam the following morning. When she'd got home after Finn's show, Simon had been on the phone to his mother. Eventually, he'd hung up and come into the bedroom, methodically undressing and folding away his clothes, before putting on his blue striped pyjamas.

'How are your folks?' Jess had said finally.

Simon had shaken his head. 'Mum gave Pops some painkillers and half a Valium. He's in bed asleep.'

Jess had frowned. 'Painkillers and valium?'

'The painkillers were for his ears, Jess. He suffers very badly.'

'You know, I'm pretty sure that's some sort of vitamin deficiency. I'll look it up.' She'd pulled out her phone.

Simon had held up his hand. 'I'm not interested, Jess, you've done enough.'

He'd apologised that morning for snapping at her, before adding that he'd ask Kate to double-check that none of the wedding music was too loud. Jess didn't know whether she was more annoyed with Simon or Kate, even though rationally she knew that neither of them was to blame for Edward's ears.

Now Adam changed up gear as they hit the motorway and turned on the radio. Jess settled back as comfortably as she could in the old jeep and let the chat and music drift over her as they drove.

Eventually, Adam said, 'Do you need a break?'

Jess pulled herself into the moment. '*Um*, no, I'm fine.'

Then, suddenly, it struck her. *Oh God, Luke's party!* That was this morning and she was supposed to be there! She pulled out her phone and sent a quick, apologetic WhatsApp to Kate, explaining that she was halfway down to Linford and had completely forgotten about the party. She was the worst friend!

Adam glanced over. 'We should be there within the hour.'

Jess nodded. 'Have you been busy? I don't think I saw you around yesterday.'

'I flew out to Switzerland on Thursday evening after work and didn't get back until late last night. I sent you that email from the airport.'

'I was in bed.' She remembered how early it had been. 'I wasn't well.'

Adam glanced over. 'How are you now?'

'Fine. It was just slight food poisoning.' Was there such a thing as slight food poisoning? 'I'm completely over it, though – I mean, I'm not going to throw up in your car or anything.'

He chuckled. 'This thing has seen far worse than that, I promise you.'

Jess looked at him for a moment. Weirdly, she believed him. The thought annoyed her. 'How was your trip?'

'Predictable.'

He shrugged, and it struck Jess as odd that he didn't want to talk about somewhere he'd lived for years. Unless he hadn't liked it there. Still, it was safer to keep the conversation about him.

'Where else in the group have you worked?'

'London, Berlin and Paris. What about you? How long have you been with us?'

There it was: the subtle reminder that Adam was part of the upper circle. But anything about her life before Simon was at least safe to talk about.

'I was lucky enough to get a job straight from college.' She glanced over, trying to gauge how much detail he wanted. 'I went Interrailing the summer I finished, then got a trainee management job at one of our hotels. When an entry position came up in the marketing department, I went for it. I know it sounds cheesy, but I feel like part of the Charleston family.'

Adam laughed. 'I'm not reporting back to Frank.'

Did he still expect her to believe that, she wondered.

He sighed. 'Have you ever been to the Isle of Man before?'

'What?' Jess was startled at the change of topic.

'I just wondered if it was your first time on the island?'

'*Yep.*' It came out as a squeak. 'You?'

'I go TT racing there.'

'TT racing?'

'Tourist Trophy – motor bikes.' He changed gear. 'We never really talked about that night, did we?'

Jess flicked him a panicked look. They'd agreed to forget it had ever happened. It was the only way she could face him every day. That, and knowing he'd be going back to Switzerland after the Linford wedding.

Adam seemed to read her mind, and they lapsed into silence until they came to their exit.

'I'd forgotten how close it is to Linford,' Jess murmured.

Adam negotiated a particularly sharp bend. 'What is?'

'*Um.*' Jess strove for casual. 'Ballygobbin, it's not far.'

Her mind wandered back to the first time she'd seen Ballygobbin village, and its tiny old church. She'd never imagined herself getting married on the other side of the country, but her mother had reminded her that it didn't matter where the wedding was, once she was marrying the right person. It would be the most exciting, wonderful day of their lives. She was absolutely sure of it.

They arrived at Linford Castle shortly before noon. As Adam wound the car up the long, tree-lined driveway, Jess waited for the first, familiar glimpse of the castle, with its four fairy-tale turrets and ivy-covered stone walls. Adam parked at the front of the hotel.

They walked through the heavy, arched doorway into Linford's vast hallway.

Inside, Jess felt the same familiar giddiness she'd felt the last couple of times she'd visited. From the enormous fireplaces and furniture to the reproduction wallpaper, rugs, chandeliers and ornate ceilings, Linford Castle looked every inch the grand Victorian house.

'Jess, Adam, lovely to see you both!'

Ian Finnegan, impeccably dressed in a three-piece suit with a mint-green shirt, dark-green tie and matching breast-pocket handkerchief, strode through the hall to greet them.

'You're right on time! Chelsea, Leo and Angel are on their way from Shannon Airport by helicopter. We have a table laid out in the orangery.'

'That sounds great.' Jess fell into step beside him. 'Who's Angel?'

'Chelsea's life coach.' Ian shot her a look. 'And their wedding planner. But judging by the amount of work he's offloaded, I get the strong impression that he's not too keen on that end of things.' He chuckled. 'Not that I mind, it's my job.'

They followed Ian to the orangery, a large conservatory on the east side of the hotel. Sun slanted in through windows in the high, domed ceiling, throwing rainbow patterns over the cool, mosaic-tiled floor. The room was filled with luxurious cane furniture and marble statues, while enormous potted palms, ferns, jasmine and citrus trees brightened up the corners and scented the air.

'This is gorgeous.' Jess took a deep breath and then sneezed a few times. 'Dammit.' She caught Ian's eye. 'Sorry, I'm just a bit allergic to flowers. I'll be fine.'

Ian produced a small remote from his pocket and pressed a button. Immediately, a number of small, high windows started to open. 'That should help.'

Adam pointed to a corner of the ceiling, where two of the small windows seemed to be boarded up. 'What happened there?'

'They're being replaced on Monday.' Ian sighed. 'We came in one morning last week to find them smashed all over the floor.'

Adam frowned. 'Has there been a storm?'

'No, I don't think so.' Ian hesitated. 'All the staff were told not to say anything – we don't want any negative publicity right now. Please, make yourselves comfortable. The manager and I are meeting our guests at the helicopter pad. We'll see you shortly.'

'I can't believe they don't know what caused two broken windows,' Adam grumbled after Ian left.

Jess ignored him as she checked her phone for a text from Kate, but the WhatsApp hadn't been read. She sighed, distracting herself by soaking up her immediate surroundings: a generous, round table laid with china tea and coffee settings, and a couple of tiered cake-stands filled with tiny savouries and petit fours.

Adam poured them both some water. 'How bad is your allergy?'

Jess grimaced. 'I usually take antihistamines at this time of the year. I just forgot how many flowers this place has.'

She remembered Úna's horror when she explained that she wouldn't be having any flowers at their own wedding. 'You have to have flowers,' she'd said, in the same tone of voice Jess imagined she'd use if Jess had suggested she get married naked. 'You could just have white roses.'

After Jess had patiently explained about pollen, Úna had sent an email with a list of 'suitable' flowers that contained very little. Jess had sent a short, polite reply to say that she didn't want so much as a daisy at her wedding.

A chorus of chatter and laughter alerted them to Chelsea and Leo's arrival and, as Ian led the trio into the room, Jess and Adam stood to greet them.

Jess had seen a couple of episodes of *California Girlfriends* and decided that Chelsea Deneuve looked much younger in real life. Unlike the over-the-top stuff she wore on TV, she was wearing a pink cashmere sweater and white jeans, her long blonde hair caught back in a ponytail. Beside her, in designer jeans, a polo shirt, and sunglasses perched on highlighted hair, Leo Dinardia looked like he'd just stepped off his yacht.

Ian stepped forward to make introductions.

'We're psyched to be here,' Leo said.

His face barely moved as he smiled, Jess noticed.

'We're delighted you've chosen Linford for your special day,' she said, and shook his outstretched hand.

Chelsea beamed as she looked around. '*Wow*, this place is awesome! It has all this positive energy. I feel really drawn to it.' She turned to Jess. 'You guys must feel it, working here every day.'

Jess smiled. 'Adam and I work in head office in Dublin, but we drove down today to meet you.'

'*Aw*, that's so sweet!' Chelsea turned to Leo. 'Isn't it, honey?'

Leo looked faintly amused. 'Hundred per cent.'

'So, is this your first time in Ireland?' Jess said.

Chelsea's smile widened. 'It's my first time in Europe. But Leo's been here before, haven't you, honey?'

'Not for the weather.'

Everyone laughed politely.

'That's what makes Ireland so beautiful,' came a soft voice.

Angel had arrived.

Jess was glad of an excuse to look at the middle-aged man who stepped into view, his white, shoulder-length curly hair framing a tanned but sparsely lined face, his squat figure swamped by a voluminous white shirt and loose white trousers.

Two female waiters, in full Victorian uniform, entered from a side door with a trolley of hot and cold drinks. Ian gave them a discreet nod and they stood to one side.

'Let's sit down.' Ian ushered them to the comfortable armchairs and sofas arranged around the table and opened up a small laptop.

While the waiters poured refreshments, Chelsea explained that they'd done the virtual tour of the hotel.

'We just fell in love with it.' Chelsea reached for a glass of water. 'It feels so authentic, like the whole castle is wearing its truth.'

Jess spotted one of the waiter's mouth twitch but, after another discreet nod from Ian, the staff left.

Chelsea continued. 'Anyway, I was super-excited after it passed the test.'

'The test?' Jess was still trying to work out how a hotel could wear its truth.

Chelsea clasped long, manicured hands together on her lap. 'It was my dream to marry in an Irish castle, but everything had to be aligned, so Angel guided me to this place.' She crossed her hands across her chest and looked earnestly at Jess. 'Being in the public eye is like, so difficult, because I have to give so much of myself. I totally depend on Angel to help me make the right life choices.'

Jess didn't dare meet Adam's eye.

Angel gave a beatific smile and produced a small tablet from the leather satchel he wore across his body. 'Which was why I couldn't refuse when Chelsea asked me to plan the wedding.'

Chelsea's smile widened. 'This man, right?'

When nobody responded, Jess said, 'I've been brushing up on Linford's history and this orangery is the most recent addition to the castle, late Victorian. Beautiful, isn't it?'

Chelsea nodded. 'It has an almost spiritual vibe.' She waggled her forefinger at Jess and Adam. 'Speaking of vibes, you guys make the most gorgeous couple.'

She meant her and Adam.

Jess tried to laugh it off. '*Uh*, no, we just work together.'

Adam flicked Jess an amused look, as she hurried to turn the attention back to Chelsea. 'You know, I'm a big fan of *California Girlfriends*. And, *um*, your TikToks are so inspiring.'

'Oh my God, that's so lovely of you!' Chelsea reached across the table and squeezed Jess's hand. 'I just knew you were a kindred spirit.' She turned to Angel. 'Don't you feel that too?'

Angel blinked. 'It was exactly what I was thinking.'

'So,' Adam flicked a quick look at Jess, before clearing his throat, 'Jess and I just wanted to meet you today, to get a feel for what's happening.' He turned to Ian. 'Why don't we get started?'

Relieved, Jess turned her attention to Ian.

'Now, all our staff have signed NDAs,' Ian began. 'We know the theme is to be kept a complete secret.'

'Because of Bobbie Grayson's movie.' Chelsea beamed at Jess. 'But you guys know it's a Cinderella theme, right? I'm having a coach with twelve white horses and everyone will be in costume.'

'Including the staff,' Ian said. 'And we've confirmed the hot-air balloons and the puppies for the petting room. They're coming with their minders on the morning of the wedding.'

Jess met Adam's eyes as he widened them comically and she had to look quickly away.

While Ian talked about fireworks displays, a private casino, wedding-favour gift baskets and a six-foot-high castle wedding cake, Jess studied Chelsea. The wedding would be completely over the top, she knew, but the younger woman's obvious excitement was contagious, and Jess found herself wanting everything to be perfect for her.

The icing on the cake was that, despite Chelsea briefly mentioning the Linford Curse on TikTok, nobody seemed to think it was a problem. Maybe the couple regarded wedding disasters for what they really were: the result of bad planning or, sometimes, just bad luck. Having both Ian and Angel to take care of the details meant there was no need to stress about anything.

Not that there was anything for her and Simon to worry about either, she mused. Especially with Kate, Úna and her mother looking after so much of the planning. Which meant the little darts of anxiety Jess felt when she thought about her big day were most likely pre-wedding jitters.

Leo poured himself some more water. 'The entertainment is gonna be first rate. We've got Joie de Vivre, a dance troupe at one of my casinos, performing with an orchestra and that Irish group, Malarky. That right, Angel?'

Angel clasped his hands across his round stomach. 'Think Steam Punk meets French classics from the thirties and forties.'

Jess took some notes. 'It sounds quite Moulin Rouge.'

Chelsea frowned. 'The Disney movie about the Chinese girl?'

'No, similar names.' Jess shot the younger woman a quick smile and wondered if she'd imagined Leo's faint look of derision.

'Angel, I believe you've organised the menu with our banqueting manager?' Ian said.

'Yes, that was interesting.' Angel's tone was dry.

'We're having a full Victorian menu,' Chelsea said. 'But most of it will be vegan, obviously.'

Leo snorted. 'Not all vegan. Some of us want to eat real food.'

Jess met Adam's eyes briefly. 'Excellent.'

Chelsea looked relieved to have a break in the conversation. 'You know, I'm totally in love with the grand hall. All those paintings and crystal chandeliers. It's like one of your casinos, isn't it, Leo? Imagine how awesome it'll look when it's decorated.'

Leo smiled indulgently.

Jess's phone buzzed. 'Sorry.' She declined the call as she saw Kate's name flash up on the screen.

'So.' Ian rubbed his hands. 'They're the broad strokes, and Angel and I will keep in touch. Now, who's for the grand tour?'

Chapter 14

AS JESS and Adam said their goodbyes, Leo pressed a card into Adam's hand. 'If you run into any problems, contact my personal assistant.'

'I can't foresee any problems that Ian and Angel can't sort,' Jess said as they walked back to Adam's jeep. 'Although it's pretty weird to ask your life coach to be your wedding planner.'

'Maybe less weird than travelling around with your life coach.' Adam grinned. 'I wonder how Leo feels about Angel.'

Jess thought back over the previous hour. 'If you ignore all the nonsense Chelsea actually believes, I think she's quite sweet. I'm not sure about Leo, though.'

She didn't mention that she'd managed to grab a private word with Ian before leaving, and he'd assured her that although he'd appreciate their help in the run-up to the celebrity wedding, it was unlikely that either of them would be needed on the big day, as the staff at Linford would have everything under control.

'I nearly forgot, I missed a call from a friend – can you give me a minute?'

'Take your time.'

Jess walked away to phone Kate, who picked up after a few rings.

Jess? she shouted down the phone.

'Yeah, is everything all right? Did you get my message?'

'*I can't hear you, hang on!*' There were some shuffling noises, followed by a bang and, when Kate came back on, she sounded like she was in a tunnel. 'I got your message.' She sighed.

'It's fine. I just wanted to let you know that I rang Simon, and he offered to come instead.'

'Simon's there now?'

'Yes.' Kate sounded distracted. 'The kids are all on the climbing wall, and I can't leave Simon on his own with them. He says he won't make dinner at your parents' place later, because he'll have to catch up on work. I'd better go, I'll see you Monday, yeah? Bye.' She hung up.

Jess sighed. She felt bad for forgetting about the party, but she wished Kate's default position wasn't always to turn to Simon. She had a niggling feeling that Kate tended to use him, because he was a soft touch where Luke was concerned. Jess knew it wasn't easy for Kate being a single mother, but her dad lived right beside her. Why hadn't she asked him, or one of her brothers or sisters-in-law for help? Sometimes the way Kate went on, people would swear she was an only child.

'Everything okay?'

Jess turned. Adam was looking closely at her, and Jess pushed Kate and Simon to the back of her mind.

'Everything's great.'

They climbed into the jeep and Adam drove slowly down the long driveway.

'So, what did you think?' Adam asked.

'About their plans?' Jess shrugged. 'They seem to have a clear idea about what they want.' She paused. 'It did strike me as a bit ironic that they're going for a Cinderella-themed wedding, though. I mean, Cinderella had only until midnight before all the magic disappeared.'

Adam shot her a look of amusement. 'I didn't miss the irony. But, to be honest, I think this will be the wedding that breaks the Linford Curse.'

'It's probably silly to overthink a themed wedding, even a Cinderella-themed one.'

Jess took a deep breath and tried to shake out the tension in her body, but it was difficult sitting in a car. She rolled down the window, wishing she wasn't facing a long journey home on such a gorgeous afternoon. She put her head back, closed her eyes and eventually drifted into a relaxed state between waking and sleeping.

'Jess?'

She started awake to see Adam, head turned, smiling at her as he drove.

'I was thinking we could take a short break before we go back? Stretch our legs somewhere.'

She hesitated. How wise was it to spend any more time with Adam? Especially on a Saturday, when she should probably be getting straight back to Simon. Except that Simon was now at Luke's birthday party.

She nodded. 'Actually, I'd love that.'

'What about that little village you mentioned? There's a river walk, I think.'

She hadn't been there since she and Simon had booked the church.

How weird would it be to go there with Adam?

He glanced over. 'The turn's coming up.'

'*Um*, sure.' It would be fine. It was a walk, nothing else.

Adam turned right onto a small road that wound around until it came to a humpback bridge over a river. The road widened slightly as they came to the outskirts of Ballygobbin village.

Moments later, they pulled into the small car park behind a pub.

Jess got out of the car and stretched, shielding her eyes against the sun and grateful for the warm wind. It was the most perfect afternoon. She slipped on some sunglasses and fell into step beside Adam as he headed towards the river.

'Pretty, isn't it?' He pushed his hands into his pockets. 'I think it's the same one that runs through Linford's grounds.'

'*Hmm?*' Jess glanced over. 'Oh probably, it's only twenty-six miles away.'

'Really?' He slanted her a smile.

She'd looked it up, she remembered, but now she realised how weirdly specific it sounded. 'Apparently.'

They walked in silence along the river path, as shards of sunlight filtered through the tall trees that lined the bank and bounced off the water. Finally, it became too narrow to walk side by side.

Adam stopped and pointed to the far bank. 'There, look!'

A heron dived into the water, surfacing moments later with a wriggling fish in its bill.

'I love it here!' Jess laughed, glancing quickly away as Adam's eyes met hers. This was insane, she couldn't flirt. Jess inched slightly away and listened for a moment to the competing sounds of birds, the buzzing of insects, and the quiet rush of the river. She'd always loved rivers and canals, but she and Simon had been under pressure to see the church and get to Burlington House the day they'd come down, and they'd had no time to explore. Now, being here with Adam felt disloyal.

'Let's get back into the sun.'

He shrugged. 'We can explore the village a bit.'

They retraced their steps, re-emerging into the village, and wandered up its hilly main street which was busy with local shoppers and children eating ice creams or running along the path in front of them. A group of bored teenagers hung around outside a pub.

Adam turned to her. 'I think that's an old church at the top of the hill. Will we take a look?'

'*Er*, well, we could always …' Jess glanced around. There wasn't a lot else to do in the village, unless they went back to the river. Or stopped at one of the local cafés, and she'd drunk enough coffee for one day. 'Okay.'

'So, how do you know this place?' Adam asked as they walked past a short row of small shops and pubs before they reached the centre of the village, with its small green, a stone statue of a local historical figure, and an old unused water pump.

'How do I know it?' Good question, how did she know it? 'A friend of mine … used to live here.' God, that sounded a bit lame. 'Well, she grew up in Dublin, but she moved here … for a while.' That was worse.

But Adam just nodded and pointed up ahead. 'Nearly there.'

This felt wrong. She should definitely tell Adam the truth. But it wasn't like she'd really lied to him – she just hadn't mentioned that she was getting married. They stopped in the church grounds to admire the exterior. Jess had fallen in love with it on first sight. It was mid-nineteenth century Gothic revival and reminded her of a church a child would draw: a small, rectangular stone building, with a central spire and slanting, tiled roof. She supposed it was quite romantic to be marrying where Simon's parents had tied the knot over thirty-five years ago. Even if it was a long way for most people to travel.

'After you.' Adam's mouth quirked into a half smile, and Jess wondered if the weird feeling in her tummy was thanks to all the miniature jam scones she'd wolfed down at Linford.

Inside, the church was cool and empty, and Jess stood, inhaling the distinct smell of the wax candles and floor polish.

As Adam walked around, Jess stayed at the back, trying to imagine the dark pews decorated with ribbons and filled with their families and friends. She'd had a difficult time persuading Úna about the ribbons but, given that she couldn't have flowers, she'd won that battle. Úna had got her way in almost every other aspect of the wedding, including the black-tie dress code, arguing that it would be simpler for guests. Jess knew her parents didn't mind, but most of her mother's extended family didn't go in for very formal wear.

'Jess?'

She looked up to see Adam standing at the top of the aisle. A shaft of late afternoon sun slanted through the window above his head, catching his dark hair.

He smiled. 'You're miles away.'

For a moment Jess couldn't breathe. She tried to picture herself walking up the aisle, in her tightly corseted, billowing white dress. She tried to imagine Simon standing where Adam stood now: tall, angular and floppy-haired, in his dinner jacket and wing collar. Would he smile at her, the way Adam smiled? Briefly, she closed her eyes, trying to conjure up a mental image of Simon. But even with her eyes closed, the only person she could see was Adam.

Well, of course it is, Jess. He's the only other person in the church.

And if you'd told him about Simon, you wouldn't be here right now.

Adam ran his hand over one of the benches. 'Look at the detail. I love the craftsmanship of these old churches.'

She tried to remember what Simon had thought of the church, but he'd seemed satisfied that it was the right size and distance from Burlington House, where they'd have their reception. At the time, she'd teased him about his practicality. Now, it bothered her.

'Maybe the Tourist Board should make this place an official stop,' she said.

'They could open a shop beside it and sell souvenirs.'

Adam gave her a long look. 'You think the only thing I care about is the bottom line?'

Jess folded her arms. 'You're being groomed for a top position. You tell me.'

He walked down the aisle towards her. 'Did Frank tell you I was made head of European operations earlier this year?'

'No.' Jess's voice became less echoey as Adam approached. So, he wasn't being groomed: he was already there. 'You sure you're not here to keep an eye on me?' She tried for a casual tone, but her throat felt tight.

It was so quiet here, so peaceful. In the space between them, the sun scattered patterns on the intricately tiled floor.

Adam stopped at the last pew. 'Frank told you the truth. I was due to come over later this year, but this wedding is too important to the group. And the reason I admire good craftsmanship is because my dad's brother is a carpenter. He rebuilt our farmhouse and pretty much everything in it. He taught me woodwork when I was a kid.' He tipped his head to one side. 'You should see my dovetails.'

'You grew up on a farm?'

He grinned. 'You latched on to that bit?'

Jess kept her arms folded, wishing she didn't feel so defensive around Adam. 'You don't look like a farmer.'

'I grew up working on the farm, I've just never run it.'

'So, let me guess. Farms are passed to the eldest son, and you lost out because you weren't born first.'

'Wrong on all counts.' Adam leaned back against the bench. 'Nowadays, farms are usually passed down to whoever in the family will run them: sons or daughters. But, as it happens, I am the eldest.'

'No pressure, then.'

His eyes narrowed slightly, but his tone was light. 'None at all. So, what about you? Judging by your accent, you grew up in a comfortable Dublin suburb. You lived at home, rent-free and totally cosseted, while you swanned around in college for four years.'

Jess drew a steady breath. As the eldest daughter of an electrician and a nurse, she'd never swanned around anywhere. Her parents had often worked long, erratic hours when she was growing up, and she'd worked hard in college, determined to do well. She shouldn't care what he thought: no doubt he already judged her after the weekend. Screw guys like Adam with their double standards.

'We should go.' She turned abruptly.

Adam reached out and caught her by the arm. 'Sorry, that was out of line. I didn't mean …'

'You didn't mean *what*?' Shame and anger battled in her.

'Any of it.' He seemed sincere as he held her eyes. 'Look, I feel we're avoiding the elephant in the room. The truth is, I wish you'd waited around that Sunday morning on the Isle of Man. Actually, I wish you'd woken me up.'

The abrupt change of topic left her momentarily stunned. 'Were you hoping for a romantic breakfast together?' The words tumbled out, as heat rushed to her face. 'Or maybe you fancied round two?'

Adam's jaw clenched but a brief hurt expression crossed his features. For a moment, she thought he'd walk out.

Instead, he spoke quietly. 'The thing is, Jess, I'm usually a pretty good judge of character. Which is why I don't believe this whole act.'

'It's not an act.' Her voice shook. She hated that he was right. But it was the perfect opportunity to tell him the truth – so he'd back off.

He looked at her closely. 'I think it is.'

She was convinced her heart was trying to escape her chest. She had to leave. If she stayed here, she didn't know if she could trust herself. All she had to do was walk away, but her feet were rooted to the tiled floor.

Adam stepped into the space between them and took her face between his hands. 'I won't kiss you if you say no.' He waited.

Say no, Jess, it's just one little word. Her breath fluttered like a butterfly in her throat, trapping the word.

Then he kissed her.

Chapter 15

NOT since the day she'd left home had Jess been so relieved to be going to her parents' house for dinner without Simon. She inched her way through rush-hour traffic towards Dunlaoghaire as she listened to the AA traffic report and tried to figure out a faster route. Not that it mattered. '*Why does any of it matter?*' she yelled at the radio, stabbing viciously at the dial to turn it off. 'I've screwed up totally, and I'll probably lose my job!'

The middle-aged woman driving in the adjacent lane shot her a worried look, and Jess quickly mouthed an apology and whizzed up her window. '*Fuck it!*' Why had she let Adam kiss her like that? She'd stood there, in the church where she and Simon would exchange their vows and let herself be kissed. She could have easily stopped him. She had a mouth on her, as her mother often pointed out when she and Zoe were growing up. She'd a mouth on her all right, and she hadn't used it to talk.

Nor had she just let it happen. In fact, if she were being perfectly honest, they were equal partners in all things intimate. The second she'd felt his lips against hers, she'd acted like nobody had kissed her in years, and her actual life depended on this particular meeting of mouths and tongues. She'd wrapped her arms around his neck and wriggled closer to him, and Adam had been more than happy to help her along. Had there been moaning? She was pretty sure she'd moaned. Her face burned at the memory. What was wrong with her? In a few weeks, she was going to be marrying the love of her life. Maybe she was a commitment-phobe. Everyone assumed that only men were afraid to commit. Why not women?

Except it couldn't be that. After the initial shock of Simon's proposal, she'd thrown herself into wedding plans with abandon. Or, at least, she'd gone along with them. She and Simon had decided on the church together, after Úna's suggestion, obviously.

Zoe had agreed to be their photographer, and her mother had picked out her dress. Strictly speaking, Jess had chosen her own dress. But only because she knew her mother had fallen in love with it.

'If Zoe ever gets married, she'll probably wear jeans,' Carmel had declared.

Zoe, who'd been with them at the time, had responded with an unladylike snort.

Jess had wanted to laugh, but wasn't sure if she could, given how tight the bodice was. Instead, she'd given one final twirl in the eighteenth-century-style instrument of torture and declared it The One.

Choosing her bridesmaid had been easy. As the official photographer, Zoe had told Jess she'd have enough to do on the day. And Kate was her oldest, closest, and most capable friend. It was Kate who'd organised the website for the wedding gifts and had her own checklist of everything to be done between now and The Big Day.

Jess hadn't even picked the wedding invitations. Úna had quickly offered to do that, and it had been easier to agree, than risk upsetting her future mother-in-law.

But if Úna was determined that her only son's wedding rose to her exacting standards of elegance, Jess was pretty sure her own family would bring a bit of balance to the day.

Because there was nothing understated about her wedding dress. Or the huge, feathery hat her mother had bought. Or any of her mother's sisters, all of whom were coming to the wedding with her equally wonderful uncles-in-law. She felt a bit better by the time she pulled up outside the dilapidated Victorian house on the coast road.

Just as she put her key in the lock, Carmel Bradley flung open the door, wearing a T-shirt and baggy jeans, and what could have been very old hospital clogs.

'Come in, Jess!'

Her mother pulled her in for a hug, and Jess wrapped her arms around her strong, tiny frame.

After a couple of moments, Carmel stepped back and briskly rubbed Jess's arm. 'Maybe you can talk to your sister. I don't know where we went wrong with her. Not a whit of sense.' Her mother turned and headed back down to the basement kitchen.

Jess took a deep breath and shrugged out of her jacket, hanging it on the end of the banisters. Judging by how loudly Daniel O'Donnell was being played in the kitchen, her mother had found her worry of the week. She took a second to check her appearance in the mirror over the table. Unbelievably, she still looked the same. How was that even possible?

Carmel roared up the stairs. '*She's in the sitting room. Go and talk to her!*'

Jess went into the slightly draughty sitting room with its well-worn, mismatched furniture, and threw herself down on a sofa beside Zoe.

'Hey, what's up?'

Zoe looked up from her phone. 'Nothing. Mam just keeps

forgetting that I'm twenty-five.'

'Where's Dad?'

'Hiding in the greenhouse.'

'It must be really bad.'

'I'm moving in with Finn.'

Jess frowned. 'Doesn't he share a house with four other people?'

'He has a double room.'

'Oh, well then.'

Zoe glared at her. 'We don't all have rich fiancés who own posh flats in Dublin four.' She glanced towards the door. 'Is he with you?'

Jess felt a flash of guilt as she remembered why he couldn't come. 'No, he's catching up on work.'

'Good, at least we'll be spared Mam feeding him up like a turkey in November. And poor Simon telling her how much he loves her good, plain cooking.' Zoe smirked.

Jess said nothing. She was too tired to argue and the part of her brain that was still working kept replaying Adam's kiss. Discussing Simon felt icky.

Zoe looked up after a minute.

'I can't live at home forever.'

'I know.' Jess studied her as she returned to her phone.

Sprawled beside her, her younger sister looked about eighteen. Fine-boned and slender, Zoe had always been able to eat whatever she wanted and not put on weight, and her long blonde tresses never frizzed like Jess's coarser, darker hair. Jess wondered if she knew how beautiful she was but, if Zoe knew, she didn't care. She was the least vain person Jess had ever met.

'Can you afford it?' she asked.

Zoe shrugged. 'I work for a studio, Jess. I won't get rich taking photos of brides and babies, but it's steady money. And I'm not exactly high maintenance.'

'What about Finn? How's his job going?'

Zoe shot her a scornful look. 'He's a waiter in a private club. What do you think?'

'He's heard nothing back from the Arts Council?'

'Not yet.' Zoe sounded a bit flat.

'Say if they turn him down?' When Zoe said nothing, Jess added, 'I know they're really good, but it might be difficult to get Arts Council money to do a new tour with his troupe.'

Zoe turned to face her, tucking one black-denim leg under her on the sofa. 'Maybe you could do something for him.'

Jess blinked. 'Like what?'

'Well, some of the hotels in your group are really fancy and the guests might love some performance art in the foyer as they're checking in, or I don't know …' Zoe cast about wildly. 'Lots of hotels have art exhibitions so why not performance art? You're the marketing manager, Jess. You must have loads of ideas and this would be totally different!'

Jess spoke carefully. 'It would be different.' Despite what had turned out to be a surprisingly skilled performance, Jess wasn't sure if Finn and his troupe would be a fit for the Charleston Group's very traditional hotels. 'I'll see what I can do, okay? I can't promise anything, but I might talk to a couple of people.'

Zoe flicked her hair off her face. 'Thanks. He's feeling a bit shite after last night.'

'Did he notice Úna and Edward leaving halfway through? Because you should just explain that Edward has something weird going on with his ears.'

'Yeah, I told him. He's just a bit down, it's his creative temperament.'

Which was a nice way of saying that the guy could be as moody as hell. Poor Zoe. Following your dream was one thing, but Finn had barely made a cent from the career he was hell-bent on pursuing.

'So, when are you moving?'

'After dinner.'

'*What?* That's a bit sudden, Zoe. No wonder Mam's upset.'

'I told her two months ago, that we were thinking about it.'

Carmel came into the sitting room. 'If you mentioned it before, I certainly didn't hear you. This is a big thing, Zoe. Something you consider properly and discuss. You don't just announce it before dinner and move out after you've had your apple tart.'

'It'll be really late to start moving in tonight, Zoe,' said Jess. 'Why don't you wait until tomorrow? I'm sure Dad would help.'

'God almighty, Jess, have you seen the place?' Her mother gave her a disappointed look. 'It looks like a squat from the outside. You're worse than her!'

'Thanks, I guess,' Zoe said, when Carmel disappeared back downstairs again.

Jess leaned back against the sofa, resting her head against the faded floral fabric. 'Maybe I'll move back in until after the wedding.'

Zoe put down her phone and gave her a hard look. 'What happened?'

'Nothing happened. It'd just be nice to spend a bit of time with Mam and Dad.'

'*Bullshit!*' Zoe's blue eyes glittered. 'Did you have a huge row?'

She'd forgotten about Zoe's inbuilt lie-detector. 'No! God, I can't open my mouth around you. You always think the worst!'

Her sister's expression softened. 'Jess, it's not too late to pull out of the wedding. Think about what you're doing. This is the rest of your life.'

The memory of the Isle of Man, and Adam's pretty spectacular kiss only hours ago, flashed to mind and panic surged through her. She'd never let anything like that happen again.

'You've never liked Simon, Zoe, so let's drop it.'

'Chill, Jess, I don't hate the guy. Just because he's not my favourite person doesn't mean I can't see things clearly. He won't make you happy.'

Jess stood and pushed her feet back into her shoes, avoiding Zoe's eyes. 'Of course he makes me happy. And we've been together for nearly three years, so it's not like we don't know what we're doing. Now leave it alone. I'm going to say hi to Dad.'

The doorbell rang.

'Is that Finn?'

Zoe shrugged. 'It might be. I wasn't sure if he was coming for dinner.'

Jess said nothing. As far as she knew, her mother always made extra food in case Finn turned up.

As Zoe went to answer the door, Jess wandered out to the garden and followed the cobbled path down to the greenhouse. Tom Bradley was wearing baggy brown shorts, an Irish football T-shirt and an old pair of runners, as he staked his tomato plants.

'Hiya, Dad!'

'How's my best girl?' He straightened and scratched his sun-speckled balding patch.

'The tomatoes look great.'

'Good crop this year. I'll give you some to take home.'

Jess nodded. 'Thanks.'

Tom cast a glance back to the sitting room. Through the open patio doors, they could hear Carmel talking to Zoe and Finn. Jess could guess what her mother was trying to do. Carmel Bradley could be extremely persuasive when she wanted. It was her nurse's training, Jess supposed. As if sensing he was being watched, Finn looked out through the patio doors and gave a friendly wave in the direction of the greenhouse.

Tom gave a fond smile and turned back to Jess. 'Don't worry about Mam. Zoe and Finn eat with us most of the time, I don't see that changing in the near future. Here, try one.' He handed Jess a perfectly ripe, yellow cherry tomato.

Jess turned it over between her hands, inhaling its scent. She dropped her voice when she spoke again. 'I don't want to interfere, Dad, but Zoe is twenty-five. Why is Mam babying her?'

He pursed his lips. 'Your mam thinks that Zoe deserves a bit better than one half of a double bed in a very rundown shared, rented house. Lookit, Zoe will make that move when she wants to, no matter what anyone thinks. In the meantime, we'll play it a bit softly around Mam, yeah? She's a bit, well, hormonal, and with the wedding coming up and everything.'

His neck and ears went pink, and Jess resisted the urge to hug him, knowing he'd be even more embarrassed if she made a fuss.

'What did you think of Finn's performance last night?'

Tom looked visibly relieved at the subject change. 'Different, anyway. Not that I've any idea what it was all about. Have to say though, I enjoyed it, and I didn't expect to. I don't see Finn earning a living from it, but sure what would I know?' He huffed a laugh.

Jess bit into the tomato, wiping away juices with the back of her hand. 'I'm just glad Zoe has a decent job.' She didn't add that, despite Zoe and Finn being a couple since college, she'd never really seen a future for them. 'How's the business?'

'As much work as I want, pet, people always need electricians. Although if your mam had her way, I'd be working two days a week. She keeps telling me I have to take it easy.'

Jess felt a stab of worry. 'She's a nurse, Dad, maybe you should listen to her.'

Tom rolled his eyes. 'Don't you start. Sure, didn't I get the all-clear? And your mam has me eating all this healthy stuff. I've forgotten what a good steak tastes like! Now, enough of that.' His expression softened. 'Do you need anything done? I'm never too busy to drop over and get your little jobs sorted, you know that.'

Jess gave him a quick hug. 'I know, thanks, Dad. Simon and I are fine.'

'Grand, so. Well, we'd better go in for dinner. Maybe you could distract Mam with some wedding talk. It shouldn't be hard – she's watched *Father of the Bride* so often, I think she must have a crush on Steve Martin.'

Great, wedding talk, that was all she needed. She smiled brightly. 'I'll do my best.'

Chapter 16

JESS saw Kate when she dropped into Butlers before work that Monday morning. She paused, knowing that Kate was probably playing advanced Sudoku on her phone, and mightn't spot her if she slipped back out straight away. She hated herself for even considering it: guilt was the worse feeling in the world. She reminded herself that she'd been working, but she still felt bad that she'd completely forgotten about Luke's birthday party. Although considering how awful she felt about sleeping with Adam, Jess wondered if it was displaced guilt. Not to mention the double pressures of keeping such a huge secret and having the celebrity wedding clash with her own.

Kate looked up and gave a small wave. Jess plastered on a huge smile, and waved back, before weaving her way through the tables to join her.

Kate put down her phone. 'Hey, how did Saturday go?'

Jess slid into the seat opposite. 'Fine, interesting, I guess. Listen, I'm so sorry about Luke's birthday. There was a last-minute change in arrangements, and the party just completely slipped my mind. Did he have a good time?'

'He had, in fairness.' Kate looked at her closely. 'Have you not been talking to Simon?'

Jess hesitated. She'd barely seen Simon all weekend. She'd arrived home late on Saturday evening, to find he'd already gone to bed. On Sunday, he'd taken himself to the spare bedroom for most of the day to finish up whatever he was doing, and then he'd gone to see his parents on Sunday evening. Jess had excused herself with a headache that hadn't been a complete lie.

'*Um*, not really, but I think he really enjoyed being there for Luke.' It was a fairly safe bet.

Kate placed her elbows on the table and rested her chin in her clasped hands. 'He made his day. I think Luke gets that Simon's genuinely interested, you know? They just really connect.'

'Absolutely.' For the millionth time, Jess tried to imagine having children with Simon. What would happen if she never wanted any? Or just not with Simon? She felt a jolt of shock as the thought slid into her head. Of course she wanted children with Simon. Eventually.

'Jess?' Kate looked a bit impatient. 'Are you listening?'

'Sorry, what were you saying?'

Kate pushed her empty cup to one side and took a small mirror from her bag to reapply her lipstick. 'Simon was saying that he's going clubbing for his stag.' She raised one eyebrow. 'I bet that's not his idea. I mean, it's not really his thing, is it?'

'I suppose not.' The last thing Jess wanted to talk about was Simon's stag. Kate might start talking about her hen weekend again. 'So, *uh*, what movie does Luke want to see for his birthday?'

Kate hesitated. 'I'm not sure he really wants to do that this year … he's a bit old.'

Jess gave a surprised laugh. 'He's ten!'

'I know.' Kate tucked her hair behind her ears. 'I mean, I just think he'd prefer to go to the cinema with his friends. Don't take it personally.'

Jess shifted in her chair as she considered this. 'Right. Well, ask him, will you? It's our thing.'

Kate said nothing, and Jess got the distinct feeling that something was off. Down the years, she'd become as close to Kate as she was to Zoe. Closer, probably. In college, she'd stood by Kate after she'd got pregnant with Luke, while Kate's other friends had dropped away, unwilling to stick around for someone who couldn't stay out partying, or take off for the summer to Europe or the States. And she'd been there for her when Kate's mother died a few years later. And, as Luke's godmother, she'd always taken him out for special occasions.

'I thought it was pretty brave of Úna and Edward to come along to Finn's performance last week.' Kate's mouth twitched. 'Although I thought your nana was going to get up and join in.'

Jess smiled. 'Finn's troupe were really good, Kate. I mean, they were out there, but people loved it.'

Kate looked unconvinced so Jess decided not to pursue it. She stirred the frothy milk into the last of her coffee.

'Okay, thoughts: how am I going to squeeze in Úna's last-minute wedding guests?'

'The hotel has said they can definitely only seat a hundred?'

'You've seen the room, Kate.'

'What does Simon think?'

Jess sighed. 'I haven't had a chance to talk to him. But he'll probably agree with Úna. She actually suggested I un-invite friends.'

'I don't envy you.' Kate looked thoughtful. 'Úna's not trying to be difficult, though.'

'You don't actually believe that, do you?' Jess huffed. There was no point arguing about it with Kate. The girl had a bit of blind spot where Simon's mother was concerned. She decided to change the subject.

'I'm organising drinks for David some evening after work.'

Kate glanced away. 'Stop playing matchmaker, Jess.'

'I'm not.' She caught Kate's expression. 'Fine, but you haven't even met him. Just give him a chance.'

'I'm not interested.'

'Kate.' Jess leaned across the table and forced Kate to look at her. 'When was the last time you went on a date. Why don't you prove to yourself that you still can?'

Kate's lips tightened. 'I don't have to prove anything to myself.'

'Then prove it to me.' Jess folded her arms. 'You deserve to be happy.'

Kate's eyes flashed. 'I *am* happy.'

'Come on, stop deliberately misunderstanding me!'

'I'll go for drinks, but that's all.' Kate scraped back her chair and stood. 'I need to get back to work.'

Jess's insides squeezed. How had that gone so badly? 'I'll come too.' She grabbed her bag.

They crossed the road in silence.

Jess stopped outside the office. 'Kate, I'm sorry if I'm being pushy.' Maybe she had been unfair to her. Although it *was* just drinks.

'No, I get it,' Kate said slowly.

Jess tried to read her expression. 'So, we're okay?'

'We're fine, I'll see you later.'

Kate went inside, walking straight through the lobby to the loos.

As Jess took the stairs to her office, her thoughts swirled through their conversation, wishing she could understand what was going on. Because whatever it was, it had caused a fundamental shift in their friendship.

Chapter 17

WHY was it, Jess thought, as she headed back to the office, that if one part of your life went wrong, other parts started to follow? What was wrong with a bit of balance? And how exactly did you get it? Kate was a firm believer in feng shui: the tidier your house, the tidier your life. Or something like that. But Simon was tidy to the point of obsessive, so that theory was starting to look a bit shaky.

Ever since that stupid, crazy night on the Isle of Man, her life had gone a bit pear-shaped. Sometimes she even found herself doubting her future with Simon. She hated keeping secrets from him, but she'd heard horror stories about people who'd destroyed their relationships by confessing one-night stands. She couldn't hurt Simon like that, especially for one awful, drunken mistake. Except … what about that kiss in Ballygobbin? She and Adam had been completely sober. Worse, it had happened in the church where she and Simon were due to marry.

Jess did a few yoga breaths and tried to calm herself down. It should be very simple. All she had to do was to be professional around Adam. She could do professional. And, in her private life, she just had to remember that she loved Simon. Which she did. He was the kindest, loveliest man and, even if he tended to be a bit pompous and was definitely allergic to all her attempts to make his flat a bit cosier and less sterile, she was very lucky to have him.

Her real worry was Kate. Ever since their first day of secondary school, when twelve-year-old Jess's books had fallen out of her locker and narrowly missed concussing Kate who'd been assigned the locker underneath, they'd been firm friends. Friends who'd always told each other everything. But Kate would never understand any of this, and she didn't blame her.

All Jess knew was that she'd somehow stepped into someone else's life that night on the Isle of Man, and even trying to make sense of it was exhausting. Tearing open the wrapping on a Mars bar, she scrolled through her phone, clicking into a short piece on Hollywood gossip site, TMZ.

California Girlfriends star Chelsea Deneuve has agreed to sign a drastic pre-nup, before her upcoming marriage to billionaire casino owner, Leo Dinardia, later this month. The pair are set to wed in a 400-year-old Irish castle, now a luxury hotel on the Atlantic coast. Although 33-year-old Dinardia is reputedly footing the bill for the lavish wedding, he has made sure that if Chelsea is unfaithful, or if the marriage lasts less than 10 years, Chelsea won't be entitled to any of his wealth.

Jess finished her chocolate and opened Twitter, where celebrity wedding and celebrity pre-nup were trending. After a quick think, she ran some searches for everything she could find about Leo and Chelsea.

Leo had no social media, although details about his casinos and gossipy articles about the break-up of his previous marriages were easy to find. Chelsea, on the other hand, had two and a half million followers on Instagram, and almost as many on TikTok, where, as far as Jess could see, she specialised in vague, inspirational soundbites.

Her phone rang and Carmel's name flashed up on the screen. 'Hi, Mam.'

'Is this a bad time, Jess? I'm just off night duty and I wanted to phone you before I get some sleep.'

'Grand.' Jess scrunched up her empty chocolate-bar wrapper as she opened TMZ on her laptop and refreshed the page. **The Fairy Tale's Poison Apple** grabbed her attention.

'I think it's a bit silly, I know your dad does,' Carmel was saying, 'but Finn found out today that his house has been condemned, and the landlord has to evict everyone.'

Jess felt a flash of pity for Finn. 'It could be an excuse for the landlord to put up the rent.'

'Well, Zoe's very upset. I'm relieved, obviously. As I said, the place looked like a squat.'

'*Hmm.*' Jess glanced over the gossip piece, which was accompanied by a photo of Chelsea and Leo, over a caption which read **Chelsea and Leo spat in Vegas nightclub.**

'Oh Jess, give me a minute, there's someone at the door.'

Jess heard her mother put down her phone, and she quickly read the article.

California Girlfriends star Chelsea Deneuve and her fiancé Leo Dinardia were seen arguing last night outside the Blue Flamingo nightclub on the Vegas strip. And a close friend of Chelsea's told TMZ that the bride-to-be is furious about the pre-nup. The couple are set to wed at the end of the month, in what should be the ultimate fairy-tale wedding at Linford Castle, a mock-Victorian five-star hotel in the West of Ireland. Chelsea, who has a loyal social media following, has talked about her dream of a wedding in an Irish castle. But some people were surprised that the couple chose Linford Castle, which comes with a curse: a history of wedding-day disasters. Could Chelsea and Leo's wedding be the latest?

'*Noooooo!*'

Carmel came back on the phone. 'Sorry about that, Jess – that was Mrs McCarthy at the door, asking about the bridal shower.'

'Mam, if that's too much for you ...'

'Don't be silly.' Carmel was firm. 'I told you I wanted to throw you a bridal shower, and that's what I'm doing. Anyway, where was I? Oh, Finn getting evicted.'

'Right. Will he move back in with his parents?'

'He can't, sure didn't they sell their house five years ago, to go globe-trotting in a camper van? I hope it keeps fine for them. So, I invited him to stay with us.'

'*He's moving in?*'

'Ah Jess, what could I do? The poor lad would have ended up on the streets. I'm sure it's just for a short while.'

'Well, I suppose he's already there a lot of the time.' Jess wasn't sure what else to say.

'Exactly.' Carmel paused. 'The thing is, would you mind if the two of them took your room? It's bigger than Zoe's and there's a better bed.'

Jess scrabbled with the idea. If she ever had to move back home ... which wouldn't happen, because she lived with Simon. And she always would.

'Jess, are you still there?'

'Still here, Mam. *Er,* that's fine.'

'Are you sure? I mean, you'll be wanting to come back here the night before the wedding, but we'll make Zoe's room lovely for you.'

'Oh, Mam, I wasn't planning to do that.'

'But it's traditional!'

'We can talk about it again. Honestly, I'm fine about the room. What about Zoe? Is she pleased Finn is moving in?'

Carmel tutted. 'You never know with Zoe. She can be as odd as two left feet sometimes.'

Maybe Zoe felt trapped. It was one thing moving in with your boyfriend, but another having him move into your parents' house. Finn was generous and easy-going, if a bit moody at times, but he was a total dreamer. Still, maybe this would make or break them.

'I'll talk to you soon, Mam, I have to go.'

'Jess?'

'Yes, Mam?'

Carmel cleared her throat. 'I just wanted to say, I'm glad things are working out for you and that you're settling down with such a nice man. You were always the sensible one. Now, I'll see you soon.' She hung up.

Jess sat still for a long moment. *Always the sensible one.* God. Her phone pinged with a message from Simon: **Meet you for lunch at Oui Monsieur, 1pm?** Oui Monsieur was one of Simon's favourite city-centre eateries, but he'd never suggested meeting there for lunch mid-week. In fact, he rarely suggested meeting for lunch at all during the week, because he usually only had time for a sandwich at his desk. It probably meant he had good news: he might have got that promotion at work. She messaged back with some food and drink emojis and put her phone away.

Early on in their relationship, she'd tried a few sexy WhatsApps, but Simon had deleted them immediately and asked her not to sext. 'Say if I mislay my phone and somebody saw those?' he'd said.

Which was hilarious, considering that Simon was the most careful person in the world, and Jess doubted he'd ever lost anything in his life. Plus, would it matter if his girlfriend sent him a few risqué messages? Still, it was just one of his little quirks. Feeling a bit better, she got back to work. Today was already improving.

Jess left shortly before 1 o'clock and hurried across town to Oui Monsieur, where Simon was already waiting. 'Sorry I'm a bit late.' She kissed him briefly on the cheek and slid into the chair opposite. 'So, any news?'

Simon pushed his glasses up his nose. 'David rang. He sounded glad to be home.'

'Brilliant! I'll organise drinks as soon as possible. I know Kate's looking forward to meeting him.'

Simon looked surprised. 'Really?'

'Well, yeah, he's the best man and she's my bridesmaid. Plus, they're both single.' She beamed.

Simon chuckled. 'You're such a romantic. Oh, before I forget, I picked you up something on the way here. He took a small box of artisan chocolates out of pocket and slid it across the table to her. 'I thought you'd like to have something with your coffee in work.'

Jess felt a rush of love for him. 'Thank you, that was really thoughtful.' She examined the beautifully wrapped box. They were a far cry from the cheap chocolate she kept in her desk drawer.

'So, do you think they'd hit it off?'

'Who?'

'David and Kate.'

Simon's eyebrows shot up again. 'Gosh no, I can't see them together at all.'

Jess said nothing. Simon could be so clueless sometimes. Now that the Big Day was imminent, it was a pretty safe bet that Kate was starting to feel a bit left out. It would certainly explain the recent tension in their friendship.

Simon took off his glasses and cleaned them with a small cloth from his inside pocket, before picking up the menu.

Jess tried to think of an interesting topic of conversation. Not the wedding. Anyway, what would they talk about once it was all over? A slight shiver ran through her, and Simon glanced up.

'Are you cold? I hope you're not coming down with something.'

'No, I'm fine.' Jess smiled and picked up the menu. He was so thoughtful.

'*Hmm*, it's just a critical time for me at work, and I can't afford to catch anything.'

Jess's smile faltered.

'While I think of it, Jess, there's something I want to discuss.'

Shit, that sounded serious. 'Is it a pre-nup?'

'What? Of course not.' He blinked. 'You don't want a pre-nup, do you?'

'*Er*, no.' She had to put work stuff out of her mind. 'Sorry, go on.'

'It's about my mother's request for those extra guests.'

'The Feely people, right.' Jess sighed, then realised that Úna hadn't sent her an email about it. 'Maybe she'll forget?'

'The Feely-Martins, and my mother won't forget, darling.' Simon's eyebrows disappeared under his fringe. 'She's not senile.'

Jess fiddled with her watch. 'I suppose we could phone the hotel and beg them to fit in a couple of extra people …'

He reached across the table and ran his thumb over the back of her hand. 'I was thinking it might be easier to ask if there's anyone who'd prefer not to come?'

Hadn't that been his mother's suggestion? Jess knew if she did that, her family and friends would think she'd lost her mind.

'Maybe someone who's not that close to either of us. Someone we rarely see.' Simon appeared to think. 'You know what weddings are like, there's always lots of people who feel they have to go but would rather not. Like that awful wedding you and I met at. It was the last place I wanted to be.'

'*Er*, that was where we met.'

Simon smiled. 'Which was very lucky. But that's not my point.'

What was the point? 'Let's think about who's coming, Simon. There's our friends.' She spoke quickly. 'And on my side, it's just family and a couple of really close friends of my parents. If I asked someone not to come, I'd upset everyone.'

Simon pushed his fringe off his forehead. 'They're not the Mafia, Jess. What about your dad's really weird brother?'

'He's my dad's only sibling and he's bringing Nana!' Jess leaned across the table and tried to sound reasonable. 'Why don't we just enjoy our lunch?'

'Jess, how are you doing?'

She jerked around at the sound of Frank Charleston's voice. Beside him stood Adam.

Oh God, this was like one of those anxiety dreams, where she was about to make a presentation, only to discover she was naked. Only this was a hundred times worse.

She forced her mouth into a smile. 'Frank, lovely to see you.' *Please just walk on!*

When he didn't move, Jess's eyes slid again to Adam. Maybe she didn't have to introduce Simon. Or she could sort of introduce him and leave them to think what they wanted. Or …

Adam stepped forward and stuck out his hand. 'Adam Rourke, how do you do?'

Simon grasped his hand. 'Simon Donohue.'

Jess was pretty sure her heart actually stopped, but Simon didn't expand, and for once she was grateful that he rarely offered unasked-for information.

Frank Charleston briefly shook Simon's hand. 'We'll leave you to enjoy your lunch.'

Adam gave them both a polite nod before striding off in the direction of their table on the far side of the restaurant.

Simon waited until they were out of earshot. 'They seem very pleasant. Who were they?'

Jess drank some water and tried to calm her heart, which was now threatening to burst through her chest. 'That's Frank Charleston, the chief executive. Adam works for the group too.'

To her relief, Simon changed the subject. Jess didn't dare look over to see where Frank and Adam had gone. With a bit of luck, she and Simon would be finished before them. Had Simon picked up on any undercurrent between her and Adam? There was no reason why he should: he trusted her. And she'd betrayed that trust in the worst possible way.

She looked him in the eye. 'Leave your mum's request with me. I'll sort it out.'

Jess braced herself for the worst when Adam walked into her office that afternoon. She hadn't talked to him since Saturday.

After their kiss in the church, she'd shut down his attempts to discuss it on the drive home. Adam had seemed frustrated by her silence, but he hadn't pushed her. She hated that he'd probably already guessed who Simon was, but it was a clear sign for her to come clean. 'Adam, have a seat.'

'Thanks.' He threw himself into the other chair, put his phone on her desk, and hitched one ankle over his leg. 'That was a nice restaurant. Bit fancy for lunch, but Frank was paying.' He gave a lopsided smile. 'How was your meal?'

Jess picked up a pencil and started to doodle a cartoonish couple on the open notebook beside her. '*Um*, good. Look, now that you're here …'

Adam cut across her. 'I want to apologise for what happened on Saturday.'

She looked at him, her heart thumping. He seemed sincere. Her eyes slid away from his, as she tried to ignore the weird little flips her stomach was doing.

'I should have just said no.'

'Right, sorry. For everything. For putting you in that position in the first place.' He dug a hand through his hair. 'It won't happen again.'

Jess probed her feelings, knowing she should feel relieved. Weirdly, she felt more confused than ever.

Adam clasped his hands behind his head.

'So, Simon seems like a nice guy. Does he work for the group?'

This was it, confession time. It was for the best: Adam would think the worst of her, but he'd back off completely. 'No, he doesn't.' She took a deep breath. 'Actually, he's getting married soon.'

Adam's face was a study in polite interest. There was clearly a deeply buried streak of masochism in her, or she would have just told him. It was like ripping off a plaster. Her mam had always done it so fast she and Zoe had hardly known it was happening.

But this wasn't the same.

Jess looked back down at the page and drew a tutu on the tiny, curvy woman. Maybe she could just leave it at that. She sat up a bit straighter. 'So, what did you want to see me about?'

'Who's he marrying?'

What was wrong with the man? Unless he'd guessed and was just messing with her head. She just needed to say it. Three little words: *He's marrying me.* 'Why? Why do you want to know?' She wiped her hands surreptitiously on her skirt.

Adam's eyes seemed to bore into her. Finally, he shrugged.

'Frank thought he recognised him from one of the company picnics.'

Jess tried not to sag in the chair. She was certain that Frank didn't have a clue she was getting married, and he obviously didn't even know she was with someone. Why should he? Frank was nice, but he wasn't the sort of boss who took a massive interest in anyone's personal life.

'He's marrying Kate, from Accounts.' She blurted out the lie.

'Kate.' Adam paused, frowning. 'I don't think I've met her.'

She was a total idiot. Was it too late to come clean? It felt too late. 'She's very private, hates people knowing her business. In fact, I shouldn't have even mentioned anything.' She leaned forward and lowered her voice. 'It's a bit odd, but nobody even knows she's getting married.'

Adam nodded slowly. 'That is a bit odd all right.'

'I know, but please don't mention anything to her. Or to anyone else, obviously.'

'Sure thing. So, why were you having lunch together?'

Jess blinked. 'I'm her bridesmaid. And, *um*, I'm organising some wedding stuff for her which I had to run by Simon.'

'So, you and Kate are good friends?'

'Best friends.'

Adam smiled. 'She's lucky to have you.'

Jess managed a weak smile in return. Okay, she hadn't actually done anything that awful to Kate. Except lie about her getting married to Simon, and hint that she was a bit odd. So, maybe it was sort of awful. She'd make it up to Kate. Anyway, it didn't matter, now that Adam had promised absolutely nothing else would happen between them. Plus, he'd be going back to Switzerland soon, and he'd be far too busy being head of European operations, to think about Kate or Simon. Or her. Which was a good thing, obviously. Sound.

'*Um*, while you're here, I'm not sure if you've seen this.'

'What?'

'Give me a sec.' Jess opened her phone and quickly found the two short gossip pieces. 'There were two pieces about Chelsea and Leo on TMZ earlier. I'm sending a link to your email.'

She waited while Adam read them.

'I wouldn't worry about it. People like Chelsea need to be in the limelight all the time – the row was probably staged. What day is the photo shoot, by the way?'

'Next week.' If she didn't know better, she'd think that Adam didn't care for one moment that Chelsea and Leo might have had a real falling-out. 'I'll have to double-check my diary.'

'Great, we'll take the jeep. Nothing like getting out of Dublin at the weekend.'

Why was it that he always wanted to be in the bloody driving seat? Literally. Still, at least there wouldn't be a repeat of their last trip.

'Jess?' Adam frowned. 'You've gone very pale.' He jumped up and took two strides to the water dispenser, filling a cup for her. 'You're not worried about the wedding, are you?'

Jess sipped some water. 'The wedding?'

'At Linford Castle.' Adam spoke slowly. 'Are you sure you're okay?'

'All good.' She had to keep it together. 'The wedding won't be a problem.'

Adam smiled again, and Jess offered a small smile in return. None of this was Adam's fault. She couldn't allow her guilt to affect their working relationship. She wished he'd move away: it felt a bit dangerous when he was this close. And that smile ... she swallowed hard. She didn't just jump into bed with any guy. Nope, he must have smiled like that a lot, the night she met him. Pathetic.

'I'll catch you later.' Adam got to his feet.

'Great.' Jess fixed her eyes on her computer screen.

After Adam left, she slithered down her chair until she was almost horizontal. How had that just happened? There were probably Russian spies leading less complicated lives than her. She opened her desk drawer and reached for a Mars bar.

Adam came back in, making her jump. 'Sorry, left my phone ...' He picked it up off her desk, as Jess, red-faced, scrambled to pull herself up on the chair.

Adam raised an eyebrow but said nothing as he slipped his phone back into his pocket.

Upright again, Jess held up a pen. 'Got it.' From the corner of her eye, Jess saw his mouth twitch as he left.

Chapter 18

TMZ has learned today that the upcoming wedding of the year, the three days' nuptials of Chelsea Deneuve and Leo Dinardia, will be almost entirely vegan. We applaud the celebrity couple for their ethical and moral choices, but it's hard to imagine some of their guests, which include body-builder Rocko Davida, will be too thrilled. Davida has publicly rubbished veganism as 'fine for people who operate on a sub-par level'. As for lots of their other Hollywood guests who don't eat gluten, or who have soy, sesame and nut allergies, we have to wonder what they'll be able to eat.

Jess flicked to the back of her notebook, where she'd written a list for her own wedding. Most of it had been ticked off, and she comforted herself with the fact that there was plenty of time to figure out everything else. The important thing was not to get panicked by the thought of two weddings on the same day. Once she stuck to her lists, everything would be fine. It was just common sense. She studied the most recent additions.

31. Sort out seating at wedding so Úna's friends can go.
32. Remind everyone about night out for David.
33. Ask Zoe to do an engagement shoot.

The last one was a fabulous idea. A couple of framed pictures of her and Simon in a relaxed setting would make a great thank-you for the two sets of parents. Their mothers would love it, they might even bond a bit over it.

She phoned Zoe, who picked up on the last ring. 'Make it fast, I'm in the middle of a kids' shoot.'

'Will you do an engagement shoot for Simon and me?' Jess grabbed a pen and absently doodled two little figures beside her list.

There was a brief silence. 'I thought you didn't want one of those.'

'I never said that.'

'You did. I offered to do one when Simon proposed, and you said you didn't want one.'

Shit, maybe she had said that. 'I've changed my mind. Please? Could you make it this weekend?' She looked at her drawing. The little figures had their arms wrapped around each other; their heads tilted towards a kiss. A photo of her and Simon kissing would be cute.

'What?' Zoe gave a disbelieving laugh. 'I need more notice than that.'

'I'll pay you the going rate.'

'As opposed to what?'

'As opposed to the sister rate.'

Zoe sighed. 'Fine. I'd better get back to the Third Circle of Hell.'

After Jess hung up, she put a small tick beside the third item on her list and waited to feel a small rush of satisfaction. Simon lived by lists, swore by them. So did Kate. She drew a tiny heart over her doodle, and then hurriedly scribbled the whole thing out, as an image of her and Adam came to mind.

Her eyes slid to number 31. It was definitely the most difficult.

In fact, it was downright impossible. She'd leave it for the moment. Meanwhile, she'd see if David was around tonight to meet them after work. The sooner she got Kate and David together, the better.

Simon pushed his fringe away from his forehead, where it flopped back immediately. 'I still don't understand why we all need to meet David tonight. Why are Zoe and Finn coming?'

Jess slipped her hand into his. 'We're busy next weekend, and I know David is dying to meet everyone.'

She followed Simon down the spiral stairs into Majors, a trendy basement bar off Dublin's main shopping area. Dimly lit, it was already packed with the after-work crowd.

'There they are.' Jess squeezed Simon's hand as she spotted Kate and David at a table, his distinctive sandy curls and darker reddish beard a foil for Kate's dark colouring. Jess felt a quiet thrill as she heard Kate laughing at something David had just said. 'They are totally into each other.'

'Oh, for goodness' sake, Jess!' Simon looked bemused. 'Kate's just making David feel welcome.'

As if she'd heard her name, Kate glanced up and waved to them both.

David got to his feet as Jess came over and pulled her in for a hug. She smiled up into his broad, freckled face.

'Great to see you, David, you haven't changed a bit.'

He grinned. 'I've a few more grey hairs, but they're kind of blending in. How's the bride to be? Not long now.'

Jess's stomach squeezed. 'Yeah, it's mad.'

Beside her, Simon leaned in to give Kate a hug and kiss. 'Ignore everything this man tells you.'

Kate seemed to glow as Simon pulled up a stool to sit on the other side of her, and Jess couldn't help feeling a bit smug about her matchmaking skills.

'I'll go get us drinks. Usual, Simon?'

He nodded.

'Kate, David, what about you?'

'We're good for now, thanks, Jess.' Kate tucked some hair behind her ears and leaned towards David as he said something to her.

Jess smiled to herself as she headed to the bar and put in the order. Kate and David were definitely giving off good vibes and, if Simon couldn't see that, he needed an eye test.

By the time Jess returned, Zoe and Finn had arrived. She put her and Simon's drinks on the table. 'Sorry, lads, bad timing.'

'Don't sweat it, I've got these,' Finn said.

As he headed to the bar, Jess sat down beside Zoe. Opposite, Kate and David were in a huddle, chatting and laughing. Jess passed Simon his drink and he nodded a thanks, before turning his attention to Kate and David again. Jess felt a bit sorry for him. He probably felt Kate and David were excluding him, and everyone else. She supposed they were, in a way, but it would be worth it to see Kate find someone special.

'Simon?' She leaned towards him. 'Simon?' He half turned, and Jess smiled at him. 'Everything okay?'

He frowned and reached over to give her hand a quick squeeze. 'Of course. You?'

'Totally.' She was about to add something else, but Simon had withdrawn his hand and glanced away again. Jess sighed and turned to Zoe. 'How's Finn?'

Zoe bundled her hair up into a topknot, before rooting around in her pocket for an elastic. 'I think he liked the photos from Friday. I've sent some to a few of the papers. By the way, if you're trying to set those two up,' she nodded towards Kate and David, 'forget it.'

Jess glanced over at Kate, before leaning in closer to Zoe. 'What are you on about? Look at them!'

'I'm looking. And I reckon he's into her. I'm just not sure about Kate.'

Zoe could be so annoying at times. 'Zoe, look at her body language.'

Zoe shook her head. 'She's putting on a good act, maybe to keep you happy. She probably knows you want them to get together.'

Jess studied Kate and David over the rim of her glass. Even after a couple of drinks, Kate tended to be quite reserved. Right now, she looked like she was in a flirting competition. It could be just an act, Jess thought. But it was far more likely that Kate was finally giving her love life a chance. If she was overplaying it with David, it was because she was out of practice.

Finn came back with pints for him and Zoe, and bags of crisps and nuts, which he deposited in the middle of the table. 'Help yourselves, lads.' He stuck out his hand to David. 'Finn.'

'David.' He grasped Finn's hand. 'Hey, proper Tayto crisps, I've missed these.' He opened a pack and offered some to Kate, who politely declined. 'Ah, come on, I can't eat them by myself. I'll have cheese-and-onion breath.'

Jess watched the exchange. Kate never ate crisps, she was too disciplined. But after a slight hesitation, Kate simply smiled and dipped her hand into the bag. 'Thanks.'

Jess met Zoe's eyes. Her sister just raised her eyebrows and reached for a bag of peanuts.

Simon insisted on getting the next round of drinks. He'd always been generous, Jess thought fondly. Unlike the guy she'd dated for a year before him, who'd never even bought her a coffee when they'd been out together.

Finn tipped some peanuts from the bag straight into his mouth, washed them down with a slug of beer, and wiped his hand across his face. He belched loudly. ''Scuse me, folks. Better out than in, though.'

As Zoe punched him on the arm, Jess was grateful that Simon had gone to the bar. Simon was always polite to Finn, but Jess knew exactly how he felt about him.

'So, Jess,' Finn took another gulp of beer, 'Zoe tells me you're sort of in charge of this very cool celeb wedding in Mayo.'

'I'm more of a bystander, really.' Jess wondered about the best way to explain her role. 'Linford needs a lot of wedding business, which to be honest it doesn't have right now. So, part of my job is to use this wedding to boost our marketing campaign.'

Finn nodded thoughtfully. 'That because of the Linford Curse?'

Jess gave a mock groan. 'Not you as well!'

Simon returned with a round of drinks for the table. 'Not Finn as well what?'

Jess grinned. 'Finn and I were just chatting about the Linford Curse.'

Simon's eyebrows disappeared beneath his fringe. 'Superstitious nonsense.'

'Well, in a way.' Jess laughed awkwardly. 'The point is, too many weddings went badly wrong, and eventually people stopped booking them. This is our first one since we bought it.'

'Aren't you getting us that golf weekend there?' Simon said.

'Absolutely, once this celebrity wedding is over.'

Simon's eyebrows disappeared beneath his fringe. 'I'm not sure why that would make any difference.'

Jess pretended not to notice Zoe and Finn exchange a look. Simon was never deliberately rude, but he was definitely in a weird mood. Although he probably had no idea that the wedding was the same day as theirs. Instinctively, it felt better not to tell him.

Kate pulled on Simon's arm.

'David's been telling me that you've known each other since your first day of school.' She giggled. 'I'll bet you were a very cute five-year-old.'

Jess tried not to laugh. Clearly Kate had had a lot more to drink than usual. Simon's face was bright red.

David grinned as he caught Jess's eye. 'Kate tells me you two have been taking dance classes. I don't have to guess whose idea that was.' He reached behind Kate to clap Simon on the back. 'You know the rest of us will be throwing ourselves drunkenly around the floor, mate?'

Jess laughed. 'I'm pretty sure we'll be the same.' She glanced at Simon, who was wiping his glasses, and immediately felt bad for laughing. 'But the classes are great fun.'

'Kate, why don't you and David take a few classes?' Zoe said.

It was the perfect excuse for getting them together again, Jess thought, making a mental note to thank Zoe.

Kate looked over at David. 'Would you want to?'

'Hey, I can't be any worse than Simon.' David winked and raised his glass to Kate's. 'I'm on if you are.'

Jess noticed Simon was staring at Kate, as if it was the first time he'd ever seen her.

If Kate noticed, she didn't react. Instead, she simply smiled and clinked her glass. 'Looks like the bride and groom have some competition.'

Simon yawned and made a show of checking his watch shortly after ten thirty. 'Jess, have you seen the time?'

David raised an eyebrow. 'What are you doing to him, Jess? You'd better not crash out this early at your stag, Simon.'

'That strip club doesn't even open until eleven,' Finn deadpanned.

Simon ignored Finn and turned to Kate. 'Can we drop you home?'

Kate shot David an almost imperceptible glance. 'No, thanks, Simon, I'll be fine. But, before I forget, Luke wanted me to ask if you'd take him to the new *Star Wars* movie.'

Jess stared at Kate, but she seemed oblivious.

Simon brightened. 'Tell him he's on.'

'Excellent.' Kate turned to David, who seemed bemused as he followed their conversation. 'Simon pitched in at Luke's birthday party last week, and Luke's friends said Simon was sound, which is as good as it gets.'

Simon and Kate exchanged a warm look, as Jess quickly swallowed the remainder of her drink, and reminded herself how lucky she was that Simon and Kate got on so well.

And now Kate and David had hit it off. She'd overheard David asking Kate out for dinner, when Simon had gone to the bathroom. It was a relief to get something right, after all the mistakes she'd made recently.

'I should head off too,' Zoe said. 'I'm up for an early shoot in the morning.'

The others were quick to take their cue.

'Talk to you soon, mate,' David said, standing and pulling Simon into a quick hug. He caught Jess's eye as he pulled away. 'Great to see you again, Jess.'

'You too, David,' Jess said and they hugged.

Jess willed Kate to look her way, but she and Simon were talking together quietly. As Zoe and Finn said their goodbyes and slipped away, Jess gave David an awkward smile. Sometimes she wished Simon didn't behave like such a protective older brother around Kate.

Finally, Kate shot her an apologetic look. 'Sorry, Jess.'

Jess wondered exactly why she was apologising. For delaying them? Or for asking Simon instead of her to take Luke to the cinema. She was being petty, she knew. Simon had rescued Kate at the birthday party, and Luke was probably at the stage where he needed good male role models. She waved away her apology, as Simon said goodnight to Kate and David, and turned to her.

'Are you ready?'

'Sure.'

Jess tried not to feel annoyed as she and Simon took the last train home from town. She made a couple of attempts to talk about the evening, but Simon's strange mood had returned. Agitated, she folded her arms and turned to stare out the window, as Dublin's brightly lit cityscape flashed by. They walked the short distance from the train station to their flat in silence, where Simon drank a full glass of water, and muttered something about feeling tired.

After he went into the bedroom, Jess leaned against the counter, surveying Simon's streamlined kitchen, all steel and pale grey. How was it always so tidy? She felt a momentary pang of longing for her parents' dated wooden kitchen with its mismatched plates and dishes, well-thumbed cookery books and a biro-marked wall that had served as a growth chart for her and Zoe. Finally, she turned off the lights and went into the bedroom, hoping Simon wouldn't sulk all night.

Simon was tucking the laces into his shoes before putting them on a slide-away rack in the wardrobe.

Jess leaned against the doorframe. 'Are you going to tell me what's wrong?'

He pushed his fringe out of his eyes. 'Nothing.' He sighed. 'Well, obviously I found it a bit strange seeing Kate and David …'

'Together?' Jess prompted.

'Hardly, they just met.' Simo frowned. 'I just hope they didn't think we were trying to push them together.'

'That would be awful.' Jess came in and plopped down on the bed beside him.

Simon pulled off his socks and dropped them into the laundry basket. 'Why are you trying to play matchmaker?'

Why was he being so ridiculous? 'Because they're both single adults who hit it off, so unless David's a serial killer …'

'Don't be dramatic.'

Jess felt herself tense. Maybe she should just drop it. But it didn't make any sense. Simon should be thrilled that Kate and David had got on so well.

'So, what's the issue?' she asked.

Simon took off his glasses and placed them in their case. 'Look, Jess, I know you think I'm overprotective. And maybe I am, but Kate has to think about Luke. And I've known David a long time. He's not the kind of guy who wants a ready-made family.'

Maybe now wasn't the moment to mention that David had asked Kate out. But it was a bit weird that Simon wouldn't want two people he cared about to get together.

'How do you know that's still the case? People change. And not every relationship has to end in happy ever after. Why does it matter if they date?'

Simon's jaw tightened. 'Kate is my friend too. I know I haven't known her as long as you have, but I care about her and Luke. Don't get me wrong, David is a good guy, and he was the best friend I ever had at school. But you have trust me when I say he isn't a good fit for Kate.'

They seemed to be going in circles. Suppressing a sigh, Jess wriggled out of her jeans before stripping off her T-shirt and letting it fall on the floor.

'Will you either fold those or put them in the laundry?' Simon took off his shirt.

Jess thought quickly. The last time they'd made love had been weeks before the hen weekend. But now she thought about it, even before that they'd been having a lot less sex. She stood, turning to face him, and unsnapped her bra.

Simon's voice was tight. 'I'm sorry, Jess, don't take this the wrong way but I'm just not in the mood.'

Jess hooked her thumbs into the top of her knickers. 'Give me a chance, I'll put you in the mood.'

Simon stood, forcing her to take a backward step. 'I'm tired, and we have my boss and our American client coming for dinner tomorrow night. Let's just get some sleep.' He offered a conciliatory smile and a quick kiss before walking past her into the en-suite bathroom, letting the door close behind him.

Jess sank back onto the bed, her face burning. Yanking open the drawer beside her, she pulled on a clean T-shirt. She couldn't put her finger on what had happened tonight.

Simon had once told her that he'd been shy and quite lonely in school, until David had joined his class when the boys were nine. Despite David being a natural extrovert, the two had become the best of friends. So it made no sense that Simon would discourage him from dating Kate.

And none of it explained the increasing tensions between her and Simon. Taking a deep breath, she released it slowly, trying not to feel hurt. She was probably overthinking things. Simon was under a lot of strain in work, and he had to be feeling the pressure of the wedding as much as she was. Once they were married, everything, including Kate, would sort itself out.

Chapter 19

JESS woke in a sweaty tangle of sheets and duvet that Wednesday morning. In her dream, she and Simon had been standing at the top of the church about to exchange vows, when Adam had burst into the church to tell Simon that she was a cheater and a liar, and he should dump her.

She reached over to Simon's side of the bed, but the sheets were already cold. He was probably finished at the gym and on his way to work. Last night had been awful, and no matter how many times she went over it, she couldn't figure out exactly what she'd done wrong. Simon had seemed uptight all evening and, after she'd gone to bed, she'd lain awake for hours. She couldn't shake the feeling that something was really wrong. Or that the reasons ran deeper than her hen weekend. All she knew was that they seemed to be pulling away from each other.

Jess forced herself to get up, heading straight for the shower. As she stepped under the hot spray, she wished things could return to the way they'd been before their engagement, and the stress of an impending wedding. What she needed was a quick win: maybe if she solved the problem of the extra wedding guests, it would help smooth things over between them.

She turned off the water, grabbed a bath towel and wrapped it around her. She'd been so excited to move in with Simon, especially as she was the first girlfriend he'd ever lived with. But even though she knew having her move in had been a culture shock for him, nothing had prepared Jess. Certainly not her years spent at home, or the couple of years where she and some college friends had rented together. At least, she reasoned, they were going into marriage with their eyes open.

She rang Burlington House as she walked to the bus stop, and waited as she was connected with the banqueting manager.

'Hi, is that Laura? This is Jess Bradley. My fiancé and I are having our wedding reception there on Saturday, July twenty-eighth.'

'Of course, how can I help today?'

'We were hoping to invite a couple more people.'

'Let me just check your details.'

There was a pause and Jess could hear the distant clicks of a keyboard.

When Laura spoke again, she sounded apologetic. 'The problem is you're already at maximum numbers. We simply can't seat any more than a hundred guests.'

'Could you make a small exception, please? You could just squash them in somewhere, they wouldn't mind.'

Jess was sure the Feely-Martins would definitely mind being squashed in somewhere, but that was the least of her worries.

'It's not that simple, I'm afraid.' Laura was firmer now. 'Our insurance won't cover us for more people in that room.'

Shit. Jess tried to think. 'Could we extend into another room? It doesn't matter if some people are sitting separately.'

'Our banqueting room only connects to a corridor, not another room. I can send you a layout of the hotel, if that helps.' The other woman hesitated. 'We're a boutique hotel – your wedding is quite large by our standards.' She let this sink in. 'Why don't you have a think about it and let me know what you'd like to do? I'll give you my direct line.'

'Thanks. Yes, that would be good.'

Jess hung up, feeling sick. There were just over two weeks to their wedding and the hotel had them over a barrel. Maybe she shouldn't have said anything to Laura and simply told Úna that it was sorted. Jess had worked in hotels long enough to know that no manager would ever risk upsetting a wedding party. If two more people simply showed up on the day, they'd have to find some way of accommodating them.

It was tempting, except the Feely-Martins would probably make a fuss, and Úna would blame her.

Jess arrived at the bus stop. What if she asked Laura to swap two of her cousins' places for the Feely-Martins? Jess knew that Faye and Sarah wouldn't panic if they couldn't find their names, and Jess would make sure that she or Kate was on hand to get it sorted. It was such a simple solution, she was surprised she hadn't thought of it sooner.

The bus arrived and she slid into one of the front seats. Taking out her phone to check her newsfeed, a headline caught her eye. **Fire at Linford Castle destroys part of the South Tower.** *Shit, no.* She steadied the phone in her hand and scrolled down, skimming over it before she realised that nothing was going in. She took a deep breath and forced herself to read slowly.

A fire that broke out overnight at Mayo's historic Linford Castle, where reality TV star Chelsea Deneuve and Casino King Leo Dinardia are due to wed at the end of this month, has

damaged part of the South Tower, which includes the newly refurbished bridal suite.

The fire seems to have started around midnight and was discovered by staff after smoke triggered the hotel's fire alarms. A spokesperson for the hotel said it was brought quickly under control, and nobody was injured. The cause is not yet known.

The celebrity duo is flying in 200 guests for their three-day wedding which begins on Saturday 28th, and all their guests will stay at the castle or in one of the self-catering cottages in the grounds.

Jess didn't bother to read the rest of the article. The bus pulled in at her stop and she walked the five minutes to the office, grateful for the chance to think.

She had just turned onto the canal when her phone rang, and Ian Finnegan's name flashed up on the screen.

'Hi, Ian, I've just read about the fire.'

'There's a Garda forensics team looking at it now.' He sounded grim.

Jess rubbed her forehead. 'How bad was it?'

'Not too awful, considering.' Ian gave an audible sigh. 'Part of the old tunnels were damaged, and we've a lot of electrical stuff hidden away there, so we think that's how it started.'

It was mindboggling to think that faulty electrics could have started a fire, just six months after a major refurbishment.

'How long did they say this will all take? I mean, do they know about the wedding?'

'They know about the wedding.' Ian sounded wry.

'Right, well keep me posted.' Jess hung up and walked into reception, where Emily waved her over.

'Oh my God, I've just read about the fire!'

'There wasn't too much damage, we'll get everything repaired in time.' Jess hoped it was true.

Emily bit her lip. 'Brandi Oliver is all over TikTok saying that it's the Linford Curse, and the wedding will be a total fail. And she's got like, one million followers, Jess!'

Was it too much to ask that this one wedding went off without a hitch? Jess muttered something about having to get back to work, before retreating to her office, where she prised open the window and grabbed a mini-Mars bar from her drawer. As she bit through the chocolate coating, there was a knock on her door. Jess shoved the bar out of sight and wiped her mouth.

'*Come in!*'

Adam opened the door and stepped inside.

Jess looked at him suspiciously. 'So now you're actually waiting outside until I say come in?'

'I am. I always seem to crash in on you when you're doing yoga or having a bit of a lie-down in your chair, and I feel bad about that.'

Jess's face heated as she stared at him. Was he winding her up?

He seemed perfectly serious.

'You've heard about the fire?' she asked.

'Yup, and I talked to Ian on the way in. They think it's electrical.' He scrubbed a hand over his face. 'As soon as we nail down the cause, we've given management carte blanche to get repairs and renovations done. We can't afford any delays.'

Jess nodded. 'Worst-case scenario, what about a plan B?'

'There's another suite on the floor below but, given that we've only twenty bedrooms in the castle, including the honeymoon suite, it would mess with our numbers a bit.' He shrugged. 'Let's not worry until we have to.'

After he left, Jess powered up her laptop and opened her emails. Ian had sent one the previous evening, with the link to the two virtual tours of Linford: above and below stairs. In the first video, two actors in Victorian costume brought the viewer on a tour of the castle that the general public saw. In the second video the same actors were dressed as head butler and housekeeper for a below-stairs tour, which included a walk-through one of the castle's old tunnels, now locked to the public.

Jess knew that if the initial theory about the fire in the south tower was right, all the tunnels would have to be checked, as much of the electrics were housed there. She checked her Twitter feed. *#FaultyTowers* was trending: **Linford Castle's Bridal Tower Fire.** Time to share the virtual tours across their social media. Linford Castle needed some positive publicity.

Chapter 20

JESS phoned Kate that afternoon. 'Hey, do you feel like grabbing a coffee?'

'I can't, sorry. I want to get away early.' Kate sounded distant.

Jess spun in her chair to look out the window. 'Just tell me quickly how last night went after we left.'

'You mean with David?' Kate paused. 'We shared a taxi, and he dropped me home.'

'And?'

'And what? I just met the guy.'

God, she was as bad as Simon. 'Kate, this is me you're talking to. I saw you, you're totally into each other. You're going to dinner with him.' When Kate said nothing, she added quickly, 'I overheard him asking you last night.'

'It sounds like you already know everything.'

'Come on, Kate, don't be like that.'

'I don't want to talk about it.' Kate huffed out a breath. 'Wait a second.' There was a shuffling on the line and, when Kate came back on a few moments later, her voice sounded different. 'Look, I've just slipped into the bathroom to talk. When I got home last night, Luke was still awake.'

'Was everything all right?'

'Not really. He had to do his family tree for homework last night.'

Jess spoke gently. 'Does he know anything about his dad?'

'He does now.' Kate was terse. 'I'm not sure he believed me when I said I didn't know his last name. Try telling a ten-year-old boy you only knew his dad for one night, before he went back to Sweden.'

'Shit, I'm sorry, Kate. How was he?'

'Shocked, I think. It was the first time he'd really pushed me to answer questions.' Her voice shook. 'I never wanted to hurt him, Jess. So, I gave him my word that if he wants to find him when he's older, I'll help.'

'Hey, it sounds like you handled it well.'

'I don't know.' Kate sounded a bit defeated. 'He seemed happy enough with that, but I know Luke. He's really starting to think about what he's missing.'

Jess tried to think of something comforting to say. 'He's got good people in his life, Kate, including good male role models.'

'Yeah.' Kate sighed. 'Look, I'd better go, I'll see you soon.'

After Kate hung up, Jess stared out at the canal, remembering the moment in college that Kate's life had changed forever. Jess hadn't been able to go out the night Kate and Jacob had met, so apart from what Kate had told her, she knew nothing about Luke's dad. Once Kate had got over the shock of finding herself pregnant, she'd decided two things: she was going to have the baby and she wasn't going to let Jacob know. 'He's an Erasmus student, and it was just a one-night stand – what can he do?' she'd said. Since then, Kate had been careful not to let any man into her life, in case it didn't work out and Luke got hurt. Jess knew that was why she valued Simon's friendship so much.

When her phone rang moments later, Jess thought Kate had changed her mind about coffee. But it was Moira.

'Hi, Nana, how are you?'

'Well, I have a bit of a problem, dear, and I've been trying to reach your dad.'

Jess frowned. 'I think it's his hill walking day with his club. Can I help?'

'I tripped on loose pavement, and it appears I've fractured my foot. I'm at Vincent's hospital. I came in style by ambulance but I've no way of getting home.' There was a wobble in Moira's voice.

'Stay right where you are, I'm coming to collect you.' Jess put her on speaker so she could shut down her computer and pack her bag.

'I feel so bad taking you away from work,' Moira was saying. 'I'd ring your mam, but I wasn't sure if she was working nights this week.'

'As far as I know, she is.' Briefly, Jess wondered if she'd tried to contact her dad's brother, but she decided not to ask. 'It's no problem at all, Nana, I'll see you shortly.' She hung up, took one last look around the office and left.

Jess sat beside Moira in Accident and Emergency, as they waited for her doctor to discharge her.

'I've no idea why I've to wait around like this,' Moira grumbled. 'I've already seen the doctor. It's only a hairline fracture and I'm well able to walk in this boot.' She stuck out the foot in question for a brief inspection.

Jess chose her words carefully. 'Who else did you see?'

Moira gave her a stern look. 'If you're asking if I saw a

geriatrician, the answer's yes. She asked me a lot of stupid questions. Nothing happened, except that I tripped on loose pavement. I wasn't dizzy, I didn't have an episode, whatever that's supposed to be.' Moira's voice grew louder, and a few people turned around. 'I should sue the bloody Council.'

A woman sitting opposite nodded in agreement. 'The paths are a disgrace in this country.'

'Mrs Bradley?' a voice said.

Moira looked up and nudged Jess. 'Here's himself.'

Jess stood as the doctor approached.

He gave her a friendly nod. 'You're Mrs Bradley's granddaughter?'

'Jess Bradley, yes.'

'Good.' He turned back to Moira. 'Here's a prescription for your painkillers, Mrs Bradley. You're going to need daily help, so the local health nurse will call on you tomorrow and assess your needs. Do you have family living nearby?'

'My older son Seamus lives in Arklow, and my other son and his family are all in Dublin. I'll be fine, won't I, Jess?'

Jess nodded reassuringly. 'Absolutely.'

The doctor seemed satisfied. 'I've spoken to the geriatrician, and she seems happy enough. We'll send you out a reminder of your next appointment, but any problems in the meantime, just phone the hospital.'

Moira grumbled as an orderly helped her into a hospital wheelchair and waited with her as Jess drove up to the hospital entrance, but Jess could see that she was secretly relieved for the help.

Jess pushed the passenger seat back and helped her into the car.

As she drove out the gates and headed towards the N11 to Wicklow, Moira yawned. 'You're so good to do this, dear.'

Jess glanced over. Moira's head, with its pink fluffy curls, was resting back against the seat and her eyes were closing. 'That's what family is for Nana.'

But Moira had already fallen asleep.

Jess was grateful that her nana lived in a small bungalow, because she doubted she'd manage any kind of steps. She'd stay with her tonight, and tomorrow she'd phone the number she'd been given in the hospital, to make sure her details had been passed to the local health nurse.

She was heating up some soup when she remembered Simon's business dinner. '*Oh crap!*'

'What is it, love?'

She turned to Moira, who was sitting at the kitchen table. She was struck by how frail she looked. She couldn't tell her about Simon's dinner. Moira would try to insist she go and, when she didn't, she'd just worry all evening. Even if she asked Zoe to step in to mind Moira, she would still feel guilty that she'd messed up Jess's plans.

'*Um*, I was just thinking it's a pity we don't have some fresh bread.'

'Oh, I think I have some slices in a bag in the icebox.'

Trying to stay calm, Jess opened the icebox behind her. 'Got them.' She popped a couple of slices in the toaster. 'That'll all be ready in two minutes. I'll just go freshen up.'

Jess hurried to the bathroom and took out her phone, almost crying when she saw it was on eleven percent. Could today get any worse? She rang Simon but his phone went straight to voicemail. She waited for the beep.

'It's me, Simon. I'm sorry but I won't make dinner, Nana fell and fractured her foot and I have to stay with her. The lamb is in a dish in the fridge, it needs an hour and a half in the oven. I meant to pick up a cheesecake on the way home, so try to think of that too. I have to go, see you tomorrow.'

She hung up and checked her phone. She hadn't brought a charger, and her nana used an old Nokia block. She turned it off.

Once Moira had eaten some soup and Jess had helped her to bed, she rang Zoe from the landline.

'Hi, Nana.'

'No, it's me.' Jess filled her in.

'Ah shite, poor Nana. I'm glad you're staying. What can I do?'

'Don't say anything to Mam before she goes to work, I don't want her worrying. But let Dad know. Nana couldn't get hold of him earlier.'

'Will do.' Zoe paused. 'She can't be on her own, can she?'

'No, we'll have to figure that out, talk to you tomorrow.'

Jess hung up and washed up the few dishes they'd used. She checked on Moira, who was fast asleep, then flicked on the TV, but couldn't concentrate on anything. She was completely lost without her phone: she couldn't even monitor how well the virtual tour videos were doing on social media.

Figuring she should try to get some sleep, she found some blankets and a spare pillow in the tiny airing cupboard in the bathroom. There was a spare bedroom, but it was full of Moira's sculptures, packets of clay and paints, so she made the couch as comfortable as possible. As she pulled the blankets up to her chin and tried to relax, she wondered for a moment how her nana would react to having a carer. She knew how fiercely Moira guarded her independence, but Jess hoped that she'd agree to accept help for the next while.

Chapter 21

JESS waited for her dad to arrive the following day before leaving for work. Despite Moira's insistence that she was fine, Jess had no intention of leaving her by herself. She felt grimy after spending the night in her blouse and underwear and planned to swing by the flat to shower and change, so she'd rung Emily to say she'd be late. To her surprise, her parents pulled up outside the house shortly before half past eight.

'Hi.' She hugged them briefly in the hall before turning to her mother. Shouldn't you be in bed, Mam?'

Carmel dumped a bag of shopping, which seemed to be full of ready-to-eat soups and dinners for one, on the table. 'Don't worry, I'm not working tonight, so I'll catch up then. How's Nana?'

'She slept well – she's having breakfast in bed.'

Carmel rubbed Jess's shoulder. 'You leave things to me. I'll organise some extra help for her.'

Tom took off his jacket. 'And Seamus and I can pick up the slack. I'll go in and say hello. Well done for stepping in yesterday, love.'

As Tom checked on Moira, Jess wrapped her arms tightly around herself and shivered with tiredness.

'I'll say goodbye before I head off. I need to change and get into work.'

Carmel nodded. 'Have you been on to poor Simon?'

Jess wondered how the dinner party went. 'I left a message yesterday evening.'

'Good, I'm sure he understood.'

Jess hugged Moira carefully before she left. 'Take care, Nana, I'll check in with you later.'

'Thank you, dear, I'll be fine. I just have to decide what outfit will look best with this boot, for your big day.' She beamed and Jess gave her another quick hug.

As she drove back to Donnybrook, Jess fought the urge to call in sick and just go home to bed. She was stiff and exhausted after the uncomfortable night on the couch.

As soon as she got to the flat, she went straight to the bathroom to shower before slipping into clean clothes, feeling slightly better as she blow-dried her hair and reapplied her make-up. Stomach rumbling, she went into the kitchen, put some bread in the toaster and started up the coffee machine, before opening the fridge.

She froze when she saw the half leg of lamb was still there. Maybe Simon hadn't had time to cook it, so he'd done something quicker instead. Like some of those fish fillets with diced vegetables in little tinfoil parcels that were dead easy to do but looked really fancy. She checked the bin, but there was no sign of any sort of leftovers.

With a growing feeling of unease, Jess plugged in her phone to charge and switched it on, to find she had three missed calls from Simon. She debated calling him in work, but decided it was better to talk to him later. The coffee machine beeped, and Jess poured herself a large cup, adding two spoons of sugar and a splash of milk.

As the first welcome shot of caffeine hit her system, she remembered Kate and David's date the night before. She rang Kate, hoping for some good news to distract her.

Kate answered immediately.

'Jess, did you get back in time for Simon's business dinner?'

Jess was a bit thrown. 'How did you ...?'

'Simon called me.'

Jess's insides squeezed. 'When?'

'Last night. I was out with David.'

'That's why I was phoning – tell me everything.'

'Jess, it was a total disaster.'

Jess leaned back against the counter. 'But you two got on so well the other night!'

Kate huffed out a breath. 'I'm talking about Simon. That was an important business dinner – he was really upset when he rang me.'

She was way too tired for this. 'Look, Kate, I'm really sorry Simon rang in the middle of your date – he shouldn't have bothered you at all. Nana broke her foot and had to go to the hospital, so I collected her and took her home. I left Simon a message to tell him I wouldn't be there.'

'Oh no! Your poor nana! How is she now?'

'She'll be fine. Mam and Dad came over this morning but I couldn't leave her on own yesterday.'

'I understand, sure.' Kate sounded puzzled when she spoke again. 'The only thing is, Simon didn't get any message.'

'What?' For a moment, Jess was speechless. 'I left him a message.'

'Well, he mustn't have got it in time.'

This was beginning to feel like a lecture. 'It's fine, Kate.' Jess knew she sounded cool, but she couldn't help herself. 'Simon's not helpless. I'm pretty sure he figured something out. Listen, how was your date?'

'It was nice.' Kate was annoyingly noncommittal. 'I just felt bad that there was nothing I could do for Simon.'

Jess felt a surge of frustration. 'Simon needs to let you have your own life. So, are you seeing David again?'

'We're coming to your dance class on Friday, remember?'

Jess suppressed a sigh. 'Great, I'll talk to you soon. Thanks again.'

She hung up, unsure why she was thanking Kate, but determined not to say something she'd regret. She felt … irritated. And she could sense Kate's annoyance too. Kate was the sister Simon had never had, and Jess had always encouraged their friendship. But there were times she wondered if she'd done too good a job.

Jess poured herself a glass of wine when she got home that evening and eyed the meat in the fridge. It was far too much for just her and Simon. Maybe they could invite Kate and Luke over at the weekend? Or Zoe and Finn. No, Zoe would spend the whole time baiting Simon. And Finn didn't eat red meat. Kate and Luke, then. Hopefully it would smooth things over with Kate, too.

She sighed and opened the icebox. There was a packet of handmade sausages that Simon liked, from their local butcher. She'd defrost them and throw them in the oven with some potatoes. They'd be perfect with a salad.

Simon arrived in and threw his keys on the counter. 'Good of you to come home.'

'Simon, I'm sorry about missing the dinner but I left you a message.' When he said nothing, she motioned to the sausages. 'I was just about to start some dinner for us, actually.'

'I'm not hungry. I'll get a bowl of soup later on.'

It was worse than she thought. Simon liked a proper dinner every evening. As far as he was concerned, soup was strictly for lunch.

He turned away, but Jess put a hand on his arm. 'Simon, can we please talk about this? I'm sorry I forgot about your business dinner. Nana fell and broke her foot, and I had to stay with her. I rang and left a message.'

He spun back. 'I'm sorry to hear that. I hope she gets better soon, Jess, really. But somebody else in your family could have stepped in.' He shook off her hand and gave a small belch. A strong smell of alcohol wafted towards her.

She stared at him. 'Have you been drinking?'

'Yes, I thought I deserved a couple of drinks after work, given the utterly shitty day I've had.'

'I'm sorry.'

'So you said.'

Jess pulled her hair out of its ponytail and tried to smooth it down. 'Look, there was nothing I could do. Nana couldn't reach Dad, so she rang me. After I left you a message, I had to turn my phone off because it was out of battery, and I'd no charger with me. And I had to stay overnight with Nana.'

Simon shook his head. 'You know, it wouldn't be so bad if I hadn't persuaded Liam to let me entertain him and the client. Liam would have taken the guy out, except that he's so weird about restaurants. And then Liam told me he'd have to get caterers into his place, just for a bloody dinner. I thought I was doing the right thing.'

He tugged off his tie and threw it beside his keys. 'Liam was depending on me, Jess, and I fucking screwed up. I didn't pick up your message until it was too late, and I'd no time to cook anything, so I ordered in, and the fucking restaurant lost the order.'

Jess blanched. Simon never cursed. 'What did you do?'

'We went out for dinner.' Simon gave a short, mirthless laugh. 'The restaurant had no atmosphere; the service was appalling and the food was mediocre. I had to sit there and watch a potential client become sourer by the minute. In the end, he cut the night short and told Liam he'd be in touch.' Almost savagely, he pushed his glasses further up the bridge of his nose. 'I lost a huge client for my firm. I haven't a hope of making partner now.'

Jess tried to think. 'Just blame it on me. Why didn't you blame me?'

'Jesus Christ, Jess, I'm not in the habit of blaming other people. I let Liam down. I let the firm down.'

Poor Simon, she thought. He was so obsessed with making partner, he was prepared to do anything. No matter how ridiculous.

He pushed his fringe out of the way. 'If it was just this, it wouldn't matter so much.'

Jess frowned. 'What do you mean?'

'I don't feel I have your support.' He gave her a long look. 'I know you think I was mad to offer to do this, but you agreed to help and then you forgot.'

Jess wasn't sure what to say. 'I said I was sorry. Of course I support you.' The words tasted hollow in her mouth.

Simon looked like he didn't care anymore. 'I'm going to rest for a while.' He went back out to the hall and, a moment later Jess heard him close their bedroom door.

'*Shit.*' Jess took her wine into the living room, curling up on the sofa and pulling the woollen tartan throw over her. Two weeks ago, everything had been fine. Not perfect, but pretty perfect. Except for the whole baby thing. Which was quite important, now she thought about it. Briefly, she wondered how different her life would be if she were single. She'd never have met Adam on the Isle of Man, but she'd still have met him in work. Would he have asked her out?

What was she even thinking? A one-night stand was nothing, less than nothing. It was just ... sex. Jess put down her wine and picked up the TV remote, flicking around until she found an episode of *Fair City*. How could Simon accuse her of not supporting him? There was no point even asking about his work, because he was never allowed to talk about it. As for the dinner party, she'd just have to find some way of making it up to him.

Chapter 22

JESS threw herself into work the following day, hoping it might help her forget the night before. She and Simon had stayed out of each other's way, and Jess could practically feel disappointment radiating from him. This morning, he'd still been upset and had barely spoken two words. She felt bad, but she wished he'd put things in perspective. Although by the sound of it, his boss and their potential client also needed a bit of perspective.

She'd always talked through her problems with Kate, because she seemed to understand Simon in ways Jess didn't, and always gave brilliant advice. But she couldn't turn to her anymore. She was frustrated that Simon had dragged Kate into this, and annoyed that Kate had taken Simon's side.

She cheered up slightly when she saw the positive reaction online to Linford's virtual tours, with hundreds of retweets and thousands of views on Instagram and TikTok. The only irritation was TMZ's latest story. *California Girlfriends* **half-sisters, Chelsea and Brandi, have massive fallout at Chelsea's hen party.**

Jess skimmed the short article. Chelsea had invited the whole cast of *California Girlfriends* to Leo's Malibu beach house for a few days, and a video of her shouting match with Brandi had gone viral within the last hour.

She opened TikTok and found Chelsea's latest video. Dressed in a short, floral beach dress, the bride-to-be looked solemn.

'Hey, everyone, I just wanted you to hear the truth about me and Brandi. I worked so hard to make sure that everyone had an awesome time here in Malibu, and I'm gutted that my generosity was abused. Holding grudges is totally toxic, but I need to do what's right for me. Remember, never make your life about the other person. Ask yourself: what do you want? What do you need? So, what I need is to cut toxic people out of my life.'

Chelsea crossed her hands on her chest as Jess had seen her doing in Linford. *'Find your truth, live your truth, be your truth.'*

Who actually believed this crap? Apart from a couple of million followers, obviously. Curious, Jess found Brandi Oliver's latest TikTok.

'Hey, y'all.' Brandi gave a sad smile. *'Thank you soooo much for all your messages and healing vibes. The last twenty-four hours have really sucked, and I've suffered deep emotional abuse from someone I've always looked up to. But when bad stuff happens, I look at the good stuff in my life, especially all my followers. And I totally get that not everyone is as blessed as I am, and I'm so grateful for what I have.'*

Maybe she was being cynical, but she could probably take a few marketing tips from Brandi, Jess thought as she clicked out of the site.

There was a WhatsApp from her mother in the family group: **Don't forget hair appointment at lunchtime for tomorrow's bridal shower.** With everything that had happened in the past twenty-four hours, Jess had completely forgotten about it.

At least nothing could go wrong at a bridal shower, and it might be exactly what she needed to get her properly in the mood for her wedding. She popped some love hearts and champagne glasses emojis into the group.

Carmel waved to her from one of the low sofas in the hairdresser's.

'You're just in time, pet.'

'Hi, Mam.'

Jess came over and collapsed into the sofa beside her, leaning her head back against the soft leather with a sigh. After their row last night, both she and Simon had slept badly, and Jess was pretty sure that she'd only drifted off just before dawn.

'You've big dark circles under your eyes, Jess.' Carmel clicked her tongue. 'You'll need to get plenty of beauty sleep between now and the wedding.'

'Yeah, because Simon's going to completely wreck you on your honeymoon. *Oops*, my bad, Simon's too busy for a honeymoon.' Zoe didn't look up from her phone.

'Behave yourself, Zoe,' Carmel said. 'Now, I made sure that we're all sitting together to get our hair done.'

Jess twisted around to face her mother, tucking one leg underneath her. 'How's Nana?'

'Absolutely fine. I've organised someone to drop in every day, and the local health nurse will keep an eye on her too. And we're only a phone call away.'

Jess ran her hand through her hair, trying to untangle some knots. 'I'm just worried that she'll get a bit down, if she can't get out to all her classes and her bridge games.'

Her mother patted her arm. 'I've already rung a few of her bridge friends and they've promised to come over to her one night a week for a game. But I might see if the carer can bring her to one of her classes.'

Zoe glanced up from her phone. 'Pity she doesn't have an iPad. Look at all the stuff she could do online, and she could video chat with anyone she wanted.'

Carmel raised her eyebrows. 'Your nana doesn't even have a smart phone, love. I don't think she'd manage an iPad.'

Zoe stretched out her legs and crossed her ankles. 'Finn and I are going down to see her at the weekend. I'll take my old iPad and see if I can teach her.'

'Is Nana not coming to the bridal shower tomorrow?' Jess chewed on a nail.

'She is. Your dad's collecting her – she said she wouldn't miss it for the world. Jess, don't chew your nails.' Carmel smiled at her. 'Nana told me she knows all about bridal showers.'

Jess wondered if Moira had been watching the same movies as her mother. Since the moment she and Simon had got engaged, Carmel had dedicated herself to watching every wedding movie she could find: *Father of the Bride*: the original and the remake, *Bride Wars, 27 Dresses, Bridesmaids, The Other Bride, Four Weddings and a Funeral*.

Apparently, she even made notes. According to Zoe, who was allergic to romantic comedies, it was their mother's perfect excuse to indulge her love of ridiculous movies, while simultaneously bonding with her daughters. Jess also knew her mother was determined that Úna McCardle-Donohue would not find any fault on the big day.

One of the hairdressers called them over to the basins.

'Hang on.' Zoe scooted over to Carmel and held her phone at arms' length. 'Pre-transformation selfie!'

'Oh dear God, do we have to, Zoe?' Carmel gave an anxious smile. 'I'm not wearing any make-up.'

Zoe put her phone away. 'Chill, Mam – I can do some touch-ups.'

Jess leaned back into the curved basin, and tried to relax as she closed her eyes.

Hair washed, she was led to a free station between Carmel and Zoe, in front of the mirrors.

'You're the bride, right?' The hair stylist ran a comb through Jess's hair. 'Will you be having an up-style?'

Jess tried to remember what Kate had suggested, but Carmel spoke before Jess had a chance to answer.

'I see all these brides, Jess. You'll be getting your hair done at the hotel, and it's an up-style you need with that dress.'

The hairdresser held up the bottom inch of Jess's hair between her fingers. 'I'll take about that much off – you'll need enough hair to work with.'

Carmel settled back into the swivel chair. 'So, how's Simon? Isn't that business dinner next week some time?'

'Actually, it was last night, but I couldn't make it. So, I left a message, but he didn't get it on time.' Jess braced herself.

'Because you were with Nana?' Carmel looked horrified as she met Jess's eyes in the mirror. 'Mother of God, you should have asked one of us to step in! What did poor Simon do?'

Jess decided to stick to the short version. 'They went out for dinner, but I don't think it went well.'

'Oh, Jess!'

'Mam, please don't start. I've heard enough from Simon.'

Zoe snorted. 'Simon's a grown man. He needs to get over himself.'

Jess shot Zoe a grateful look. 'Normally I'd agree with you, but he's probably lost his promotion.'

'Poor Simon!' Carmel shook her head.

Jess fisted her hands in her lap and wished she'd said nothing.

'If you've any ideas, Mam, feel free to share them.'

Carmel sighed. 'All you can do is promise the poor man that you'll be more attentive to his needs in future.' She ignored Zoe's snort of laughter. 'With a career like his, he needs your support.'

Attentive to his needs? Her mother made it sound like Stepford Wife meets BDSM sub.

Carmel gave her hand a reassuring squeeze. 'Simon will come round. Try to be there for him a bit more.'

'Hot sex.' Zoe smirked. 'That'll sort him.'

The girl cutting Jess's hair struggled not to laugh, as Carmel pretended not to hear.

Jess strongly doubted that sex was going to solve this. She just had to figure out what would.

Jess felt a bit more optimistic by the time her hair was finished. Her hairdresser had trimmed the ends and given her a feathered fringe and a tiny bit of layering around her face, and the overall look was lighter, more sophisticated.

By the time she headed back to the office, she'd decided to tackle the forgotten dinner, the same way she'd tackle a work problem – with a combination of creative thinking and practical solutions. Which meant there was no point trying to make it up to Simon at home, if things were still tricky for him in the office.

She passed Emily's desk and gave her a wave.

Emily put down the phone. 'Omigod, I love your hair! Okay, I don't want to ruin your day, but are you up to speed on Chelsea and Brandi's fight?'

'Yep.' Jess stopped for a moment. 'Maybe it's just a publicity stunt?'

Emily's eyes widened. 'You do know they can't stand the sight of each other.' She did a quick search on her phone and passed it to Jess. 'TMZ posted that a few minutes ago.'

Jess read the short piece: **Although the theme of Chelsea Deneuve and Leo Dinardia's wedding is a closely guarded secret, TMZ has learned from sources close to Chelsea that the bride to be is likely to be heavily influenced by her love of fairy tales. We can only think of one fairy tale that would fit a grand ballroom in a 400-year-old castle.**

Jess wrinkled her nose. 'It's pretty vague, they could be guessing.'

Emily looked unconvinced. 'I wouldn't put it past Brandi to leak stuff. You know Chelsea and Brandi's mother was a model?' When Jess said nothing, she hurried on. 'Basically, she wanted Chelsea to be exactly like her – only, after she and Chelsea's dad got divorced, Chelsea took her dad's side. She hated her mam, so she quit her dance classes and those weird kids' beauty pageants her mam had her in. Then, when Chelsea was eight, Brandi was born, and she became the favourite kid who did everything their mother wanted. Sad, right?'

So Chelsea was the poor little rich girl, Jess thought, as she headed back upstairs. It explained why she was so dependent on Angel. She needed a guiding figure in her life, even if it meant paying somebody to fill the role.

Back in her office, she sat down and thought about Simon.

Maybe his boss, what was his name – Liam – would enjoy a luxury weekend break.

Taking a book of Charleston Hotels vouchers from her drawer,

Jess carefully filled one in: *Entitles bearer to two nights Bed & Breakfast and two evening meals for two people, in Linford Castle.* She signed it and, on a separate note, wrote: *Dear Liam, so sorry I couldn't be there for Simon's business dinner. I had a family emergency, and Simon didn't get my message in time! I hope you and your wife enjoy a lovely break at Linford. Yours sincerely, Jess Bradley.*

She slid the voucher and note into an envelope, checked the website of Simon's firm for Liam's last name, and addressed it to his office. She wasn't naive enough to think it would make up for the ruined business dinner, but it was an important gesture. One problem solved.

Chapter 23

'LAST dance class before the wedding, we'll be experts after tonight!' Jess attempted to lighten the atmosphere in the car that Friday evening, as she and Simon drove to Ranelagh.

Simon indicated and turned carefully off the main road.

'Simon, I really am sorry about the dinner.' She decided not to add that he should listen to his messages.

'I know.' Simon's tone was even. 'Did you sort those extra guests, by the way?'

Jess thought about the pointless phone call with Laura from Burlington House. 'All sorted.'

'I'm glad, thank you.'

They lapsed into silence. Jess was grateful it was their last class. She dreaded the weekly torture and they definitely hadn't got any better at waltzes or foxtrots, or whatever it was they were supposed to be learning. How did they make it look so easy on *Celebrity Come Dancing?* Jess figured that even if she and Simon spent all day every day for a week learning one dance, they'd still mess it up. She could imagine Úna's face at the wedding, as she watched them make a show of themselves. Hopefully, Kate and David would make this evening a bit more fun.

'Maybe we could go for a drink with Kate and David afterwards?'

Simon reversed the car neatly into a space outside the community centre. 'Maybe.'

Jess suppressed a sigh. Clearly, he was still annoyed.

In the hall, Simon excused himself to talk to the dance teacher, and Jess made a beeline for Kate and David.

'I'm so glad you came!' She gave them each a hug.

David shoved his hands in his pockets. 'That makes two of you. I'll be tripping over my own feet as soon as we get going.'

Kate smirked. 'I'll go easy on you.' She looked around. 'How's Simon?'

'Fine, he's just chatting with the instructor.'

Jess wondered if Kate had told David about the business dinner. Probably, given that Simon had interrupted their date when he'd rung Kate.

David turned to scan the room. 'I'll go say hi, back in a few.'

After he left, Kate arched an eyebrow. 'So?'

Jess slipped her hands into the pockets of her dress. 'He's still annoyed with me.'

Kate glanced over to where Simon and David stood talking. 'He'll forgive you, Jess, you know that.'

Jess sighed. 'Eventually.'

Kate appeared to think. 'How about we swap partners after the first dance? I'm not promising anything, but I'll talk to him.'

'Kate, it's not fair that we keep dragging you into our problems.'

Kate tucked her hair behind her ears. 'You're not, I offered.'

Jess hesitated, then smiled gratefully. Maybe Kate regretted having taken Simon's side in Dinnergate, 'Thanks, I owe you one.'

The dance instructor announced a fast waltz, and Jess made her way over to Simon. For the next couple of minutes, she smiled and said nothing, as they shuffled around the floor. Looking around, it was clear that almost everyone else wasn't just better than them but were discreetly staying out of their way. When the instructor stopped the music to demonstrate head and shoulders positions, Kate and David moved in beside them.

'Kate thinks we should swap partners for a couple of dances,' David said. 'Because you two will have to dance with other people at the wedding.' He grimaced. 'How formal is this wedding going to be anyway? Tell me you guys got a decent band.'

'Yes, but we're having a half-hour of ballroom dancing first,' Jess said, 'so some of the older guests won't feel left out.'

Simon held out his hand to Kate.

'Come on, Kate, let's show them how it's done.'

'My pleasure.' Kate beamed as she stepped into Simon's arms, and Jess breathed in relief.

David raised an eyebrow as he watched them for a moment.

The music started again, and they moved away from Kate and Simon.

'Jess, why do I get the feeling you and Kate set that up?'

Jess released a tense laugh. 'Don't tell Simon. He still hasn't got over the fact that I missed his dinner party. If anyone can bring him around, it'll be Kate.'

David looked over at Simon and Kate before turning back to Jess. 'Really?'

Jess shrugged. 'Kate gets him.'

'Right.' David hesitated. 'Look, it's not really any of my business, but I get the feeling Simon relies on Kate a fair bit. Apparently, she was the first person he called the other night when he was looking for you.'

Jess stumbled and quickly righted herself. 'Well, yeah, Simon thought she'd know where I was. But you've got it backwards: it's Kate and Luke who rely on Simon.'

'And you don't mind?' He frowned.

Did she mind? She'd never minded before now. 'No, not at all.' She smiled brightly. 'Simon's like a brother to Kate.'

She ignored the strange look David gave her and glanced over at Simon and Kate. The two of them seemed to be dancing pretty well together, but maybe Kate was easier to lead. Jess watched as they both laughed quietly at some shared joke. She remembered how her nana had once advised her to marry her best friend. Jess was fairly sure that Simon was still her best friend. But for the first time, she wondered if she was his.

Chapter 24

'I'M OFF now, Simon.' Jess tried not to sound relieved as she said goodbye.

Simon glanced up from his work. 'You're working on a Saturday?'

She wouldn't point out the irony. Right now, their relationship was fragile enough. 'It's my bridal shower, over at my parents' house.' She gestured to her wrap-around, floral dress. 'What do you think?'

'You look beautiful.' He adjusted his glasses. 'I don't have to be there, do I?'

'Girls only.'

'Enjoy it.'

'Thanks.' Jess turned to go.

'Jess?'

'Yep?' She turned.

He offered a half-smile. 'Let's just forget about the dinner, okay?'

She released a breath. Everything would be fine once this month was over. The celebrity wedding would be a success, and her and Simon's wedding would be a good day out and photos on people's Instagram accounts. She walked over to where he was sitting and hugged him. 'It'll be okay, you know.'

Simon frowned. 'What will?'

'Everything.' Jess shrugged. 'See you later.'

This afternoon would be great, Jess told herself as she arrived at her parents' house. She'd always been close to her family, especially on her mother's side. This was what mattered: love and family. And Simon, obviously. She took a deep breath and let herself in.

Her mother's eldest sister, Maggie, was in the hall.

'There's the girl of the hour!'

Maggie held out her arms and Jess allowed herself to be hugged tightly before Maggie planted a lipsticky kiss on her cheek. She breathed in her aunt's familiar perfume.

'Great to see you, Maggie.'

Maggie pulled away and searched Jess's face. 'Everything all right now, love?'

Jess nodded vigorously. Maggie could sniff out people's worries in a minute: it was her superpower. 'Absolutely. Just excited about seeing you all.'

Maggie linked her. 'We're all in here. Your mam doesn't want too many people in the kitchen. Zoe's giving her a hand.'

'What about Kate?'

'I haven't seen her yet. Come in and let everyone make a fuss.' Maggie led her into the sitting room, where the dividing doors to the rarely used dining room at the front of the house had been opened. The ancient dining-room table was pushed back against the wall, covered in the good tablecloth and piled high with sandwiches, sausage rolls, vol-au-vents and small, heart-shaped iced cakes, bottles of Prosecco, sparkling water and orange juice. Chairs and sofas were grouped around the two rooms and the whole area was decorated with pink and white helium balloons and a huge *Congratulations* banner that Jess recognised from her engagement party.

'*There she is now!*'

The volume of voices rose and, for a few minutes, Jess was surrounded by her aunts and cousins, who took it in turns to hug her and kiss her.

'*Jess!*' Faye and Sarah hugged her in a three-way embrace.

'I'm so glad we had a hen weekend,' Faye whispered. 'Today is going to be pretty tame.'

'Speaking of tame, is anyone coming from Simon's side of the family?' Sarah winked and Jess suppressed a sigh. They'd clearly been listening to Zoe.

'I don't think Úna is coming, and he has no sisters.'

'Just us lunatics, then.' Faye grinned. 'Uncle Tom, how are you?'

Jess turned to see her dad escorting Moira into the dining room.

'Nana, let me help.' Jess let Moira link her until she was sitting in the best armchair, her booted foot raised on a footstool.

'Let me look at all you beautiful girls.' Moira beamed and thanked one of Jess's aunts as she handed her a drink. 'I've never been to a bridal shower, you know. Will there be chocolate willies and crotchless knickers?'

Faye and Sarah started to giggle. 'They're for the hen weekend, Moira,' Faye said when she composed herself. 'Your hair is great, by the way.'

Moira put a hand to her curls. 'Thank you, sweetheart. I was thinking of getting a few red streaks put in.' She sipped her Prosecco. '*Ooh*, that's lovely. Pity about the chocolate willies, though. Did you get any on your hen weekend, Jess?'

The doorbell rang again, sparing Jess an answer. Thank goodness Úna wasn't coming. Her poor nana was obviously experiencing a rush of euphoria after being cooped up at home.

Kate stood outside, holding a bunch of flowers.

'Kate, you're here! *Wow!* Gorgeous flowers, are they for –?'

'They're for your mam.' Kate's eyes slid past Jess.

'Oh, she's in the kitchen. I'll head down with you; I haven't seen her yet.'

Jess turned to her as they descended the stairs to the basement kitchen.

'Nana arrived a few minutes ago. I think she was hoping for a few chocolate willies!' She laughed.

Kate gave a tight smile but said nothing.

Jess quickly changed the subject. 'Hey, whatever you said to Simon last night did the trick. He told me earlier that he forgives me.'

Kate sighed but her smile gentled a bit. 'I didn't do very much, Jess. It wasn't like he was never going to forgive you.'

'Right – but still.' Jess nodded. 'Did Luke have a match this morning?'

'No, that's tomorrow. I went out shopping with Dad this morning, he had to get his tux for the wedding.'

Jess stepped aside so Kate could go downstairs first. 'Maybe he should have rented it.'

Kate shrugged. 'It doesn't matter. We had a lovely morning. Dad insisted on treating Luke and me in Bewleys afterwards.' She pursed her lips. 'I just wish he wasn't so obsessed with my love life.'

Jess wondered how much Kate had told her dad about David, but she didn't get a chance to ask, because they'd stepped into the kitchen.

Jess hung back while Carmel hugged Kate and thanked her for the flowers. No wonder Kate was so tense – she was clearly under pressure, Jess thought. Everyone close to her was pushing her towards David, except for Simon, who seemed to think she shouldn't date anyone.

Carmel interrupted her thoughts.

'Hello, pet, I didn't hear you come in. You look lovely, doesn't she, Kate?'

Kate clasped her hands in front of her. 'Jess always does.'

'You both do,' Carmel said firmly. 'Jess, did I hear your dad's voice upstairs?'

'Yeah, he came in with Nana. I think he's gone out to the greenhouse now.'

Carmel clicked her tongue. 'Zoe, will you take up that plate of biscuits? Now Úna rang to say she's on her way.'

'Úna's coming?' Jess snagged a biscuit off the plate as Zoe passed. 'Are you sure? She more or less told Simon she thought bridal showers were a vulgar American import.'

Kate frowned. 'I'm sure she didn't mean that, Jess. When I was talking to her, I said you'd be really pleased to see her.'

'You asked her to come?'

'No, I just told her you'd be pleased if she did.' Kate looked closely at Jess. 'You did invite her, didn't you?'

Jess caught her mother's eye just as Carmel intervened. 'I organised today, and I asked her to come, so I'm delighted she can make it. Now, Kate, would you mind checking with Maggie that we have everything we need upstairs?'

'Sure.'

After Kate went upstairs, Carmel turned to Jess. 'Are you all right, love? You seem a bit tense.'

Jess tried to relax her features. 'I'm fine, Mam.'

Carmel looked unconvinced. 'Don't worry about Úna – she'll have a lovely time. She won't be able to fault a thing.'

Her mother had gone to so much trouble, Jess thought with a stab of guilt. 'Nobody could fault a thing, Mam, thanks so much for everything.' She gave her mother a quick hug, stepping back as Kate came back down to the kitchen.

'Everything looks fine upstairs, Carmel.'

Carmel nodded. 'Thanks, Kate.'

'Jess, I have some party games,' Kate added, 'but your cousins said you might want to start with some presents.'

Jess turned to her. 'There are party games?' She really needed to gear herself up for games. '*Um*, let's open a couple of presents first.'

'Okay.' Kate turned to Carmel. 'I nearly forgot, Úna's just arrived and I offered to get her some tea.'

'I'll make it,' Jess offered.

Kate crossed the kitchen. 'Jess, you should be with your guests.' She waved her away. 'Go on, it's your day, I'll be there in a minute.'

Trying to shake a feeling of unease, Jess went back upstairs, followed by Carmel.

Jess was relieved to see that Úna was sitting on the three-seater sofa between Maggie and her parents' elderly next-door neighbour, Mrs McCarthy. Knowing Maggie, she had taken charge to make sure Úna felt comfortable.

Carmel pitched her voice to be heard over the chatter. '*If I could have everyone's attention for a minute?*' She paused for a moment as all eyes turned to her. 'Thank you all for coming today. There's plenty of food and drink so please help yourselves. And while you're doing that, Jess is going to open some of her presents.' She beamed at Jess, who offered an awkward smile in return.

This was starting to feel a bit like a teenage birthday party. Jess looked around at the pile of brightly wrapped gifts, wondering where she should begin.

'That's a little something from me, Jess.' Mrs McCarthy handed Jess a rectangular box which Jess unwrapped to reveal a tablecloth, edged with a tiny floral pattern. 'It opens out to six feet long,'

Úna and Carmel made all the right noises.

'Thank you, it's beautiful.' Jess caught Zoe's eye.

Zoe seemed to read her mind, and quickly found some music on her phone.

'Oh, that reminds me.' Úna turned to Jess. 'I forgot to thank you for sorting out the extra guests for the wedding.'

Crap, she could see where Simon got his sense of timing.

'No problem.' Jess flashed Úna a quick smile. Why couldn't she have sent one of her annoying emails, and left it at that? 'Maybe I'll open another gift.'

'There's extra guests coming?' Carmel looked puzzled.

Nooo, this wasn't happening. Jess willed her mother to drop the subject.

'It's fine, Mam, all sorted.'

'Just two.' Úna turned to Carmel. 'The Feely-Martins, terribly nice people, very good friends of ours.'

Carmel gave Úna a steady look. 'So, does that bring the numbers up to a hundred and two?'

You could get nothing past her mother. Desperately, Jess tried to send her meaningful looks, but Carmel was on a roll.

'Has the hotel softened a bit on numbers, Jess? Because if that's the case, your cousins could bring their partners.'

Faye started to say something, but Jess quickly asked her to pass her another present from the pile beside the sofa.

'*Ooh*, open this one!' Faye passed her a prettily wrapped gift, which looked like a book.

'That's something we all put together.' Faye and Sarah's mother, Susan, gave a proud smile.

Jess opened an ornate, spiral notebook. On the first page was a handwritten inscription, *Favourite Family Recipes*.

'I talked to your Mam and your aunts, to gather all our best recipes,' Susan said. 'Sarah typed them all and we divided them up seasonally.' She watched eagerly as Jess carefully turned the pages.

'I love it. It's so thoughtful.' Jess could feel her eyes stinging and she took a deep breath. She knew why she was teary, and it was all her own fault. '*Wow*, Gran's Christmas pudding is in here. It was always my favourite.' She realised her faux pas and shot Moira a look of apology. 'No offence, Nana.'

Moira chuckled. 'None taken. I hated making Christmas pudding.'

'Carmel, didn't you tell me that the hotel is very strict about numbers and that's why you couldn't invite a lot of your own friends?' Mrs McCarthy's voice rang clearly through the room.

Jess felt a bit sick. She knew it had been tricky for her parents, not being able to invite their close neighbours to the wedding.

Carmel looked a bit flustered. 'That's right, Mrs McCarthy, they were very firm about that.'

'But didn't you just say that there's extra coming now?'

It was getting worse.

Faye handed Jess another gift. 'That's from me and Sarah.'

Jess smiled her thanks, but her fingers fumbled as Úna explained the guest situation to Mrs McCarthy.

'I think Jess organised that a couple of her friends would come along in the evening.'

Susan leaned across from the other sofa, to catch Úna's attention. 'I hope you don't mind me saying, but that would have been quite tricky for Jess.'

'I can't imagine why,' Úna said.

Carmel looked confused. 'There's evening guests too?'

'No, no.' Jess could feel her neck and face heat under Susan's scrutiny. 'There was no need, it all worked out.' *Why couldn't everyone just leave it alone?*

'Well, I talked to that banqueting manager, to make sure the Feely-Martins would be at the right table.' Úna sipped her tea. 'She told me you'd put them in instead of two friends of yours. I can't remember their names.'

There was a brief, uncomfortable silence in the room. Out of the corner of her eye, Jess saw her mother mouth something to Zoe, but she didn't dare look at anyone else. Palms sweating, she tore the wrapping off her cousins' gift, to reveal an enlarged framed photo of herself, Zoe, Faye and Sarah as teenagers.

'That was the summer you all went down to the caravan in Wexford without us, remember?' Susan laughed. 'You three promised you'd mind Zoe.'

Carmel came over to admire it. 'Look at that!' She exchanged a smile with Susan. 'We only let them go because the rest of the family were already down there, and they were dying to see Sarah and Faye. Poor Zoe was only there a day when she fell and broke her arm.'

'Those were the names,' said Úna.

Jess looked up in horror.

Úna seemed pleased to have remembered. 'The woman from the hotel told me she was replacing Sarah and Faye with the Feely-Martins.'

In the silence that followed, all eyes turned to look at Jess.

'I can explain. But maybe now isn't the best time.' Jess gave Faye and Sarah a pleading look, but their expressions as they stared back were a mix of hurt and disbelief.

Susan turned to Carmel. 'Did you know about this?'

Carmel was exasperated now. 'There's nothing to know. Faye and Sarah are both coming to the wedding. Anyway, this is nonsense about evening guests. I don't think they're allowed, are they, Jess?'

Jess could barely get the words out. 'No, the hotel doesn't have room.'

'Oh.' Bright spots of colour flashed to Úna's cheeks, as she seemed to realise what had happened. She turned to Sarah and Faye. 'I'm dreadfully sorry, I didn't mean to cause any hurt.'

Jess felt a stab of annoyance. What did Úna imagine would happen when she asked her to un-invite people?

'Kate, Zoe, please pour everyone more drinks.' Carmel stood. 'Jess, would you, Faye and Sarah give me a hand in the kitchen?'

'Sure.' Jess scrambled to her feet, feeling like a teenager in trouble.

Wordlessly, she and her cousins left the room and trooped downstairs.

In the kitchen, Carmel turned to her. 'What's going on, Jess?'

Jess turned from her mother's worried expression to meet her cousins' silent stares. 'I should have explained. The only way I could squeeze in Úna's guests was by saying they could take your places at the table.'

Faye folded her arms. 'Why would you do that? When were you planning on telling us?'

'I wasn't, there was no need. Look, the hotel says they're strict on numbers, but a good hotel manager will do everything they can for a wedding party. If extra wedding guests turn up on the day, places will be found very quickly.'

Sarah gasped. 'So, you were okay with having us just turn up and face all that embarrassment?'

Jess shook her head. 'Sarah, I'd have made sure that wouldn't happen.'

'How?' Faye's voice rose. 'I guess it doesn't matter, though. It's just us, not Úna's precious last-minute guests.'

'That's not fair.' Jess felt sick. 'Look, nothing has changed, you'll be at the wedding.'

Her cousins exchanged another look.

'Actually, we *won't* be.' Sarah looked pointedly at her watch. 'Thanks for inviting us today, Carmel, it was lovely. But I have to go.'

'Girls, please stay and sort this out!' Carmel was upset.

Shit, this was awful. 'Mam's right,' Jess said. 'We can sort this – it's all my fault!'

Faye gave her a cold look. 'You're right, it is all your fault and you need to sort it.' She gave Carmel a brief hug. 'See you soon, Carmel.'

Jess sat down heavily at the kitchen table after they left. 'I can't believe this has happened, Mam. I'm so sorry, I've been trying to keep everyone happy.'

Carmel sighed and leaned back against the work counter. 'I know you're trying to keep *Úna* happy.'

'And Simon.'

'Yes, and Simon. It's a juggling act, but you can't alienate your own family in the process.'

Jess propped her elbows on the table and rested her head in her hands. 'I should never have agreed to let Úna bully me into squeezing in last-minute guests. I'll message the girls later and make this right.'

Carmel spoke slowly. 'I'm not sure how you can make this right without making changes. Faye and Sarah are your closest cousins, and they were invited first.'

Jess looked up. 'I know.' She massaged her temples. 'God, Mam, the last thing I want to do is to go back upstairs to everyone.'

Carmel flashed her a sympathetic look. 'We have guests. Come on, we'll take the cake up and play some of Kate's games.'

'I'll take it.' Jess took the chocolate cake carefully off the counter, steeling herself as she walked back upstairs, where she was relieved to hear music and chatter. Taking a deep breath, she went back into the living room. She just had to get through the next hour. It took her a few moments to realise that Susan had gone as well as her daughters.

That had been the longest hour of her life, Jess thought, as she said her goodbyes to everyone at the door, and thanked people for coming. She wondered if they'd all been as conscious of the strained atmosphere after Faye, Sarah and Susan had left. If so, everyone had made a huge effort for her and Carmel's sake, even if they weren't keen to hang around afterward.

To Jess's surprise, Úna was one of the last to leave.

'I know I've created some problems between you and your family, Jess.' Her hand fluttered to the pearls at her throat. 'I'm so sorry. Maybe I can explain the situation to the Feely-Martins.'

Jess was tempted to ask her to do just that. But Úna looked so worried she felt a bit sorry for her. And it still wouldn't fix what she had done to her cousins.

'It's fine, we'd better not mess with it anymore.' Jess gave her a hug. 'I should have just come clean with the girls at the start. I'll figure it out.'

Úna appeared to be at a complete loss. 'I don't know how we managed to pick a hotel that doesn't allow after-dinner guests at a wedding, even if there is a limit on numbers.'

Jess decided not to remind her that the church and hotel had been her suggestions.

'Well, thank you for a lovely afternoon, Carmel. We'll see you at the wedding.' Úna clasped Carmel's hands briefly in her own.

Jess felt a flash of respect for her as she watched her leave. It would have been easy for Úna to make her excuses today, and she wouldn't have blamed her if she'd left early after what happened.

She closed the door and went back into the living room, where her mother, Zoe and Kate were clearing up. Suddenly, all she wanted was to be alone with her own family.

'Thanks, Kate, we've got this, honestly.'

Carmel caught Jess's eye before turning to Kate. 'We have a lot of leftover food. Will you come down to the kitchen to help me wrap some of it? I might give a few things in to Mrs McCarthy, and you'll take some cake and biscuits home for Luke, won't you?'

Kate nodded and with downcast eyes followed Carmel downstairs.

Zoe rounded on Jess. 'What's up with her?'

Jess perched on the arm of the long sofa. 'Kate? She might be feeling under a bit of pressure because of David, I'm not really sure. To be honest, I have bigger problems.'

Zoe found a clean glass and poured herself some warm Prosecco. 'Jess, this is your wedding. Just tell the hotel you need extra space. Full stop.'

'I tried that. The banqueting manager reminded me that it's all they can fit in their room. It all comes down to insurance.'

Zoe pulled a face just as Kate stuck her head around the door. 'I'm off.'

Jess got up and went out to the hall. 'Hey, thanks again.' She moved to hug her, but Kate reached for the door instead.

'See you Monday, Jess.'

Jess sagged against the door after she left. Kate had seemed fine the night before at the dance class, so she couldn't understand why she'd been in such bad form today. After the awful incident with her cousins, the old Kate would have hugged her tightly, and told her everything would work out. Jess missed that person.

The guest book, another of her mother's ideas, was open on the hall table and Jess spotted Faye's distinctive, loopy handwriting. Beside her signature, she'd written: *Here's to a fab day on the 28th. Can't wait. xx* She felt like a total bitch. She should have told Úna and Edward straight out that she wouldn't hurt her friends or family, but she'd been too much of a coward.

She ran her eye over the other comments, stopping when she got to Mrs McCarthy's. Opposite her name, in careful, spidery writing, she'd written: *The key to a happy marriage is to keep a few secrets.* Jess sighed. Mrs McCarthy was a smart woman. And possibly a mind-reader.

Chapter 25

'I'M GLAD we came out tonight.' Jess reached across the table at La Vivanda and took hold of Simon's long, slim hands.

Simon rolled his shoulders as if easing out some tension. 'Well, at least I got my work finished. Although I'm not sure going out on a Sunday night is a very good idea.'

Jess squeezed his hands. 'I know, but I feel bad about Thursday, and this was the only night we were both free.'

'Was that the reason for the engagement photos?' Simon smiled tiredly. 'I appreciate the effort, Jess. I'm just sorry I can't enjoy it a bit more.'

Jess thought about their engagement shoot in Malahide Castle earlier in the day. Zoe had done her best to relax them, but had finally said that if Simon didn't smile, she wouldn't Photoshop out his bad bits.

'I don't expect you to Photoshop anything, thank you, Zoe. My parents like me exactly the way I am,' Simon had replied.

Zoe had unclipped a lens cover and given Simon a pointed look. 'I suppose they have to, they're your parents.'

Jess had imagined an engagement shoot would be a lot of fun, but after about twenty-five minutes it had been easier to call it a day.

Zoe had shrugged. 'Suits me. Finn and I promised Nana we'd go down this evening to make her dinner and do a bit of cleaning.'

'Actually, I asked Zoe to do our photos ages ago.' It was tempting to tell him what she'd done on Friday for his boss, but it was better to make it a surprise. She caught their waiter's eye, and he hurried over to their table.

'Such a pleasure to see my two favourite people. How are you both this evening?'

Jess beamed. She was convinced that Italian men had to attend charm school. 'We're celebrating, Luca.'

Simon looked astonished. Luca looked delighted.

'Birthday? No, a baby?' His eyes flicked briefly over Jess's slightly rounded tummy.

She sucked it in, feeling a bit annoyed now.

'Actually, Luca, we're just celebrating the fact that we're getting married in a couple of weeks' time, so we'll have …' she glanced at Simon, who was looking at her as if she'd sprouted an extra head, '*er*, our usual bottle of wine, please. You know the one.'

Simon cleared his throat. 'Cabernet Sauvignon.'

Jess nodded. 'Right, that one.'

After Luca left, Jess took Simon's hands again. 'This is nice, isn't it? Just the two of us. I mean, I feel like we don't see each other anymore.'

Simon extracted one hand to push his glasses up his nose. 'We see each other every day.'

'Well, yes, obviously. I just feel it's important for us to make time to really talk to each other.'

He sighed. 'It's also important we don't break promises to each other.'

Jess felt colour flash to her cheeks, as a sharp memory of her night with Adam on the Isle of Man caught her unawares. She forced herself to concentrate.

'I know, I should have asked Zoe to step in. But I thought that was behind us?'

Simon pushed his fringe out of the way. 'It is, I'm sorry, I'm just a bit caught up with work right now. Liam has spoken to Bill, and he thinks we might win him over, but I still let the firm down.'

Jess tried to think of something comforting to say. 'A lot of that was outside your control, Simon. He can't blame you for bad food or terrible service in a restaurant. You did your best.'

Simon folded his hands on the table. 'Jess, you do understand how important my career is, don't you?'

Jess nodded. 'Of course, I love what I do too.'

Simon seemed to be trying to choose his words. 'Look, Jess, I don't want you to get upset but …'

'*Okaaay* …' Jess shifted in her chair.

Luca reappeared with the Cabernet Sauvignon, as well as two flutes of sparkling Italian wine. 'On the house, with our very best wishes.' He gave Jess a little wink.

'Thank you, Luca.' She smiled and took a sip.

'The thing is,' Simon said, after Luca left, 'my career is very different to yours.'

Jess drank some more sparkling wine. 'I agree.' Where was this going?

'And the reality is that once we have children, it'll probably suit you to take a career break. Otherwise, neither of us would see our children very much.' Simon held up a hand. 'Let me finish, please. Financially, it makes sense to put my career first.'

Jess's mouth opened and closed, but she couldn't speak.

Oblivious, Simon turned to study the menu. Jess didn't know why: he always ordered the lasagne.

She put down her glass carefully. It was best to say nothing. She couldn't make a scene here, in their favourite restaurant. That was the trouble with having a favourite restaurant. Simon was probably still hurting after the failed business dinner; he didn't literally mean that his career was more important than hers. Except that he'd hinted at it before. Still, saying something and really meaning it were different things.

Simon closed the menu. 'I know what I want.'

Maybe he wouldn't ask for the lasagne. 'They have great specials tonight.'

'*Hmm*, maybe.' Simon raised his eyebrows. 'So.'

'So.' Jess smiled.

'Was there something in particular you wanted to talk about?'

A change of topic! Jess released a breath. 'Well, nothing in particular. I thought we could chat about *er* … silly stuff.'

'Silly stuff?' Simon's eyebrows disappeared under his fringe.

'*Er*, well, not literally.' She lifted her glass. 'Anyway, here's to us!'

Simon pulled a face as he took a sip. 'It's that awful cheap stuff. I'll stick to the bottle we ordered. You should too.'

Jess drank half a glass. 'I like it. And it's kind of rude not to drink it.'

Simon gave her a patient look. 'Not when we didn't ask for it.'

Jess maintained a firm smile. Would this be their regular restaurant in years to come? Would they have date nights? Celebrate birthdays and wedding anniversaries? Bring their kids, eventually? She couldn't picture any of it. Maybe if there was less pressure to have children ... she stopped herself from taking another deep breath. She was starting to hyperventilate.

'Actually, I've been thinking, how about we start looking around for a house?' Simon said, swirling the wine gently in his glass before taking a sip.

'*Um.*' Their flat was very spacious for two people. Just not for a family. Her chest felt tight, and she quickly drank some water.

Simon looked worried. 'Jess?'

'I'm fine.' She flashed him a smile. 'Just ... hungry.'

'Right, hang on.'

He signalled to Luca, who approached their table, smiling broadly and flourishing a small notebook.

Crap, she hadn't even had a chance to look at the menu. It didn't matter, she'd already mentioned the specials. She slanted Simon what she was pretty sure was her sexiest look. 'Why don't you order for me?'

Simon cleared his throat and turned to Luca. 'Two lasagnes and the house salad to share.'

Chapter 26

JESS crept into work the following morning. Something had taken up residence in her stomach overnight and died there. Whatever it was, was also affecting her head. Had she drunk too much? Hardly, not in front of Simon. But now she thought about it, she'd probably thrown that sparkling wine back too quickly, followed by more than half of the Cabernet, despite Simon's insistence that they take the rest of it home.

'Nobody does that, Simon,' she'd hissed, mortified when he asked Luca to re-cork it. 'There's only about a glassful left. Let's just finish it or leave it.'

'Don't be ridiculous, Jess.' Simon had sounded a bit exasperated as he paid, added a ten percent tip, and collected his coat.

He'd dismissed her suggestion that they go to see a late movie. 'I want to get you straight home to bed.' He'd sounded firmer than usual.

This was more like it, Jess thought, suddenly keen to get home quickly. Their relationship needed something exciting. Because after only three years, their sex life was fairly predictable. But right at that moment, it seemed, Simon had decided to take charge. Maybe he wanted to surprise her. Shock her, even.

Now she snapped back to reality as she crossed the foyer, giving

Emily a small wave. Emily shot her a sympathetic look in return. 'Hey, Jess, don't take this the wrong way, but you look stressed out. I totally get it, though, if this wedding doesn't go ahead ...'

Jess stopped. 'What are you talking about?'

'You haven't seen it? TMZ are saying that Chelsea and Leo aren't with each other, like, they're not even talking to each other. He's accusing her of being a gold-digger and she's saying he's just using her for her fame.' Emily's eyes narrowed. 'I still think Brandi is the leak – she knows everything that Chelsea does.' She arched her eyebrows meaningfully. 'She's meant to be pretty close to Leo too.'

God, it was way too early for this. She needed more coffee. Or a lie-down. Or both. 'Emily, it's just gossip. I'm sure Chelsea and Leo have already made a statement.'

Emily flicked back her hair. 'Nope.'

Jess suppressed a sigh. 'Well, let's not worry until we have a reason to worry.' Or the energy to worry. 'Talk to you later.'

Jess hit the button for the lift, and leaned back against the wall as she waited, her thoughts drifting again to the previous night.

Simon had shocked her all right. He'd helped her off with her shoes and coat before disappearing to the kitchen. Encouraged by the prospect of something exciting, she'd stripped off, thrown on her sexiest underwear, generously spritzed on some *Good Girl Eau de Parfum*, and sprawled in the middle of the bed with her arms above her head. Moments later, Simon had returned with a glass of water and ordered her to drink it. Right before he changed into his stripy pyjamas, lay down and turned on his side to go to sleep.

The lift appeared and she stepped in, relieved to be on her own. This morning, as always, Simon had been up at ridiculous o'clock to go to the gym, where he'd no doubt done a thirty-minute aerobic workout, showered, changed and gone straight to work. Off to fight for clients in the heady world of big finance and save the world from injustice ... or was it justice? Whilst she got on with ... well, staying upright and not getting sick would be a major achievement. The lift stopped and she peered out.

The corridor was clear, so she sprinted down to her office and slunk in, closing the door. Okay, things might be a bit terrible right now, but at least she still had a brilliant job that she absolutely loved. She also had a responsible, hardworking, decent fiancé. So, basically amazing. So why didn't she feel that buzz of excitement she used to feel? She could understand relationships going stale after ten years. No, that didn't sound very long. Twenty years: that was ages. A lifetime, in fact. But three years?

Oh God, she was starting to feel faint. She needed chocolate.

The office phone rang before she had a chance to eat anything, and with a slightly uneasy feeling she answered.

It was Ian Finnegan.

'Jess, I'm sure you know why I'm calling.'

She hadn't thought it was possible for her headache to get any worse. 'Please don't tell me the wedding is off.'

'Let's not jinx anything now.' Ian paused. 'I'm not sure what to believe, though. We've had reporters phoning the hotel all morning, and I've left messages with Angel and Leo's PA, but I've heard nothing back yet. I wanted to keep you updated, that's all.'

'Yeah, no, hopefully it'll all work out.'

'Fingers crossed, Jess. We need this mad wedding.' Ian sighed. 'I'll be in touch.'

After Jess hung up, she kicked off her shoes and lay down on her back, stretching her legs up against the wall. That felt quite good.

She wondered if it was an actual yoga position: it definitely should be. Her mobile rang and she sat up and reached for her bag.

It was Simon. Hoping it wouldn't be another lecture, she swiped to answer. 'Hi.'

'Jess, did you send my boss some bloody letter offering him and his wife a weekend in one of your bloody hotels?'

Maybe she should have told him about that. But it wasn't like she'd done anything wrong. Jess frowned. Was Simon gritting his teeth? 'Yes, with a voucher. I thought it would be …'

'His *dead* wife.'

Jess felt a ringing in her ears. '*What?*'

'I can't believe you, Jess.'

'I can't believe his wife is dead.'

'She died last year. We went to her funeral!'

Jess gasped. 'That's whose funeral we were at! Oh my God, I totally mixed Liam up with someone else.'

'Who? Never mind, I don't want to know. I had to tell Liam that you've been on very strong antibiotics, and they've made you delirious.'

'What?' Jess massaged her forehead. 'Actually, that's quite good. Did he believe you?'

She thought she heard him swear.

'If he does, it's because he knows I couldn't make that up.'

'But you did.'

'Kate did.' Simon spoke stiffly.

Jess gave a nervous laugh. 'What?' Why would he talk to Kate before her? And ask her to help? 'When did you talk to her?'

'Earlier this morning. That's not the point.'

'You're right.' Jess's mouth dried. 'Did you phone her?'

'Kate phoned to talk to me about something just after Liam called me into his office. When I told her ...'

'You told her before you told me.'

'*Because I happened to be talking to her!*' Simon sounded furious. 'Why are we arguing about something so stupid?'

'We're not.' Jess felt like she was free-floating.

'Fine.' Simon took an audible breath. 'Please, don't do anything else.'

'I wasn't going to. I have to go, bye.' She hung up.

The phone dropped to the carpet with a soft thud, and she buried her head in her hands. She was such an idiot. But how the hell was she supposed to remember the personal details of everyone Simon worked with? And now Kate was involved. Again. She couldn't believe he'd told her.

It didn't matter that Kate and Simon were friends: there were things that should stay between Simon and her. Hypocrite: the word slid into her mind. Determinedly, she pushed it out and phoned Simon back.

'What now, Jess?'

She flinched. 'Sorry.' She had no right to ask. Not after she'd cheated. She went to hang up but instead she blurted out, 'How often have you confided in Kate instead of me?'

There was a long silence on the phone.

'You can hardly blame me if I didn't ask for your advice after what you did,' he said finally.

'I'm not talking about that.' Jess took a shallow breath. 'I'm talking about usually.'

Simon's tone was cool. 'Kate's a good friend, Jess. She's intelligent and reasonable, and I trust her.'

'And you don't trust me?' *Why would you? I cheated on you. But you don't know that.* Jess felt close to tears. 'Why would you undermine me by running to Kate?'

Simon's voice rose. '*I didn't run to Kate.*'

She gripped the phone, forcing herself not to hang up as Simon continued, his voice laced with hurt and anger.

'You undermined me when you screwed up my business dinner. And you made things worse with that bloody voucher.'

He was right to be angry. But he'd had no right to drag Kate into it. Maybe once the two weddings were over ... she stopped. Then they'd be married. How would things be any different?

'Simon, I need a break.' The words rushed out.

'Sorry?'

Jess faltered. 'I think we need a break, Simon. I'm going to move back home for a few days at least. I ... we need to think.'

There was another long silence. She thought he had hung up.

When he spoke again, his tone was cool. 'Take all the time you need, Jess. I'm working late tonight. I expect you to be gone by the time I get home.'

He hung up and Jess ran to the bathroom, turning on the cold tap to rinse her hands. Her stomach heaved and she threw up into the sink. With shaky hands, she turned on the other tap, rinsing the sink clean. She stared at her reflection, eyes puffy and bloodshot in a white face. What had she done?

Chapter 27

CARMEL opened the door to Jess, who stood, suitcase by her feet, a large handbag slung across her body. 'Hi, Mam. Sorry, I couldn't find my key.'

Carmel's gaze went to her case and then swept back up to Jess. 'Please tell me your washing machine has broken.'

She wished she didn't have to do this to her family. 'Not exactly.'

'I'm putting the kettle on.' Carmel ushered her into the hall.

A while later, Jess finished her second mug of tea.

Carmel folded her arms on the kitchen table. 'I'm still no wiser, love. You had a row with Simon because you forgot that his boss is a widower. I'm sure he'll understand your heart was in the right place.'

'Maybe.' Jess huffed out a breath. 'But that wasn't why we rowed. He got Kate involved, instead of talking to me.'

Carmel gave a sympathetic nod. 'He probably shouldn't have done that. But you can't move out every time you have a row.'

Jess glanced at her empty ring finger. Her engagement ring was still in its box at Simon's apartment, and she hadn't thought to pack it. Maybe it was a sign that they should make a clean break. Who was she fooling, anyway? She'd cheated just weeks before their wedding. If she really loved Simon, she wouldn't have even considered a one-night stand. A wave of exhaustion hit her.

'This feels different, Mam – I needed to get away.'

'Oh Jess.' Carmel squeezed her hand. 'Have you talked to Kate since?'

'No, I don't want to right now.'

Carmel ran her hands back through her fine, fair hair, so like her younger daughter's. 'You girls are close, and it sounds like she was just trying to help.'

Jess felt her chest tighten. 'Then she should have told Simon it was none of her business and he should talk to me. Look, do you mind if we don't talk about this anymore now?'

Carmel nodded reassuringly. 'Of course.' She hesitated. 'You'll be in Zoe's old room tonight, remember. Oh, Finn has moved into the spare room in Nana's for the moment.'

Jess blinked. 'When did that happen? I only saw Zoe yesterday.'

'The pair of them went down yesterday evening, and Finn did some jobs for Moira. By the time they were leaving she had a proposition for him. He'll stay rent free, while her foot is healing, and help her with the shopping and cleaning, and whatever else she wants done.'

Jess took a moment to digest this. 'Were he and Zoe getting on all right here?'

'As far as I could see.' Carmel was matter of fact. 'Although I think Finn felt a bit awkward. At least at Nana's he's being useful. She actually needs him.'

'How does Dad feel about it, Mam? Finn isn't even family.'

'If your dad had any doubts about him, he'd have said something. Finn's a decent lad, Jess, and sure it's not like he's doing anything personal for her. Nana's quite independent, and she has the carer coming in to check on her every day. But he's company. She loves his performance art, so they'll have things to talk about.'

Her mother made it sound like Finn was dropping in for afternoon tea. He might be well-intentioned, but he was a total flake. Jess made a mental note to visit Moira soon.

'I'll leave clean sheets in Zoe's room for you.' Carmel looked at her properly. 'You do look quite tired. Do you want to go to bed now?'

Despite everything, Jess started to laugh. 'It's only half past nine. I think I'll chill for a while. Where's Dad?'

'In the greenhouse.'

Jess pushed back her chair. 'Mam, if you want, I can pretend we're having the flat painted.'

Carmel looked puzzled. 'Why would you do that?'

'In case Mrs McCarthy asks why I'm back.'

Her mother clicked her tongue. 'Mrs McCarthy has a lot of time on her hands, pet. Let her think what she wants. It's nobody's business except yours and Simon's. Now, stop worrying: things will look better in the morning.'

Which was hilarious advice from the professional worrier in the family.

But Jess shot her a grateful smile. 'Thanks, Mam, you're probably right.'

Chapter 28

THINGS had looked only slightly better the following morning. Jess had got up early after a night of fitful sleep and nightmares, and eaten a quick breakfast, leaving for work before her parents were out of bed. To her relief, Leo Dinardia had released a statement denying the allegations on TMZ and insisting that their relationship was as strong as ever. What struck Jess was Chelsea's silence. She was usually keen to talk directly to her fans, but her social media sites were quiet.

Now Jess sat on the floor in her office, her back against the wall, and tried to concentrate on her breathing. A little over two weeks ago, she'd had a best friend she could depend upon, and a fiancé she was sure she loved. One whom she was positive she'd marry.

Her phone buzzed at her hip, and she pulled it out, wondering if it was Simon. But it was Úna. Suppressing a sigh, she swiped to answer.

'Hi, Úna, how are things?'

In a corner of ceiling, Jess noticed a fly struggling to free itself from a web.

'Hello, Jess, I'll come straight to the point. I'm a bit worried.'

Crap, Simon must have told his mother too. 'Úna, I know you only want what's best, but this is between Simon and me. We'll sort things out between us.'

Úna sounded puzzled. 'I'm not quite following. What have you done?'

What had *she* done? Irritation made her flippant. 'Since Simon and I decided to take a break yesterday? Not a lot, to be honest. Got up this morning, came into work.' Her eyes fell on the spider web. The fly had almost stopped struggling.

'A break? To do what?'

For a smart woman, Úna could be surprisingly slow. Which meant now she'd have to spell it out. '*Crap.*'

'I beg your pardon?'

'Sorry, Úna.' Jess tried to sound matter of fact. 'Simon and I are taking a bit of a break. I moved back home yesterday.'

She heard Úna's slight intake of breath. 'Did you know that Simon lost his promotion?'

'Oh no, definitely?' Jess sat up a bit straighter.

'He was told yesterday afternoon that he didn't get it. His boss gave him a plethora of excuses about it not being the right time.' Úna cleared her throat. 'I'm not one to interfere, Jess, but I am upset. Simon worked tremendously hard for that promotion, and he had his heart set on it. That's why I phoned.'

'Úna …'

'Please, Jess, just listen.' Úna's voice softened. 'We both love Simon. At least, I hope you still do. So, whatever has happened, please resolve it quickly. Simon is a bit stubborn – he gets that from The Judge, so you might have to make the first move. Now, I know this can be a stressful time, but I do hope you take my advice. I know you and I will be great friends.'

It would be a lot easier if she could just dislike Úna. But she wasn't a bad person. Even if she tended to be quite blunt and had no compunction about interfering.

Before she could reply, there was a sharp knock on the door, and Adam came in.

'What happened?' He hunkered down beside her. 'Are you feeling dizzy?'

Jess met his eyes. How had she never noticed those really long, dark eyelashes? Especially as she'd noticed everything else about him. She really needed to try harder not to. 'I'm fine.'

'Jess? Are you still there? Who are you talking to?'

'I'm sorry, Úna, I have to go. My boss just walked in. I'll think about what you said.' She hung up.

'Your boss?' Adam smirked.

Jess sighed. 'That was … it doesn't matter. I'm kind of glad you came in. And I'm not dizzy, but thanks for asking.'

'Good to know. Now that I'm here, can I get you anything? A pillow and blanket?'

'Wow, you're a regular comedian.'

'Hang on.' He stood and took hold of her hands. As he pulled her to her feet, Jess caught a hint of his scent, light, but spicy.

'I don't mean to be rude, but have you got shorter?'

A sharp memory of their night together flashed to mind, Jess standing on tiptoe to reach his mouth, Adam slipping his hands under her bottom to lift her into his arms, as she wrapped her legs around him. Flushing hotly, she turned abruptly away, wondering if it was possible to be a masochist and not know it. She stepped into her shoes.

'Do you want to sit down?'

'Sure.' Adam threw himself into the other chair, as Jess took refuge behind her desk.

He studied her for a minute. 'You seem a bit stressed.'

'I'm fine, really.' When he said nothing, she relented. 'It's kind of personal.'

Adam gave a brief nod. 'You've been following the latest Leo and Chelsea drama, I assume?'

'Yes.' It was almost a relief to worry about work. 'I saw Leo's statement this morning.'

He folded his arms. 'I managed to get hold of Angel yesterday evening. He admitted that there's been some tension since Leo made Chelsea sign the pre-nup.'

'But there's no major problem, is there?'

'I got the impression there was a lot Angel wasn't saying. Look, I think we do need to have a plan B, in case this wedding doesn't go ahead.'

'You don't really believe that's a possibility, do you?' Jess shook her head. 'They've already spent so much, asked all their guests, and there's that huge TV deal with Bobbie Grayson.'

'I agree, it wouldn't make much sense.' Adam raised an eyebrow. 'But things have gone very quiet at their end. Ian Finnegan has heard nothing from Angel and, until yesterday, Angel was phoning or emailing daily with new requests.'

Jess forced herself to think rationally. 'If the wedding didn't happen, we'd have to seriously tailor our marketing strategy.'

Adam looked like he was choosing his words. 'Linford is a big place, lots of potential, we just need to be creative.'

Jess guessed what he was trying not to say. If this wedding fell through, it would take them years to come back from the Linford

Curse. In the meantime, she'd have to work ten times as hard on a new campaign, which would probably only have a fraction of the success.

Adam got to his feet. 'The good news is there was a small problem identified with the electrics in Linford's south tower, so we're getting it repaired and the whole place checked. The refurbishment will begin as soon as that's done.'

Jess nodded, her mind still on the possibility of a wedding falling through. 'Will it be done in time?'

'It'll go down to the wire, but that's the plan.'

There was a knock on the door, and Kate came in.

'Oh, hi, Adam. I can come back when you're free, Jess.'

She seemed a bit edgy, Jess thought. They really needed to clear the air between them.

'You're fine, I'm going.' Adam glanced at Jess. 'Catch you later.'

After he left, Jess got up and walked around to sit on the edge of her desk.

'Hey, I'm glad you dropped by,' she said. 'I wanted to say sorry if Simon dragged you into the middle of our ... row.'

Kate raised a hand, cutting her short. 'He didn't mean to. I'd phoned him about tonight, and he mentioned it.'

Jess frowned. 'Tonight?'

'Simon's taking Luke to the new *Star Wars* movie.'

'Sorry, right. Thanks for trying to help.' Jess felt bad for being annoyed with Kate. None of this was her fault.

'Anyway, don't forget your final dress fitting next Saturday afternoon.' Kate pursed her lips. 'You need to make a decision, Jess.'

'About what?'

'Whether or not you're getting married. Stop messing around

and apologise to Simon. I know it sounds harsh, but don't screw this up.' Kate opened the door and gave Jess one final look. 'I'd better get back to work.'

After she left, Jess stayed where she was, trying to analyse her feelings. She knew Kate was right, but it felt like she was judging her. She'd never really thought about it before, but in just three years, Kate had managed to become as close to Simon as she was to Jess. If she and Simon were to break up permanently, Jess knew Kate's loyalties would be torn.

And now the celebrity wedding looked uncertain too. Jess's stomach knotted tighter. Maybe she could market Linford as a luxury retreat from the world and advertise the cottages on the grounds to writers and artists for short-term lets. Which might work, except that it wouldn't fit in with Frank's vision. Not when they'd spent so much money on its Victorian makeover. The truth was, if Chelsea and Leo's wedding didn't go ahead, Linford Castle could bankrupt them.

Chapter 29

THE PHOTO shoot was underway by the time Jess and Adam arrived at Linford on Wednesday.

Adam had been quiet during the drive down, apparently lost in his own thoughts. He was probably worried about the celebrity wedding, Jess reasoned. But she also suspected that Adam had the same restless energy as Zoe. She couldn't imagine him wanting to stay in the one place for too long. Maybe being head of European operations suited him: it was bound to mean a lot of travel.

'See you in a minute.' Adam parked to the west of the hotel and headed inside.

Jess wandered around to the East lawn. Under a white and pink rose-festooned canopy, a number of hotel staff were putting out rows of white, silk-covered chairs either side of a central aisle littered with matching rose petals, while three more staff carried a huge, fake wedding cake to a nearby table. Jess eventually found Zoe in the middle of a shoot in the formal walled rose garden and waited for her to call for a break.

'Why didn't I think of a white tuxedo?' Jess gestured to one of the female models as Zoe changed a lens on the camera.

Zoe raised an eyebrow. 'Mam would have written you out of the will. And poor Simon strikes me as old school.'

Jess decided to let that go. 'Have you everything you need?'

'Yeah, I think so. I didn't have any time to look around when I got down, but Gemma and her team have their shit together.' Zoe glanced up at the sky. 'I'm hoping to get the outside shots done while the light is good and the weather holds.'

'You're clear about the evening scenes?'

'Don't fuss, Jess, I know what I'm doing.'

'I know.' Jess glanced over her shoulder to make sure Adam wasn't around. '*Um*, I have a favour to ask, but you can't ask questions.'

Zoe smirked. 'Not sure if I can promise anything if I can't ask questions.'

This had been a bad idea. She should have known that having Adam and Zoe work so closely together was crazy. 'Zoe, please.'

Zoe rolled her eyes. 'What is it?'

'If you're talking to Adam, who's the guy I came down with, my boss's nephew ...' Jess stopped, experiencing another stab of panic.

Zoe gave her a curious look. 'You okay?'

Jess lowered her voice and spoke quickly. 'You can't tell him I'm about to get married. Don't even tell him I'm with someone – he doesn't know about Simon. Well, he does, but he thinks Simon is marrying Kate.'

Zoe's eyes narrowed. 'I won't say a word if you tell me what's going on.'

'Just promise me.'

'*Okaaay*, I promise.' Zoe stared at her.

Jess nodded, relieved. 'I've to go find Gemma, see you later.'

Adam and Ian were chatting by one of the two grand fireplaces in the foyer.

'Jess.' Ian shook her hand. 'Great to see you again.'

Jess smiled. 'You too, Ian. How's the repair work coming along?'

'We've a team working around the clock.' Ian adjusted a crisp white handkerchief in his top breast pocket. 'Gemma's making sure they clear out while the photos are being done. Anyway, busy day ahead, but I'm around if you need me for anything. Take it handy.'

After he left, Adam turned to Jess and sighed. 'Zoe's already here?'

'She's getting the outside shots done first.'

'I need to make a phone call, excuse me.' Without another word, he turned and went back outside.

Jess breathed out. The sun was shining and she was away from the stuffy confines of the office. She'd try not to worry about anything else.

Ian had organised a buffet lunch in one of the conference rooms.

Zoe grabbed Jess at the door when she came in with Gemma.

'Jess, a quick word?' Zoe took Jess's hand and marched her into a quiet corner before rounding on her. 'Tell me what's going on with you and Adam.'

'Nothing! I can't believe you even asked me that.' Jess wiped her hands quickly on her long linen dress.

Zoe sighed heavily. 'Cut the crap, Jess. I'm lying for you. And Adam has been asking about you being bridesmaid at Kate's wedding.'

'*What? Shit.*' Why had she ever agreed to a hen weekend? She'd actually suggested it. Why hadn't someone talked her out of it? 'Tell me exactly what you said, Zoe.'

Zoe folded her arms. 'As little as possible. That's not the point. The guy's clearly into you. Why didn't you tell him you're engaged to Simon? Why does he think Kate is?'

It was her own fault, asking Zoe to do the photo shoot. Even as a child, she'd demanded to know everything.

'Keep your voice down, Zoe,' she hissed. 'There's no time for the long version.'

'Give me the CliffNotes.'

Jess massaged her temples, frantically trying to work out how much to tell her. 'I might have let Adam think I was single and *um*, interested. In my defence, I was a bit drunk and so was he.'

Zoe looked perplexed for a moment, then her eyes widened. '*Shut the front door! The hen weekend? Did you two actually ...?*'

Jess checked that nobody was within earshot. 'Yes, okay? Obviously, I completely regret it. You're the only person I've told. I just can't tell Adam the truth. Anyway, I don't have to because he's going back to head office in Switzerland after this wedding.'

'So why does he think Kate and Simon are engaged?'

'Because he saw Simon and me together and I told him I was Kate's bridesmaid. It was the first thing that came to mind.'

Zoe gaped at her. 'You do get how screwed-up that is?'

'Which is why you can't say anything to Adam.'

'Adam is the least of your worries.'

'He's my boss's nephew.'

'What's your boss going to do? Fire you for having a one-night stand?' Zoe put her hands on her hips. 'Never mind. How can you still think you want to marry Simon?'

Gemma appeared at Jess's elbow, making her jump. 'Sorry to interrupt, Zoe. I need to run through some stuff with you.'

Zoe gave Jess a final look. 'Coming.'

After Zoe disappeared with Gemma, Jess found a large wingback chair and sat down, trying to make herself as inconspicuous as possible. Even though she'd sworn to herself never to breathe a word about the Isle of Man, she felt oddly relieved that Zoe knew, and guilty that she'd ever mistrusted her.

'Are you hungry?'

She looked up to see Adam, holding a plate of sandwiches. 'Starved actually.'

'Hang on.' He pulled a small table towards her chair and put down the plate, before dragging over another chair for himself. 'I took these from the buffet table. There's someone coming around with tea and coffee.'

'Thanks.' She picked up a dainty turkey and salad sandwich and took a bite. They were miniscule: she'd need a dozen to fill her.

Adam hitched one ankle onto the opposite knee. 'I had a bit of a chat with your sister about you.'

Jess tried not to look nervous. 'Why?'

He grinned and reached for another sandwich. 'You're kind of difficult to get to know.'

Jess swallowed hard to dislodge some bread that had stuck in her throat. 'There's not much to know.'

'So Zoe would have me believe.'

Jess said nothing.

'Look,' Adam said, finally, 'I know we got off on the wrong foot, but I'd like to get to know you better.'

She gave him a wary look. 'How do you mean?'

He met her eyes. 'What would you say if I asked you out for a drink?'

The pulse in Jess's neck started to throb. He *was* interested. He was asking her on a date! God, not in a million years could she ever admit the truth now. 'That's not a good idea, we work together.'

Adam shrugged. 'For now. '

'Exactly, you'll be going back to Switzerland after the wedding, so it's better to keep things simple.' Not to mention that if Adam really knew her, he'd want nothing to do with her. Jess hated how much that thought hurt.

'Say if I wasn't going back after the wedding?'

'But you are.' She was depending on it.

'Yes, but if I wasn't?'

For a brief moment, Jess imagined what it would be like to date Adam. The thought of it was so exciting, it was downright terrifying. It would never last, she told herself.

Adam wasn't like Simon. In fact, he was the opposite of Simon. She folded her arms. 'Then we'd be working together, and it would still be a terrible idea.'

Adam stood and brushed away some crumbs. 'Looks like I lose, either way.' He tipped his fingers to his forehead in a casual salute. 'I've a few things to do. Catch you later.'

Jess sat, heart thumping, feeling strangely deflated. She could hardly blame Adam for asking her out, given what had happened between them, the last time they'd been down here. But she should be happy he'd finally got the message.

She badly needed to believe that if Zoe hadn't put her on the ferry, she and Simon would be blissfully counting down the days. But they still had to sort out their problems, or there wouldn't be a wedding at all. And even though Zoe knew the truth now, there was no point asking for her opinion, because she was completely against her marrying Simon.

She also needed to fix things with Kate. Jess just hoped that whatever had happened between her and Simon, and her and Kate, was a temporary glitch in the matrix.

Chapter 30

THAT was possibly the best coffee she'd ever had. Jess finished her latte and put the cup on the glass table beside her. The surroundings helped, of course. For the last hour she'd had a whole wing of the orangery to herself. With the blinds shuttered across the stained-glass windows to temper the July sun, Jess had enjoyed tasters from their pastry chef with her coffee, and spring water from their own well.

She hardly noticed the waitress until she placed another steaming latte on the table, with a fresh plate of delicate pastries. Jess looked up and laughed. 'How did you even know I was finished?'

The young woman blushed. 'I've personal responsibility for your group this afternoon, ma'am. My name's Holly, so if you need anything please press the bell.' She indicated the discreet buzzer on the table, disguised to look like a Victorian bell.

'Thanks, Holly.' Jess tried to guess her age. The waiting staff wore full Victorian costume: knee-britches, stiff white shirts and dark navy waistcoats for the men, ankle-length dark navy dresses, white aprons and white caps for the women. Female staff with long hair had to secure it in a low bun, while minimal make-up with no nail polish or jewellery completed the illusion.

'Will there be anything else for now, ma'am?'

Jess grinned. 'You could agree not to call me "ma'am".' She held up a hand. 'I know it's the rule, but we both work for the group.'

'Yes, ma'am – Ms Bradley.'

'How long have you worked here, Holly?' Jess saw the confusion on her face. 'What I mean is, did you work for the previous owners?'

'No, I was still in college. I got my diploma in hospitality and when Linford Castle was doing interviews late last year, I went for this job.' Holly glanced discreetly around. 'It helps that I'm a local. Mam said she thought I'd get the job, because our family has a sort of connection to Linford.'

Jess helped herself to a tiny cinnamon bun, half wishing she could ask Holly to sit down. 'What sort of connection?'

Holly stood up a bit straighter. 'We're actually related to the Linford family.'

Jess blinked. 'Really?'

'Honestly.' Holly looked pleased. 'So, you know Helen Linford? She was an only child, like, and even if she hadn't been I don't know if this place could have gone to her, because she wasn't a man.' She rolled her eyes. 'Anyway, when her dad, Lord Linford, died, this place passed to Manus Linford, his nephew. Manus was my great-uncle.'

'*Wow*.' Jess tried to process this. 'Do any of your family remember this place before it was sold out of the family?'

Holly shrugged. 'Maybe my gran.'

Jess smiled. 'Well, that's really interesting – your family connection.'

'I never tell guests, in case it's unprofessional,' Holly said. 'Well, except for Chelsea. But only because she was massively interested in the history of the place and, like, the manager told us we're to be well clued up. She's lovely, like. Way nicer than she comes across on *California Girlfriends*.'

'Right.' Jess wondered what else Holly had told her.

'Anyway,' Holly continued, 'I think she's amazing coming all the way to Ireland to get married. Like, if I lived in the States, I'd find somewhere warm like the beach for my wedding. I wouldn't want to get married somewhere with a wedding curse.'

'Did you say that to Chelsea?' Jess spoke slowly.

'No way, honest!' Holly's eyes widened. 'I just answered her questions.'

She turned as Adam came into the room and slid back into her professional role. 'Good morning, sir, may I get you a special tea or coffee? There's also French filtered coffee and fresh breakfast tea on the table.'

Adam sat down. 'Thanks, no, I'll stick with the coffee in the pot.'

Holly poured a cup and once they'd both assured her there was nothing else they needed, she left.

Jess turned to Adam, determined to keep the focus on work. 'Zoe's sent me some of the stuff she's already done.' She opened a photo on her iPad of a bridal party standing at the hotel's grand front entrance. Flowers arched around the door, with more in huge pots on the stone steps, and lined up either side, were some of the hotel staff. 'We could go with: *Linford Castle: 400 years of history, five-star luxury, memories you'll treasure forever.*'

'It's fine.' Adam paused. 'Maybe a bit generic, though?'

Jess raised an eyebrow. 'We'll have more pictures inside the hotel. We'll be showcasing the Victorian restoration.'

Adam helped himself to a pastry. 'You could get sucked into

Linford's fantasy, couldn't you?'

Which was exactly what she wanted to capitalise on. 'It's fun. I know Frank wants our guests to feel like they're completely immersed in the past.'

Adam nodded. 'When I came out of college, I spent a couple of years working as a waiter in our five-star hotel in Paris. It's not like Linford, obviously, but it has an old-world feel about it.'

Jess regarded Adam over the rim of her china cup. So, he'd worked the normal jobs: his uncle hadn't simply handed him a title. A movement at the door caught her eye and she turned as Zoe, in her uniform of skinny black jeans and T-shirt, strode into the room.

'Hey, Zoe, coffee?'

'No, thanks. I've a bit of a problem: two of the models have dropped out. One of the lads has a stomach bug and one of the girls had a family emergency. I can manage, except for a big group shot I hadn't got.'

Jess put down her cup. 'Are you sure? I mean, it's only two models.'

'Who's the photographer here, Jess?'

'I can get back onto the agency.' Jess picked up her phone.

'It'll take too long. Can the two of you stand in?'

Jess stared at her. 'We're not models.'

'I did a bit of modelling when I was in college.' Adam shrugged. 'Handy money.'

Jess met his eyes, before glancing quickly away. She knew exactly what sort of shape Adam was in.

Zoe clapped her hands. 'Sound. Okay, time is money.'

For reasons she didn't want to examine, Jess didn't want to model with Adam. 'Zoe, I'm kind of tied up here – can you find someone else?'

'One hour, tops. I promise not to tie either of you up longer than that.' Zoe gave Adam a flirty wink.

Jess stifled a sigh. Zoe was right: they needed to get everything done today.

'Fine.' Jess tried to sound matter of fact. 'But there's no way I'll squeeze into anything those models were wearing.'

'Chill, Jess. Adam will fit the wardrobe and we can be clever with your shots.'

Clever? Still, they couldn't afford to miss their deadline. 'Lead the way.'

Why had she agreed to this, Jess thought, as Gemma helped her into the first wedding dress: a form-hugging fitted sheath. Terrified she'd rip it, she held onto a chair and slipped her feet into the highest shoes she'd worn since her hen weekend.

Gemma ran a critical eye over her.

'It's a bit tight, but it'll do.'

Jess peered down at the dress and wondered how she'd walk in it. 'I still can't believe I got into it.'

Gemma shrugged. 'Some of the stuff is bigger, so if we don't have the right size, we just pin the dress around the model. But this looks okay.' She consulted a clipboard. 'Come on, your sister's waiting for you in the great hall.'

Jess attempted a couple of steps before slipping off the shoes and hitching up the dress so she could walk barefoot through the hotel and into the great hall.

Gemma had created a Christmas wedding theme at one end, the summer flowers now replaced with garlands of poinsettias, amaryllis and holly, and hundreds of tiny, white fairy lights. The whole area was lit with storm lanterns, open candles and discreet modern lighting.

'Impressive, isn't it?'

Jess spun as Adam walked towards her, hands in the pockets of a dark, three-piece suit, the collar of a crisp white shirt open at the neck. She reminded herself firmly that everyone looked good in a three-piece suit.

'Short dress and no shoes.' Adam grinned. 'You own the look.'

Despite her nerves, Jess laughed.

Zoe checked her viewfinder. 'Jess and Adam, stand over beside the fireplace.'

Jess stepped carefully into the shot and Gemma hurried over to fix her dress around her.

'I wonder if those candles might be a bit close?' Jess pulled a bit of the train slightly closer to herself.

'Any further away, Zoe won't get the look she needs.' Gemma straightened up. 'Come on, put your shoes back on.'

Adam steadied her elbow, and Jess tried to ignore the tingle that ran through her, as she stepped into the stilettos again.

'Let's get started.' Zoe walked over and turned Adam slightly towards Jess. 'Look slightly away towards the camera and tip your head slightly down. Now just put your left arm around Jess's waist.'

As Adam's hand rested on her back, Jess tried to ignore the ripples of warmth that travelled right to the pit of her stomach. Was Zoe doing this deliberately, because she knew about her and Adam? *'I'll kill her.'*

'Sorry?' Adam pulled his arm away.

She'd said that out loud? Heat flashed to her cheeks. 'Nothing.'

Zoe cleared her throat loudly. 'Jess, turn towards Adam, put your right hand on his shoulder and look towards that shoulder. No, don't turn your head too much … that's it.'

'Try not to move, either of you.' She ran back behind her tripod and snapped a few photos before taking the camera in her hand and moving around them, taking some more shots.

'You sure you're all right?' Adam whispered.

Jess blinked and met his eyes. 'Yes.'

'Jess, turn your head back,' Zoe said.

Jess moved her head back into position, grateful to have an excuse not to look at Adam for too long. It felt too intimate, standing like this, the heat of his hand on her back, burning through the silky material of the dress.

Zoe's voice cut through her thoughts.

'Gemma, can you get the others in for the rest of the shot?'

Gemma reappeared a few minutes later with three female and three male models, the men in dark suits, the women in sophisticated, deep purple bridesmaid dresses.

Jess rolled her eyes. 'Why isn't one of the models the bride, Zoe?'

'It's good to get a real look,' Zoe deadpanned. 'Okay, line up beside our happy couple. Girls beside Jess and boys beside Adam.' The models stepped quickly into place. 'Right, Jess, Adam, turn to face each other and hold hands.'

Jess turned stiffly towards Adam, who took hold of her hands.

'*This is ridiculous,*' she said in a furious whisper, aware that her face was probably blazing red. '*There's so much other stuff we could be doing!*'

'*It won't take long,*' Adam whispered back.

'Jess, Adam, can you smile adoringly at each other, please?'

Zoe was enjoying this way too much.

'Okay, last shot.' Zoe approached Jess and Adam. 'I'm going to need you to kiss.'

Jess whipped her head around to Zoe.

'It's not real,' said Zoe hurriedly. 'I'll show you how.'

'I know how,' Adam said.

Zoe glanced at Jess. 'If that's okay with Jess?'

Adam dropped his voice so only Jess could hear. 'Trust me.'

'Fine!' Jess tried not to snap. It wasn't Adam's fault, but this was too close for comfort. No wonder Zoe had made them bride and groom. She'd never talk to her again.

Zoe gave some instructions to the models, put the camera back on its tripod and peered down the viewfinder. 'Whenever you're ready.'

Jess's heart hammered as Adam angled his head and leaned in, his nearness sending heat racing through her.

'Ready?' he said quietly. Instead of his lips landing on hers, she felt them just above her mouth. Jess's eyes closed as she tried not to think about their kiss that day in the church and tried harder to ignore the instinct to move her mouth up to meet his. This felt unnatural and a bit uncomfortable. If she could just shift her weight a bit …

As she moved, she realised her mistake. Now her lips were pressing on the lower part of Adam's mouth. She felt his hand squeeze her waist slightly, but he didn't move. Despite the heat of Adam's body, a shiver ran through her. Had someone suddenly turned up the air conditioning?

'*Move, everyone!*' Gemma suddenly screamed.

Before Jess realised what was happening, Adam was stamping hard on her train, then he was pulling her towards the middle of the room. Lights flickered and flashed around them, as the other models jumped out of the way, seconds before hundreds of fairy lights swung down to where they'd been standing seconds before. As Jess stumbled over her dress, Adam quickly put an arm around her back and another under her knees, picking her up.

'Adam, put me down.' Jess struggled to stand.

'Hang on!'

'I'm fine, will you just ...'

Adam put her down. and Jess turned to face the end of the room where they'd been. The fairy lights now lay scattered across the ornate panelled floor. Moments later, every last one flickered out.

Zoe turned to Gemma. 'What happened?'

'They're safety lights. If something goes wrong, they're supposed to turn off like that. They're just not supposed to fall.' Gemma looked around. 'Is everyone all right? Those lights are quite heavy.'

'That was well spooky,' one of the models said. 'Anyone else feel that? Just before the lights fell, it got super cold. And this room was really warm when we came in.'

The noise levels rose again as everyone started to talk at once.

Shit, Jess thought, this was the last thing they needed. She raised her voice over the others. 'Could I have everyone's attention, please?' The room quietened. 'If it's okay with Zoe and Gemma, we might take a break. Go get some refreshments in the orangery, while we get this sorted.'

The models left, visibly keen to be in a newer, brighter part of the castle.

Gemma came over to Jess and Adam.

'I'm really sorry. Nothing like this has ever happened before.' She turned back to survey the mess. 'I'm still not sure what happened this time. Those lights were all secure.'

Adam dug a hand back through his hair. 'I'll talk to the manager;

we'll have to get the electrics double checked in this part of the hotel. It's the most likely reason for ...' he waved a hand in front of him, 'all this.'

Gemma frowned. 'Except the lights went out after they fell. I don't think any of them shorted first. Bloody nuisance.'

'It could have been worse.' Adam pointed to the chandelier above their heads.

Gemma grimaced. 'I've messaged my crew to come down. They've just finished setting up for the next shoot in the honeymoon suite. They'll get this lot cleaned up.'

Gemma walked away and Jess turned to Adam.

'Thanks.'

He shrugged. 'Any time. Look, I don't think the others noticed, but the train of your dress got singed when one of the candles fell over.'

Jess looked down at the end of the dress, which was now badly discoloured. 'Oh God.' She met Adam's eyes. 'That's why you were stamping on it like that.' She shivered. 'I should change.'

'Will you be okay?'

Adam looked at her closely and, for a moment, Jess couldn't look away.

His phone rang, breaking the spell. 'Sorry, I'd better take this, excuse me.' As he walked away, Jess slipped out of her shoes and hitched up the dress. Right now, she needed some fresh air.

She just hoped that Zoe had got all her shots in the Great Hall before the lights collapsed, because there was no way she was going to get back into this dress again to pose with Adam. Falling fairy lights and open flames scorching her dress were bad enough. But playing happy couples with Adam was far more dangerous.

Chapter 31

ZOE and Gemma finished the shoot shortly after 5 o'clock and once the models left Ian invited the rest of the crew to stay on for dinner.

'What are you going to do?' Jess helped Zoe to pack her cameras and lighting equipment into the boot of her battered old Ford Fiesta.

Zoe grinned. 'What do you think? How many chances do I get to eat for free in a five-star hotel? I've already stuffed my rucksack with bread rolls from lunch.'

Jess hesitated. The dinner would be amazing. But there'd also be far too much food and even more wedding chat, and she'd had enough of the latter for one day.

She bumped into Adam in the foyer.

'Hey, are you staying for dinner or going straight home?' she asked.

Adam inclined his head to one side. 'What are you doing?'

Jess flushed. 'I asked you first.'

His mouth twitched. 'I'm not staying for dinner.'

'Right, so could I get a lift with you?'

'Really? You'd prefer to come with me than have dinner here?'

Did he just enjoy making her squirm? 'I'm just not in the mood for small talk over a big meal.'

His expression changed. 'Actually, you might prefer it.'

Was he still annoyed because she'd turned him down for that drink earlier? He didn't strike her as petty, but maybe she'd misread him.

'It's cool, I didn't mean to ...'

Adam cut across her. 'I need to take a small detour on the way home.'

She could stay and get a lift back with Zoe. But Zoe would spend the whole drive home interrogating her about Adam and telling her not to marry Simon.

The truth was, she'd much prefer to spend the evening with Adam. He had no idea she was getting married. For a few blissful hours, she could forget about the wedding hurtling towards her.

'It's up to you.'

Adam's eyes glinted. 'I don't mind, if you don't.'

So they were playing that game. She gave her sweetest smile. 'Ready when you are.'

Adam slanted Jess a glance as he drove down the curving, tree-lined driveway. 'I didn't tell you what my detour was.'

'Is it something illegal?' Jess allowed herself to feel excited at the prospect of a mini-adventure.

'I'll try for that next time, I promise.' Adam's mouth pulled upwards into a half smile. 'I told Mam I'd stop by the farm. Dad went into hospital for a routine operation a couple of days ago, and he came home today.'

Jess stared at him. Maybe that was why he'd seemed so distracted earlier. 'Why didn't you tell me? The last thing your parents need is a stranger showing up.'

Adam burst out laughing. 'You're very Dublin, aren't you? According to Mam, Dad is fine. But you'll have to have dinner, they'll insist. I can even arrange a tour, wellies included.'

'Adam, it sounds lovely, but …'

'We're against the traffic, we'll be there in less than an hour. And we have horses.'

Jess'ss eyes widened. 'How did you know?'

Adam looked smug. 'Zoe.'

She'd deal with Zoe later. But Adam had clearly done his homework.

He couldn't have predicted her request for a lift home, but it had been a fair guess, given that they'd driven down that morning. She was overthinking it: the detour sounded perfectly legitimate. And it wouldn't bother her if Simon spent time with a female colleague: he often spent time with Kate, and she trusted them both completely.

Why wouldn't she, she thought guiltily. Their friendship was completely different from the weird and slightly dangerous relationship she had with Adam.

'You're not worrying about earlier, are you?' Adam said.

Jess looked over, hoping he wasn't talking about their near kiss.

'The lights? Your dress getting burnt?'

'It was just an accident.' She paused. 'Do you really think the Linford Curse is what's stopping people booking weddings there?'

Adam shrugged. 'We've cut our prices, offered fantastic wedding packages. When did Kate get engaged, by the way?'

'Kate?'

'Yeah, I just wondered where she's having her wedding. Maybe we should offer Charleston Group staff an extra discount to marry at Linford.'

'Right, excellent idea.' Jess wiped her palms on her trousers.

'So, how's the bridesmaid speech coming along?'

'I've made a start.'

Adam glanced over. 'You have to wonder what the speeches at Chelsea and Leo's wedding will be like.'

Jess laughed, relaxing a bit. 'Chelsea will probably have to run them by Angel first.'

Adam slowed, as a hare hopped out in front of the car, before disappearing into the hedgerows. She decided to change the subject. 'Do you get down to see your parents a lot?'

'Since I've been home, I've been down to see them every weekend. And I've been able to catch up with my brothers, who live nearby. What about you? Have you a big family?'

'Apart from the one annoying younger sister?' Jess laughed. 'I'm lucky – my mam's from a very big family, so I have lots of cousins I'm close to. And there's my nana, who's my dad's mam. She's eighty-two, and she's great fun. And, apparently, totally mad when she was younger.'

'Like her granddaughter, then.' Adam smirked.

Heat flashed to Jess's face. In spite of his teasing, she'd got used to him being around, she'd even miss him after he left. But it would be a disaster if he stayed. Once Adam found out about Simon, he would never trust her again. She'd just enjoy the rest of his time here.

Jess tried some surreptitious deep breathing when Adam finally took the exit off the motorway onto a smaller road. 'Are you sure this is okay with your parents?'

He glanced over. 'Mam will be delighted to have somebody else to feed.'

The jeep rumbled over the cattle grid at the gate to the farm.

'I got the distinct feeling you disapproved of my jeep.' He pulled up outside the yard at the rear of the house and turned off the engine.

'I was just annoyed that you always insisted we take your car,' Jess admitted. 'But I'll admit the jeep is great to have for driving down the country.'

'Maybe we misjudged each other.' Adam's voice was light, but Jess got the distinct impression he was interested in her reaction. Pretending not to notice, she turned to inspect the yard, which was littered with straw and walled on three sides with sheds.

'This way.'

Adam got out, and Jess followed him to the back door of the house, avoiding a number of cats and some very relaxed looking hens.

'You keep chickens?'

Adam laughed. 'Mam and Dad keep about a dozen for themselves. They don't sell the eggs. Let's say hello, and I'll show you around.' He stepped back to usher Jess into an enclosed porch, which led straight into a large, warm kitchen.

A petite, dark-haired woman in jeans and an old T-shirt sat at a pottery wheel at one end of a large pine table, elbow-deep in pottery clay.

Jess recognised one of Ed Sheeran's songs playing quietly in the background.

'Adam, how are you, love? And you must be Jess, Adam sent me a quick message to expect you. It's lovely to meet you. Mightn't shake your hand just yet though.' She grinned and blew a lock of dark hair out of her eyes, as she slowed the pedal at her foot, and smoothed down the rough pot.

Adam strode over and bent to kiss her on the cheek. They had the same shape and colour eyes, Jess noticed.

'Where will you fit this one, Mam?' Adam gestured to the old-fashioned dresser, overflowing with colourful earthenware.

'These are all yours, Mrs Rourke?' Jess walked over to take a closer look. 'They're gorgeous.'

'Call me Anna. You'll have to pick a favourite piece to take home. Adam's right: I need to make room.'

Jess turned. 'Oh, I couldn't.'

'I insist. Now, your dad's having a bit of a rest, Adam, so you'll see him at dinner. The pair of you should get some fresh air and let me clean up here. I've put a shepherd's pie in the oven. It's from our local deli and it's very good. I've a vegetarian version, Jess, if you prefer?'

'Oh no, I eat everything.' Jess smiled gratefully.

'That's easy, so.' Anna waved them away. 'Go on, I'll see you back here in an hour and a half.'

As Adam and Jess went back outside, the final sounds of Ed Sheeran drifted into the yard.

'Your mam's great.' Jess tried not to compare her to Úna.

Adam looked over at her. 'She likes you too. She tends to make snap decisions about people, and she rarely offers strangers her pottery. Choose something you really like; she'll be offended if you don't.'

Jess met his eyes. 'She's very different to how I might have imagined her. Not that I really had time to speculate about your parents, obviously …' She felt herself flush.

'Did you imagine someone feeding chickens with one hand, and milking cows with the other?' Adam's eyes glinted. 'You know that milking is all done by machine?'

'You must think I know nothing about farming.' Or anything else, Jess thought as she followed Adam through the gate in the corner of the main yard.

He pushed his hands into his pockets. 'I'm sorry, I didn't mean to sound dismissive. Do your parents have farming backgrounds?'

'No,' Jess admitted. 'Dad's from Wicklow and Mam's from a village about ten miles outside Waterford town.'

'They'll pass as culchies, so.' He winked. 'Here's the milking shed. We've come at the right time.'

A trail of straw and dried mud paved the way to the shed, and Jess lingered just inside the door, trying not to cough, as a mixture of smells invaded her senses.

Adam pointed to an older man at the other end of the long room, overseeing the rows of cows being milked. 'That's Michael.'

The man looked up, and came over, wiping his hands on dark overalls. He was younger than Jess had initially thought, mid-fifties, at most.

'Not planning on getting your hands dirty dressed like that, are you, Adam?' He raised an eyebrow at Jess. 'You must be special, if he's showing you around the farm.'

Jess shifted a bit uncomfortably, but Adam gave an easy laugh.

'Jess and I work together. We had to come to Linford Castle for the day, so we stopped by on our way back to Dublin. Jess, this is Michael Brady, our manager of ten years.'

'Eleven.' Michael shook Jess's hand. 'Lovely to meet you, Jess. Watch this fellah, though. He's a bit of a dark horse.'

Except Adam had already shown his hand, Jess thought with a

stab of guilt. And he knew she wasn't interested. Even if he didn't know the real reason, he'd accepted it.

Adam turned to her. 'Speaking of horses, how about riding out before dinner?'

'Really?' She glanced down at her clothes.

'You could borrow some stuff from Mam.'

Jess beamed. 'You're on.'

As Jess and Adam brought the horses back into the yard later, Jess realised she couldn't remember the last time she'd felt this happy. They'd ridden out across his parents' land, starting slowly with the horses to let Jess get used to the mare, before finally letting the two animals canter for a while. Adam had stayed beside Jess, pointing out various landmarks as they skirted the farm's boundaries, but mostly they'd ridden in contented silence and Jess had let herself forget about everything except Adam's easy company and the joy she always felt on horseback.

Almost reluctantly, they'd circled back around to the stables. 'Do you always come out for a ride when you're visiting your parents?' she asked, as they gently slowed the horses down again.

Adam flashed her a smile. 'As often as I can. I find it's the perfect antidote to corporate burnout. And the horses need to be ridden. Mam takes Sable out when she can, but Dad hasn't been riding for a while. What about you? Do you ride often?'

'Not now, but I took lessons as a teenager.' Jess slowed the mare down even more to match Adam's pace. As the two animals fell into step beside each other, her leg brushed continually against Adam's and little bolts of electricity sparked deliciously through her. To distract herself, she added, 'It kept me out of trouble.'

'Maybe I should be grateful you don't ride that often now.' Adam gave a wicked smile and as Jess caught his meaning, she looked away, glad of cool air on her face.

They got back to the yard and Adam quickly dismounted, then steadied Jess's mare as she dismounted moments later.

'So, what did you think of her?' Adam patted Sable, Jess's mare, as he led his own towards the stable.

'She handles beautifully, I love her.'

'Sable prefers women, in general, but she doesn't respond the same way to everyone. You did well.'

Jess smiled and shook her head.

'What?' Adam gave her a curious look.

'Nothing, it just feels good to talk about horses.'

Adam nodded. 'I thought the break would do you good. Let's clean up. I don't know about you, but I'm starving.'

Jess scraped her boots on an outside mat, and followed Adam back into the house, feeling strangely comfortable as she left the riding boots in the mud room, before collecting her own clothes from the bedroom where she'd changed earlier.

'You can freshen up in here.' Adam opened a door further down the hall, to reveal a small, pristine shower room. 'Take your time.'

Jess locked the door behind her and gave herself a few moments to take stock. It felt a bit surreal being in Adam's family home, about to have dinner with him and his parents. Weirder still was how natural it felt. Maybe if things had been different, she and Adam could be friends. She sighed. Who was she kidding? If things were different, she'd either be single and free to date Adam, or Adam would know about Simon and none of this would be happening.

She tried to tell herself that it was okay: Adam would be returning to Switzerland soon, and then she could forget about him and move on.

Leaving the clothes she'd borrowed from Anna in a neat pile, she turned on the shower and stepped in under the hot spray. It struck her that she'd hardly thought about Simon all day. But realistically, who thought about their partner the whole time? Even if they weren't on a break from each other. This evening, she just wanted to forget about everything.

'Have you and Adam known each other long?' Declan Rourke sat down beside his wife at the kitchen table.

Jess had been momentarily stunned into silence after he'd introduced himself, terrified she might let something slip about how Adam had used the same name on the Isle of Man. Careful to avoid Adam's eye, she'd simply smiled and shook his hand.

She supposed it was common for eldest sons to be named after their father, but clearly Declan Adam Rourke had had his own ideas.

'*Er*, no, not long.' Jess cleared her throat. 'Just a couple of weeks, since Adam came to work in the Dublin office.'

'A couple of weeks?' Declan exchanged a glance with his wife. 'Tell us now, where are you from, Jess?'

'Dublin. I grew up in Dun Laoghaire.'

'Oh, do you sail at all? Or swim? Anna's brother, Frank, was only telling us recently that the Forty Foot is full of people diving into the sea in all weathers. I think he's a bit of a regular there, himself.'

Jess couldn't imagine Frank Charleston diving into the Forty Foot, or anywhere else. 'I'm a fair-weather swimmer, to be honest.'

'Jess rides very well, Dad,' Adam said. 'She handled Sable beautifully.'

'Well done.' Declan gave a nod of approval. 'Been around farms much?'

Anna tutted. 'Stop quizzing the poor woman, Declan, and let her eat. Adam, how's Frank? Have you seen much of him recently?'

'Yes, he was asking for you both.' He turned to his father. 'How are you feeling, Dad?'

'Nothing wrong with me that a bit of work won't cure,' Declan said firmly. 'In fact, I've been giving more thought to what you said about the dairy herd …'

'*Er*, Dad, can we talk about this another time?'

'Good a time as any, son.' Declan helped himself to more shepherd's pie. 'And while I'm at it, that parcel of land is free and clear for you to build your own house. Get out of Dublin and back to your roots.'

Anna put a hand on her husband's arm. 'I don't think this is the right time, Declan.'

Declan frowned. 'It never seems to be the right time.' He waved his fork at Adam. 'What are you going to do, Adam? Head back to Switzerland? Work at something your heart isn't in? How's this fellah's time-keeping these days, Jess? We used to have to drag him out of bed when he was a teenager.'

Adam's jaw tightened. 'Please, Dad, we have a guest.'

Anna shot her husband a stern look, before turning to Jess with a smile. 'Has Adam told you about his two younger brothers?'

'Yes, he's mentioned them.' Jess injected a note of interest into her voice, to hide the fact that she was dying to know what Declan meant. Was Adam annoyed about the reference to his job? It was hardly the quip about his teenage years.

'Shay's the engineer, he's married with two little boys under two.' Anna smiled over at her husband. 'We see a lot of them and they're wonderful. And our youngest, Neil, lives with his girlfriend in the next town. They're both primary school teachers.'

Declan's expression softened for a moment. 'They're great lads, both of them. We love having them all so close, don't we, Anna?' Before Anna could reply, he turned back to Adam. 'Have you not told Jess anything about your plans for the farm?'

Jess took pity on Adam. 'Mainly we talk about work.'

Adam cleared his throat. 'Dad, Jess and I are just colleagues.'

'Oh.' He stared at them in confusion. 'Well now, Jess, I hope I didn't embarrass you.'

Jess smiled brightly. 'No, of course not. Adam was being kind, he thought I could do with some fresh air and relaxation.'

Declan's sudden, deep laughter sounded exactly like Adam's. 'Being kind? Give the man a bit of credit, love!'

'Dad!' Adam shot her a quick look of apology as heat flashed to Jess's cheeks.

This was all her fault. She should have had the guts to come clean with Adam. She was being incredibly selfish.

But for a while longer, she wanted to pretend it was just her and Adam and his lovely, normal, down-to-earth parents. Real life could wait.

Chapter 32

'THANKS again for a lovely evening, Adam.' Jess unsnapped her seat belt as Adam pulled up outside her parents' house in Dunlaoghaire, later that night. It had just got dark, and the road was quiet. They'd talked during the drive up from his family home, the atmosphere between them warm and relaxed. Now, in the stillness, the mood had started to shift to something more intimate.

Jess reached for the door. 'I'll see you tomorrow.'

'Hang on, please?' Adam's voice was low.

Jess's hand stayed on the door, but she turned back to face him. Adam ran a hand through his hair. 'Nice house.'

She swallowed. 'It's my parents' house. I've moved back for a while.'

He nodded. 'Can I just say something?'

'Sure.' Jess was amazed at how steady her voice sounded.

'I'm a bit confused.' Adam spread his hands. 'The whole Isle of Man thing aside, you definitely didn't seem to like me when we first met.'

'Adam, I …'

'Look, I get that was my fault, I was a complete bollix to you. But now we know each other better, I get the feeling …' He stopped and seemed to gather his thoughts. 'We've just spent a lovely evening together. And you could have gone home with Zoe, but you came with me instead. Tell me I'm reading this wrong.'

For a few moments, Jess didn't trust herself to speak. She'd cheated on Simon, and now she'd given Adam the wrong idea. 'I'm sorry, Adam. I love horses, and it was too good an opportunity to pass up. That's all.'

Adam's expression closed. 'No worries, you're welcome any time.'

Briefly, Jess indulged in a fantasy where she could escape to Adam's farm, and ride horses whenever she wanted. 'I'd better go in, it's late.' She tried to smile, but she was a bit afraid she might cry instead. 'Goodnight.' Carefully, she picked up the colourful earthenware pot she'd chosen. 'Please thank your mam again.'

'Goodnight, Jess.' Adam made no effort to move as she got out, but waited until she'd let herself in, before he drove away.

In her parents' hall, Jess leaned against the door, listening to the sound of the engine grow fainter. Finally, she forced herself to move. She found Zoe in the garden, sprawled in a faded deck chair, a blanket warding off the cool evening air.

Zoe shot her a sly look. 'Thought you'd run away with the sexy Adam.'

'Don't.' Jess dropped into the other chair. 'We stopped at his family farm on the way home and had dinner with his parents.'

'*Shut the front door!*' Zoe let out a whoop of laughter. 'You know I'm supposed to be the wild one in our family, don't you?'

'Zoe, keep your voice down.' Jess turned to make sure neither of their parents was around. 'Anyway, there's nothing wild about a family dinner.' She pushed her hair tiredly back from her face. The evening had been perfect. Or as perfect as anything based on a lie could be.

Zoe closed her eyes. 'Can I just say something?'

'You will anyway.' Jess yawned.

'You're supposed to be getting married in ten days and you're still on a break. I just think if this were about Simon being pissed off at you, you guys would have had a yelling contest and lots of make-up sex, or whatever it is you do.'

She didn't want to talk about Simon right now. Especially with Zoe. 'How are Nana and Finn getting on?'

'Finn thinks Nana is the coolest eighty-something he's ever met.'

'What's he going to do when Nana's back on her feet?'

'Don't think he's thought that far ahead.' Zoe turned to look at her. 'I know I'm totally pointing out the obvious here, but you have a bigger fucking problem than where my boyfriend will live when Nana's better.'

Jess gave a flick of her hand. 'I don't want to talk about it.'

'Thank fuck.' Zoe grinned.

'So, what did you think of the Linford job?'

'Dinner was good. What happened in the big hall was a bit *woo-woo*.'

Jess rolled her eyes. 'It was just the electrics.'

'Maybe you could pretend there's ghosts.'

'*Haha*, that'd work.'

Zoe stared at her. 'Why wouldn't it?'

'Because I can't just lie, Zoe. We've done the research and, weirdly, there's no mention of a single ghost in the whole history of Linford.' Jess sighed. 'Anyway, it could totally backfire, and we have enough problems with the curse. That's why we're so dependent on this wedding going ahead.'

'You're missing a trick, Jess.' Zoe rolled her eyes. 'People either believe in ghosts or they don't. Tell everyone that Linford is haunted and, if people don't believe in ghosts, it won't make any difference. But it might attract the supernatural crowd. Make one of the bedrooms haunted and give me and Finn a mates' rate. We could do with a break.'

Jess said nothing. Beneath Zoe's flippant remarks was frustration that she and Finn could barely afford rent in Dublin. What would happen if she and Simon did split up? She could rent somewhere small but, at thirty, she'd be starting all over again, on her own. God, she had to stop thinking like that. What mattered was whether she loved Simon enough to marry him. But for the first time ever, she wasn't so sure anymore.

Chapter 33

JESS brought a change of clothes with her to work the following day, for the awards ceremony that evening. She'd sent Kate a quick text, to ask if Luke had enjoyed the new *Star Wars* movie. Kate had texted a *y* in response. Jess had stared at the single letter text. It was very un-Kate-like. But now she thought about it, she hadn't even heard from her since Tuesday.

She plugged her phone into her laptop port to charge. All this radio silence from Kate radiated disapproval. But she couldn't tackle her about it, partly because Kate's judgement was based on what she knew. Only Jess knew the full truth: her awful betrayal of Simon, the reason she needed time to think.

The problem was, it was difficult to think about Simon when she couldn't stop thinking about Adam. Spending all that time with him and his family on their farm had almost felt more intimate than their kiss.

As if on cue, Adam appeared at the open door of her office.

'Hi.' He smiled and Jess felt her defences weaken further. Why was the man being so nice to her? 'I thought you might be missing this.' He crossed the room and placed a small item on her desk.

'My watch!'

'You left it on the shelf in my parents' guest bathroom. I found it last night before we left and meant to give it to you.'

'Thanks.' She swallowed. 'I missed it earlier. I was terrified I'd lost it.'

'It's beautiful. Is it old?'

'It was my gran's.' Jess hesitated, wondering if she should she say anything else about the evening before. But it felt strange now that things were back to normal.

She almost laughed. As if things had ever been normal between them.

'Glad it wasn't lost.' Adam pushed his hand through his hair. 'Anyway, I won't delay you.'

After he left, Jess tried to shake off a feeling of unease. It was clear Adam also thought they'd overstepped a line.

With an effort, she turned back to her work. Speculation about Chelsea and Leo's relationship had settled a bit, and the celebrity wedding was getting tons of international interest. Linford was getting plenty of small bookings, just no wedding bookings. With a bit of luck, they would happen.

She couldn't put her personal problems off any longer. She needed to make things right with Simon. She dismissed the idea of messaging him to meet for a drink: it was time to break his no-calls-in-work rule. Picking up the office phone, she rang his direct line.

'Simon Donohue.'

'It's me.'

'Kate?' He sounded delighted.

'It's Jess.' She almost stumbled over the words.

'Sorry, Jess, I wasn't ...' He hesitated. 'How are you?'

'I'm fine.' The phone felt sticky in her hand. 'Were you expecting Kate?'

'I thought she might have been calling about the cinema the other night.'

'Oh, right.' This felt a bit strange. 'Did Kate go too?'

'No, she wasn't feeling well, I was a bit worried about her.'

An unsettling thought slid into her head but disappeared before she could examine it. There was a brief silence before Simon spoke again.

'So, I was just about to meet a client, Jess … was there anything you …'

'No, nothing.' Jess's mouth dried, making it harder to speak. 'I just rang to say hi.'

'Look, I'm sorry to rush you.'

'No, *um*, I'd better go too. Take care.' She stabbed the off-button and stared at the phone. She'd no idea what was going on between Simon and Kate, but she hoped he hadn't dragged Kate further into the mess she had made.

She worked fitfully for another hour, before finally accepting she wouldn't be able to concentrate until she found out what was wrong. She texted Kate. **Going to get a coffee, can I get you one?** She added a coffee cup emoji, a cake emoji, and a pink heart emoji. A moment later Kate replied, **Meet you in the foyer.** Jess gave a small sigh of relief. Maybe things were okay.

Kate was in the foyer, doing a word puzzle on her phone, when Jess got there.

'Hey, how are things?'

Kate gave a distracted smile. 'Fine.' She stood and followed Jess across the road to Butlers.

As they stepped inside, Jess took a deep breath and tried to sound casual. 'I was talking to Simon earlier. He said you weren't feeling well the other night, when he took Luke to see *Star Wars*.'

Kate didn't look at her. 'Luke enjoyed it, that's all that matters.'

'Yeah, absolutely.' Jess had an urge to shake her. They took their place in the queue for coffee and she tried again. 'It's a pity you couldn't go. How are you now?'

Kate folded her arms. 'I'm fine, okay? I was fine the other night too, but I'd prefer if you didn't tell Simon that.'

'I won't.' Jess was tentative. 'Why?'

For a long moment, Kate said nothing. 'It felt wrong, Jess, that's all.' She looked at her. 'You and Simon are on a break and then, what? It's me and Luke and Simon off playing happy families?'

Jess found her voice. 'That was why you didn't go?' She tried to understand exactly what Kate was saying. 'But you and Simon are friends, you often do stuff together. Why wouldn't you go to the cinema when he's taking Luke anyway?'

'Next?' The barista looked a bit impatient, and Jess and Kate stepped up and put in their order.

Jess gestured towards the counter by the window. 'Let's sit down for five minutes.'

After they sat down, Jess cut her slice of chocolate biscuit cake in half and offered some to Kate, who shook her head.

'You don't think I'm worried about you and Simon out together, do you?' Jess said, finally.

'What?' Kate went bright red. 'No, of course not.'

'Sorry.' Jess flapped a hand. 'My bad. I'll shut up.'

They drank their coffees in silence for the next few minutes.

'So, the photo shoot in Linford –'

'Simon dropped in for a few –'

'You first.' Jess's insides squeezed.

'Simon came in for a coffee after he dropped Luke home. He wanted to know how things were going with David.' Jess relaxed a bit. 'How are things going? You never tell me.'

'There's not much to tell.' Kate focused on the countertop. 'We've been on a couple of dates.'

'What does Simon think?' Jess wondered how blunt he'd been.

Kate wrapped both hands around her cup. 'He told me that David's a good guy, the best. He also said that he'd been in a two-year relationship in London with a single mother. Her little girl became attached to David and when he and the mother split, the child was pretty upset.'

Jess tried to keep the frustration out of her voice. 'Did David tell you anything about this himself?'

'We've had two dates, Jess!' Kate's voice rose, and a few people glanced around. 'Look, I'm seeing the guy. That's what you wanted, isn't it?'

'Yes, but is it what you want, Kate? I mean, I don't believe that –'

'That what?' Kate stared at her. 'Anyway, you've no right to ask me what I want. You don't even know what you want for yourself.'

'Yes, I do, I want to marry Simon.'

'*Do you?*' Kate's voice held an undercurrent of anger. 'Does Simon know? Because he needs to know. He needs to be sure it's what you really want.'

Only it wasn't just about her anymore, Jess realised. The moment she'd cheated on Simon, was the moment she'd completely messed up her life. Briefly, she closed her eyes. She seemed to be going around in circles. Her phone buzzed and she opened a message from Zoe. **Sent you a file with the pix from yesterday. Hard copies should be with you now too.**

'Is that Simon?' Kate looked closely at Jess.

'No, just a work thing.'

'He has his stag tomorrow night.' Kate's voice was flat.

Shit, she'd completely forgotten that. There was no point trying to arrange to meet him then. Jess's smile felt strained. 'I hadn't forgotten.'

Jess returned to the office, feeling worse than ever, and collected the photos at reception. 'Thanks, Emily.' She squinted at her. 'Are you okay? You look very warm.'

'Yeah, cool.' Emily lowered her voice. 'So, I was just wondering, like, is Adam seeing anyone? Only, we were talking a few minutes ago and he's so sweet.'

Jess told herself firmly that it was none of her business if Emily and Adam got together.

In fact, it would probably be a good thing. She hated herself for hesitating. 'Is he not a bit old for you?'

'Whoever he is, he's probably not good enough for you, Emily.'

Jess and Emily both jumped as Adam strode up behind Jess. He stopped, frowning.

'You okay, Emily? You look a bit hot.' He nodded to the envelope in Jess's hands. 'What's that?'

'Just photos from the shoot. I'm about to take a look at them.'

'Mind if I join you?'

The thought of her and Adam in close proximity after the weekend was unsettling, but Jess couldn't think of a reason to say no. 'The boardroom is free. Let's work there.'

'These photos are incredible,' Adam said, a while later, as he passed more of his favourites to Jess, who was sorting through a selection of black-and-white, sepia and colour shots Zoe and her team had taken.

'*Hmmm ...*' Jess slipped some into an A4 folder and scribbled some ideas on the outside.

'This is marked private.' Adam handed Jess a separate envelope. She peeked inside: they were the photos of the engagement shoot with her and Simon. She shoved the envelope into her bag, just as the lights flickered out and the room was plunged into darkness.

'Did we lose our power?' Jess glanced around.

'I think so. Trust us to pick a room with no windows.' Adam scraped back his chair and walked over to open the door. 'The building's out. Our own generator should kick in shortly. In the meantime, we could tell ghost stories.'

Jess laughed, feeling some of the earlier tension of the day disappear.

'Hey, did you see the photos of us?' Adam said.

'Not yet.'

'I have them here. You look pretty good.' Adam sounded gruff and Jess was glad the room was dark. He cleared his throat. 'You know, we have our own generator on the farm? It's used more than you'd imagine.'

Jess latched on to the change of subject. 'You know, about the farm ...'

The lights flickered back on, and Jess met Adam's eyes. He gave a half smile.

'What about the farm?'

Before Jess had a chance to speak, his phone rang.

'Better take this.'

Adam left the room and Jess heard him talking in the corridor outside. Quickly, she found the photos of her and Adam at Linford and flicked through them. It was incredible, Zoe had made her and Adam look like a real, happy couple.

Checking that Adam was still on the phone, she took the smaller envelope out of her bag and glanced through the photos of her and Simon. Technically, they were stunning, but she couldn't find a single photo she liked. A bit panicked, she shuffled through them again. It wasn't possible: she and Adam looked happier together than she and Simon did. She remembered how stressed Simon had been that day. And, if she were being honest, she knew she'd been different around Simon since her hen weekend.

She'd been so stupid to think that cheating on her fiancé, even once, could be dismissed as a drunken mistake. Not when it had stained every relationship in her life. Jess looked over the photos one last time. She'd have to pick something for the two sets of parents. But if it was up to her, she wouldn't use any of them.

Chapter 34

'FRANK looks like he's about to burst with happiness.' Jess regarded the chief executive with a mixture of awe and affection at the awards ceremony across town later that evening.

'Three awards in one night.' Adam raised his glass to his uncle. 'And he told me he was swimming at the Forty Foot this morning.'

Jess grinned. 'That's an image I'll never get out of my head. But hey, you must be proud, too.'

'I'm happy for Frank.' Adam rolled his wineglass gently between his hands. 'You get as much credit as anyone.'

'Thanks.' Jess tugged self-consciously at the deep-blue, three-quarter-length, slim-fitting dress she'd changed into after work. She hadn't worn it since the previous summer and now she was dying to get home and take it off. Why was it that other stressed brides-to-be lost weight in the run up to their big day, while she'd piled it on?

Adam pulled off his bowtie and opened the top button of his dress shirt.

'What?'

He gave a bemused smile and Jess realised she'd been staring. 'Nothing.' She felt her face warm. 'I was just thinking you've probably been to tons of these.'

He glanced around the room. 'Actually, they're not really my thing.'

There was so much about him that didn't add up, she thought, especially given his promotion within the company. 'Too many speeches?' She realised she sounded flippant.

Adam just smiled wryly and gestured to his dinner jacket. 'Not a huge fan of the clothes either.'

Jess tried not to compare him to Simon, who had four dinner suits in his wardrobe. She wondered if he was this honest with everyone. By rights, things should be incredibly awkward between them, but the more time they spent together, the more she liked him.

It was just as well he'd be gone soon.

Adam leaned back in his chair.

'So, can I buy you a drink?'

Jess's heart crashed against her chest and, as she met Adam's eyes, she guessed he'd experienced the same flash of déjà vu.

'Or how about we get out of here?' he said hurriedly. 'I'll have to leave the car in town, so we could share a taxi.'

Jess thought for a moment. Now that the main part of the night was over, people were mingling at other tables, or getting drinks from the bar. Under normal circumstances, she'd stay until the bitter end.

Frank came over back to the table. 'What are you pair up to?' His shrewd gaze belied his jovial tone, and Jess briefly wondered if Adam's mother had told Frank that she and Adam had been to visit.

'I was about to leave.' Adam looked at Jess. 'I'm not sure what Jess is doing.'

'You've worked hard. Go home, get some rest.' Frank shook Jess's hand and clapped Adam on the back.

After Frank left, Adam lifted an eyebrow. 'What do you think?'

Jess nodded, and they left the noise of the big room behind them, walked along the corridor to the stylish reception, and out into the cool night.

'Do you feel like walking for a while?' Adam said.

Right now, the only thing she wanted was to spend more time with Adam. Which probably meant it was the worst thing she could do.

He pushed his hands into his pockets. 'Unless you'd rather just get a taxi home.'

She was completely overthinking this. 'A walk would be great.'

'I hope you didn't feel pressured to leave early tonight?' Adam kept to Jess's pace as they passed the grand Georgian houses of Merrion Square, all of them now converted into offices.

Jess shook her head. 'You didn't pressure me.'

He spoke quietly. 'I'm glad.'

They walked in comfortable silence until they reached one end of the square, which was quiet and lit by late Victorian streetlamps, and a half-moon in a near cloudless sky.

Jess stood and breathed in the crisp air, wishing she could freeze the moment.

'What are you thinking?'

Jess looked over at him. That it's a perfect night, Adam, and there's nowhere else I want to be, and nobody else I'd prefer to be with. It was a total head-wreck.

'What did your dad mean about this not being the job you really want?' She tried to read his expression. 'It's just, you seemed so relaxed at the farm.'

He looked amused. 'I'm always relaxed on the farm, it's where I grew up.'

Jess shook her head. 'It was more than that.'

Adam sighed and looked around the elegant city square. 'I love cities at night, don't you? They've a sort of magical quality. But you're right, I'm a country lad at heart, Jess. And I haven't been quite truthful about the farm.' He met her eyes. 'The thing is, it was always my plan to manage it for Dad, and eventually take it over. But I have my own ideas.'

Jess looked at him curiously. 'Go on.'

He shrugged. 'Dad is totally reliant on dairy farming. I want to phase out a lot of the herd and introduce specialist animals: ostriches, game, maybe a couple of species of pig, see if we can establish direct relationships with restaurants. That might mean starting with some farmers' markets to build our brand.'

She tried to imagine Adam standing behind a stall at a farmers' market. 'Would that not be a lot more work?'

'Different work. The farm would need to be adapted.' He shook his head. 'It doesn't matter, anyway … it's a bit complicated.'

'Of course it matters, if that's what you want to do.' Jess remembered something else. 'Why does your dad think you don't like what you're doing now?'

Adam was quiet for a moment. 'It doesn't matter. I gave a commitment to Frank.' His expression closed.

Jess tried to lighten the mood again.

'What about the horses? Will you keep them?'

Adam smiled. 'I meant to ask you about that. On the farm you said you don't ride out very often. You know there's lots of stables around Dublin and Wicklow.'

'I know.' Jess pulled her wrap a bit tighter, wishing she didn't have to fudge the truth. She couldn't tell Adam that she used to ride every weekend. When she and Simon started to get serious, she'd told herself that she didn't have as much time. With both of them working so hard during the week, they only had the weekends together.

She'd always spent Saturday mornings at the stables. When Simon had suggested they spend that time together, Jess had convinced herself it was nicer to spend her weekends wandering around bookshops, or through food markets, or visiting a new art exhibition, than grooming horses and mucking out stables. After she moved in with Simon, a morning at the stables meant having to shower and change at her parents' house, before going back to the flat, as Simon seemed to be allergic to the smell. And it had become easier to stop going.

She realised Adam had said something. 'Sorry, I was miles away.'

'I said don't worry about the horses, we'll keep them. How else would I get you to come visit?' His tone was light.

'Oh, I'd still come visit.' Jess suddenly realised how much she'd love it, and how unlikely it was. How could she visit Adam's family farm if she was married to Simon? Her stomach squeezed. She should be trying to work things out with Simon. Every moment she spent with Adam, she found herself forgetting about her real life. Like the time they'd walked by the river in Ballygobbin. And now, in this beautiful square on a summer's night.

It was the perfect setting with the wrong person.

A taxi turned the corner, and Jess flagged it down. 'I really need to get home. Do you want to share?'

Adam gave her a puzzled look. 'Is everything okay?'

She smiled brightly. 'Yeah, I'm just tired. You coming?'

'Actually, I might walk for a while longer.' He sounded a bit dismissive. 'Safe home.'

'You too.' Jess ignored the tightness in her chest as she slipped into the back of the waiting taxi. 'Dun Laoghaire, please.'

Had she done the right thing? Maybe she should have stayed and talked a while longer. She'd have asked him why he was working at something he didn't want to do. Although he'd made it pretty clear he wouldn't talk about it. As the driver pulled away from the kerb, Jess turned around to wave, but Adam had already walked away.

Chapter 35

JESS stared at her wedding dress, which hung in the mirrored dressing room of the bridal shop that Saturday. At this moment, she deeply regretted every cheesy pizza and Mars bar she'd eaten in the last six months. Worse, with exactly one week to her wedding, she and Simon still hadn't made up. The whole thing felt like a pretence, and she felt like a total fraud.

'Have you got the dress on yet?' Kate stuck her head around the door.

Jess turned. 'What if it doesn't fit?'

Kate smothered a yawn as she came into the dressing room and took it off the hanger. 'There's still time for it to be let out. Oh, your mam wants to know if you'd like another glass of Prosecco?' She gestured to the half-full glass Jess had left on the shelf. 'Zoe has started on her third out there.'

Jess grimaced. 'I don't think so. You can tell Zoe she can have the rest of mine.'

'Everything all right in there, ladies?' The owner's melodic voice floated through the door.

'Great, thanks!' Kate called back. She held the dress out for Jess, who stepped carefully into it, and tried to adjust the bodice so the boning didn't dig into her ribs. 'Turn around, there's all these buttons.'

Jess's phone pinged and she reached for it, mindful of Kate fastening the dress. Maybe it was Simon to tell her how his stag had gone. One of them needed to make the first move. But it was a notification.

'I'd better watch this – Brandi Oliver is going live.'

'Who?' Kate muttered.

'Chelsea's half-sister.' Jess clicked onto the TikTok.

'*Hey y'all.*' Brandi Oliver smiled and gave a little wave. '*So, I'm over on the East Coast right now, visiting some of my dad's family, because family is everything, right?*'

'Jess? Can you straighten up a minute?'

'Oh, yeah, sorry.' Jess turned the volume down on her phone and stood up straight, pulling at the voluminous skirt. 'I look like a Disney princess. Úna's going to hate it.'

Kate met her eyes in the mirror. 'Stop demonising Úna. She'll probably hug you and tell you how beautiful you look.'

Jess's insides squeezed. 'Úna doesn't do hugs, she does air kisses. And she'll be hoping I chose the simplest wedding dress possible. You know, one of those tasteful sheath things, no lace or embroidery.' She fluffed out the layers of tulle. 'Basically, nothing like this. Oh, hang on.' Jess turned up the volume for the end of the TikTok.

'*... and I'm, like, devastated that she doesn't want me now as her maid of honour. It's easy to forget about the people who care about you the most.*' Brandi finished the video by bringing her fingers together in a heart shape.

Jess shook her head. '*Wow*, she could give lessons in passive aggression.'

Kate fastened the final button. 'Good news: it closes.'

Jess put down the phone. 'Bad news: I can't breathe.'

'What are you talking about?' Kate poked a finger down the back of the dress. 'You've loads of room.'

'It just feels so tight.' Jess tugged at the bodice.

Kate stared at her. 'It's supposed to be a bit tight, but it fits.'

Jess tried lifting her arms above her head, but the dress dug into her armpits, and she let them flop to her side. 'Is that normal? I mean, I know I have these squidgy bits,' she pinched a couple of inches under one arm, 'but I think I should be able to lift my arms.'

Kate smothered another yawn and Jess threw her a sympathetic look.

'Bad night?'

'Late one.' Kate's eyes slid away.

'You and David?' Jess frowned. 'No, hang on, he was at Simon's stag.'

'I know.' Kate started to fuss with the back of the wedding dress, ruffling out the layers of tulle. 'I was at a club with the gang from accounting and we bumped into them.'

'You've never gone clubbing with them before.'

'They're always asking me.' Kate sounded defensive.

'That was a coincidence, running into the lads like that.' Jess spoke slowly, her mind whirring. 'Did Simon or David tell you where they were having the stag?'

Kate blushed furiously. 'Obviously not. It's not like I *planned* to run into them.'

'No, fair enough.' Jess tried to sound casual. 'So did you and David hang out for a while?'

Kate moved to the Jess's left side, arranging more of the skirt. 'We, *uh*, we weren't with them for long.' She straightened and met

Jess's eyes in the mirror. 'Look, I need to ask you something, and it's not very easy to say it, so please hear me out.'

'Okay?'

'Do you really want to marry Simon?'

Jess turned to look at her, the bodice tightening more. 'Is this because we're on a break?'

'No, it's not just that.' Kate's voice shook. 'Okay, here's the thing, Jess. I think you love Simon, in a way. But in the last year you've changed quite a lot.' She folded her arms. 'Maybe it's not just you, it could be Simon too, but I can see it. And I really feel that the two of you are about to make the worst mistake ever.'

Jess's mouth dried. 'Is this a weird joke, Kate?'

Kate paled. 'You honestly think I'd joke about something like this? Look, I'm sorry, Jess, I can't do this. Forget I said anything. The dress is gorgeous, you look wonderful. And I have to go, I have to get home to Luke.'

Jess felt a bit dizzy. 'What else is going on? What aren't you saying?' She knew she was pleading, but she didn't care. 'Ever since my hen weekend, you've been different. I don't feel like you have my back.'

Kate's eyes flashed. 'I've had your back every step of the way, Jess. Why can't you understand? You're the one who's changed. And I'm the only one telling you the truth.'

Kate was right: it *was* her. But Jess was falling, and nobody was going to catch her. She'd nothing to lose.

Jess gulped in some air. 'Nobody undermines their best friend like that.'

'I'm not trying to undermine you.'

What was she missing? 'Did something happen at the stag?'

'It's nothing to do with that.' Kate's voice sounded strangely thick. 'I'm sorry, Jess, I know you don't want to hear this, but I think you've sleep-walked through the last three years and you're about to sleep-walk into a marriage. You and Simon are amazing people and I love you both, but you're not right for each other.'

Vaguely, Jess realised that she might be going into shock. 'I don't believe you're doing this,' she whispered. 'I thought you were my friend.'

'I am.' Tears had begun to roll down Kate's face. 'That's why I can't do this, I can't pretend everything is fine when it's not.'

Anger bubbled up. '*Get out!*' The words seemed to come from someone else, but Jess knew she'd screamed them.

With a sob, Kate turned and flung open the changing-room door. A moment later, Jess heard the old-fashioned bell clang, as the shop door banged. Then Carmel was guiding her into a chair and saying something soothing.

'What?' Jess tried to focus on her mother, but the room had started to spin.

Her mother's hand was on her back, gently pushing her forward.

'Head between your knees, Jess. *Breathe.*'

This stupid dress: she needed to get out of it. Her throat was as tight as the bodice.

'I can't.' Panic flared in her chest.

'*Breathe.*'

As her mother rubbed circles on her back, Jess's anger dissolved, and she felt the first tears on her cheeks.

The shop owner produced a clean towel, and draped it across the top of the dress, tucking it in at the back. 'Cry away,' she said. 'It's good to release tension.' She hesitated. 'I'll be outside if you need me but take your time. There's nobody booked in for another half hour.'

She left, and Carmel pulled another chair close to Jess, sitting down so she could put an arm around her. For a long while, Jess sat, sniffling and hiccupping until her tears subsided. Carmel handed her a packet of tissues, and Jess wiped her face and blew her nose.

Zoe stood in the doorway, pulling at some skin around her thumb. 'What can I do?'

Jess felt exhausted. 'Nothing.' Her whole face felt swollen, and most of her make-up seemed to be on the balled-up, soggy tissues in her hand.

'That girl certainly picks her moments.' Carmel sounded grim.

'It's complicated, Mam.' Far more complicated than she'd ever know.

But Zoe did. And Jess knew she could trust her not to say a word.

'How is it complicated?' Carmel said. 'Am I right in thinking she doesn't want to come to the wedding?' She pursed her lips. 'It doesn't make sense. Unless she's jealous.'

Why would she be jealous? Maybe she was afraid that Jess and Simon would move on with their lives without her. Or that if Simon became a dad, he'd forget about Luke. Then there was David, the first guy Kate had let into her life in ages. On the one hand, Jess was pushing them together, on the other, Simon was warning Kate away.

That had to be it. All this time, Jess had been so caught up in her own problems, so focused on her own secrets, that she hadn't appreciated just how worried Kate was. If she was Kate, she'd probably have lashed out too. When she calmed down, they'd talk properly. Everything would work out.

Chapter 36

ADAM was waiting in Jess's office when she arrived in on Monday morning. She took one look at his expression and knew there was something wrong. Whatever it was, Jess thought a bit grimly, it might distract her from what had happened over the weekend, and from her own wedding which was now hurtling towards her like an asteroid.

He got straight to the point. 'I wanted to let you know that you'll be on your own after today. I'm flying back to Switzerland.'

Jess blinked. 'Before the wedding? I thought ...'

'I won't be needed.' Adam's face was unreadable. 'You and Ian have this: there's no need for me to hang around. And I've spent long enough in Dublin.'

Something was off. She'd known Adam wouldn't be staying, but this was too sudden. And even though she'd been betting on it, now that it was happening it felt like a punishment.

He opened the door, then, almost as an afterthought, turned back. 'Congratulations, by the way. Seems I was the last to know.'

Jess felt the colour drain from her face. She knew instinctively what he meant. She'd somehow known the second she'd walked into her office.

A muscle in Adam's jaw visibly tightened. 'I bumped into Kate on Saturday afternoon when I was running in the Phoenix Park. We had a coffee together and she told me the happy news.'

Oh God, Kate must have gone straight there after she'd left the bridal shop. She'd finally broken her promise to Jess, not to tell Adam anything personal about her, by revealing the most damning thing of all.

'I'm sorry, I know I should have told you, Adam.' She swallowed, trying to think. In the beginning, she'd pretended she didn't care about his opinion of her. Then, when she'd finally accepted how much she liked him, his opinion had meant everything to her. It was so messed up – and now he'd hate her anyway.

His eyes bored into her. 'Save the apology for the poor bastard you're about to marry. For the record, we wouldn't have slept together that night if I'd known you were in a relationship. Especially if I'd known you were about to get married. No matter how much we'd had to drink.'

'It wasn't like ...'

A movement in the corridor behind him caught her attention and, as Kate stepped into view, Jess saw the horror on her face.

Kate stumbled as she turned, briefly catching the edge of the door to steady herself. Before Jess could react, she had left. *Shit*, how had everything got so bad, so quickly? She braced herself.

'Adam, I know you've every right to be angry ...'

'Forget about it.'

Jess wished he'd have a good rant, demand a few answers. At least that way, she might have a chance to explain. But the truth was, she couldn't explain herself: she'd had no excuse for what she'd done.

Adam barely looked at her when he spoke again. 'You have five days to this wedding; you need to focus on that.'

He left without another word, and Jess sank weakly into her chair. Sugar was supposed to be good for shock, she remembered. She found a KitKat in her desk and tore off the top, but after a single bite felt too sick to eat. She couldn't put off the inevitable: she needed to talk to Kate.

She eventually found Kate in the loos near Accounts. She was leaning against the wall, hands braced behind her, eyes tightly closed.

'Kate?' Jess spoke quietly.

Kate's eyes snapped open. 'Stay away from me.'

'Please, Kate, let me explain.'

Kate's eyes glittered. 'Explain what? That you've been screwing around behind Simon's back? I got that.'

Jess swallowed hard. 'It happened once, that night on the Isle of Man, when I was drunk.'

Kate took a step towards her. 'Is that supposed to be an excuse?'

'No, if I could change ...'

'Does Simon know?'

Jess shook her head.

Kate looked at Jess like she was a stranger. 'I can't believe you'd do something like that, hurt someone you love. It isn't you.' She gave a disbelieving laugh. 'But I guess it is.'

Jess felt a fresh wave of nausea. 'You've no idea how guilty I've felt since that night.'

'Not guilty enough to tell Simon and beg his forgiveness.' Kate was trembling. 'Because you're too ashamed to be with a man who loves you, and who would never do that to you? Or because you've realised you don't love him?'

Jess folded her arms, pushing them hard into her stomach. 'Stop judging me. Look, I didn't even want to tell you because I knew it'd be like this. I didn't want you caught in the middle, as you always seem to be.' She stopped, wishing she could find the right thing to say. 'Just try to understand.'

Kate's dark-brown eyes were full of hurt and disgust. 'I get it, Jess, more than you think. But here's where you and I are different. Just because I really want to do something, doesn't mean I do it. Sometimes things are just wrong. It's not that hard to figure out.' Without another word, she walked out.

Jess sagged against the nearest washbasin. If things had been bad on Saturday, this was a hundred times worse.

But she also knew that no matter how angry Kate was, she wouldn't say anything to Simon. It was up to her to come clean with him.

She thought about her mother, who'd poured so much time and energy into the wedding. And Úna? No, she couldn't worry about Úna right now. In the last three years, she'd been stupid enough to think her life was sorted. Until that hen weekend, she and Simon had been happy. Not ecstatically happy, but who was constantly, ecstatically happy? Now she didn't know where she stood. Simon hadn't made a single move to get her back, Kate hated her, and the half of her family who weren't worried about her, weren't talking to her.

Her stomach gave one final heave and she dived into a cubicle to throw up. Grateful there was nobody else in the bathroom, she rinsed out her mouth at the washbasin, and stared bleakly into the mirror. The woman who stared back was unrecognisable. And it went way beyond her dishevelled hair and ruined make-up. It was official: her life was a total mess.

Chapter 37

'WHY are you home in the middle of the day?' Zoe looked up from her laptop at the dining-room table as Jess collapsed into the chair beside her an hour and a half later.

Jess rested her head in her hands. 'I wasn't feeling well.'

'Oh solid, share your germs.'

'It's just stress.' After she'd thrown up, Jess had struggled through for another while, unable to stop replaying the awful scenes with Adam and Kate. By then, she'd developed the worst headache since her hen-weekend hangover and was now dosed up on the strongest painkillers she could get without a prescription. 'What about you?'

'Day off.' Zoe pushed her chair away from the table. 'Actually, I have some news, but you need to keep an open mind.'

Grateful for the distraction, Jess took her hands away from her face and sat up a bit straighter. 'I'm listening.'

Zoe caught back her hair, knotting it loosely on top of her head. 'Finn's been offered a job in Limerick city, teaching modern dance and performance art at a theatre school.'

Jess blinked. 'That sounds great.'

'Yeah, that's not all. You remember I was telling you about that old cottage his friends are selling in Limerick?'

'I remember.' Jess realised that Zoe was trying her best to appear cool.

'We've checked with them that they're still selling. It's a private sale, no agent.'

This was it, Jess thought, Zoe was moving out, moving on with her life. Jess wouldn't see her when she came home to visit. Apart from the time Jess spent a term in Germany during college, it'd be the first time in twenty-five years that they'd really be apart.

'What's the catch?'

Zoe shrugged. 'It's quite rural and it's really rundown. Like, it would take a lot of work. But it's a total steal. I mean, I have some savings, and we'll have a small mortgage and Mam and Dad have offered to help a bit.' Before Jess could reply, she added, 'Dad said he'd take a look at it. He won't let us buy anything that's not structurally sound. And he's promised he'll do loads of the work for us.'

'So, you're buying it?'

'We're buying it together, Jess.' Zoe sounded firm. 'There's a large shed at the back, that could be a studio. In the meantime, I'll try to get a job down here. Worse case, I can freelance.'

'It sounds like you've thought it through.'

Zoe gave an unladylike snort. 'What's there to think about? It's either that, or I stay here with Mam and Dad while Finn moves down on his own. I love him too much to split.'

Jess tried to imagine Zoe living in a crumbling, rural cottage. 'Zoe, if this is what you want to do, do it. You're young, and if it doesn't work out, it doesn't matter. Just do what makes you happy.'

'So, I shouldn't stay in my safe job?'

Jess released a tense laugh. 'Did Mam say that?'

Zoe rolled her eyes. 'She said we should try a long-distance relationship for a while. Mad stuff.'

'It'll be an adventure, Zoe. I'm kind of surprised though. Finn doesn't strike me as the teacher type.'

'Fuck it, Jess, you can be completely clueless.' Zoe gave her a hard look. 'Who do you think does all the choreography for the troupe? You've all judged Finn for years. You think he's a waste of space.'

'Zoe!'

Her sister's voice rose. 'The only reason Finn stayed in those crappy jobs was to eat and pay his rent. But he can't hang around forever for his big break. So, this is him getting real. He'll be on a steady wage. It's not performing, but he'll be happier than working as a waiter.'

Jess was quiet for a moment. 'Sorry.'

Zoe sighed. 'Yeah, don't sweat it.'

Jess rubbed her eyes. It was starting to feel like the longest day of her life. 'When are you moving?'

'I don't know. We can't put in an offer until Dad has seen it. But if we buy it, he'll help me hire builders. There's two bedrooms. You could come stay … on your own, or with Simon, obviously.'

Jess managed a smile. Zoe knew well that unless Simon was heading off to a four-star hotel, preferably with a golf course, he rarely ventured beyond the confines of South County Dublin. 'It sounds great.'

'Hey, if you decide to move home, you'll get your old room back.' Zoe tried to make it sound like a joke.

'I think I'll go lie down for a while.' Jess stood.

'You sure you're okay?' Zoe narrowed her eyes. 'Mam set her

alarm clock for two, so she could take a look at you then.'

'I'll be fine, I just need some rest. See you later.' Jess tried to avoid the creaky steps as she headed up to her room, before remembering that Zoe slept there now.

She headed down the corridor to Zoe's old room, stepping out of her suit and slipping between the clean, cool covers of the bed. When the tears came, they rolled down her cheeks, wetting the pillow. As her eyes shut, she wondered if she could just stay here forever.

Carmel was in the kitchen heating up some soup, when she got up. She gave Jess a quick look over. 'Zoe told me you were home. How are you feeling, love?'

'Better, Mam.' As well as anyone could feel when their life was falling apart.

'What do you feel like eating?'

It was almost like she'd never left home at all, Jess thought. Despite, or maybe because of her nursing background, her mother's solutions for most of life's problems were tea, food and sleep. 'I'm not sure.'

'Well, you don't like tomato soup, so I'll make you an omelette.' Carmel got up and took a small frying pan out of the drawer. 'Have you any plans for the rest of the day?'

Anxiety curled through her. Her mother meant well, but if she stayed at home she'd have to talk about Simon and the wedding. She remembered hearing a dry weather forecast for the afternoon.

'I think I might go to the stables.'

A couple of hours later, Jess slowed her horse from a gallop to a canter, as she crossed the final half mile back to Glenwood Stables.

She'd never been so grateful that she'd kept all her riding clothes in her parents' house. Her headache and the earlier tension in her body gone, she slowed to a trot and dipped forward to stroke the horse's head, remembering how she'd felt riding out with Adam on his family farm. This afternoon had been almost as good.

Back in the yard, she dismounted and led the gelding to his stable. She was hanging up her tack when the stable manager came in. 'Seán!' She threw her arms around him, hugging him tightly.

'Hey, you.' He returned the hug. 'Thought you'd given up on us.'

She pulled back, smiling up at him. His skin was deeply tanned from a life spent outdoors, his fair hair bleached in the sun. 'How have you been?'

He rubbed his chin. 'I've a bit of news: Catriona's agreed to make an honest man of me.'

'Hey, I'm so happy for you guys!'

'Yeah, well.' He laughed. 'We haven't set a date or anything. You know us, we'll probably just do up the barn in the far field, maybe attach a marquee and have a massive buffet. Sure, there's about five hundred people we'd want to invite.'

'That sounds amazing.' Jess felt a pang of envy. Compared to her own wedding, it sounded fun and relaxed.

'It'll be a bit of craic. But listen, we're really looking forward to your big day out. Catriona bought a new outfit, and I have the good suit.'

Jess could feel some of her earlier tension return. 'Have you been busy?' She started to brush down the gelding's coat.

'Ah, the usual. Although we had a bit of a hike in numbers after your fiancé came for that lesson. A lot of people hoping for a repeat performance, until they realised it was a one-off.' He winked. 'Pity,

I think he was a natural.'

Despite herself, Jess laughed, remembering how she'd persuaded Simon to take his first and only riding lesson. 'In his defence, he'd never been on a horse before.'

'He wasn't on one that time either. We gave him one of the kid's ponies, remember?'

Jess hung up the brush and shut the half-gate on the gelding's stall, before feeding him a small treat from her hand.

'Yeah, well, it's not something I see us doing together. Maybe I'll take up golf.'

'You're wounding me now, Jess.' He placed a hand on her shoulder. 'You sure everything's okay?'

She gave a quick smile. 'Everything's perfect. And I'm joking about the golf.'

Seán checked the time. 'I'd better head off, I've a few things to do before our next class.'

Jess was tempted to stay on for another hour and help out. But she'd only be delaying the inevitable. She had to face her real, messy life and the sooner the better. 'Give my love to Catriona.'

'I will. Don't be a stranger, now.'

She watched Seán stride away across the stable yard, then collected her things and headed back to the car. As she drove up the narrow lane that led to the back roads of the foothills of the Dublin mountains, she remembered her first time at Glenwood. She'd been fourteen, Zoe just nine. Her confidence had hit a new low, after puberty brought an alarming weight gain. Their mother had refused to discuss dieting and instead decided that both girls would take up riding. Gradually, fresh air and regular exercise, combined with the confidence that came from being around horses, had proved a winning combination.

Seán was right, she should get back to riding. Especially as Simon usually worked part of his Saturdays now. She missed the camaraderie at the stables, and it wasn't like she and Simon had any real shared interests. She hated golf and opera and despite attending a few matches, still had no interest in rugby. She'd tried to learn chess, but she found it too slow. Simon dismissed *Celebrity Come Dancing* and *The Great British Bake Off* as cheap TV, and he thought yoga was for conspiracy theorists. They even had different taste in holidays.

While Jess loved beaches, horse trekking on country roads and cosy pubs in the evening, Simon's ideal holiday was a good golf course and plenty of culture. But none of it had ever mattered before, they'd always found things to talk about. And Simon had been a steady, reliable presence in her life. It was she who'd let him down.

But recently she'd started to realise something else. Kate understood Simon far better than her. Simon might be her fiancé, but Kate was the glue holding them together. Kate was the person Jess had always turned to for advice when she and Simon disagreed, and to her shame Jess had never questioned it.

For a brief moment she allowed herself to imagine her life if Simon had never proposed. She wouldn't have had a hen weekend. She wouldn't have slept with Adam or fallen out with Kate.

She'd never have hurt her cousins, because of Úna's insistence that she try to squeeze in last-minute guests.

But the reality was, Simon wanted marriage and a family. Jess just wasn't sure what she wanted anymore.

'Are you going to tell me what's really wrong?' Zoe looked up from her phone that evening as Jess tidied up the sitting room. 'And don't bullshit me about this celebrity wedding.'

Jess glanced over her shoulder. 'Where's Dad?'

'He's upstairs. I think he's trying to give us some space.'

Poor Dad, Jess thought. Neither of her parents had any idea what was going on. She stacked some gardening magazines and straightened up.

'Kate found out that I had a one-night stand with Adam.'

'Oh shit.'

Jess sighed. 'It gets better. She ran into Adam on Saturday, and she told him about me and Simon.'

Zoe stared at her. 'You know, I used to think your life was really boring.'

'Cheers.' Jess threw herself into her dad's armchair. Maybe if she stopped thinking about her problems for a while, they'd all somehow sort themselves out. Because the more she tried to fix things, the worse she made things. 'What about you? How's Finn?'

Zoe shrugged. 'He's cool.'

'Are you two okay?'

'Yeah, we just need to get on with our lives, and we can't do it in Dublin. I know you think it's weird that he's staying with Nana, but it was weirder having him living here. Mam and Dad were trying to be chill, but it was a total turn-off having Dad snoring on the other side of the wall.' She pulled a face and Jess gave a tired laugh. 'Anyway, stop changing the subject. What are you going to do?'

Jess found a bobbin on the coffee table and pulled her hair back off her face. 'All I know is that I've managed to screw up everything. I still don't know what to do about Simon, and Kate …' She swallowed. 'She'll probably never talk to me again.'

Zoe rolled her eyes. 'Kate needs to cop herself on. She's been a third wheel for so long that she can't get her head around the two of you splitting up. That's why she's so pissed off.'

Jess tried to pin down her thoughts, but her head felt like wool. 'I get that she's angry at me, but she's been pulling away from Simon too. I just don't get it.'

'Don't overthink it, Jess, she'll come around. You're her person.'

'I used to be.' And then Simon had become Kate's person. Until recently, anyway.

'You girls in here?'

Jess looked up as their dad stuck his head around the door.

'Zoe, would you mind if I had a quick word with Jess?'

'I'll go help Mam with the dinner.'

Zoe left and Tom sat down on the sofa. Jess turned in the chair to face him, tucking her legs up.

'Everything all right, Dad?'

He looked at her steadily. 'You tell me, Jessie.'

A laugh caught in her throat. 'You haven't called me that since I was a little girl.'

Tom rubbed his nose. 'I'll come straight out with it, love: do you want to marry him? Because if you're having second thoughts ... look, none of it matters, that's all. Everything can be cancelled; wedding gifts can be returned.' He reached over and took her hand. 'Your Mam and I just want you to be happy.'

Jess blinked rapidly as she squeezed her dad's hand. For a while they sat in silence. Maybe he was right. She would tell Simon that she couldn't marry him. She wouldn't even have to tell him about Adam, just that she'd used the break to think about things.

It was the perfect solution. And the coward's way out. Not to mention that she wasn't convinced breaking up with Simon was the answer. She shook her head. 'Simon and I need to talk, Dad.'

'I'll leave it with you, Jessie. Mam and I are here for you, no matter what you decide.'

Jess heard her mother's footsteps on the stairs as she came up from the kitchen and then Carmel appeared, hovering at the door of the living room.

'Is everything all right, pet?' Carmel gave Jess an overly bright smile, the one Jess guessed she used to calm and reassure her patients, even when she knew everything wasn't all right. That was it: she'd put her parents through enough.

'Everything's great, Mam. Actually, I've been thinking about things and I'm moving back in with Simon after dinner.'

'Oh Jess!' Relief washed over Carmel's face. 'I'm sure he's been missing you like mad.'

Jess felt her dad's eyes on her. 'Do you need some help downstairs, Mam?'

'Not at all, Zoe came down to make the rice for the curry. I'm ready to serve up now.' Carmel's smile was genuine. 'And I'll give you some dessert to take home to Simon.'

Almost reluctantly, Jess's eyes met her dad's again. She knew she hadn't fooled him for a moment.

Chapter 38

SIMON'S flat was quiet when Jess got back later that night. She dropped her case in the hall and walked through to the living room. She hadn't thought it was possible, but the whole place looked even tidier than usual, and a faint smell of beeswax lingered in the air. It was the first time she and Simon had spent more than a day apart since she'd moved in, and it struck her that despite her best efforts it still felt like his flat, rather than theirs. Behind her, the front door closed.

'Jess?'

'I'm in here.'

Simon came into the living room, and stopped a couple of feet from her, his expression unreadable. Jess managed a smile.

'Mam sent you over some dessert.' She held it out like a peace offering. 'Brownies, they're really fudgy. I'll put them in the kitchen.' She turned and walked over to the kitchen area, grateful for something to do.

'That was good of her.' Simon pushed his glasses up his nose. 'I won't have any now, I've just eaten with my folks.'

Jess came back into the living room. 'How are they?'

'Fine, I suppose.' He frowned. 'They'll be pleased that you're back. If you are back.' Without waiting for a reply, he pulled a clean white envelope out of his pocket and handed it to her. 'They gave us this.' Jess opened it and took out a voucher.

'It's a two-weeks' stay at the Ritz Carlton in Rome, where my folks stayed on their honeymoon.' Simon cleared his throat. 'I thought we could go in September, when the weather's cooler.'

'*Wow!*' Jess looked up, brushing aside the uncharitable thought that as well as deciding where they'd get married, Úna had now chosen their honeymoon destination. 'That's incredibly kind. I thought the dance lessons was their wedding gift.'

Simon gave a slight smile. 'Mum didn't want us to disgrace ourselves. Apparently, our generation can't dance properly.'

This was agony: she couldn't put it off for any longer. 'Simon, we need to talk.'

He didn't quite meet her eyes. 'Are you calling off the wedding?'

Jess swallowed. What she was about to do was cruel, but Simon deserved to know. 'No, but I need to tell you something.'

He looked at her properly. 'I'm going to have a gin and tonic. Would you like one?'

Jess shook her head and Simon strode past her into the kitchen, taking down a single tumbler. Drink in hand, he went into the living room and sat down.

Jess perched on the edge of the sofa and took a deep breath.

'I have something to tell you first.' Simon threw back half his drink.

Jess released the breath she was still holding. Shit, if she didn't say this quickly, she was going to chicken out. 'Okay.'

'I kissed Kate.'

She stared at him. He'd kissed Kate? She hadn't seen that coming.

Simon gulped some more of his drink. 'We bumped into her and her friends at the stag.'

'She told me.' Jess blinked. 'Well, she didn't mention the kiss.' Was that why Kate had been so angry and self-righteous? Had she been trying to justify her actions, by telling herself that Jess didn't love Simon? Except it made no sense. But not owning up to a harmless kiss at a stag party made no sense either.

'It was just a kiss.' God, if she didn't tell him now ... 'Simon, it was just a stupid kiss on your stag night.'

He took an audible breath. 'I want you to know how it happened.'

This was insane. But it was clear he wanted to get everything off his chest.

Simon stared into his glass.

'We were dancing, and I think ... I know I'd had a lot to drink. Not that it's any excuse. Anyway, I kissed her.'

Jess's heart thumped loudly. Had Kate kissed him back? Had she kissed him first? It would be so like Simon to be gallant about the whole thing. He seemed to be waiting for some sort of response.

'How does Kate feel? I mean, did you talk about it?'

A vein throbbed in Simon's neck. 'I hope she sees it for what it was.'

Jess didn't care. None of it mattered, not the hows or whys. It was nothing compared with what she'd done. 'Simon, really, it's okay.'

'How is it okay, Jess?' Simon looked up, his eyes glittering. 'I shouldn't have done that to Kate. She trusted me, Luke trusts me. And what about you and Kate? I've put myself between the two of you.' He pushed a hand roughly through his hair. 'I've no idea how Kate feels, because I've been too much of a coward to contact her and apologise properly. But I feel like such a shit.'

A memory of her and Adam kissing in the church slid to mind. Was that how Simon and Kate had kissed? It wasn't impossible, especially when she thought about how close they were, how easy it would have been for them to take that next small step. She finally knew why Kate had lashed out. It was guilt.

Jess tried to take a deep breath, but her chest was too tight. 'Simon, I need to say this before I lose my nerve.'

Simon shifted in his chair. 'Wait, do I really need to hear it?'

She was speechless. Did he guess? Was he giving her an out? If she said nothing, could Simon pretend it was nothing? Jess tried to imagine that, and for a few moments she let herself believe it was possible. Only what if he guessed wrong, and discovered later that it was far worse than he'd imagined? Her insides squeezed. 'I need to tell you so you can decide whether to go ahead with the wedding.'

Simon looked sharply at her, before tossing back the rest of his drink.

Jess spoke quickly to her tightly clenched hands. 'I got drunk on my hen night and, as a joke, the girls put me and Zoe on a ferry to the Isle of Man. I had a one-night stand.'

She glanced up at Simon, who looked paler than she'd ever seen. When he finally spoke, his voice was dull. 'Did you know him?'

'No.'

'So, he was a total stranger.' A look of horror crossed his face. 'Was it rape? You said you were drunk.'

Jess spoke quickly. 'We'd both been drinking, but there was consent, Simon. It wasn't rape.' She tried to guess what he was thinking. 'He used protection. The following morning ... I left before he woke. I'm desperately sorry, I've never cheated on you before, that's the truth.' Jess's face burned as Simon continued to stare coldly at her. Her voice wavered, a whisper now. 'I'll understand if you want to end things.'

Simon put his glass down on the table. 'Is that what you want?'

She shook her head, not trusting herself to speak.

Simon sat forward and rested his elbows on his knees, pressing the heels of his hands into his eyes. '*Fuuuuck!*'

Jess didn't think it was possible for her heart to beat any louder. 'I'm sorry,' she said again, starting as Simon sprang to his feet.

'No wonder you wanted a break.' His eyes were bright with tears as he gave her a brief, hard stare. 'I'm such a fucking idiot.' He turned on his heel and strode over to the window, where he stood with his back to her, staring out.

Jess didn't move: her whole body felt frozen, her brain incapable of thought. After what seemed like an eternity, Simon spoke again.

'Is there anything else I need to know?'

'No.' She'd rather throw herself out their third-floor window, than tell him Adam was the man she'd slept with. She couldn't be that cruel.

But she'd thought that coming clean about her hen weekend might be cathartic. At least for her, if she was being honest. She hadn't thought about the amount of pain she'd cause Simon. Jess tried to wet her lips. 'I thought about not telling you ... but it wouldn't have been right.'

Simon seemed emotionless. Maybe he was in shock. She wouldn't blame him: it was a lot to throw at someone you were about to marry. Eventually he turned, a grim expression on his face. 'I can't do this now. I'm going to bed. I'll give you my decision in the morning.'

Briefly, he met her eyes, and another wave of shame washed through her.

'I'll sleep on the sofa bed.' She wrapped her arms around herself. 'Unless you'd prefer I went home again.'

'I actually don't care, Jess.' He walked out and moments later, Jess heard the bedroom door close. Drawing her knees up, she hugged them tightly to her chest. She'd half expected Simon to throw her out, tell her he never wanted to see her again. He still might. She knew she'd done the right thing, but she didn't know if she'd made things worse. It definitely hadn't made them better.

Instead, it felt like she and Simon were standing on the edge of a cliff. She'd no idea how she'd feel if Simon called off their wedding. Even more terrifying was that she'd no idea how she'd feel if he didn't.

Chapter 39

JESS tried to feel relieved as she left for work the following morning, but so much had happened that all she felt was numb.

After the worst night's sleep she could remember, she'd finally got up around dawn to make coffee, only to find Simon had beat her to it. His face had been the same shade of grey as his stripy pyjamas as he'd handed her a cup, made exactly how she liked it. Somehow, that had made her feel worse.

'I won't pretend I'm not devastated by what you did, Jess.' Simon had leaned against the counter, staring at the floor. 'To be honest, I don't know what to do. Part of me thinks we should just call the whole thing off.'

Jess's face had burned. So, this was it. This was how their three-year relationship would end: just days before their wedding. Simon probably hated her, but she could never hate him – he had every right to end it.

She'd sat down. 'Right.' Her voice had been as wobbly as her legs.

Simon had given a humourless laugh. 'It's a very different feeling for me, not knowing what to do.'

He'd looked at her and Jess had felt another wave of shame.

After a long pause, Simon had spoken slowly. 'I've no road map for this, Jess, and I'm not used to making important decisions based on feelings. So, I've tried to take everything into consideration, including the circumstances of that weekend and the amount you had to drink. I think we should go ahead with the wedding; I hope we won't regret it.'

'Thank you.' Jess had expected to feel a flood of happiness, or at least relief, but she'd been too exhausted to feel anything.

'Promise me this was a horrible mistake, one that could never, ever be repeated.' He'd given her a long look.

Jess had simply nodded.

'No more secrets?'

She'd thought briefly about Adam. It didn't matter anymore: he was already gone. She'd shook her head.

'If this is to work, Jess, we have to put this behind us. And, in future, we need to be completely honest with each other.'

'I'm so sorry I hurt you, Simon.'

'Yes.' He'd sighed. 'I know.' He'd seemed too exhausted to talk any more about it, and Jess had been grateful.

Now she wondered if she'd be so forgiving if Simon cheated. But she knew it would take him a long time to trust her again.

She hadn't told him about her fight with Kate. In spite of what Kate had done, she couldn't bear the thought of losing her friendship. The friendship they'd once had – not the slightly weird relationship they'd had in recent months. And Simon would lose Kate's friendship too. When she thought about that, she felt weirdly guilty and confused. After everything that had happened recently, she wasn't sure which of them would miss Kate more. The only thing she could do was to focus on the moment and, for now,

Simon seemed willing to forgive. She knew that had to be enough.

She was walking through reception when she overheard Emily on the phone.

'I want you to listen very carefully to me. I'm getting rid of all the toxic people in my life and that means *you*!' She slammed down the phone and caught Jess's eye. 'Ooh, just the person I was looking for.'

Jess sidled over to the desk. 'Please tell me that was your latest boyfriend.'

Emily started to giggle. 'Well, it wasn't a client.'

'Right, look, just don't let Frank catch you making personal calls.'

'No, it's all good, he rang me.'

Jess stifled a sigh. 'Why were you looking for me?'

Emily flicked her hair back off her shoulders. 'I was wondering if you could put in a good word for me at Linford Castle? For a receptionist job.'

Jess blinked. 'You want to move to Mayo? Do you not like working here?'

Emily shrugged. 'It's not that I don't like it, it's just Linford would be kind of cool. I'd meet loads of people from all around the world, I'd get to see big celebrity weddings, and I wouldn't be living at home with my parents. I could actually like, afford to rent somewhere, because unless I want to live in somebody's attic, I can't afford anywhere in Dublin.'

Jess thought of Zoe and Finn. 'Yeah, I can see that.'

'Plus,' Emily lowered her voice, 'I'd have no problem finding a decent fellah. Everyone knows the west of Ireland is full of single men looking for women. I could end up with a rich farmer.'

'True.' Jess grinned. 'But I think they might be a lot older than you.'

Emily gave a dramatic sigh. 'I need an older man. All the guys my age are complete tools. And I don't think Adam's interested in me.'

Jess made her excuses quickly before Emily started to talk about Adam.

Zoe rang her at lunchtime. Jess was eating a tuna-and-sweet-corn roll at her desk, because she couldn't face bumping into anyone, least of all Kate.

'Hey, Zoe.' Jess brushed away some crumbs.

'Have you taken refuge in Cadbury Land?'

'I'm having lunch. I'm okay, I told Simon last night.'

There was a brief silence. 'About Adam?'

Jess sighed. 'I didn't exactly mention him, I told him I had a drunken one-night stand on my hen night. Honestly, Zoe, that was enough to dump on him.'

'So, what happened? Don't leave anything out.'

Jesus, Zoe made it sound like she was catching up on an episode of *Fair City*. 'What do you think happened? He was shocked and devastated, and I was lucky he didn't kick me out there and then. Eventually, he said he wanted to sleep on it, so I spent the night on the sofa bed.'

'*Wow.*' Zoe breathed the word. 'And this morning he said it was all good?'

Jess tried to swallow, but the food was stuck in her throat. She swigged down some water.

'You still there, Jess?'

'Yeah. Look, things are so far from all good, but he wants to put it behind us.' She dropped the rest of her roll in the waste basket. 'Oh, and he kissed Kate at his stag.'

'*Holy shit*. That probably explains the meltdown at your dress fitting.' When Jess didn't reply, Zoe said, 'Do you want me to come in and meet you?'

'No, I'm fine.' Jess pressed the heels of her hands into her eyes. 'Okay, I'm not fine, but I can't overthink the kiss. Simon had a couple of drinks, and we were on a break and Kate was there, and one thing led to another. It was a kiss. Compared to what I've done, I don't know how he can even forgive me.'

'I guess he loves you.' Zoe sounded uncertain. 'Isn't that what you wanted?'

'Yeah.' Jess spoke quietly. 'I'm lucky to have him.' She moved her hands up to rub her forehead. 'And I really need one thing in my life to be normal right now.'

'What about Kate, have you talked to her?'

'I can't face her, Zoe, she hates me for what I've done.'

'Maybe it's not that, though.' Zoe spoke slowly. 'Maybe Mam's right about her being jealous.'

'I could almost cope with that, but you weren't here yesterday when she found out about Adam.'

'Yeah, well, she's had a chance to cool down. She's probably scarlet she overreacted.'

'You think?'

'Jess, she's your best friend.'

Jess swallowed hard. 'Actually, that would be you. Thanks for not judging.'

'I'd never judge you, you sap. Are you going to be okay? Like, really?'

'Yeah, really.'

'Okay, go do what you have to do.'

Zoe hung up and Jess took a slightly shaky breath. She'd have a five-minute lie-down on the floor. Then she'd try to talk to Kate again.

'How can I help, Jess?' Kate didn't look up from her keyboard when Jess came into the Accounts department.

Kate's female co-worker shot Jess an odd look and Jess wondered if she'd said anything. Until yesterday, she'd never have doubted her friend's loyalty, now she wasn't so sure.

'Can we talk in private?'

'Is it about work?'

'No.'

'It'll have to wait, I'm busy.' Kate continued to tap at the keyboard.

The other woman murmured an excuse about lunch and left.

When they were alone, Jess said, 'I came to say sorry, I want everything to be all right between us.'

Kate continued to input figures into a spreadsheet.

'Kate, please just stop for a minute and listen.'

Kate spun her chair around to face her. 'Fine, I'm listening.' She folded her arms.

'I'm sorry, okay?' Jess's voice shook a bit.

'For what, exactly?'

'That I didn't tell you what happened with Adam. I couldn't tell you and not Simon. He's the one I hurt.'

Kate's eyes glittered. 'So, he knows? You told him?'

'Yes.' As the colour left Kate's face. Jess rushed on. 'Look, I get it, you and Simon are friends and you probably felt I didn't love him …'

'You don't.' Kate's voice had hardened.

Jess's skin prickled. 'Kate, you can't judge a relationship from the outside.'

Kate got to her feet so quickly Jess was forced to take a step backwards. 'We're finished here. I'm not coming to the wedding because it'll be a joke, and deep down you know that.'

'Please don't make me choose between you and Simon, Kate,' Jess's voice was barely more than a whisper. 'That's just nuts.'

Kate took a step towards her, and Jess was shaken at the hurt and anger in her expression. 'There's no more to talk about. I want you to leave me alone.'

For a moment, Jess was tempted to beg. But she knew she'd be wasting her time. 'Have it your way.'

She left, suddenly needing to clear her head, and took the stairs down to the foyer. She didn't stop until she was outside on the street.

Crossing the road, Jess walked along the canal until she found a free bench. When had her friendship with Kate started to change? Her mother and Zoe both thought Kate was jealous, but Jess had a feeling it wasn't that simple: she had to be missing something. Had their friendship started to shift three years ago when she'd met Simon? No, if anything they'd got closer because Kate and Simon had always got on so well.

She tried to pinpoint anything odd that had happened since the engagement, but nothing stood out. She understood why Kate was hurt that she hadn't told her about the Isle of Man, but it didn't explain her anger. Kate and Simon might be good friends, but if

Jess and Simon were prepared to give things another try, why wasn't Kate happy for them?

Even stranger was that Kate had voiced doubts about Jess and Simon, before she'd even found out about Adam. Nor had she trusted Jess to see the stag party kiss as a bit of harmless fun. Only, what if it hadn't been?

Half-formed thoughts that Jess had previously dismissed rushed back. Kate was beautiful and smart and kind. Men had always been interested in her: it had rarely made any difference that she'd been a single mum. But in the last few years, she'd made no effort to date.

In fact, now she thought about it, David was the only man Kate had gone out with more than once in the past three years. Bumping into him at Simon's stag should have been an ideal opportunity for her to have some fun. But at Jess's final dress fitting, Kate had barely mentioned David. In fact, she never talked about him. By contrast, she never stopped talking about Simon. But then, Kate saw almost as much of Simon as she did.

Her thoughts swirled to a stop as a final jigsaw piece slotted into place. She knew why Kate never dated, why she was happy to be a third wheel in their relationship. And it was suddenly crystal clear why Kate had pulled away from Simon, when she and Simon had been on a break: she'd been afraid to overstep a sacred boundary. It was also why Kate believed that she was about to marry the wrong man. Kate was in love with Simon.

Chapter 40

KATE was in love with Simon. It was all Jess had thought about since yesterday. No wonder Kate wouldn't talk to her. How had she never seen it? The only reason that made any sense was that Kate hadn't realised it either. It seemed she'd been too focused on Luke, and on the delicate nature of her friendship with her best friend's fiancé.

Somehow, all that had changed after the hen weekend. Long before Jess had accepted it, Kate had somehow guessed that something had shifted, and Jess was different. Because one thing was certain: if Jess had been lying to other people, she'd also been lying to herself.

But she wanted to marry Simon. They'd been together three years, and their relationship pointed in one direction. Still, one thing niggled: Jess didn't know how Simon really felt about Kate. She knew a quick snog at a stag usually meant nothing, but she also knew how much Simon genuinely cared for Kate. Jess had taken their friendship for granted and now, even if she didn't marry Simon, she couldn't see how things could ever return to normal between the three of them.

Her phone pinged: Chelsea had just started a live video. Jess clicked on the link and Chelsea waved at her from a large white sofa with pale pink and white scatter cushions, that looked a bit like a giant marshmallow.

'*Hi, everyone.*' Chelsea smiled broadly. '*So, three more sleeps to my special day and I'm sooo excited, I can't even. As you know, Bobbie Grayson is gonna be filming on the day, so I've been sworn to secrecy. But we have awesome surprises lined up for our two hundred guests, and you guys will get to see everything afterwards, that's a promise.*' She thrust her hand into her long, loose hair and it fell across her other shoulder. '*The one thing I've tried to do every day of my life is to live my truth. But I also believe in the power of forgiveness.*'

She nodded to someone off camera and a moment later, Brandi Oliver came into view and sat beside her. Jess was struck by how alike they were: same long, blond hair and deep blue eyes, same delicate, sculpted faces, cleverly made up to appear natural. Chelsea continued. '*I wanted you all to know that I've made up with Brandi, because there's nobody else I want on my special day as my maid of honour.*' She turned to Brandi, who was wiping away some seemingly imaginary tears.

'*Thanks, Chelsea. I'm truly blessed to have a big sister like you. And I'm so psyched.*'

'*Thanks, Bran.*' Chelsea swung the camera back to her. '*I've still got so much to do, so I'm gonna go. I love you all.*' Massive smile. '*Find your truth, live your truth, be your truth.*'

The video ended. Jess wondered if their fallout had been one giant publicity stunt but was grateful they'd ended it on a happy note.

Her phone rang and she swiped quickly when Moira's name flashed up. 'Hi, Nana, how are things?'

'Very good, all things considering. Now, a little word: I'm giving you some money.'

Jess frowned. 'For what?'

'For you, dear, for your wedding.'

Jess felt a stab of unease. Was Moira becoming forgetful? She knew it was the one thing she dreaded. 'Nana, you've already given Simon and me a wedding present, that beautiful antique dinner service.' It was one of Jess's favourite wedding gifts: a 1930s full Wedgewood service that Moira had tracked down on eBay. Jess suspected Zoe had helped her.

'That was for you both.' Moira clicked her tongue. 'This is just for you. Only you, do you hear me? You're not even to mention it to Simon.'

Oh God, this was even worse. 'Nana, please don't think you have to do that.'

Moira gave a sniff. 'Listen, Jess, and you know I think Simon's a grand young fellah. Bit stiff for my liking, but he's a good lad. But it doesn't matter one bit whether you've got a big, high-powered career, or you're at home rearing your children, every woman needs running-away money.'

Jess blinked rapidly, feeling a rush of love for Moira.

Moira seemed to read her mind. 'I can afford to do this, Jess. I've had my own running-away money all these years and not even your granddad knew. Always have a few secrets, pet.'

Jess suddenly remembered what Mrs McCarthy had written in the bridal shower guest book: *The key to a happy marriage is to keep a few secrets.*

It took Jess a moment before she could speak. 'Thanks, Nana.'

'Good girl.' Moira sounded brisk. 'Now, text me your bank details and I'll put it straight into your account today. After that, I'd advise you to transfer it. I've always found post office savings reliable, but that's up to you. Just one last thing.' Moira paused. 'If you decided you weren't going to get married after all, I'd still give you the money. It might help you to get out on your own.'

Jess tried to process this. Did Moira privately think she was doing the wrong thing also? And how much money was she planning to give her? She might have a bit of a chat with her dad, to make sure Moira wasn't leaving herself short. She thought about having a nest egg that she'd never tell Simon. Until her hen weekend, she'd never kept secrets from him. But maybe having a few secrets was the key to a successful relationship. Small ones, anyway. Just not the whopper she'd been keeping.

He'd suggested booking their honeymoon tonight, so Jess guessed he saw this as their fresh start, and he wasn't taking anything for granted. Moira was worrying for nothing. Her phone buzzed and she opened a text from Moira: *Please let me know when you get the full amount later today.* Jess's eyes widened when she saw the figure Moira had included. With a flash of insight, she knew how she was going to use a little of that money. With a bit of luck, it wasn't too late to make one more thing right.

Carmel sounded a bit worried when Jess phoned her later. 'Jess, love, is anything wrong?'

God, she'd been so wrapped up in herself, so focused on keeping secrets that she hadn't seen the hurt she'd caused. Jess deliberately injected an upbeat tone into her voice. 'Everything's great, Mam. Actually, I've a bit of good news.'

'I'm all ears.' Carmel sounded relieved.

'A while ago, Laura from Burlington House sent me the hotel's floor plan, and I noticed our dining area has French doors that open into the grounds. Anyway, I rang her today, and she's agreed to attach a small marquee, so we can invite extra guests.' Jess's flash of inspiration had come after she remembered Seán telling her that he and Catriona might use a marquee for their own wedding.

Carmel didn't reply immediately. 'Won't that be dreadfully expensive?'

'You have to trust me; I have the money.'

'Okay, love, but it's very last minute.'

Her mother was right, but Jess was determined to fix things. 'Just tell people the truth, Mam. Invite whatever friends and neighbours you like and tell them to wear what they want. Oh, and offer to split it with Úna. Just make sure we don't go above forty.'

'You'll have to make it up with Faye and Sarah first – they were very hurt.'

Jess was dreading it. 'I know. I'm going to phone them now and grovel.'

'I'll get busy my end.' Her mother sounded brisker. 'Well done for sorting this, Jess. I'm proud of you.'

After she hung up, Jess tried Sarah, but her phone was busy.

Faye sounded cool when she picked up. Jess spoke quickly. 'Hi, I wasn't sure if you'd answer.'

'I wasn't sure either,' said Faye.

Jess turned her chair to face the window. There were no sign of the swans on the canal this morning but it was warm and dry enough that a number of people were sitting at the picnic benches outside Butlers. She wondered if Kate was among them. Maybe she'd start having coffee with her colleagues in Accounts, the same ones she'd been out with on Simon's stag night.

'I don't blame you. I screwed up completely, but I never meant to hurt you or Sarah.'

'You've already said sorry, it's fine.'

Jess took a breath. 'It's not fine. Look, I called to say that Burlington House just agreed to attach a marquee to our reception room, so we can have forty more people. I'm an idiot for not thinking of it sooner, but I'm hoping everyone we couldn't invite will be able to come. Especially you and Sarah. And I'll move people around so you'll be in the main room. You can come by yourselves or bring partners. Please say yes.'

In the silence that followed, Jess dug her fingers into the palm of her other hand.

Finally, Faye spoke. 'Have you talked to Sarah?'

'I couldn't get her.'

'I'll talk to her.'

'Does that mean you'll come?'

'Yeah, hun, we both will.'

Jess breathed out. 'Thank you. I don't deserve you guys.'

'I think you were put in a difficult position. I know Simon's mam is probably okay, but she's not exactly chill.'

'She's definitely not chill.' Jess laughed.

'Look, I have to go, hun, my coffee break's over.'

'See you Saturday.'

'Thanks for making things right.' Faye hung up.

Jess cradled the phone in her hands. She'd have to mention the extra guests to Simon, but she'd make it clear she'd pay for them. Not that Simon would mind, it had never been about the money for him. Or his parents, to be fair. Now the only dark cloud over the wedding was that Kate wouldn't be there.

As she left the office that evening, she realised how strange her day had felt without Kate and Adam.

Emily was packing a gold lamé rucksack, as Jess walked through reception.

'Hi Jess.' Emily looked concerned. 'You're not sick again, are you?'

'No, all good.' Jess tried to hide her surprise.

'Oh.' Emily flushed. 'It's just you never go home this early.'

She meant on time. Emily was right, but she and Simon needed to talk. And the sooner, the better. 'Did you see Chelsea's Instagram live earlier today? The one Brandi was in too?'

Emily's face lit up. 'I saw it! Omigod, Jess, Chelsea is *sooo* sweet. Like, I was so over Brandi, after she outed Chelsea for ditching her last boyfriend at the altar.' She stopped. 'I just remembered, I heard the weirdest rumour today but I'm not sure whether to say anything to you in case it's like, not true and then ...'

'Emily, just say it.'

Emily took a breath. 'Somebody said you're getting married.'

'Who?'

'So it's not true.' The younger woman looked crushed.

'It is. I just didn't ...'

Emily gave a little squeal. 'When? Did you just get engaged? This is awesome, Jess, when are you getting married?'

'*Uh*, soon.' She couldn't tell her she was getting married on Saturday and have to fend off a million questions about why she'd said nothing.

All this time, she'd told herself it was because she didn't want Frank to think her focus was off, while she was still trying to prove herself. Now it seemed like such a lame excuse. Maybe she'd just never wear her wedding ring to work. 'I'd better shoot off.'

'Are you seeing him tonight?'

'Yep.' Jess nodded enthusiastically.

'You are so lucky.' Emily sighed. 'I just want to find a lovely guy and have loads of cute kids together.'

Jess's face hurt from holding her smile. 'See you tomorrow.'

Chapter 41

SIMON was at his laptop at the dining table when she got home, a glass of white wine on a coaster beside him. There was some fresh fish and stir-fry vegetables laid neatly out beside the stove in the kitchen. He glanced up as she came into the room.

'I thought you could cook, while I start checking flights in September.'

'Right.' Jess studied the ingredients. She couldn't believe Simon had bought stir-fry vegetables. 'What do you want with this?'

'What do you mean?'

'I think we're out of pasta, will I do potatoes?'

'I think there might be some brown rice in the press.'

Jess remembered she'd bought it in a moment of madness, after seeing a programme on vegan cooking. The TV chef had made brown rice look like the most exciting whole grain ever. Now she imagined gravel probably tasted the same.

'You don't like brown rice. Or stir-fry.'

'It's probably better for us.' He didn't look up from the screen. 'I got a call from the dress shop to say you can collect it tomorrow. They said they tried to contact you earlier?'

Jess frowned. She definitely hadn't missed a call. But why would she have? Kate had been managing all that and had been the wedding dress shop's first port of call. If they'd rung her, Kate must have given them Simon's number. It was petty, but it was also a sign of how angry she was.

Jess took a deep breath and found a pot for the rice. Right now she couldn't care less about her wedding dress, but it hurt to see how quickly Kate had distanced herself. She dreaded what she had to say next.

'Simon, I need to tell you something about Kate.'

Simon's shoulders stiffened. 'What about her?'

'She's not coming to the wedding.'

He turned to face her, his face white. 'Since when?'

'It happened over the weekend. It was Kate's decision.'

'Because of our kiss?'

Her heart was going to shatter. 'It's more complicated than that.'

'Does she know about your hen weekend?'

Jess didn't answer. Instead, she said, 'I need to ask you something.'

'What?'

Maybe she should sit down. Although depending on Simon's reaction, it might be easier for both of them if she just stayed here. Did she even have to ask how he felt about Kate? Wouldn't he have just told her the other night, after she'd confessed to a one-night stand and given him the ultimate get-out clause? But she needed to know for sure.

'Do you love Kate?'

Simon looked at her for a moment. 'Because I kissed her?'

Jess swallowed hard. 'Partly.'

'I said I was sorry.'

The tone of his voice challenged her to pursue it. He was right.

He'd kissed a friend; she'd slept with a stranger. She reminded herself why she was asking.

'It's just that you and she are so close, and you're so great with Luke and ...' Oh God, she couldn't just tell him that she was pretty sure Kate was in love with him.

'We are close.' Simon seemed to be trying to figure it out for himself. 'And you're right, it's a privilege to be a small part of Luke's life. So yes, I love Kate, she's an incredible person.' He paused and Jess's stomach clenched. 'But I love you differently, Jess. And I'm marrying you.'

Jess breathed out, the rush of blood her head making her dizzy. So, she'd been wrong: Simon's feelings for Kate were purely platonic.

Simon took off his glasses and rubbed a hand across his face. 'I never meant to come between you, maybe I should talk to her.'

Shit, she couldn't have that, not now that Kate knew about her and Adam. 'It'd be better if you didn't.'

He stared at her. 'What aren't you telling me? Have I hurt Kate?'

'It's not that.' He was about to hurt her more than he'd ever know.

'So, what do we do?'

'Nothing.' Jess shook her head. 'We give her some space.'

'But she's your best friend, Jess, I can't believe you're just ...'

'*I'm not just anything.*' Jess was fierce. '*Trust me.*'

There was a charged silence. Finally, Simon turned back to his laptop. 'It looks like I don't have a choice.'

Jess stared at the ingredients on the counter. Her life was a ball of twine that had started to unravel the night she'd met Adam. She and Simon might eventually move past this, but she wasn't sure if she and Kate ever would. Crucially, their delicate three-way friendship would be broken forever.

But what if Kate could find a way back into their lives? How would she feel, knowing that Kate wanted more than friendship from Simon? For the moment, at least, despite Simon's feelings for Kate and Luke, he guessed his relationship with Jess was too fragile to mess up. For the first time in ages, it seemed they were on exactly the same page.

Chapter 42

THE celebrity wedding was the lead item on the news the following day. Jess felt a small thrill as she watched coverage of TV crews descending on the small village of Linford, as national and international journalists interviewed the locals and did to-camera reports from outside the gates of the castle. It was exactly the kind of publicity they needed.

She and Simon had booked their flights and hotel for the last two weeks in September. After swearing for so long that he wanted a short winter break, he'd agreed that Rome in September would be perfect. Maybe he'd guessed that his parents wanted to make them a present of their honeymoon. Or he simply had more time now he hadn't made partner, Jess thought a bit guiltily. Either way, their wedding suddenly felt much more real.

Jess was on the bus to work when she got a text from Ian to check out the latest story on iNews. With a feeling of dread, she clicked onto the site.

Vegas Entertainers forced to pull out of Dinardia/Deneuve fairy-tale Irish Wedding

American dance troupe Joie de Vivre has been forced to pull out of the celebrity wedding of American reality TV star, Chelsea Deneuve to Vegas casino king Leo Dinardia, after eighteen of the

thirty-strong group were hospitalised when the coach in which they were travelling overturned on the highway. All of the injured are reported to be in a stable condition.

The troupe, which performs regularly at Leo's Vegas hotels, had been due to arrive in Ireland today.

Jess skipped past the details of the wedding, Chelsea's last abandoned wedding in Vegas, and her and Leo's recent problems, to read the last paragraph.

All of this has fuelled speculation that the celebrity couple could become the latest victims of the Linford Curse ...

She stopped reading and quickly checked the other news sites, knowing that the Linford Curse would be all across the media again.

She rang Ian as she took the stairs to her office. 'Any idea what Leo and Chelsea are planning to do?'

Ian sighed. 'Not a clue. Sure look, there have to be hundreds of professional dance troupes that could do the job, but the way Angel's going on, you'd swear the world was about to end. I know they'll have less than two days' notice, and Leo and Chelsea might have to compromise a bit, but I sometimes wonder whose side Angel is on.'

Jess shouldered open her office door. 'Listen, I might have another idea. Leave it with me.' She hung up and rang Moira who picked up on the final ring. 'Hi, Nana, is this a good time?'

'Jess, how are you? Always a good time to talk to one of my favourite granddaughters. But I get the feeling that you're not phoning for a chat.'

'I promise I'll phone you this evening.' Jess smiled. 'I need to talk to Finn if he's there.'

'He's bringing in my shopping.' Jess heard her call him. 'Here he is now, pet.'

'Jess?' Finn sounded worried. 'Is Zoe all right?'

'She's fine, this isn't about Zoe.' Maybe she'd been a bit hard on Finn. 'I have a proposition for you. For your whole troupe, actually. But you'd have to do an awful lot of work very quickly.'

'What's it for?'

'The Linford celebrity wedding. It's in two days' time, but we're really stuck.'

'Weren't they supposed to have a troupe of Vegas dancers at their wedding?'

'They've been in an accident. Look, can you wing it? Adapt some of your *um*, performances? We'd supply all the costumes. Think *Moulin Rouge* costumes with French music from the thirties and forties.'

There was a short silence on the phone. Then Finn gave a snort of laughter. 'Not exactly ground-breaking stuff. We've all done loads of improv, so it'll be no bother. What's the money like?'

Jess released a breath. 'That's the best part. But we're not there yet. I still have to convince the guy calling the shots.'

Chapter 43

TOM handed Jess a list when he collected her from Simon's flat on Saturday morning. 'Your mother told me to give you this, love, so you wouldn't forget anything.'

Jess glanced through it. 'Everything's packed, Dad, and Mam has the dress.'

Simon kissed her briefly and told her he wouldn't be late. As her dad drove them back to Dunlaoghaire to pick up Carmel and Zoe, Jess wondered if Simon had felt the need to reassure her after her recent confession. He was the most punctual person she knew.

'We got a grand day for it.' Tom Bradley flipped down his sun visor. 'Mam says your Auntie Anne has been lighting candles all week in the church for you.' He grinned over at her. 'They seemed to work.' They drove in silence for a few minutes. 'Are you all right, Jess? You're not worried, are you?'

'*Um*, I was thinking about Leo and Chelsea's wedding. I just hope everything goes well for Finn.'

'Don't you worry about Finn. No matter what I think about that weird dancing he does, I can see he's good. And sure, all those American celebrities love Irish performers.'

Jess nodded. After she'd got Finn to agree, her biggest job had been persuading Angel.

'Please tell me this is your Irish sense of humour. We'll have the whole world watching us.' He'd sniffed loudly. 'This isn't amateur hour.'

'They're not amateurs, Angel. And they're quick studies. You need a group that can go with the flow, not dancers who need weeks or months of rehearsals.'

Angel had given another disdainful sniff. 'I'm the one who'll be blamed if their flow doesn't cut it at this wedding.'

Jess had held her ground. Finn and his troupe were good, and she knew instinctively that Leo and Chelsea and their guests would love their energy and flamboyance.

'Angel, if you try to bring another troupe in from abroad at this stage, you'll be doing it blindly. I can personally vouch for Finn's troupe.'

He'd sighed dramatically. 'Joie de Vivre were booked for the three days of the wedding. I assume these performers can deliver the same commitment and stamina?'

'Of course. You'll see for yourself.'

Angel had sounded less sure. 'I'll hold you to that.'

With Angel on board, Finn had had a video call with Chelsea and Leo. After he'd watched a video of Joie de Vivre's final dress rehearsal, he'd assured the couple that once they agreed to trust the performers, he and his troupe would honour their broad vision. Jess wondered why she'd ever worried about the celebrity wedding: Ian had assured her that the management and staff at Linford had all the details under control. Everything was falling into place.

Tom seemed to read her mind as he pulled up outside the house. 'You've done your job, pet. Let your colleagues look after that big celebrity shindig. You've your own day to look forward to. So, are you ready for your mam? Because she's as excited and anxious as I've ever seen her.' He glanced towards the house but made no effort to get out of the car.

She was ready, wasn't she? Everything had been building to today, and she knew she should be more excited. But that would probably come later.

Jess took a deep breath and squeezed his hand. 'It's going to be an amazing day.'

By the time Jess, Carmel and Tom arrived at Burlington House shortly before midday, Zoe was already there, having insisted on driving down by herself.

Carmel had been a bit surprised that Zoe didn't want to come with them, but Jess guessed she was feeling a bit smothered.

Jess figured it was an actual miracle they'd got there so early, given that her dad kept to a steady seventy-five kilometres an hour, even on the biggest motorways. Standing there in the foyer with her family, she had a fleeting memory of childhood holidays. When she was little, they'd taken self-catering breaks in Ireland, but by the time she'd turned twelve, her parents had opted for annual package trips to France or Spain. Her mam had read, swam and sunbathed, while her dad pottered about, trying his best not to burn his pale skin.

The manager shook everyone's hand and handed Jess an old-fashioned key. 'A very warm welcome, Ms Bradley. This is for our honeymoon suite. I believe your fiancé will use the best man's room until after the ceremony. If there's anything you'd like, please just ask.'

Carmel turned to Zoe. 'Isn't it a pity all the same, that Finn won't be here.'

'Finn is making his name and fortune at the celebrity wedding.

Who knows, this time next year, he could be heading to Hollywood.' Zoe winked at Jess.

'Have the Donohues arrived yet?' Carmel peered around, as if they might be hiding behind the furniture.

The manager checked his screen. 'Not just yet. I see the mother of the groom is also booked into our beauty salon.'

'Would you look, I'd nearly forgotten.' Carmel tapped her watch. 'We all have hair and makeup appointments.'

The manager picked up the phone. 'I'll let them know you'll be there in about ten minutes. And one of my staff will bring Dr McCardle-Donohue down to join you when she arrives. After that, we can offer you all a light lunch.'

'That sounds perfect.' Carmel beamed at her daughters. 'So, hair, makeup and manicures. Your dad is even getting one of those wet shaves.'

Behind Carmel, Tom Bradley gave Jess a wry smile, and grabbed a suitcase.

At least she'd have some company, Jess thought, as she sat around trying to keep her hair and make-up from getting messed up. This was it: in a few hours, she'd be married. She just wished her best friend was here with her. No matter what Kate had said or done, she missed her desperately.

The manager cleared his throat. 'Would you like a hand with your luggage?'

'We'll manage, thanks.' Tom grabbed the big case Carmel had brought for the two of them.

Carmel put a hand to her mouth as she checked the bags. 'Your dress, love, I checked three times that it was packed. Where is it?'

Jess glanced around. 'It's okay, Mam, I think I left it in the car.'

Chapter 44

JESS hardly recognised herself in the full-length mirror of the honeymoon suite. The makeup artist and hair stylist had done an amazing job. She turned her head, admiring the ivory silk ribbon woven through her intricate hair style. She'd been unsure when Kate had suggested it, but it really worked. She blinked back tears, trying not to think about Kate. If she started crying now, her makeup would be ruined.

Earlier, she'd thought about asking Zoe to get ready with her, before quickly dismissing the idea. Even though she was pretty sure her sister wouldn't say anything to upset her hours before the wedding, it was enough knowing that she didn't like Simon.

She shuffled over to the bed in the complimentary robe and slippers and fantasised briefly about walking down the aisle in the comfy white bathrobe. Her mother would have heart failure, of course. As would Úna. Jess knew it wouldn't matter at all to her dad, who was more of a big picture kind of person. And Simon? Some guys would find the whole thing hilarious, but Simon wasn't one of them. He'd be mortified. She eyed the instrument of torture hanging on the outside of the wardrobe. There was nothing for it. A few hours from now, she'd be shackled into it, before heading to the church.

Jess pulled open the sash of her robe and contemplated her wedding lingerie. She'd been so tempted to wear the full tummy support knickers she'd bought, but after trying them on, she realised they'd make her sweat. Instead, she'd opted for what had definitely looked sexier on the shop hanger: a white lacy thong and matching strapless push-up bra.

'They'd take your eye out,' her mother had said a bit uncertainly, the first time Jess had tried the bra under the dress. It was her own fault, forgetting to buy the underwear first. But it was this or go braless. And given how revealing the bodice was, it was safer not to risk too many surprises.

For a brief moment she thought about Adam, before pushing him firmly from her mind and pulling the robe back around her.

Her phone rang and Jess reached across the bed for it. It would be Simon: he'd promised to phone when he arrived. Maybe all she needed was to hear his voice. But it was an unfamiliar number on her screen. She swiped her finger across the screen. 'Hello?'

'Jess? It's Emily, look, sorry to phone you on a Saturday, but have you seen Chelsea's TikTok?'

Jess felt a bit sick. She'd deliberately turned off all her notifications, so she wouldn't be distracted today. 'What's wrong?'

'Just hang up, Jess. It's live now.'

Jess hung up, her heart racing as she found Chelsea's TikTok.

'*My feelings towards Brandi will never change,*' Chelsea was saying, '*because what she doesn't understand is that I totally get her. Even when she was little, all she wanted was to be me. So today I'm making the decision to walk away from the drama.* Chelsea gave a small wave. *Just remember, everyone, live your truth.*'

The screen went blank, and Jess almost dropped her phone in

her efforts to phone Emily back. The younger woman picked up immediately. 'Jess, did you see it?'

'I saw the bit after she mentions her feelings for Brandi not changing. What did she say before that?'

'Nothing much.' Emily sounded tense. 'She said she knows her fans want the best for her, and that she appreciates us all.' She hesitated. 'It's not really the TikTok you make on your wedding day, is it?'

'Definitely not.' Jess was starting to get a bad feeling. 'I might check it out. Listen, I'd better go, there's somebody else trying to call me.'

'Good luck, Jess.'

Jess hung up and tried to compose herself for Simon's call. But the name flashing up on her phone was Ian's.

'Ian? Is everything all right?'

'Jess, I'm sorry to bother you and, believe me, if I had any choice in the matter I wouldn't. But Chelsea has locked herself into her suite and doesn't want to speak to anyone except you. I've tried to explain that you're in Dublin, but she's insisting. I thought we could set up a video call?'

'She won't talk to Leo? Or Angel?'

'Apparently Leo tried to talk to her earlier. He told me he's leaving her to "sort out her shit", his words, not mine. As for Angel, Chelsea fired him after they had the mother of all rows. Now, between you and me, I'm not surprised. We expect most brides are a bit hyper on their wedding day, but Angel was the one throwing shapes all over the bloody place. We're well shot of him.'

He was lucky he was gone, Jess thought grimly, or she'd find him and throw him off one of the turrets for trying to screw things up.

'Is there anyone else in the suite with her, Ian? Bridesmaids? Stylists?'

'Nobody. She's on her own, Jess.'

Jess checked the time. 'I'll talk to her, Ian. But you needn't bother with a call. I'm not in Dublin. Actually, I can probably be there in about half an hour.'

Ian barely hesitated. 'Thank you, Jess, I appreciate it.'

Jess hung up. She could do this, but she'd need some help. And there was only one person she could trust.

Chapter 45

'YOU KNOW this is completely nuts.' Zoe drove at speed in the direction of Linford Castle. Beside her, Jess looked at her watch for the millionth time. 'I know, what's your point?'

Zoe shot her a sly look. 'That it's probably the most exciting thing you've done in the past three years. Apart from your hen weekend. And after today, you're doomed to a lifetime of safety!'

Jess huffed out a breath, rooting out her phone to check if Chelsea had posted anything else, but there was nothing. Her earlier TikTok had started to trend, along with speculation about what it meant.

Chelsea Deneuve posts cryptic TikTok on her wedding day: will the California Girlfriends star be a no-show?

Jess scrolled down.

Speculation grows that Chelsea Deneuve has fled Linford Castle hours before she's due to marry fiancé, Leo Dinardia.

She refreshed her feed.

Is Chelsea's wedding day TikTok code for Leo and Brandi's secret affair?

'Shit.'

Zoe glanced over. 'What?'

Jess shook her head. 'It's starting to hit the fan.'

Zoe grinned. 'Hey, your wedding day will be memorable.'

'Right, because weddings are usually so forgettable.' Jess leaned back against the headrest and tried to stay calm. So far, the day had been fine. Úna had arrived not long after them, and they'd been treated to champagne and strawberries while having their hair and makeup done. If Jess managed the next hour cleverly, she'd make her own wedding, without anyone even knowing she'd been gone.

'Hey, you might get to see Finn.'

Zoe snorted. 'That's what you're thinking about?' When Jess said nothing, she added, 'Just ring her, Jess.'

Jess blinked hard. 'She doesn't want to …'

'It's your wedding day, what have you got to lose? Anyway, stop apologising. Tell her what she deserves to hear, not what you think she wants to hear.'

Heart thumping, Jess picked up her phone again. 'I'm just not sure what to say. I don't want to say something I'll regret, Zoe. And to be honest, I don't think I'm …' She jumped, nearly dropping her phone as it started to ring. 'Oh God, it's probably Ian … shit, it's Kate.' She swiped the screen. 'Hi.'

Kate's voice crackled on the other end. 'Jess? I'm really sorry. For everything. I'm on my way to the hotel. If I'm still welcome.' She paused. 'Because I'd totally get it if you didn't want me there.'

'You're coming?' Jess's eyes stung.

'It's your wedding, Jess, and you're my best friend. There's nothing between me and Simon, I promise you.'

There was a loud noise in the distance.

'Kate? Are you there?' Jess strained to hear.

'Yes, but I've pulled in illegally. I have to move; I'll see you in about an hour.'

'About that, Kate. Zoe and I are on our way to Linford. There's a slight problem with the celebrity wedding, and I want to see if I can help sort it. I have my dress with me, I'll be back on time.'

After a brief silence, Kate spoke firmly. 'Don't worry, if I don't see you back at the hotel before I go to the church, I'll let your mam and dad know. Just keep an eye on the time.'

She hung up.

Jess turned to Zoe. 'She's coming.'

'I got that.' Zoe gave her a critical look. 'You might want to fix your eye makeup. There's some tissues in the glove box.'

'Thanks.' Jess leaned forward and rooted through the overstuffed glove compartment. She was jerked back as Zoe braked hard.

'Sorry about that.' Zoe started to reverse. 'The road ahead is closed, but Google Maps is taking me another way.'

Jess glanced back over her shoulder. Her wedding dress, which Zoe had suggested bringing in case they had to go straight to the church, slid in its zipped cover across the back seat. On the floor were her wedding shoes: beautiful, nude Manola Blahniks, a gift from her Auntie Anne.

Zoe turned the car up the small road that led to the enormous front gates of the hotel.

As she rounded the final corner, Jess stared at the scene that greeted them. 'There's easily a hundred paparazzi here, Zoe.'

Zoe slowed down, as photographers snapped pictures around the car, before they seemed to realise they weren't wedding guests. 'They're just doing their job, Jess. Any idea how we're going to get in?'

Before Jess could reply, a man banged on her window, making her jump.

'What's your deal, girls? You heading to this? You working at it? Did you hear that Leo's been screwing Brandi Oliver?' The photographer put his phone against the window.

Jess pulled out her own phone, her thumbs flying over the keypad to find the article. There it was: **Leo Dinardia cheated on fiancée Chelsea Deneuve with her half-sister,** *California Girlfriends* **co-star Brandi Oliver.** '*Oh crap.*' She scanned the first few lines, barely able to take it in. This wasn't just gossip or speculation anymore: the article was on one of the more reputable sites. Chelsea must have found out just before it broke, no wonder she was upset.

She almost dropped her phone when the reporter banged again on her window.

'Is there going to be a wedding? Come on, girls, give us something. What's her dress like?'

Jess phoned Ian. 'It's Jess, I'm right outside the front gate. But I think we're going to need extra security to get us in.'

It took over a dozen security guards to get Zoe's car through the front gates, while keeping the press out. Jess noticed that Zoe seemed as shaken as she was when they finally drove around to the hotel's west side.

'Zoe, you okay?'

'I'm cool. I didn't think today would be this exciting.' She grinned and Jess gave a strained smile.

'I could probably do with a bit less excitement. Park here, we're right near the door.'

Ian met them inside, dressed in a billowy white shirt, red waistcoat and pale-brown knee-length britches.

'He looks like a giant, fat robin,' Zoe muttered.

'Jess, thank you for coming.' Ian was grim. 'We'd better not waste time; you'll have to change so you can blend in.' He turned and walked quickly down the corridor, leaving Jess and Zoe to catch up. They followed him to a small room with a dressing table and a rail of costumes. He turned to them. 'You should find something to fit you both there. Jess, have you seen the latest online?'

Jess nodded. 'A few minutes ago.'

'Leo's just tweeted this.' Ian took a mobile phone from a pocket in his britches.

'Here it is: **Chelsea and I really hurt to see these lies about us, but we hope the media can respect our privacy on our special day.** I'm just hoping Chelsea will agree to listen to him.'

'Right.' Jess scanned the bewildering array of costumes on the rail in front of her. 'Did you say he tried to phone her?'

Ian raised an eyebrow. 'He did, she's turned her phone off now too. Then he phoned Angel, but he's not answering either.'

Jess shook her head. 'When did Angel leave?'

'Mid-morning, after Chelsea fired him.'

Zoe dug her hands into her jeans. 'It's all a bit convenient. Like, if the press knew something, why did they leave it until now?'

'I've been thinking the same thing myself.' Ian scrubbed his face with both hands. 'So obviously they didn't know. But somebody did. And they wanted to cause maximum damage by releasing it today to the press.'

'So, Brandi, right?' Zoe said.

Jess sighed. 'Give us a minute, Ian, we'll get ready.'

As Jess and Zoe helped each other into the Cinderella-style ball gowns, Jess tried to imagine how Chelsea was feeling. It was bad enough to discover on the day of her wedding that her fiancé had cheated with her half-sister, but a hundred times more humiliating to have the world's media talking about it.

A celebrity wedding was huge, but a celebrity breakup hours beforehand, was even bigger. There was always a chance the rumours weren't true, but the damage was already done. Right now, she had to get Chelsea and Leo talking.

It was the only possibly way to save this wedding.

Chapter 46

THE LIFT stopped, and Jess and Ian stepped into the south tower's circular foyer. Ian swept a hand towards the door to the suite.

'It's up to you now, Jess. Good luck.'

After he left, Jess sent up a quick prayer.

She knocked loudly. *'Chelsea? It's Jess Bradley.'*

There was silence for a few minutes, and then Chelsea opened the door just enough to let Jess squeeze in, before locking it behind them.

'Oh my God, thank you for coming.'

To Jess's surprise, Chelsea threw her arms around her, giving her a long hug before stepping back.

'Sorry they made you wear a stupid costume.'

'It's fine.' Jess gave what she hoped was an encouraging smile. 'It's all part of the fun.'

Chelsea stared at her, and Jess looked properly at the younger woman for the first time. Her eyes were puffy and red in her pale, makeup-free face, and with her tiny frame hidden under sweatpants and a dark hoodie, the reality TV star looked more like a teenager. One who'd just realised that she was at the wrong party and wanted to go home.

Chelsea caught Jess's hand, and led her into the suite's sitting room, a lavishly furnished, curved space, its walls intricately papered and hung with romantic, period paintings. In one corner, a walnut coffee table was laid with champagne, still and sparkling water, fresh and candied fruit and a variety of artisan confectionary, all of which looked untouched.

'It's the fairy tale, right?' Chelsea gave a sad laugh. 'And I'm just Cinderella after the clock has struck midnight, My fairy godfather has gone, and the prince is screwing around with my half-sister.'

She sat down in one of the large Victorian armchairs, and drew up her legs, hugging them to her chest. Jess sat down in the other armchair, ignoring the corset digging into her ribs, and tried to think.

'Chelsea, I know this is an awful thing to happen on your wedding day, but it's a bit of a coincidence, isn't it? Say if someone is making it up to try to get to you?'

Chelsea swiped at a tear. 'Yeah, well, they've succeeded.'

Jess felt a surge of sympathy for her. 'I know, I'm sorry. But how do you know it's true, and not some awful lie to destroy your day?'

Chelsea shook her head. 'I really liked you when we first met, Jess. I mean, everyone here is lovely, and Ian has been awesome. But I kinda thought we had a real connection, you know?' Chelsea shrugged a bit shyly, and Jess felt mean for having dismissed the younger woman before.

'So that's why you said you'd only talk to me?'

'I have to trust someone, Jess. And I just get the vibe that you'll do the right thing here.'

None of this made any sense. 'Chelsea, maybe you should just talk to Leo, hear what he has to say.'

'We've talked.' Chelsea's mouth set in a hard line. 'He swears he's done nothing wrong.'

'And you don't believe him?'

'No.' Chelsea's eyes flashed. 'I always know when someone is lying to me. At least Brandi didn't bother denying it, she knows me better.'

'You mean she actually admitted it?' Jess felt sick.

Chelsea gave Jess a long look. 'She didn't have to.'

She was missing something, Jess thought. 'Chelsea, what happened with Angel? Is he a part of this?'

Chelsea blinked rapidly. 'He knew.'

'I'm sorry.' For a moment, Jess wasn't sure what else to say.

'It's a shit-storm, isn't it?'

Jess tried to sound positive. 'Is there anyone else you'd like to talk to? A friend, maybe?'

Chelsea shook her head. 'I don't want to talk to anyone.'

'Right.' This felt like a waste of time. '*Um*, so why exactly am I here?'

The younger woman swung her legs to the ground and leaned forward, her gaze fierce. '*I want you to get me out of here.*'

Crap, she hadn't seen that coming. Jess scrabbled for the right words. 'Chelsea, think about what you're saying. A couple of hundred people have flown in to see you and Leo get married.' Not to mention the orchestra, the singers, the Irish band, Malarky, and Finn and his troupe. This was to be Finn's big break. As for Linford, if this wedding fell apart, it would cement the Curse forever.

'I can't go through with it.' Chelsea's voice broke. 'I don't even know how long Leo and Brandi have been hooking up, but I don't care anymore. I tell my followers to live their truth. If I don't do the same thing, nobody will ever take me seriously again.' Chelsea's eyes filled with tears. 'And I'll hate myself.'

Jess felt sick. The other woman was right: nothing mattered. Not the fairy-tale location, or their two hundred guests. Not even the small matter of the multi-million-dollar TV deal with Bobbie Grayson. If Leo and Brandi had nothing to hide, they'd be here right now, determined to prove it. But there was still the problem of logistics.

'Chelsea, nobody is going to force you to do anything you don't want. But there's a TV crew filming downstairs, and probably waiting to get footage of you getting ready.

And then there's the paparazzi outside the gates. If you try to leave, you'll be hounded.' It was a horrible situation: Linford Castle was a gilded cage, and Chelsea was trapped.

'Say if I use one of the tunnels?'

Jess stared at her. Had she any idea what she was asking? Things would be bad enough when the wedding didn't happen, but if she helped Chelsea escape, she could probably say goodbye to her career. She wished she'd never answered Ian's phone call.

'Listen, I know it's a big ask,' Chelsea said, 'but I'm begging you. I can't be here; I just want to get away. Only I've no idea where any of the tunnels are, or if only some of them are safe or –'

Jess's phone rang, and she jumped. 'Hang on.' She swiped to answer. 'Hi, Ian.' She listened for a few minutes, her heart hammering, as she tried to focus on what he was saying. 'She's not ready yet. I'll do my best.'

Jess hung up and looked at Chelsea. Her face seemed to have got even paler, and there were dark circles under her eyes. She was the most miserable-looking bride she'd ever seen. Jess got to her feet.

'Where are you going?' Chelsea jumped up after her.

'If there's a tunnel in here, it'll be in the bedroom.' What she was about to do was completely insane, but deep-down Jess knew she couldn't worry about that now.

'Oh my God, you're like my real Fairy Godmother!' Chelsea ran ahead of her into the bedroom. 'I knew you'd know about the tunnels when I saw those virtual tours online.'

Jess stopped at the door. 'Is that why you asked to see me?'

Chelsea looked hurt. 'Of course not. Look, one of the staff, Holly, told me there are probably tunnels in all the towers, but she's just a kid. You're the only person I can trust.'

Jess sighed and walked over to the fireplace; its grate filled with a huge arrangement of fresh flowers, and started to sneeze. 'Sorry, I'm a bit allergic.' She looked around. 'I've just remembered, the fire was in this room.'

Chelsea looked at her blankly. 'Okay?'

'It started in the tunnel, where the electrics are.' Jess shivered.

There was a draught coming from somewhere, but it didn't seem to be coming directly from the chimney, because not a single flower petal was moving.

'I know some of the old panelling around the chimney was damaged.' Jess peered closely at the wood surrounding the mantelpiece. To the right, was a large, slightly newer-looking panel. If she was correct, this was one of tunnels that had been used for the virtual tour, which meant it should be safe. Taking a deep breath, Jess pushed, and as the panel shifted to one side, a blast of icy air rushed into the room. In silence, the two women stared into the dark space.

Jess found her voice. 'I guess they didn't lock it again.' She turned to Chelsea. 'Please don't do this. I'll go down and tell them that you don't want to go through with it. But if you go ahead, I can't guarantee that you'll be safe.'

Chelsea grabbed hold of Jess's hands. 'I'll be okay, I promise. But if Leo finds out that you've helped me, he'll sue. So, I need you to do one more thing.'

Chapter 47

JESS didn't have time to phone Ian, before there was a loud banging on the door to the suite. Checking that Chelsea had locked the bedroom door from the inside, she hurried over and peeked through the spyhole. Ian and Leo stood in the hallway.

'*Shit.*' She wiped her hands on her dress.

'Jess, can you open the door please?' Ian's voice was strained.

Jess swallowed hard. 'Hang on.' Fumbling with the key, she unlocked it, jumping back when Leo practically knocked her over as he burst past her into the room.

'Where is she? Chelsea?' He marched into the sitting room and Jess heard him curse again, before he started to rattle the bedroom door. 'Fuck sake, now she's locked herself into the bedroom.'

'How did it go, Jess?' Ian whispered. Before Jess had a chance to reply, there was another shouted expletive from Leo, before he reappeared in the little hallway.

'Why has she locked herself in the bedroom?'

Jess flashed Ian a quick look. 'Chelsea said she needed some time to herself. In fact, I was just about to call Ian when you knocked on the door.'

Leo dropped his voice. 'So, she's come to her senses? We can actually get on with this? Because Bobbi Grayson is wrecking my head about her schedule, and our guests are starting to get edgy. All I can say is thank fuck they all agreed to hand over their phones when they got here.'

'Your guests are fine, Leo.' Ian sounded firm. 'There's plenty of entertainment for them, and we're passing around finger food now, to help soak up some of the alcohol.

As for Ms Grayson, she should know that even the finest weddings are never one hundred percent on track.'

Jess tried not to gag as vomit rose to the back of her throat. How would they react when they realised that this particular wedding had been completely derailed? But she'd promised Chelsea she would help. Which meant playing for time.

'Why don't you just give her a few minutes, Leo? Go and relax in the sitting room, get a glass of champagne. I'm sure you'd appreciate a bit of downtime, if you've been mingling with your guests all morning.'

Leo shot her a filthy look, but he turned on his heel and stalked past them.

Ian turned to Jess. 'What happened, Jess? Why did Chelsea want to talk to you?'

This was it, Jess thought. She could destroy her career, or she could fudge the truth. Chelsea had given her a way out, there was no reason why she shouldn't take it. All she had to tell Ian was what she'd just told Leo. When they eventually discovered that Chelsea was gone, they'd all assume that she'd discovered the tunnel by herself. It was the easier option, she knew. But she'd told enough lies this past month, to last a lifetime.

'I found the tunnel in the bedroom beside the fireplace.'

For a split second, Ian looked confused, but his expression

quickly cleared to one of horror. 'Please tell me you didn't ...'

'It wasn't locked, Ian. After the fire, I'm guessing you didn't get a chance to lock it again.'

He turned white. 'We meant to get around to it. There was so much to do, we didn't get time.' His hands closed around Jess's arms. 'What have you done?'

'*She asked me, Ian, she begged me,*' Jess whispered furiously.

'Ian?'

Ian jumped as Leo shouted at him from inside the suite.

'Coming.' He looked at Jess. 'I'll have to write a full report, Jess, you know that?' His voice cracked.

'This will destroy Linford; it'll destroy the group. Leo will probably sue us for everything we've got.' He released her arms so quickly she almost lost her balance. His mouth set in a thin line, he walked into the sitting room. 'I think we've waited long enough, Leo. I'm going to get somebody up here to take off the lock on the bedroom door.'

'*There's a fucking tunnel?*' Leo stared in disbelief at the castle's old escape route, before whirling to glare at Jess. 'Did you tell her? Did you show her this?'

Before Jess had a chance to answer, Ian spoke. 'Leo, calm down, Jess isn't to blame. She told you what happened. Chelsea obviously discovered the tunnel herself. It's not exactly a secret. Anyone who's viewed our website, or seen the virtual tours of the castle, knows these tunnels exist.'

'And how do you know it's even safe?' Leo's voice rose.

'It's safe. After the fire in this tower, the electrics had to be repaired, and the whole tunnel was checked for wiring. Our electricians were able to walk right through to the other exit.'

Thank God, Jess thought, feeling a bit faint. Hopefully Chelsea was already out the other side.

'Could she still be in there?' Leo said.

'It all depends how long ago she left, but it's unlikely. It's not a very long tunnel.' Ian gave Jess a hard look. 'I'll radio for security now. But if she's already through, she'll be in Linford Wood, which is small, or she'll have got to the village. I can get security out there. Chelsea will be easy to spot.'

'Don't bet on it,' Leo muttered. 'She can blend in when she wants to. She's done it before.'

Ian produced a walkie-talkie from his pocket. 'What was she wearing, Jess?' There were small beads of sweat on his forehead and upper lip, Jess noticed, and for a moment, she wondered whether she'd made the right decision.

'The last time I saw her, she was in a sweatpants and hoodie.' Jess glanced at Leo. 'But I didn't see her after that, so she could have changed.'

Ian walked back out into the sitting room, where Jess could hear him talking in a low, urgent voice. Her phone vibrated and she took it out.

There was a message from Zoe. **have u talked her round, just watch the time.**

Say nothing, she's done a runner, Jess messaged back.

A moment later Zoe replied, **shit, not surprised tho, wonder does Brandi know.**

Jess put her phone away and watched Leo pace up and down the room, before peering briefly into the tunnel again.

'Fuck it, I hope you don't expect me to go in there. I'm claustrophobic.'

'There's no need,' Jess reassured him, secretly impressed that Chelsea had managed it. Then again, Chelsea had been desperate. And desperation made people do crazy things. Except that in the end, Chelsea had seemed quite clear-headed.

She turned as two security guards came into the bedroom with Ian, standing back as they headed into the tunnel with torches and walkie-talkies.

Ian turned to Leo. 'Our manager has ordered a discreet search party. If Chelsea is still in the woods or the village, we'll find her.'

'Yeah? Well, it won't make any difference now, will it? All she wanted was to marry in an Irish castle.' He gave a harsh laugh. 'And here we are, in her fucking cursed Irish castle. And she doesn't want to marry me anymore.'

And whose fault was that Jess thought, anger surging through her. She wished she could message Chelsea to check she was all right, but she couldn't risk asking Leo for her number. He was already suspicious enough.

Turning away, Jess pulled up Chelsea's Instagram and TikTok accounts, but there was nothing new. Frustrated, she opened Twitter, tagged Chelsea and Leo, and then typed **The Charleston Group wishes our special couple a wonderful wedding day at the stunning Linford Castle, here in the west of Ireland.** She included a few hashtags, then posted the tweet, knowing it was as much as she could risk. Within moments, Chelsea liked it.

'Leo, I need to show you something.' She walked over to where he sat in the turret's curved window seat, staring out at the gardens and showed him the tweet. 'Chelsea liked it, she's okay.'

'She's also not coming back,' he snapped.

'No.' Jess gave him a steady look. 'It doesn't look like it.'

'This is supposed to be a five-star hotel,' Leo's voice rose, and he jumped up, walking over to Ian and stabbing him in the chest with his finger. 'You're gonna hear from my lawyers, because somebody's gonna pay for this mess. You've made me a fucking laughing-stock on my wedding day.'

Jess walked back across the room, her stomach churning, and her eye fell on Chelsea's wedding dress, carefully laid out on the bed. How had she not spotted it before? She ran her hand lightly across the material. It was a fairy-tale dress: a silk, beaded bodice and huge skirt, the layers of silk and white tulle shot through with silver. A full-length, white-and-silver veil lay beside it.

It would have been a beautiful wedding. The dress alone must have cost thousands, and now, everything was ruined. Unless ... her stomach squeezed as a thought occurred.

'Ian, could I have a quick word? In private?'

For a moment, Ian looked like he was about to say no, but then he nodded tiredly. 'Outside. Excuse us, Leo.'

Jess followed him out to the suite's little hallway. Ian folded his arms. 'Talk fast, Jess.'

'Everyone's expecting a celebrity wedding here today, Ian. I might have an idea, a crazy one. But we'll have to convince Leo.'

Chapter 48

'*HE'S proposing to Brandi?*' Zoe almost dropped her glass of champagne when Jess found her in the great hall. 'Oh hey, is that one of the Kardashians over there? Look.'

'I don't have time. And keep your voice down.' Jess took Zoe's glass and put it on a passing waiter's tray. 'We've got to go, it's after three.'

'Crap, okay, lead the way.'

Jess grabbed Zoe's hand and they wove their way through the guests, heading for the entrance they'd come in earlier, Jess's mind racing over what she'd done.

'I'm going to be straight with you, Leo,' she'd said, after she'd run her proposal by Ian. Leo's eyes had narrowed.

'That'd be a start.'

Jess had taken a deep breath. 'We both need a wedding here today. Linford Castle needs it, but so do you. You don't want to let your guests down, and more importantly you've negotiated a huge deal with Bobbie Grayson, so if there's no wedding she could sue you.' She'd paused, her heart hammering. 'That rumour about you and Brandi: is it true?'

Leo had stared at her for a long moment, but Jess hadn't flinched.

Finally, he said, 'what if it was?'

Jess had tried not to look relieved. 'Then I may have a proposition.'

After Leo had left to find Brandi, Jess had turned to Ian. 'I'm sorry for what I did, Ian, I take full responsibility for it. But thanks for covering for me in front of Leo.'

Ian had taken a large clean handkerchief from his pocket and wiped his forehead. 'To be fair, Jess, it wasn't all your fault. Leo's a dick, and if Chelsea were my daughter, I'd do everything in my power to stop her marrying him.'

Jess had simply nodded.

'Listen, Ian, this'll sound bonkers, but I'm actually getting married shortly. The church is half an hour away and I have to get going.'

Ian's smile had been genuine. 'I knew today would be full of surprises, but I couldn't have guessed any of this. Well done on your quick thinking – we'll cross our fingers now for a miracle. And Jess, I hope your fellah's a good one?'

Jess hadn't hesitated. 'He is.'

'Finally!' Jess recognised the corridor where they'd changed earlier. Her phone buzzed and she stopped to check it, praying it wasn't a frantic message from her mother. But it was from Ian.

Brandi said yes!

'There is a God!'

Zoe shot her a look. 'What?'

'She said yes!' Jess grinned. 'Now, let's get out of here.'

'You still have to change.'

Jess hitched up her long skirt. 'We're going to have to run.'

'Maybe I should phone Simon, tell him I'm running late.' Jess slowed to catch her breath as she and Zoe reached the castle's west entrance.

Zoe didn't bother to hide her impatience. 'You really think he'll have his phone on in the church?'

'Shit, you're right. It'll be fine, brides are allowed to be a bit late.'

'I'll get your dress. Stay here.' Zoe ran out to the car and reappeared a few moments later with the wedding dress.

'What about you?' Jess let Zoe undo the zip before stepping out of the heavy costume.

'No time.' Zoe shook out the wedding dress and slipped it over her sister's head.

Jess suppressed an hysterical giggle at the thought of Zoe in costume for the day, then tried to calm her breathing, as Zoe buttoned up the dress, before finally stepping into her shoes. When she was ready, she gave Zoe a quick hug. 'In case I forget to say it later, you're the world's best sister.'

'I know, come on!'

With some effort, Zoe slid in behind the wheel, bundled the long skirts of her dress into her lap and threw her shoes into the back. Jess eyed the passenger seat: the whole car seemed to have shrunk.

'I'll have to push the seat back.' As Jess reached down for the lever, she heard a shout.

'*There she is! Chelsea? Turn this way!*'

'*Chelsea, over here! Are you leaving because Leo cheated?*'

'*Chelsea, where are you going? Give us your side of the story?*'

Jess hesitated. Should she stop and let them know she wasn't Chelsea? Only how would she explain why she was at Linford on the day of her own wedding? No, this was the less terrible option.

She threw herself into the car, yanked in her dress and pulled the door shut. The press would find out soon enough that there had been a celebrity wedding. Just not the one they'd expected. '*Drive, Zoe.*'

'Is there another way out?' Zoe reversed sharply.

'Around the back.'

Zoe drove out of the car park and found the short avenue that lead to the gates at the rear of the castle.

'*There she is!*'

'Shit, the paparazzi are everywhere.' Jess slid down in the seat. 'I don't even look like her.'

Zoe glanced over. 'You do, a bit, from a distance. Anyway, who else would they think it is, in a wedding dress?'

Jess tried to take a steady breath, which was almost impossible given how restricting the bodice was in this position. 'There's motion sensors near the gate. Just keep driving.'

Zoe accelerated, as Jess ducked lower in the seat, and tucked her head into her arms. Around them, reporters shouted and cameras flashed, non-stop.

'Okay, we've passed them,' Zoe said a few minutes later. 'That was wild.' She glanced over her shoulder. 'Shit, Jess, stay low. We're being followed.'

'What?' Jess tried to peer around the back of her seat, without being seen.

'At least two cars, and a couple of motorbikes.' Zoe cursed. 'Somehow, I don't think they believed Leo's tweet.' A deafening sound directly above their heads, made Jess jump.

'Don't look up.' Zoe checked her mirrors. 'I think that's the World News helicopter.'

'I'm in a car chase on my wedding day,' Jess wailed. 'And I think I've got makeup all over my dress.'

'Maybe we should just stop? Once they see that you're not Chelsea, they'll –'

'Don't stop, Zoe, I don't have time. And I don't want to talk to the press looking like this. Frank Charleston would kill me. After he fires me.'

'Your call. Hang on.'

Jess sat up a bit in her seat. She was nearly there; it would be fine. She could get another job, too. Maybe it wouldn't be so bad. 'I can never tell Simon about this.'

Zoe checked her rear-view mirror and drove faster. 'Why not?'

'He wouldn't understand.'

Zoe glanced over. 'You sure this is the wedding you want to go to? Just say the word and I'll turn around and go back to Linford.' When Jess didn't reply, she flicked her another look. 'Jess?'

'Listen, I know this sounds a bit out there, but what if Chelsea leaked that story about Leo and Brandi?'

Zoe braked as they approached a corner and yanked the car down a gear. Jess slid towards the door, and wondered vaguely if the dress would work like an airbag if they crashed. Probably not.

'Shit, the road's closed.'

Jess gripped the underside of the seat. If they turned back now, they'd run straight into the paparazzi. But they had no choice. 'Turn around, Zoe.'

Zoe pursed her lips, executed the fastest three-point turn Jess had ever seen, and accelerated back up the way they'd come. As they approached the top of the road, one of the cars that had been behind them skidded to a halt, almost blocking their exit.

'*Put your head down,*' Zoe yelled.

This was it: she was going to die on her wedding day. Jess ducked, bracing herself for the worst. Instead of slowing, Zoe floored the accelerator and swerved out onto the road. There was a squeal of brakes and Jess's whole body tensed, but as Zoe kept driving, she struggled back up and looked around. 'Where's the other car?'

Zoe looked grim. 'In the ditch. He had to swerve at the last second, or I'd have run straight into him. With a bit of luck, he'll be ages getting out. Like, have you seen the ditches around here?'

Jess stared at her.

'Just forget about it,' Zoe said. 'Forget about the press, forget about Chelsea and Leo. They'll be fine. Crazy, rich people usually are. Anyway, if you want my opinion, Leo got what he deserved.' She snorted. 'Even Brandi. That girl is poison. I mean, imagine doing that to your sister?'

'Imagine doing it to your fiancée.' Jess spoke quietly, and if Zoe heard, she said nothing. The car started to shudder, and Zoe swore loudly. Jess tried to formulate her thoughts, which was proving difficult during a car chase. In fact, the whole day was turning out radically different than she'd imagined.

'I think Chelsea leaked that story to take control of the situation,' Jess said.

Zoe shook her head. 'I guess we're still talking about this. Okay, let's pretend Chelsea leaked the story. How is that taking control?'

'She told me she'd found out about Leo and Brandi.' Jess spoke slowly. 'Angel knew, and he'd been keeping it from her.'

'The wedding planner? That's so fucked up.'

Jess glanced in her side mirror. The three motor cyclists they'd seen earlier, were behind them again. 'Yeah, but this way, Chelsea gets the public on her side.'

The car gave another shudder. Jess flashed Zoe a panicked look. 'Have we dropped speed?'

'Maybe, it's been doing this recently.' Zoe peered at the dashboard.

'What? Why didn't you bring it to a mechanic?'

'I meant to say it to Dad.'

Before Jess could reply, the car jerked to a stop, throwing the two of them forward in their seats. Jess struggled out, stepping straight into a ditch. 'Crap, my Manola Blahniks. C'mon, Zoe, I think we're pretty close to the church.' She slipped out of her shoes, holding them in one hand while holding the train of her dress, and started to run.

'I can see the sign for the church,' she yelled back over her shoulder.

'I'm coming.' Zoe kicked off her own shoes. Jess reached the junction. 'There it is.'

At that moment, the paparazzi rounded the corner, sending up dust as they skidded to a halt beside Jess. She turned, gasping. 'Please, leave me alone. I'm late for my wedding.'

'Fuck it, you're not Chelsea.'

'Who the hell are you?'

'We've been taken for a ride. Did Chelsea and Leo pay you to be a decoy?' Camera flashes blinded her momentarily as they snapped photo after photo.

'Stop!' Jess put her hands up to the cameras. 'I'm not trying to mess with you. My name is Jess Bradley and I really am getting married today.'

'Why were you at Linford earlier?'

'Is it true that Leo and Brandi have been having an affair?'

'Are you a friend of the couple?'

'Who are you marrying?'

Jess looked past the photographers, to the tiny church. Her father and Simon's mother both stood like statues in the doorway. In front of them, a horrified expression on his face, was Simon.

Jess pointed shakily. 'Him.'

Chapter 49

JESS slowly became aware that Simon hadn't moved. He seemed frozen to the spot. Still shaking, she managed to step back into her shoes, dimly aware of the photographers leaving.

'Jess?'

She turned and saw the question in her sister's eyes. 'I need a minute, Zoe.'

'Solid.' Zoe brushed herself down. 'I'll wait at the back of the church for you.' Squaring her shoulders, she walked up to the entrance and after a brief exchange with their dad, stepped inside.

With as much dignity as she could manage, Jess walked up to the others. Tom reached towards her and gave her hand a reassuring squeeze. 'We'll leave you to get sorted. I'll wait at the back of the church, and I'll come to get you when Simon comes in.' He held her hand a bit longer. 'Take your time, pet.'

Jess felt a rush of emotion. 'Thanks, Dad.'

Tom turned and spoke gently to Úna. 'Why don't I walk you back to your seat, Úna? I'm sure Edward is wondering what's happening.'

Jess held her breath, but Úna just nodded.

Once she and Simon were alone, Jess tried to shake out her dress, as she searched for the right words. 'I know I'm late,' she said finally, 'and I'm a bit of a mess. I just need five minutes and …'

'Please don't.' Simon met her eyes and Jess almost crumpled at the hurt she saw. 'David and I went to wait in the sacristy. I couldn't bear to stand there, wondering if you were going to show up.'

'Simon, I'm so sorry, I didn't mean to worry you…'

'David had his phone, so we saw the chase. I didn't know it was you until I recognised Zoe's car.' He pushed his hand through his hair. 'This is our wedding day, Jess.'

'Simon.' Jess closed her eyes briefly. 'I know, I had to go to Linford.' There was no point trying to explain everything now. 'It's complicated.'

'I'm not interested, to be honest.' Simon's voice was so low Jess had to strain to hear him.

Jess swallowed. 'For what's it's worth, I didn't think I'd be delayed like that.'

'Now's not the time.' He pinched the bridge of his nose. 'We shouldn't keep our guests waiting any longer. So, are you ready or do you need a minute?'

Jess glanced down at her dress. The bodice seemed fine, except for the faintest trace of makeup, and she could probably wipe the worst of the dirt off the bottom of the skirt. There wasn't much she could do about her shoes. But she doubted Simon had noticed any of that: it wasn't what he meant. She looked at him now: handsome in his tuxedo, his freshly washed hair flopping across his forehead. Right inside the door, her dad was waiting to walk her up the aisle. It was time.

'I'll see you in there.' Shoulders slightly hunched, Simon turned to walk back towards the church.

'*Stop.*'

Simon turned to face her. 'What is it, Jess?'

Her mouth had dried and when she spoke, her voice was little more than a whisper. 'I'm so very sorry, Simon. I don't think I can marry you.'

Chapter 50

SIMON didn't speak for so long, Jess wondered if he'd heard her properly. Finally, he nodded. 'Are you sure?'

Jess could feel a pulse beating hard at her throat. He sounded ... resigned. Definitely not shocked. 'I know my timing is terrible.' She forced herself to go on. 'But I think it'd be a mistake.'

'I agree.'

She swallowed hard. Not resignation, then. More relief.

'Things haven't been right for a while, have they, Jess?'

How had it come down to this? But part of her already knew the answer. 'I suppose not.'

'Maybe it's my fault….'

'It's definitely not your fault, Simon.'

He sighed. 'It's enough that we've both had doubts.'

Jess's insides squeezed. How long had Simon had doubts? Deep down, she guessed they'd started long before her hen weekend. 'Why do you think it's your fault?'

Simon didn't flinch. 'I was wrong to propose to you. To be honest, I think I proposed for the wrong reasons.' He ran a hand back through his hair. 'My life has been on this upward trajectory, and I really thought we were doing the right thing. I mean, we were living together, and…' he stopped, apparently lost for words.

'And marriage felt like the next step, I know.' Jess chose her next words carefully. 'I sort of felt things started going wrong for us after we got engaged.'

Simon winced. 'I couldn't even commit to a honeymoon, could I? I made dozens of excuses, mainly to myself.' He released a slow breath. 'We're not really in love, are we?'

Jess shook her head. 'No.'

She'd known for a while, she realised. It didn't matter how they'd got together, or how good Simon had been to her and her family. The fact was, they'd stayed together for all the wrong reasons.

He glanced back towards the church door and straightened his tie. 'I'd better make an announcement.'

'Right.'

It was surreal. Less than an hour ago, all that had mattered was making it to her own wedding on time. Now, she felt sick at the thought of their guests waiting inside. But she couldn't let Simon do this by himself.

'We'll make the announcement together.'

Simon gave her a grateful look. 'What about the meal? Will we just go ahead with it? It's paid for, and people have come a long way.'

Jess thought of Chelsea and experienced a brief flash of jealousy, then reminded herself that Simon had done nothing wrong. He was one of the best people she knew, and deep down she knew the right thing was to get through the day together.

'Good idea.'

Simon looked relieved. 'I nearly forgot.' He indicated towards the church. 'Kate is here.'

'So, she made it.'

'Yes.' A slight colour spread from his neck. 'She made it.'

She gave him a long look. It was stone mad how she and Kate had known Simon for the last three years, and none of them had seen what was happening.

'Are you ready?' He shook out his hands, and Jess realised he was as nervous as she was.

'Not really, to be honest.'

Simon opened his arms, and for the last time she stepped into his embrace, wrapping her own arms around his back, as she tucked her head under his chin. Eventually, he pulled away and held out his hand to her. She took it, and together they walked into the church.

As Simon gave her hand one last, reassuring squeeze, Jess walked off the altar, slipping into the sacristy at the other side. Closing the old wooden door behind her, she allowed herself a few moments to lean against it, and wish the day was already over.

Kate and David had known, she thought. She'd seen it on their faces the moment she and Simon had entered the church. Her dad had known too. Jess had a feeling he'd known from the moment she and Zoe had arrived. And she suspected everyone else had quickly put two and two together, when she and Simon had walked up the aisle together.

But Simon's short speech on the altar had been perfect. He'd left their guests in no doubt that he and Jess cared for each other but were no longer in love. She'd even managed a smile when he'd said it would mean a lot to them both, if everyone came to the meal. She couldn't help but wonder what his wedding speech would have been like. Now she'd never know.

When Simon had finished and they'd thanked everyone for coming, every person in the church had stood and applauded. Jess had tried to focus on that, rather than on the looks of sympathy on the faces of her family and friends. She hadn't dared to look in Úna and Edward's direction.

Now she started to shiver. Unlike the church, which had been heated, the sacristy was a cold, slightly damp little room. The door started to open behind her.

'Jess, it's me.'

She stepped back and Zoe slipped in and handed Jess a fuchsia pink wrap. 'Hey, are you all right?' She draped the wrap around Jess's bare shoulders. 'It's Nana's, she said you'd need it. I told you we should have stayed at Linford.' When Jess didn't answer, Zoe's voice softened. 'Are you sure about this? You both want to call things off?'

Jess managed a nod, shivering almost uncontrollably, as the enormity of what had happened began to sink in. Zoe put her arm around her.

'It's not too late. It doesn't matter what other people think. I know I'm not Simon's biggest fan, but if you really love him …'

'I don't.' Jess met her eyes. 'I mean, in a way I do, but not enough to spend the whole of my life with him. And he deserves better than me, Zoe. He deserves someone who'd never, ever cheat on him, who wants to have children with him and generally loves him to bits.'

'So, you did the right thing.'

'You know, Simon felt the same way? Why didn't I see that?' Jess sat down on a hard plastic chair. 'God, I thought we had our lives sorted. I actually felt sorry for you and Finn.'

Zoe perched on the edge of the formica table. 'I know.'

Jess looked up at her. 'Sorry for being a smug bitch.'

'You're forgiven. Hey, you did Finn and me a massive favour by getting him that gig today.' She paused. 'Do you think anyone will notice that it's a different bride?' She grinned and Jess giggled weakly, wondering if she'd ever be able to stand again, now her limbs had turned to lead.

'How are Mam and Dad?'

'They'll be fine. As far as I can tell, I don't think they're as shocked as Úna and Edward. The meal should be fun.'

Jess pulled the wrap a bit tighter around her. 'We just didn't want to waste it.'

Zoe shrugged. 'Yeah, screw that. How do you feel?'

'A bit numb right now, it all feels a bit unreal. But I'm sad for Mam and Dad.'

'Are you sad for yourself?'

Jess looked at her. 'Mainly, I just feel guilty. Look at all the trouble everyone's gone to, Zoe. I'm letting so many people down.'

'You won't be the first couple that called things off at the altar,' Zoe said.

'Seriously, stop overthinking it, it'll wreck your head. Simon feels the same way, right?'

'Yeah, I know it doesn't make much sense, but I think that's one of the reasons I feel guilty. I'm just so relieved.'

Chapter 51

'JESS, Kate is here to see you.'

Carmel came into the sitting room that Sunday morning and regarded her daughter anxiously. For the last few hours, Jess had sat looking out through the French doors into the garden. In spite of everything, the previous day hadn't been as awful as she'd feared. Simon had come back to the sacristy to check on her, and Zoe had surprised Jess by giving him a hug before leaving them alone.

Simon had sat down and pulled off his tie. 'You okay?'

Jess had nodded. 'What about you? What happened out there after I left?'

He'd given a small smile. 'Nothing much. I had a quick chat with the folks. I'm glad we're going ahead with the meal. People need to talk, and they need to know we're all right.'

'When did you get so wise?' she'd joked, before adding, 'I'm kind of dreading this.'

He'd looked thoughtful. 'I'll make sure my mother doesn't say anything to upset you. This was our decision.'

It had been the first time ever that Simon had admitted he needed to stand up to his mother. Without hurting his parents, he'd been as good as his word. And even though she'd spent the day in a daze, Jess knew that everyone had been kind.

They'd been halfway through the meal when the news about Leo and Brandi's wedding had broken, with wild speculation about Chelsea. Jess skimmed the headlines with growing dread: **California Girlfriend bride Chelsea Deneuve disappears from 400-year-old Irish castle under the noses of the world's press,** and **Chelsea uses decoy runaway bride to flee cheating groom.**

The latter was accompanied by photos of Jess struggling to get into Zoe's twelve-year-old car, and arriving at the church in Ballygobbin, barefoot and caked in mud.

The headlines and photos were nothing compared with what had followed, as people took to social media.

From what Jess could see, most divided into two camps: *Team Brandi* or *Team Chelsea*, although a sizeable minority, mainly men, were definitely *Team Leo*. *Celebrity Wedding* and *Linford Curse* had still been trending, by the time Jess had crawled into bed in her parents' house later that night.

Now she pulled her gaze away from the garden and looked up at her mother. 'Kate's here now? In the hall?'

'I'll tell her you're not up to seeing anyone, will I?'

'No, Mam, it's fine.'

Her mother seemed to have aged overnight.

Jess got up and crossed the room, drawing her into a hug. 'I'm so sorry for everything,' she whispered. 'What I've put you and Dad through.'

'Ah, love.' Carmel's voice cracked. 'We just want you to be happy.' She pulled back, her eyes watery as she searched Jess's face. 'We thought you were, you and Simon.'

'We were happy enough.' Jess squared her shoulders. 'But he deserves better. I'm not the right person for him.' Before her mother could reply, she hurried on. 'I'll see Kate. Please don't worry, Mam. This is the first really right thing I've done in ages.'

'If you're sure, love.' Carmel went to the door. 'Kate, come in, I was about to make tea.'

Jess and Kate waited until they heard her go downstairs to the basement, Kate hovering just inside the door, twisting her mother's ring around her finger.

'I came to see how you are.'

Jess wandered back over to the sofa and sat down again, pulling her legs up under her.

'Surprisingly okay.' She looked at Kate. 'You were right.' Despite everything, she couldn't help grinning at Kate's stricken expression. 'I know you'd never say I told you so. But I'm glad you were there yesterday. You and Zoe never left my side.'

Looking slightly relieved, Kate came in and sat down beside her on the sofa.

'Going ahead with the meal took a lot of courage.'

Jess picked at a loose thread on the sofa. 'Simon thought it was better to face everyone together and get it over with. Good thing we scrapped the table plan, though.' She grimaced. 'We certainly weren't stuck for space. I don't think everyone came back to the hotel.'

Kate reached over and lightly touched Jess's arm. 'Hey, the people that mattered were there. To be honest, once everyone got a bit of drink into them, it was grand. Even Úna and Edward were all right about it.'

Jess gave a tired laugh. The thread on the sofa came away, and she met Kate's eyes. 'You love Simon.'

Colour flashed to Kate's cheeks. 'Jess, this isn't the right time.'

'Why not?' She noticed Kate's discomfort and spoke quickly. 'I don't blame you for anything, what happened yesterday was about me and Simon. But I need to know he'll be happy.'

Kate seemed to be studying her hands. 'I think I've always loved him, but I didn't realise it.' She looked up, her face red. 'Honestly, Jess, that's the truth.'

Jess gave a small smile. 'I believe you.'

Kate twisted her ring. 'After your hen weekend, I started to get the feeling that you didn't. I mean, obviously I didn't know what had happened. But I couldn't pretend, not when I could see there was something really wrong.'

Jess took a moment to absorb Kate's words. She'd tried to pretend her one-night stand had meant nothing, but even if she'd never met Adam again, the damage had been done. She should have seen it for what it was: a massive red flag. 'What about David? Why did you go out with him?'

Kate shrugged. 'Because he's a nice guy and I thought if we tried, there might be a spark.'

'But there wasn't.'

'No.' Kate spoke slowly. 'I think we both knew after a couple of dates.'

'Do you think he knew how you felt about Simon?'

'I think he guessed.' Kate gave a shaky laugh. 'I think he knew before I did.'

Jess fell silent for a few moments. 'It sounds like everyone except me, could see what was right in front of me.'

'I pulled away as soon as I realised, Jess.' Kate balled her fists. 'It freaked me out, I kept hoping I'd get over it.'

'But you kissed him.' Jess realised it didn't bother her to say it.

'Nothing else happened, I swear. I know what I said, but I drove down to Mayo yesterday to be there for you. If you'd gone ahead with the wedding, my heart would have broken, but I couldn't bear to lose either of you.'

Jess's eyes stung and she noticed that Kate was blinking quickly. 'I don't want to lose you either.'

They lapsed into silence for a few moments. Finally, Kate said, 'I did kind of envy you when you and Simon got together.'

Jess frowned. 'I always just felt we were both in the right place at the right time. Simon was the first guy who didn't mess me around. It felt like a proper, grown-up relationship.'

Carmel came into the room, carrying a tea tray, and Kate jumped up to help her. 'Thanks, Carmel.'

'I got Hobnobs. You girls always loved them when you were little.'

Jess met Kate's eyes, and they exchanged a grin. 'Thanks, Mam.'

When Carmel left, Jess turned back to Kate. 'I think Simon and I just realised in time that we were about to make a mistake. Not because you guys kissed, but because we really hadn't sorted out the big stuff. We wanted different things from our relationship.' Jess reached for a biscuit, then changed her mind. 'I knew things weren't right, Kate, but I kept putting it down to pre-wedding nerves and the pressure of the new job.' She sighed. 'I think I may have spent the last six months stress eating, by the way.'

Kate gave her a sympathetic look. 'Have you talked to Simon today?'

'No.' Jess wrapped her hands around her cup. 'We agreed to give each other some space.'

'What about us?'

It took a moment for Jess to understand Kate's meaning. 'You think we need space, too?'

'I don't know.' Kate hesitated. 'Is it going to be weird between us?'

'You mean if you and Simon get together?'

Kate went even redder. 'I don't know if that would ever happen.'

Jess was pretty sure it would, but she was determined not to interfere. She suddenly remembered something. 'Kate, do you feel you owe me?'

'What?'

'It was something Zoe said.'

Kate sipped her tea. 'I'm grateful for everything you've done for me down the years, you've been an amazing friend.' She looked a bit sheepish. 'I know I haven't been lately.'

When Jess said nothing, Kate added, 'What about you? Will you take some time off?'

Jess folded her arms, pushing them into her stomach. 'I'm not sure it'll be time off. I think I might be fired.'

Kate looked horrified. 'Because of the car chase? I don't think so, Jess. Look, Frank's pretty fair, I'm pretty sure you can plead your case. Anyway, Zoe told me you saved that wedding by persuading Leo and Brandi to get married.'

Obviously Zoe hadn't told anyone that she'd helped Chelsea escape.

Jess felt a rush of gratitude for her sister.

'Take a few days, okay? Look, I hope you don't mind, but I have to go. Luke has a match.' Kate tucked her hair behind her ears. 'I'll see you back in work? Or I'll drop by again. Soon.'

Jess started to stand.

'It's okay, I'll see myself out.'

'Yeah, I just felt like a hug.'

Kate blinked back tears before wrapping her arms around her oldest friend. 'Actually, me too.'

Chapter 52

JESS went straight to Accounts on Monday. Kate looked startled to see her and abandoned her work to march her back out the door.

'Where are we going?' Jess said.

'Out. Anywhere.' Kate hit the button on the lift. 'What are you doing in work? I thought you were taking a few days off.'

'I told you yesterday I'd be in.'

'Yes, but I didn't believe you.'

'I couldn't take time off. The next few days might be busy.'

Kate rolled her eyes. 'I think things might quieten down a bit with that celebrity wedding out of the way.'

Jess had serious doubts that things were about to quieten down any time soon, but she allowed Kate to hurry her out of the building, and across the road to Butlers, where they ordered coffees and took a table near the counter. Jess blew gently across her latté to cool it down. 'Have you talked to Simon?'

Kate met Jess's gaze evenly. 'He dropped by yesterday. He wanted to know how Luke was, and if I knew how you were.'

'What did you say?'

'I told him I'd seen you.'

'What did he say?' Jess winced. 'Actually, scratch that, I don't have the right to know anymore. Whatever he said is between you guys.' She noticed colour creeping into Kate's face. 'Look, I admit it's still a bit weird, but I'm not falling apart or anything.'

Kate's expression softened. 'I don't think Simon is either. But maybe you should talk to him yourself.'

'I know, I will.' It was a relief to have everything out in the open, Jess realised. She hadn't felt this relaxed with Kate in a long time, although she knew things would be very different if she and Simon had gone ahead with the wedding. But that didn't matter anymore: they'd done the right thing.

Kate gave a quick glance around the café. 'You know that everyone's talking about that chase on World News.'

Jess swore quietly. 'Still?'

Kate sighed. 'I know you think I wasn't interested in the celebrity wedding, but even I know that a decoy bride being chased half-way across Mayo, is going to be news for a while.'

'Well, it won't make any difference to me.' Jess tried to sound calm. 'Not if I'm fired.'

'They're not going to fire you for that,' Kate said fiercely.

Eventually she'd tell Kate about how she'd helped Chelsea, but right now, Jess couldn't face a million questions. Instead, she said, 'It wasn't exactly the image we were going for on Saturday.'

'You weren't going for the whole celebrity bride-swap either,' said Kate, 'but if it hadn't been for you, there wouldn't have been a stupid wedding.'

'And let's face it, it was a really stupid wedding.' Jess gave a reluctant smile.

'Why don't you talk to Adam? I'm sure if he knew exactly...'

'If he knew exactly what happened, he'd make things all right?' Jess pressed her lips tightly together. 'I'd rather quit than ask Adam for help. Anyway, he's gone, he went back to Switzerland.'

Kate tucked her hair behind her ears. 'Well, now he's back. I saw him first thing this morning.'

Adam was back? Jess felt nauseas as she walked back through reception. The only possible reason for his return was that Frank was about to fire her, and he needed Adam to hold the fort until he found a new marketing manager. Maybe she shouldn't have come to work. Although she'd only be putting off the inevitable. Just thinking about it sent another wave of nausea surging through her.

As she got out of the lift, she spotted a TikTok notification: Chelsea had posted a new video. Jess slipped into her office and opened it. Linford Castle's newest runaway bride beamed into the camera. *'Hi everyone.'* Chelsea gave a little wave. *'Firstly, I wanna thank you all for your kind messages, I'm just so overwhelmed by them all.'* She paused. *'So, I wanna say that even though I didn't go through with the wedding, I'm leaving the past in the past. Because what I've learned is that it's super important not to hold grudges. The people I thought I could trust betrayed me badly, but that's also made me stronger.'*

Jess found herself holding her breath as Chelsea continued. *'The truth is, Angel Bruno knew about Leo and Brandi, and he was being paid by my ex to keep quiet.'* Shit, Jess thought, she'd been right. *'In a way, that's hurt me the most, because I've known him a long time, and trusted him to guide me in my life decisions. Now I know that the only person I can really depend on is myself.*

'Lastly, I want to thank the amazing Irish people and especially the awesome staff at Linford Castle. It's truly a magical place.' Chelsea gave a coy smile. *'There's someone else who helped me on Saturday.'*

There was a longer pause, and Jess held her breath. '*Lady Helen Linford was the same age as me, when she knew she couldn't go through with her wedding. She guided me when I needed her, showing me my way out, the very same way she escaped in 1937.*' Her smile widened. '*Find your truth, live your truth, be your truth.*' The video ended.

Jess stared at her phone. Was Chelsea pretending that Linford had a ghost?

In fairness, it was a lot more exciting than admitting an actual person had shown her an escape tunnel. One thing was certain: her two and a half million followers would lap it up.

And once this spread beyond TikTok, there'd be a lot more than that. It might even work for the group, Jess thought. Or it might backfire horribly. In which case, Frank would have his pick of reasons to fire her.

Jess tried to think. She was tempted to drop by Adam's office. A part of her dreaded seeing him again, but the other part couldn't stop thinking about him. She needed to see him. Either way, Ian would have sent his report to Frank by now, so whatever Frank had decided, Adam would know. And if the last while had taught her anything, it was that it was better to face things head on.

Adam's door was open, and for a moment, he looked startled to see her.

'Take a seat, Jess, I didn't expect to see you this morning.' He lifted an eyebrow. 'I heard what happened. I'm sorry you ended up under so much pressure trying to get to your own wedding.'

'I didn't …'

Adam's phone rang, and as he picked it up to answer, Jess wiped her palms on her skirt. 'Frank, I'm here with Jess, can I ring you back? Will do.'

Adam hung up and looked at Jess.

This was it, she thought, bracing herself. Frank had phoned Adam to talk about her and had maybe even asked him to fire her.

He cleared his throat. 'So, a couple of problems with the wedding.'

Jess couldn't speak. She could barely breathe. Adam scrubbed a hand across his face, and Jess wondered if he was trying to figure out how to break the bad news.

'I spoke to Ian first thing this morning,' he said.

Jess realised she was clutching the seat. 'He told me you rescued the wedding. The only way it could be rescued.'

Jess felt the breath rush out of her, leaving her momentarily lightheaded. 'What else did he say?'

Adam frowned. 'Nothing, really, apart from what you'd expect, given that the groom married a different bride on the day.'

'Right.' Jess tried to focus. Was it possible that Ian had decided not to write that report? 'So, what's the problem?'

'Just that the group's marketing manager looked like a hired decoy for Chelsea.' Adam's tone was expressionless.

Jess reddened. She shouldn't have to defend herself: Adam knew exactly why she'd had to leave like that. But she was determined not to make the conversation all about her. 'Did you see the TikTok Chelsea posted twenty minutes ago?'

'Give me the highlights.'

'She says she's no regrets, and that she was guided by Lady Helen Linford.'

'Guided?'

'That's what she said.'

'Right.' Adam looked thoughtful. 'Let's see how that plays out.

In the meantime, we have to explain why you were there, without making Leo look stupid.'

Jess folded her arms. 'Give me a break, Adam, Leo made himself look stupid.'

'I know.' He sighed. 'He's still our client. The moment Chelsea left like that, she stopped being our client, so it's Leo we have to concentrate on. Right now, we're trying to convince him that you and Chelsea didn't come up with that plan between you.'

Jess's mouth dried. Had Adam guessed? Or had Ian in fact told him, and Adam was simply waiting to hear it from her?

'Ian said you did everything you could to persuade Chelsea to go ahead with the wedding, but she gave everyone the slip.' Adam swept a hand through his hair. 'I know this wedding is making us money, and raising our international profile, but I'm just worried that after what happened, we may have managed to cement the Linford Curse.'

Jess knew he was right. She also knew that if she were to do it all again, she wouldn't do anything differently. 'Was there anything else?'

He shook his head. 'Not for the moment, just keep your head down.'

Feeling strangely deflated, Jess got up to leave.

'Oh, I nearly forgot,' he said.

Jess turned back, and Adam gave a polite smile. 'Congratulations on your wedding.'

Chapter 53

Jess stared at the screen in front of her. Nothing made sense anymore. In the last three years, her whole life had been heading in one direction: career, husband, children. Well, she wouldn't have rushed that last bit. Still, if things had turned out differently, she'd have ended up doing something she'd have regretted. She and Simon had done the right thing. Now, it was probably normal to feel a bit adrift. And more than a little worried.

What hurt most, she realised, was that Adam hated her. After he'd congratulated her on her wedding, she'd had her chance to come clean about everything, but fear had held her back. She was terrified that, even if he knew the truth, he wouldn't be interested. Or that he'd be disgusted that she'd put the group's reputation at risk for nothing.

There was also the strong chance that even if Ian kept her secret, Frank might still fire her, or at least demote her, for her unprofessional behaviour. Feeling miserable, she got up and went over to the window to lean her head against the cool glass. The swans were back on the canal, this time with a family of half a dozen brown, fluffy cygnets.

She jumped when her phone rang, but it was just Zoe.

'Hi, Zoe, I'm fine.' In a way, it was a relief to be back at work, no matter how long she had left. The day after the wedding had been stressful. Apart from Kate, everyone had tiptoed around her, while her mother had fielded calls from well-meaning relatives and friends.

'Good, but that's not why I'm phoning.'

Jess turned away from the view. 'Is everything all right? Is it Nana?'

'Nana's fine, chill. I have amazing news.'

'I could do with some amazing news.'

'Okay, get this. Leo Dinardia was so impressed by Finn that he's booked the whole troupe for two months at one of his big casinos in Vegas.'

Jess blinked. '*Wow!* Maybe Leo wasn't the worst. 'Wait, what if they want him to stay longer?'

'Yeah, that'd be terrible. I'd have to pack up the kids and rent out our semi-detached.' Zoe gave a mock sigh. 'He got noticed, Jess! Not just by Leo, but by a lot of really influential people. And he's let the school in Limerick know. They said they'd hire someone to fill in, until he needs the job. He's so stoked.'

'You're right, it's amazing.' Jess laughed. Zoe's excitement was contagious. 'Tell him I'm really happy for him.'

'You can tell him yourself when you see him. He wants to thank you in person. You got him this break.'

Jess felt better as she checked her emails. There was a new one from Ian Finnegan, and she took a deep breath before she read it.

Hi Jess, I wanted to let you know that we've had a lot of online enquiries about Linford since Saturday. It's hard to be sure, but people seem very taken with how we fooled the world's media with a decoy bride. We've had two wedding bookings this morning, but we're also getting enquiries from people who want

to stay in our haunted rooms. It seems the public are ready for Helen Linford's ghost!

Meanwhile, our manager appreciates how resourceful you were, and will be talking with Frank this morning. For now, from myself and all the staff, a sincere thank you.

By the way, despite the last-minute change of bride, our guests are enjoying a very successful third day of celebrations.

Chat soon, Ian.

Jess read the email a second time. There was nothing about how she'd helped Chelsea escape, and judging by what Adam had said earlier, Ian had decided not to tell Frank either. She felt a weight lift.

Having Ian in her corner would make a huge difference, if Frank did decide to haul her over the coals.

There was a knock on the door, and she braced herself.

'Yes.'

Adam came in. 'You busy?'

Jess sat up a bit straighter. . 'Actually, I've just had an email from Ian Finnegan. Two wedding bookings this morning, and people are also interested in staying in Linford's haunted rooms.' She met his gaze squarely. 'We might have that high concept we need to stand out.'

Adam closed the door. 'It sounds good, but that's not what I came to talk about. I need to ask you something.'

Shit, maybe Ian had said something after all. 'Okay.'

'Why did you not go through with your wedding?'

She sucked in a breath. 'How do you know?'

'I ran into Kate.' He sounded half amused. 'Actually, she marched into my office and told me to sit down and listen to her.'

A pulse began to beat rapidly at Jess's throat. 'If you already know what happened, why are you asking me?'

He gave her a steady look. 'I know you didn't get married, Jess. It's the rest I'm interested in.'

Where did she start? And why did he want to know? She'd had enough drama in her life in the last few days, and she wasn't sure she could handle Adam's judgement.

He ran a hand through his hair. 'Sorry, look, it's none of my business. Take the rest of the day off if you want, I'll cover for you.'

As he turned to leave, Jess caught his expression: it was the same one she'd noticed before, when he'd tried to get close, and she'd pushed him away.

Say something, Jess. 'Wait.'

Adam stood still.

She swallowed hard. 'That's not all.'

He reached behind him and shut the door with a soft click but made no attempt to move.

Jess tried to organise her thoughts. 'Simon wasn't the right person for me. I wasn't the right person for him either, to be fair. But that wasn't the only reason I didn't marry him. I, that is, what happened on the Isle of Man made me realise that things weren't right with us. I don't do one-night stands, and I shouldn't have cheated on Simon, or lied to him. I shouldn't have lied to you either.'

He appeared to be listening closely. Feeling strangely calm now, Jess continued. 'The other thing I've realised in the last few weeks is that I like you. A lot.' Adam's mouth twitched slightly, but Jess wasn't sure if it was a smile. 'I don't know if you feel the same way anymore, but …'

The rest of the sentence disappeared, as he walked over to her. 'Did you just say you like me?'

Jess tried to wet her lips. 'Um, you're a good guy.'

'So, we're friends?' Adam's eyes glinted as she looked down at her, but she took a slight step back, her mouth drying at the thought of what she had to say next.

'There's something else. And I need to make it very clear that this had nothing to do with me not going through with my wedding. Because the thing is … ' She swallowed again. 'The thing is that night on the Isle of Man I'd been drinking a lot and I threw up on the ferry.'

Adam frowned. 'Okay.'

Oh God. 'Right. And if you're on the pill, sometimes it doesn't work when you're sick.' She stopped, hoping he'd piece the rest of it together. For a long moment, Adam said nothing.

'I used a condom.' He spoke slowly.

A tear rolled down Jess's cheek and she swiped it away.

'I know. I'm sorry.' She tried to read his expression. 'You don't have to do anything, Adam. I mean, I'm not asking you for anything. But if you want to change your mind about us, I'll completely understand.' In that moment, Jess knew that no matter what Adam decided, she was going to keep her baby. And if that meant she'd be on her own, she'd manage.

'How can you be so sure the baby's mine, Jess?' Now, something in his expression made her hope.

'The timing,' she said, simply. 'Simon and I hadn't, you know … been together in the weeks before my hen weekend. And this last month since you and I …' She shrugged. 'The thing is, it's just not possible that it's Simon's. I did a test last night. It's very early days, but I'm definitely …'

Before Jess got a chance to finish, Adam had wrapped one arm around her waist and was pulling her close.

Excitement and relief shivered through her as she met his eyes.

'What are you doing?' she whispered.

'Getting you to stop talking for a minute.' He grinned, then tipping up her chin with his other hand, he lowered his mouth to hers.

With a sigh, Jess wound both arms around his neck. As Adam angled his mouth to deepen the kiss, Jess shifted her body against his, a breathless laugh escaping her, as he groaned into her mouth. He moved his lips away from hers, kissing along her jaw and down to her neck and, vaguely, Jess wondered if they should lock the door.

Abruptly, Adam muttered something and pulled away. Jess swayed, blinking at him, as she tried to calm her breathing.

'Why did you stop?'

He ran his thumb across her lips, and she felt a tingle race through her. 'I just thought we should stop. We're in work, and it's a bit unprofessional. Also, I wasn't sure how you felt about having sex on your desk.' Judging by the gleam in his eyes, he was probably joking about the last part, she thought. Still, she'd never be able to look at her desk again, without wondering what that would be like. His thumb stroked her cheek and along her collar bone. 'So, let me get this straight: you're definitely single?'

'Definitely.' Why had he stopped doing that amazing thing with his thumb?

'No other fiancés I should know about? No stalker ex-boyfriends?'

'None of the above.' She wished he'd just kiss her again. 'I'm also definitely pregnant, Adam. You heard that bit too, right?'

His smile widened. 'I did.' He paused. 'Hang on, I don't want to pressure you either way about the baby. I mean, whatever you decide … what I'm trying to say is that I'll support whatever decision you make.'

Jess nodded. A part of her couldn't believe what she was going to admit, but suddenly it felt like the most natural, wonderful thing in the world.

'I want the baby.' She noticed that Adam's eyes looked suspiciously bright.

'I'm so bloody glad to hear you say that.'

She made a half-crying, half-laughing sound. 'Really?'

He nodded, tucking some stray hair back from her face.

'I suppose for now we should get back to work.'

Was he serious? How was she supposed to work after that? 'Right, of course.' Almost reluctantly, Jess's brain caught up. 'Hang on, aren't you going back to Switzerland? I mean, why did you come back?'

'Ah.' Adam rubbed his nose. 'I did go back to Switzerland for a few days. But Frank wanted me back here to help sort …' he spread his hands, 'this.'

Jess stared at him. 'So you're going back?' She couldn't cry. After everything that had happened during the past forty-eight hours, she wasn't about to burst into tears now. No matter how messed up her hormones were.

'No.' Adam's voice gentled. 'Since about twenty minutes ago, I've decided to base myself here.'

'Oh.' Her voice cracked. 'I'm glad. I mean, your parents will be delighted, won't they?'

Adam smiled. 'Hopefully. But they don't know yet. Nor does Frank. I was waiting to talk to you.'

THE LAST SATURDAY IN JULY

Jess felt a warm glow spread through her, as the full impact of Adam's words hit home. He looked thoughtful. 'Do you want to get out of here for an hour?'

'That's a fairly brilliant idea.'

'I've been known to have one or two.' Adam opened the door. 'You know we should probably take this slowly, don't you? You were engaged about two minutes ago. And now, with you being pregnant ... '

'No, yes, I see that.' Jess was determined to be honest. 'I was telling the truth when I said things hadn't been right between me and Simon for ages, but he's a good person. I want to make sure I'm not on the rebound.'

'Do you think you are?'

'Nope, but just in case, we probably shouldn't have sex.' Jess was deadpan. 'Not for a while, anyway.'

Adam took her hand. 'So, delayed gratification?'

Jess's breath caught in her throat, as she met his eyes. 'You up for it?'

'Oh, I'm up for it.' Adam was equally deadpan. 'And I'm also good at delayed gratification, so we'll take it slowly.'

Jess felt a stab of disappointment. 'Really?'

Adam's eyes glittered. 'Well, maybe we shouldn't wait too long, either. It might get a bit trickier later on.' He glanced down at her tummy, then back up at her again and as Jess felt her face heat, he winked. More seriously, he added, 'Are you sure you're all right? This isn't exactly a perfect situation.'

Jess smiled. 'To be honest, Adam, I've found that perfect is very overrated.'

THE END

Printed in Great Britain
by Amazon